who'd have thought

G BENSON

ACKNOWLEDGMENTS

Thanks to my incredible beta team Katja, Katie, Erin, Angela, and Alex. Thanks to people who read for sensitivity and for language. You're all fantastic.

A huge thanks to the editors who worked with me, especially Michelle and Zee. Your feedback and hard work are so appreciated. Michelle, this is book number four! Boom.

Thanks to Ylva, for everything that went on in the background to make this book a reality.

DEDICATION

For Concha, an endless well of support in everything I do.
And my bringer of coffee.

CHAPTER 1

Hayden had to be up in four hours.

Four hours did not enough sleep make, and her eyes were burning. But after the stressful day she'd had, her brain wouldn't shut down. At the end of a week of night shifts, her body was taking its time settling back into its normal rhythm, even after her first shift back in the land of the living today. For about a minute, she'd contemplated going for a run—as if—but instead had eaten an entire frozen pizza. Frank, her oversized fluff-ball of a cat, had judged her from his place on top of her DVD player where he'd sat, accruing all the heat. There'd been narrowed eyes and everything. So, in a cheese-and-bread coma, Hayden had watched a movie and waited for her eyes to get heavy.

And waited.

Eventually, she'd given up and gone to bed, in the hope it would lead to sleep.

It had not.

Which meant Hayden had been left with three options: go for that run (really, never gonna happen), stare at the ceiling and count water stains, or do what she usually did when she couldn't sleep. She'd gone for option three, which consisted of trolling the Internet in the twilight hours of the morning. It was a pastime that bordered on embarrassing, but the strategy was one that almost never failed her.

She scrolled through Internet forums and advertisements to find the funniest. One guy was selling a goat he'd "accidentally" bought—Hayden wasn't sure she wanted to ask questions there. The goat did look pretty cute. It was still a baby.

Frank would hate her.

That was almost enough to make Hayden click *reply* and ask for it, but the image of a clawed-up goat and an unforgiving Frank in her tiny New York City apartment gave her pause. She huffed and kept scrolling. That cat needed to stop ruling her life. She could barely afford to feed herself, yet here she was, with the same grizzled beast she'd adopted eight years ago.

Someone was looking for a woman he swore he'd had a connection with on the subway. Apparently there'd been a spark. Snorting, Hayden scrolled on.

Spark. Sure. That, or he was stalkerish, and the poor woman had actually been edging away.

Though, that wasn't a fair thought. What if it had been love? Love that started on a dirty train car among all the germs and disdain? Did anyone ever find people on these missed connection posts? She opened another page, tapped a wrong button and watched the screen go black before opening up to her front camera. Looking back at her was the three-chinned version of herself that made her want to weep, even as she snorted. Front cameras were one of the worst inventions ever. Every time she turned it on, it was her face, looking like a thumb, that greeted her. She grinned to make herself look as hideous as possible and took the photo. Yup. She looked like a thumb. She sent it to her best friend with the caption: *Luce—why am I single?*

That would give Luce a laugh when they woke up.

Because Luce was most likely asleep, like Hayden should be.

It was now 3:21 a.m. This was getting ridiculous.

Exiting the messaging app, Hayden ended up at an empty browser page again. What was she doing? Oh. Yeah. She typed into the search bar *do people actually find each other through missed connections*. Her eyebrows rose. Whoa. There were a lot of hits. The first few articles listed announced that, yes, people did find each other that way. How romantic. And kind of gross. They could make a movie out of that crap.

She exited out of that page and went back to scrolling through junk posts. Some were clearly trolls:

For a small payment, I can clear your soul and ensure you reach your full potential!

That sounded creepy. And kind of like they were going to perform an exorcism.

Looking to trade my canoe for a shark, must not be full grown or have lasers on its head.

Sure.

Right person sought for a personal deal, will require at least one year of involvement, compensation promised.

Well, that was lacking the usual absurdity. Or details. Hayden's thumb hovered over the link, the sound of her faucet dripping in her kitchen reaching her ears. The super ignored her complaints, and she had no cash herself to fix it. *Compensation promised* sounded pretty heavenly. She clicked the link.

The message made her roll her eyes.

What a waste of time.

Looking for a woman who is discreet and reliable and interested in a long-term commitment, one year minimum. Person sought to fulfil all legal requirements necessary for a valid marriage within the state of New York. Compensation will be more than reasonable and only payable once all components of deal are completed. However, upon confirmation of the agreement, a smaller payment will be given as a show of good faith.

One, a small payment before generous compensation? Was that a joke? Two, this was clearly utter crap. No one would seriously want a fake marriage and offer money. God, Hayden loved Craigslist. This was better than the goat.

Or maybe it wasn't crap. Maybe someone needed a green card?

Though, with whatever money this was, if it were as generous as this person was hinting, Hayden would be able to afford the goat.

She laughed at herself, switched her phone off, and dumped it next to her bed.

Two hours of sleep, here she came.

~ ~ ~

All it took was five minutes of being in the hospital building for Hayden to walk into a doorway. She'd love to blame her tiredness, but it was an almost daily occurrence. Really, it was a good week if she managed to have a solitary bruise rather than several. And this one was definitely going to bruise. Rolling her eyes at herself, she rubbed the spot on her elbow. Seriously, ow. Whoever called it a funny bone could go to hell.

Once upon a time, in a different life, Hayden had studied so much anatomy her head had been left spinning with it all. You'd think it would have left her more aware of her body, but still she walked into anything and everything.

People would be surprised how many parts of the body they could live without. There were twenty-six bones in your foot, and the fifty-two that made up both feet consisted of twenty-five percent of all the bones in the human body. People could lose up to two liters of blood before death. Sometimes a little more. But really, they hit shock before that.

As an emergency nurse, Hayden saw a lot of that.

Like, a lot.

The lights in the locker room were dim. It was barely seven, and handover was about to start. She needed to wake up so she'd be able to take in the huge info dump about the patients soon to be in her care.

Other people stood around, as bleary-looking as Hayden felt, pulling on scrubs and stuffing their pockets with flashlights, swabs, and anything else they usually needed. Someone laughed, and Hayden flinched. Who were these people that could function enough to laugh in the morning?

"You look like hell."

Hayden sighed, smiling despite herself. Bloody Luce. "Thanks. That's just what a person likes to hear in the morning."

Blowing their bangs out of their eyes, Luce shrugged. "Yeah, well, I live for truth."

Well, that was true. They were the most honest person Hayden knew. Some might say tactless, but once you got to know them, you realized it was a love for a lack of bullshit. Once, over beers, Luce had made a joke that they'd spent the first twenty-five years of their life bullshitting their gender and had used up all the bullshit they had to give. Hayden had choked on her beer as Luce had thrown their arms wide, declaring, "Look at all the shits I do not give! Alas, my non-binary field of shits is barren." The bartender had cut the both of them off after that.

"I wouldn't have you any other way. Ready for handover?"

Luce's shoulders slumped. "Ugh. Yes. I suppose."

Hayden bumped her arm against her best friend's. "We can find coffee if we manage a break. Maybe at the cart with that cute coffee girl…"

Luce brightened considerably, a sly grin curling their lips up. "Well, if I must."

"Oh. You must. For me."

They sighed theatrically and pushed the double doors open to the emergency room. It was blissfully quiet. A rare thing. "You know, you really are selfish. But fine. For you, I shall."

"You could just ask her out."

"Don't be silly. I have to stare wistfully at her for at least another six months."

"Ah, yes, of course. The time-honored tradition of drooling from afar." Hayden had that down pat. She had some courage, and could approach someone she was interested in if needed, but mostly it was all a bit too scary. Staring while hoping the other person made the first move usually worked best for her.

Except often the other person was doing that too, and so no one got anywhere.

At the emergency station, they both checked the board delegating who was where.

"Same beds as yesterday," Hayden said. "I wonder what delights I'll get today."

"You had the two from that car crash yesterday, didn't you?"

"Mhm." It had been a long, long day. "They were transferred to surgery. My friend in ICU messaged me and said they're both stable."

"Well, Thomson was the surgeon on, so that's not surprising."

"Ugh." Hayden made a disgusted face to match the noise she'd made. "Don't remind me." Hayden had had to deal with Samantha Thomson showing up and taking over the scene.

"Look," Luce said, "she's stone cold, but she's the best neurosurgeon in the state."

"More like the country. And she knows it."

Luce snorted. "True. She's got an ego."

"And she's rude."

"What the hell happened to make you dislike her so much?"

"Well—"

"Ladies, are we keeping you?" They both turned on the spot, grimacing at the emergency coordinator and the team behind him, eyes shot red after their night shift and no doubt dying to go home and sleep. Or, for some, to go home and get their kids up for school. The coordinator winced. "Sorry, Nakano, *folks*. Not ladies."

Luce gave him a salute. "No problem, Ben. We're good to go."

"Hayden."

She froze as he turned his intense gaze onto her.

"You look like you need coffee more than us."

"Doubtful, but close. I'm just still getting back into day shifts after last week's nights."

"Yeah, can't wait for that in a few days." His gaze swept over the rest of the day shift that trundled through the double doors. "All right, guys—er, people, your assignments are written up. Grab your nurse for handover, and I'll be handing over to this morning's coordinator, Blessing."

Interesting to see Blessing was coordinating. She was a superstar, completely organized, and she rocked at handling difficult patients. Because of that, she often ended up on the floor rather than coordinating the shift. But Hayden wasn't complaining. It was always a smoother day when she was running things.

Everyone started to disperse, Luce disappearing to the code team's corner. Jealousy swirled up in Hayden's chest. She loved being on the code team. Luce poked their tongue out at her, so Hayden pretended to be the more mature one and ignored the gesture.

She glanced at the board again and headed for Tasha, standing near one of the nurses' stations with a pile of folders in front of her.

"Morning."

Tasha gave a weary wave, somehow not looking as half-dead as most of the others. "Hey, Hayden. How was your night?"

"Better than yours, I'd wager."

"It wasn't so bad, actually. One arrest, but other than that, mostly smooth." She pulled one of the files out. "Bed three has a homeless guy that was brought in. He's sleeping it off. Once he's awake, if you could do the usual—try getting him in the shower if you can. He hasn't passed urine yet, BSL stable..."

Hayden sunk into the language she knew and understood better than English at times.

She had three of her four beds full, one ready to transfer out in bed four. Tasha, the goddess that she was, had already arranged everything for the transfer. All Hayden had to do was some intravenous antibiotics in twenty minutes. The homeless man was another story. Unfortunately, he was a regular through their doors and would refuse all help and discharge himself once he was awake. Hayden had met him once, and she might have some luck getting some of the mediocre hospital sandwiches into him and getting him into a shower beforehand. Maybe. The third patient, bed one, was an elderly woman, found by the nurses in her assisted-living facility in her bathroom, bleeding from a head wound. She had been dazed and confused, disoriented to time, place, and person, though according to the family member who came in, she was usually lucid. One of her pupils was bigger than the other, and she had a suspected brain bleed. They were waiting on the results from her scan, and she was on thirty-minute neurological observations.

"Neuro?" Hayden sighed and made her disgusted face again. "Ugh."

"You don't like neuro patients?" Tasha asked. After her detailed handover, she finally looked ready to fall asleep on her feet. Out of nowhere, though, she brightened, a gleam in her eye. "Oh, wait. I know. It means Dr. Thomson will be down."

"Exactly." Hayden tugged the folders over to herself, checking the medication charts and notes as per protocol so she could ask any questions or check any missed medications. It all meant she wouldn't have to call Tasha later and wake her up. "Another patient shared with Thomson."

And, yeah, okay, maybe neuro patients weren't always her favorite.

A patient started yelling from the other side of the emergency room, and they both turned around. One of the other nurses bustled over, waving her hand in the general direction of everyone looking over to see if she needed help. Medical language for *I've got this.*

Tasha turned back to Hayden. "You really don't like her."

"She's rude."

"She's damn good at her job. And easy on the eyes."

"I'll tell your boyfriend."

She waved her hand dismissively. "Like he'd care. He thinks the same."

"She's, like, fifty."

Okay, Hayden was exaggerating. And also didn't want to agree that, yes, the rude surgeon was easy on the eyes. Surgeons' egos could be big enough, especially neurosurgeons', but Thomson's rivalled any other she'd seen. And she was rude. In case Hayden hadn't mentioned that.

"She is not fifty." Tasha sounded as exasperated as she looked. "She's, like, forty-two."

"How do you know that?"

Hayden really needed to start her day. And stop gossiping.

"Pablo's often her scrub nurse. He feeds me information. He also says she's not that arrogant."

"Your boyfriend is useful."

"Oh, he's more than that." Tasha winked and Hayden straightened.

"Okay. Time for you to go home and enjoy that, then. And leave me to my sexless day."

Tasha pouted. "He's on day shift."

"Oh, poor you. At least he'll come home and make you dinner. I'm going home to a giant, angry cat."

"How is Frank?"

"As cantankerous as ever. I love him."

"Such a cat lady."

"Yes, I am. Now go away. I'm busy."

Hayden threw her a grin, and Tasha turned to leave, saying over her shoulder, "Have a good day. Enjoy Thomson! Maybe she'll send a resident."

"Here's hoping."

Hayden hugged the folders to her chest and looked around the room. Half the beds were full. But anything could happen in the next few hours. For now, it was strangely calm and qu—no, she couldn't even think the *Q* word. Every nurse ever knew that it was cursed. Hayden didn't even believe in that crap, but it was such a taboo that even she couldn't say it.

The second someone said the *Q* word, the phones always started ringing off the hook, the patients kicked up, and the waiting room filled. And she was far too tired to deal with that today.

Before doing anything else, she walked around and checked her three patients, ensuring they were who Tasha had said they were, plus that they were still breathing. Bed three was still out cold, his breath rising in a steady rhythm and not due anything else for an hour. Not a lot she could do there for now. Everyone knew his story. They'd all learned he had been in the Vietnam War and had been on the streets for far too long. There'd been a family, long ago, with three young kids before he'd ended up homeless. He didn't see them. Nor did he want to, from what she could gather.

He'd been failed on so many levels by the government. And the hospital system couldn't do much for him. It was a mess.

Bed four gave her a merry wave, his apple cheeks rounding even more. She introduced herself and let him know he'd be off to the cardiovascular ward within the next two hours.

It would probably be more like four.

Bed one was asleep, curled into a tiny ball in the middle of her sheets. The family member, a son, was next to the bed in a chair, head tipped back as he snored.

She had twenty minutes until the next neuro observations were due on bed one. So she went to the medication room and started making up the antibiotic she'd need soon. At this rate, she'd be getting a coffee at a normal coffee break time, not at lunchtime.

"Hayden, I'm bored."

Who else but Luce? Hayden laughed, swirling the vial filled with saline gently. "Careful, that's awfully close to the *Q* word."

"Close but not. I was all excited to get the code team, but nothing's happening."

"That's generally considered a good thing, Luce." Hayden smirked as she checked the vial to see if all the powder had dissolved. Nope. She kept swirling her wrist. "Come check this for me."

Since it was second nature for all injectables to be checked by two nurses, Luce looked it over and signed the chart even as they kept talking.

"Yeah, I know. But this is weird. I haven't seen the emergency room this empty in a long time."

"Well, that means we get our coffee." Hayden grabbed a syringe and drew up the antibiotic into it, capping it off with a sterile lid.

"True. I heard you have a neuro patient."

"Yup. Hopefully the scan shows nothing so there will be no Dr. Thomson for me."

"I won't lie. I hope she shows up. I can watch you get all frustrated."

Hayden put all her things in a kidney dish and balanced it on the folder. "She's arrogant."

"She's not *that* bad."

"Okay, fine, she's rude."

"They can all be rude. As can we. Why does this one have you so annoyed?"

Already back out on the floor near where patients could overhear, Hayden threw her hand in the air. "Later."

She laughed to herself when she heard the indignant huff from back in the treatment room.

It turned out bed four was a delightful, jolly man who had her laughing in seconds. She gave him his antibiotic, had a quick listen to his heart, and gave him a once-over, ensuring nothing about his condition had changed. Nothing had, and she documented it, and made her way to bed one.

"Mrs. Botvinnik?"

There was no movement from the bed, so Hayden drew the curtains around it. The man sitting in the chair stirred, and Hayden gave him her attention.

"Hi. I'm Hayden, your mother's nurse today. I'm here to do her neurological observations."

"Stewart." He glanced around, rubbing at his eyes. "I didn't mean to fall asleep."

"Never mind. You need rest too." Hayden turned her eyes back to her patient. "Mrs Botvinnik?"

"She'll prefer Winnie."

Hayden flashed Stewart a smile. "Winnie?" No stirring. Not even a facial twitch. She rubbed her shoulder. "Winnie?" This time a little harder. "Winnie, can you wake up? I know you're tired, but I need to see how you're doing."

A flinch this time, and with one more shake, she stirred. A touch more difficult to rouse than what Tasha had said.

Winnie stared up at her with watery blue eyes.

"Good morning, Winnie. I'm sorry to wake you up. I'm Hayden, your nurse. Do you know where you are?"

She looked around. "At home."

Nope. "Do you know what the date is?"

She pursed her lips, clearly thinking. "It's March. 1994. I... I don't know what day."

"Good job." It was August 2016. But there was no point in distressing her. "And who's this here?"

Turning her head, she beamed dazzlingly. Her entire face lit up, the lines deepening to make her look like the happiest woman on earth. And Hayden watched Stewart's heart break, hers twinging in empathy. "That's my Hans."

Stewart looked at Hayden, a muscle clenching in his jaw even as he gave a tight-lipped smile. "That's my dad. He's been gone for nearly ten years."

"Okay."

Same result as for Tasha. She ran through some of the other tests before turning the light on Winnie's eyes. One pupil still larger than the other. However, now neither reacted to light. Hayden checked the chart to be sure, but Tasha had clearly documented that both had reacted to light on her check. Keeping her face placid, she marked it down beside the 'Glasgow Coma Scale' field on the patient chart, and tucked the folder under her arm. "Great job, Winnie. You can rest again now. Stewart, I'm going to see if I can hurry the doctor up."

"All right." He took his mother's hand in his own. She gazed at him blankly.

Walking quickly to the nurses' desk, she paged the Neuro number and stood by the phone, bouncing on her toes.

"All okay?" Blessing asked.

"Bed one, elderly woman who had a fall."

Blessing grabbed her patient list, flicking through to find the bed and look at the notes she'd scrawled all over it at her handover with Ben.

"Her consciousness level isn't good—her GCS has fallen two more points. Neuro needs to come and review her."

Yay. Samantha Thomson.

"Okay." Blessing jotted it all down on her sheet. "Keep me posted."

"Will do," Hayden said. "She's only seventy."

By the age of twenty-seven, nursing had changed Hayden's perspective of old. Seventy years old wasn't old. Fifty was young.

The phone rang, and Hayden snatched it up, telling the Neuro resident the situation and asking him to come down. He said he'd be there as soon as possible. She hoped he got the hint that it needed to be soon.

It only took five minutes. The double doors opened, and Dr. Thomson walked through, an intern hurrying in her wake. Sighing, she turned back to watch Winnie from the desk. In a swirl of some kind of understated perfume, Samantha Thomson strode up to the desk.

"You're bed one's nurse?"

Good morning, Dr. Thomson. Yes, I'm well, thank you. Tired. I know, isn't going from night shift to day shift a bitch?

"Yes, I am."

"Her GCS has dropped?" Thomson held her hand out for the folder, her bright green eyes far too alert for so early. She had a fan of lines around them, but Hayden could never place how that had happened. You usually got lines from making some kind of expression. Thomson's go-to expression was perpetually stony.

"Yes, two points." Never say Hayden couldn't be professional. "She's harder to rouse than her night nurse described. One pupil is still blown, but now neither reacts to light. Still no orientation to time, place, or person."

"She was fully orientated before the fall?"

"According to her son, yes."

Without saying anything further, Thomson turned and walked to bed one. The intern scurried after her, and Hayden was left feeling abandoned. She'd at least thought they could share a grimace or something. Camaraderie. She followed quickly, her hands deep in her scrub pockets. It was obviously a bleed, but how bad?

Dr. Thomson was running her own neuro tests when Hayden slipped past the curtains the jumpy intern had at least thought to pull around the bed. Thomson had a pixie cut, her hair a deep auburn color. Keeping it so short must stop it from falling in front of her face as she leaned over patients. Hayden had thought of doing that but was pretty attached to her curls. Her *abuela* would probably kill her if she cut it all off.

Stewart watched on, his brow furrowed. Thomson flashed her flashlight around and straightened.

"Your mother has suffered an intracranial bleed from her fall. She requires emergency surgery. I'll leave my intern available for any questions you may have."

And she turned, slipping her flashlight into the breast pocket in her lab coat. Hayden followed her. Thomson had the worst bedside manner.

"Do you have a time for the surgery?" Hayden asked.

Thomson had her tablet open as she zoomed in on a scan of the patient's brain. She didn't look up. "This bleed is complicated. When did she last eat and drink?"

"She refused food overnight, and Tasha told her son not to give her any more water from 0300 in case surgery was needed."

"Then she'll be next on the list."

And she was gone.

"Great. Thanks."

Muttering to herself was never a good look. Across the room, Luce caught her eye, clearly trying to smother their smirk. Hayden made a face and turned around to make sure Stewart and Winnie were okay and not suffering hypothermia from their surgeon's visit.

And also to make sure the intern didn't scar them.

~ ~ ~

"I'm just saying it's your fault."

Luce shook their head. "Nope. You have no basis for that."

"You said you were bored."

"So?"

"That's like saying it was quiet." Hayden dropped her head back against the booth in the sticky, old diner they were in. Both had finished the shift from hell craving junk food. Their day had not stayed chill. And there had definitely not been a fun coffee break. All Hayden had managed was to shove a sandwich into her mouth sometime around two p.m. The seat under her creaked, and the stuffing splitting out of a crack in the vinyl under her was a weird gray color. But the burgers here were to die for.

"That's a ridiculous superstition, and you know it. It's like saying it's going to be cold in winter and getting surprised when it is, which is always. It's *never* quiet for long in the ER. It's far more unlikely that *nothing* happens when you say it's quiet."

"Yeah, all right. I just want someone to blame."

"Blame the idiot who thought driving drunk on a main highway was a great idea."

The waitress put a plate filled with dirty burgers and fries in front of each of them.

"Or that patient that sliced his arm half off with his power saw." Hayden's mouth watered as the smell of grease hit her nostrils. It was layered with the scent of ketchup: everything good in the world. "There was so much blood, I have no idea how he drove himself in. At least the bone was clean-cut, though. God, I'm hungry."

The waitress, slightly green tinged, threw her a highly unimpressed look and walked away. Sometimes Hayden forgot that these conversations weren't normal for other people.

"Thank you!" she called after her.

The waitress kept walking, and Hayden couldn't blame her.

"Think she'll vomit?" Luce asked.

"Maybe."

"At least you weren't on the code team."

Hayden smirked as she stuffed a fry in her mouth. It was too hot, deliciously so. And so salty. "What happened to being all smug about getting my favorite spot?"

Neither had had the time today to speak to each other, let alone find out what was going on in the other's little corner of the ER world. Hayden took a huge bite of her burger, her moan bordering on orgasmic.

"We had two people on meth come in," Luce said. "One coded twice. One of the crash victims was coding when they came in, and after that we had a couple of patients, one after the other. I didn't pee for so long, my bladder ballooned so much I looked pregnant."

Hayden would never admit it, but she was now pretty glad she hadn't been on the code team. She wiped some ketchup off her finger and asked, "Want to know the best part?"

"What?"

"We get to do it again tomorrow. Twelve-hour shift, my pal."

Luce threw the closest thing to their hand at Hayden's head. Since it was only the plastic cover off a toothpick, it fell woefully short. "Why would you do that?"

"I'm a masochist."

"One who needs to learn manners. Don't speak with your mouth full."

"Do you like seafood?" Hayden opened her mouth wider.

"Oh my God. Seriously?"

Hayden swallowed and grinned. "You find me charming."

"Not even at all."

By the time they finished their burgers, both of them were heavy-lidded. It was almost nine and the unpaid extra forty minutes they'd had to stay behind to finish their paperwork had been painful. When the bill arrived, Hayden brought out her card and waved off the bills Luce sleepily tried to hand her.

"I've got this one. You got the last one."

"Thanks."

A loud beep rang out as her card was run through the machine. Declined. The waitress frowned at her. "Want me to run it again?"

"Yeah, please."

Heat was crawling up Hayden's neck, and she gnawed at her lip. It couldn't be empty yet, surely? She still had another full week before payday. The resounding beep almost made her flinch. She plastered a smile across her face.

"No problem. I think I forgot to activate that card."

Luce tried to push the bills back at her, but Hayden waved her off. She pulled her wallet open again and grabbed some bills, handing them over to the waitress with a tip that could only just be called sufficient.

They pulled their jackets on and stepped outside. How was her account empty already? She'd tried so hard to budget properly this month.

"Hey." Luce's voice was softer than usual. "You okay?"

Hayden put on that same smile that would probably fail any kind of happy test. "Yeah. Yeah, I'm good. Just thinking about the day. I'll see you tomorrow?"

For a second, Hayden thought Luce was going to say something else, but then they said, "Yeah, of course. Wanna share a cab?"

She shook her head. "Thanks, I'll take the bus."

"You sure?"

"Yep."

"Okay, bye. And thanks again for dinner."

Hayden watched Luce walk towards the street. Her lip stung where her teeth were biting at it, and she made herself stop. Money was the worst. She'd had to send more away to her family than usual this month, but she'd still thought she had some left over. Now it looked like it would be ramen with a side of peanut butter and jelly for the next week or two. She had some cans of soup too. Yum.

Sighing, she started the walk home. The area turned shabbier as she left the busier, more affluent areas behind.

Her building came up quickly, blending in with the other older ones around it. As usual, the door stuck as she turned her key, so she shoved her shoulder into it, and it budged with a squawk. Yawning, she still took the stairs to the third floor, stumbling into her apartment. Frank sat in the middle of the living room, glaring at her reproachfully.

"Hi, Frank. Good day?"

He made a chirrup noise that sounded like a growl to most people. Not to her, though. She loved his noises. He'd been in the cat shelter for three years before she'd brought him home. She scooped him up, and his face made him look as if he hated it, but she knew better. He purred, once, then struggled to be put down, running to his food bowl.

Which was still half-full, but apparently if it was not completely full, he was starving. Grumbling to herself, she went to the pantry. The shelves were mostly empty. There were those cans of soup. Enough for a few days. Some beans to mix into some vegetables. Some jars of sauce, some pasta.

She'd be fine.

If she walked home until payday and didn't eat out, it would all be okay.

Frank let out a meow that sounded too deep to be from a cat, and Hayden grabbed the bag of cat food, something she never ran out of. She poured it out and he set to scarfing it down, purring so loudly she could barely hear the crunch as he chewed.

"You better want to cuddle me tonight, Frank. I've had a long day."

He didn't even pause.

On her scratched-up old coffee table, Hayden spotted the mail she'd left there the night before. She fell back onto the sofa, groaning so loudly even Frank looked up.

"Sorry."

He sniffed and went back to his food. She went through the first two things, junk and some election stuff she was never going to read. The last one in the pile made her groan again. It was a late notice on her cell bill. She'd completely forgotten.

She should just make it in time to payday before they cut it off. *Again.* She was really sick of always being one paycheck away from disaster.

"Frank, can't you get out on the street and earn us some dough?"

He stalked over from his bowl and jumped up on the couch, licking his face. He settled himself a few feet away.

"Or, you know, sit next to me?"

He turned so his butt was facing her.

"Cool. Thanks."

What if something else came up before payday? What would she do? She could stop sending that money each month. Skip paying her student loans.

Neither of those were going to happen, though. Couldn't she just win the lottery?

That would involve buying a ticket. Hayden always forgot that part.

She yanked her phone out of her back pocket, wriggling so she didn't have to stand up to do it. The jostling made Frank throw her a dirty look over his shoulder, so she poked her phone into his butt. He shuffled away a tiny bit more. She grinned.

She typed *how to get rich quick* into the search bar. She wasted a good twenty minutes that way, blinking heavily at the screen. For once, Google held no answers. She found a page about saving money, and the first option made her nope out pretty quickly.

"Stop buying that five-dollar coffee each day?" She turned to look at Frank, who sat steadily facing the opposite direction and ignored her. "How is that helpful to people with actual money issues? I get my coffee for a buck at the hospital coffee cart maybe three times a week. What is three dollars extra a week really going to do? Idiots."

Frank still didn't turn around. He could be so rude.

The number in the right-hand corner of her browser caught her eye; how did she have thirty-two browser pages open? This is what happened when she opened up a new page to ask all the inane questions that entered her head each day. She started exiting out of them all one by one, pausing at last night's Craigslist adventures.

Compensation.

That stupid word.

Also, you know, money. How much even was "generous compensation"?

Well, her student loans were probably way more than whatever that amount was. Ugh.

Curiosity piqued, she clicked on the *answer* button. She was a little buzzed from the one beer with dinner. Why not? They were never going to answer anyway. She quickly typed a response.

> *Hey. I saw your ad requiring a spouse for a year. I won't lie, it was the promise of compensation that caught my attention. I do come with a cat called Frank who has a stink eye to rival angry grandparents in the supermarket, but beyond that I come with no baggage. I'm clean, work full-time, and can be a bit too sarcastic at times. I'm also a klutz. I'm fluent in Spanish, if that's any use. Let me know if you'd like to meet.*

She hit *send* and dragged herself off the couch for a shower.

Sleep was going to be bliss.

That message wasn't going to go anywhere.

CHAPTER 2

"Go talk to her."

"No."

"Luce. Do it."

"She's too pretty!"

Sitting at one of the tables outside the coffee cart, Hayden rolled her eyes. She'd found a dollar in her locker and decided to splurge on a coffee. It was worth it to watch Luce melt at the sight of the coffee girl. Who *was* cute. Her high cheekbones and black skin were complemented by a very mischievous smile. Whenever one was directed at Luce, they practically went nonverbal.

It was a little embarrassing to watch, and entirely entertaining.

But Hayden was being nice about the second part, because Luce had paid for both their coffees, being great like that. Hayden didn't think they knew about her money issues. Not in their entirety. But still.

"There's no such thing as *too* pretty."

Luce turned around. "Oh, I'm sorry, Miss-I-Can't-Even-Look-At-The-Waitress-At-My-Local-Café."

Hayden pursed her lips and held their eye contact. "Yeah, okay, fine. But she really *was* pretty."

"So is Clemmie."

Hayden felt her grin turn wicked. "Oh, Clemmie? Not Clementine, like on her nametag?"

"Shit."

"When did you get her nickname?"

"She told me, the other day."

Hayden took a smug sip of her coffee. "And did you give her your name?"

"I mumbled something. Then paid and ran away."

"Good job."

"Thanks." Luce grabbed both paper cups and stood. "Hayden, your phone's been lighting up."

"Oh." Luce wandered off to the trash can, and Hayden grabbed her phone. She had an e-mail, the name only a generic string of numbers, and something strange rolled over in her stomach. Could it be?

Apparently it could.

> *Is tonight suitable for you to meet? Somewhere public, as I do believe there can be issues with meeting people from the Internet privately. If that's agreeable to you, we could meet at, say, 8:30 p.m. Location to be sent if you agree. I'll wear a black beanie. If you could let me know what you will be wearing, that would be helpful—though I don't recommend bringing your cat. Thank you.*

"Oh, my fucking hell."

"What?"

Hayden closed her mouth and looked up. Luce was watching her, their head cocked.

"Oh, nothing. My horoscope said something surprising."

Hayden worked so well under pressure in the ER. But making something up on the spot? Not her thing at all. She hated lying. But no way was she admitting to this.

"You told me you thought horoscopes were a load of crap."

Sometimes, Hayden thought it would be easier to have a friend who hadn't started out with her in the ER. Years of long and deliriously tiring shifts had a way of making the two of them divulge more random bits of information to each other than they might have normally.

"Yeah, well, it said to watch my back, and I'm tired, so I overreacted."

Luce was still looking at her weirdly, and it was difficult not to squirm under the attention.

"Whatever," they finally said. "We need to get back."

Their fifteen-minute coffee break was up. Really, they should have accrued hours for all the ones they'd missed over the last few years, but that wasn't how it worked.

"I'll come in a sec. I just need to go to the bathroom."

"Okay."

Once Luce had walked away, Hayden dropped back down into her seat and chewed her lip. Did she reply? Hayden's response had been on a desperate whim; she'd never expected anything back. Did the reply she'd just gotten read like an axe murderer reply? Maybe it was an axe murderer. Wherever this person suggested to meet probably wouldn't even be a real place; there'd just be an empty warehouse, and then next week Hayden would be found chopped to bits.

Wow, what an embarrassing way to go.

Local queer killed by axe murderer in fake pay-to-wed scheme.

After a second's consideration, she quickly typed a response.

> *Barring complications with work, I can meet at that time. I'll be wearing a red jacket and will be without Frank. You should thank me personally for that.*

She hit *send*, swallowed heavily, and jammed her phone back in her pocket. There was work to do, and Hayden had to go deal with a neuro consult.

~ ~ ~

This was ludicrous. Insanity.

It took three attempts to walk inside the café at the address that had been immediately messaged back to her.

Oh hell, Hayden was going to end up on the news. Some kind of special report. Last seen wearing a red jacket and a face of regret as she was pulled into unmarked van with a sign offering free candy.

She took a deep breath.

Clearly, Hayden had never grown out of her histrionics.

She pushed the door open, and the warmth and smells of coffee and sweeteners washed over her. Divine. The café gave an instant feel of coziness. It was like its own little world, with squishy chairs and people sitting around with laptops. Her cousin was one of those people who sat in cafés with their computer. Hayden had asked him if he wrote much while there, and he'd laughed and said the idea was to write more but usually he ended up on social media.

The café was maybe half-full. It was quite late, really, in the middle of the week. Someone sat with a stroller they were jiggling with their leg, clutching their coffee with an almost desperate gleam in their eye. Steer clear of that one, then.

And Hayden spotted it.

Black beanie, the person wearing it facing the other way. Maybe it wasn't them? Why would they face the other way when waiting for someone? Hayden walked up, her hands in her pockets. A few feet away, she stopped.

Walking away would be so simple. Turn, get swallowed up by the cool air outside, and delete the e-mails and pretend none of this had ever happened.

But if they'd shown up, maybe it was all real?

Hayden cleared her throat, loudly. Then paused. Had she really just done that?

The person turned halfway, and finally stood and turned properly.

And, for a split second at least, Hayden's heart stopped.

Samantha Thomson.

Samantha Thomson, the coldhearted neurosurgeon, wanted to pay someone to marry her. And Hayden had sent an e-mail of interest. And joked about her cat.

It was wildly inappropriate, and completely the wrong thing to do, but Hayden burst out laughing.

And for the first time ever, Hayden saw something like an emotion flash over Thomson's face. Her eyes actually widened, ever so slightly.

Or maybe she imagined it, because they narrowed immediately.

Hayden stopped laughing, swallowing it down so fast she almost hiccupped. Her lips twitched, and the laughter died out, the feeling dissipating as if it had never existed.

This was awkward.

"Uh, hi, Thomson."

She didn't answer. Those cool, green eyes were still appraising Hayden. If only Thomson wasn't a good half-foot taller, because right now, even in a neutral place like this, the power dynamic was way off.

"Hello…" Finally, Thomson had spoken. And obviously hadn't remembered Hayden's name.

"Hayden. Hayden Pérez."

"Of course."

Hands still in her pockets, Hayden rocked back on her heels. "So…"

Thomson was clearly trying to process this turn of events. To be honest, so was Hayden. This was not what she had been expecting. And right now, she wasn't sure if this outcome was better or *worse* than the axe murderer theory.

Unless Thomson was an axe murderer?

"Uh, are you going to get a coffee?" Thomson asked.

"A cof—what?"

"A beverage. Something to drink. It's what one usually does in a café."

"Uh…right. Yeah. I'll just go order one." Hayden turned to leave, remembered her manners, and turned back. "Do you want something?"

"I have tea."

"Right. I'll be back in a sec." Hayden turned to join the short line.

Oh. My. God.

Brain numb, Hayden ordered a chai latte, not wanting to be awake all night again, and gave her name. She used the last twenty-dollar bill in her wallet and tried not to cry at the tiny amount of change she received as she waited by the pickup area. The drink came far too quickly, the barista calling her name within minutes. She almost wanted to glare at him, but he was about sixteen, and looked like he might have peed his pants if she did. So she settled for a polite look and grabbed her drink, hoping it would ward off the chill Thomson constantly emitted.

Hayden took a deep breath and straightened her shoulders. The glass of her chai was burning her fingers, but she held it tighter anyway.

Was this real life? Were there candid cameras in the room? As she walked back over to Thomson, Hayden actually found herself checking the corners of the room for any sign of film equipment.

She slid into the chair across from Thomson—one of those armchair-like seats that were always too uncomfortable to sit up straight in, yet made you look like a bored teenager if you rested your back against it. Deciding for comfortable, Hayden sat back and crossed her legs.

Surprise, Thomson was sitting up. Her posture was impeccable. Lots of surgeons had a very subtle stoop, the by-product of bending over bodies all day, eyes tight with concentration. Not this woman, though.

"You work in the ER." Thomson poured some of her tea out. It was a green color. Was this woman even real?

"Yes."

"That's unfortunate."

Well, it wasn't as if Hayden liked working with her either. Wait. Unless that wasn't what she meant. "What—"

"It's unfortunate, because now you know about—" she waved her hand vaguely in the air "—this." She paused to take a sip of her tea and swallowed slowly, as if considering this entire situation much more carefully than Hayden was. Hayden was too busy tripping out and trying to sip her chai nonchalantly and then hiding that she'd burned her tongue. "But I suppose that would make it less suspicious. We would be able to say we met there."

"You're still thinking you would want…"

"As I said, in many ways, this makes more sense."

"Ah."

This was so awkward. For something to do with her hands, Hayden picked her warm glass back up and wrapped her fingers around it, holding it to her chest as she stared at Thomson, who was staring at Hayden.

"Why did you answer my ad?" Those eyes were on her again, and Hayden watched the woman with the stroller sit down with her second coffee. Poor woman.

Should she answer that one truthfully? It couldn't hurt.

"The idea of cash, and I really did think it was a joke. I didn't think anything would come of it."

"Why did you come if you thought it was a joke?"

"I almost didn't. So, why did you reply to my response?"

Hayden looked back to Thomson and expected her to look away at the bold question as Hayden herself had done. But no. She kept that solid gaze on her.

"I've had a lot of responses. Many were easy to screen. I met a few people. Most thought it was a joke or they left me feeling uncomfortable. I was about to give up on it altogether, but your response was…amusing." There'd been another word on the tip of her tongue, Hayden could tell.

"I'm a regular comedian."

Thomson's face didn't even twitch. She sipped her tea again.

"So, why do you need to get fake married?" Hayden asked.

"One rule, if we do agree to this, is that you don't ask me that." For some reason, Hayden's cheeks went hot, as if she'd already known the question was taboo. "When it becomes necessary, I'll tell you. But, for now, it's not necessary."

"You think it's not necessary for me, the person you may want to fake marry, to know *why* you want to fake marry me?"

"Precisely."

"If I'm going to agree to this, I want part of the deal to be that you tell me eventually."

Thomson's lips pursed, and Hayden held her eye. "If we go through with it? Fine. But only when I feel the need to divulge that information."

"Fine." The reason wasn't actually so important. But damn, was Hayden curious. What could it be? Unless—"Wait. Is it for a green card? Because I *will* need to know that. I don't know a lot beyond what B-grade movies have taught me, but I do know that I'll need to do a hell of a lot to prove the marriage is legit."

Which required, you know, defrauding the government. Which was illegal.

"No, it is not for that reason."

"Oh. Okay." Damn. That would have solved that puzzle. So then why? "Can I ask why it had to be a woman?"

"There were a few reasons, but I prefer women, so it worked."

A few reasons beyond preferring women? This mystery was not getting any closer to being solved.

"Was there a reason you didn't disclose your gender?"

"I simply forgot. Plus, for all intents and purposes, it didn't really matter. Did you think I was a man?"

Hayden shrugged. "I'm pansexual, so it didn't really bother me either way. And, well, it would all be fake, so like you said, it didn't really matter."

Had it been Hayden's imagination, or had Thomson flinched at the word "pansexual" and flicked her gaze around the other tables? Why would a lesbian, or however Thomson identified, care if someone heard that word?

"Well, that works for both of us, then," Thomson said.

And so it did.

"So you really want to do this?" Hayden asked.

"Do you think I put that ad out on a whim?"

God, she was so pompous.

"I don't know. You looked almost surprised that it was someone from work. Maybe you don't want to do it."

"I was surprised. I really did think that ad was a sure way to avoid anyone I knew. But it does add a certain…authenticity to it."

Hayden straightened up in her chair, a thought occurring to her. "Plus, you would be worried that, unless I was involved, I would tell everyone what you were doing."

Thomson's eyes narrowed, just slightly. "That did occur to me, yes."

"As much fun as it would be, I wouldn't do that. If you decide I'm not appropriate, I won't breathe a word."

And why did Hayden keep speaking like this was something she was considering? Marriage had zero importance to her, but surely to marry someone with the intent of divorcing them pretty quickly wasn't the best idea.

Though it was only a piece of paper.

And money.

"That is good to know." Thomson sat back in her chair, but somehow managed to remain looking as composed as ever and not like a rebellious and sulky teenager. "We should discuss what it would entail, and once we're through, perhaps you should take some time and think about it."

"Okay."

Thomson nodded once. "Good. I would require the marriage to continue for a year, perhaps more, should things get complicated. But I do not foresee that happening. I do not require the wedding—" Hayden's stomach turned over at the word "—to be big nor public. An appointment at the courthouse would be sufficient. However..." Thomson actually hesitated, and Hayden almost felt her mouth drop open. "I do require that we wait a month and do be seen in public together a few times. And that we live together for that year. I have a large apartment with a spare room."

If not for a green card, why would she need to appear married? And a month was actually a short time to convince people it was legitimate. Hayden took a long sip of her latte. She really was going to have to think about this. Most of this could probably be kept from her family; they were in separate states, after all, as her sister liked to point out fairly bitterly. But her colleagues would all have to know. If they had to at least seem like a couple on the outside, there would be no hiding it from them.

Luce was going to pee themself laughing.

"So, what about at work?"

Thomson actually paled, though her expression didn't change. "We don't have to be exceptionally public. But as we both work there, I would need them to think it was real. This was an added bonus to not having the person be someone I work with. I could have kept work and my private life separate. I have no friends at work to complicate the issue."

No friends at work? Really? But she was so warm.

Literal pee. There would be genuine pee from Luce. And worse, Hayden wouldn't be able to tell them the truth, because even though she might be able to swear Luce to absolute secrecy, she couldn't take any chances on this insane arrangement getting out somehow and Thomson refusing to pay after Hayden had put in all that effort.

Which meant lying.

"Okay."

"As for...compensation," she paused here, and Hayden had no idea why, "I would pay you twenty thousand when we agree, and twenty thousand once the papers were signed and you were moved in."

Forty thousand? This would net her forty thousand? Plus not having to pay rent for at least a year?

Was this all real? Was she dreaming?

"Ah—"

"And at the conclusion, a payment of two hundred thousand. I do understand that this is a large commitment—around a year of your life, not to mention other issues such as having to move out of your apartment and not dating for that time. Plus, there's the deceit this entails."

Hayden barely heard anything after the words "two hundred thousand." Two hundred thousand? *Dollars?* That type of money seemed like a joke. Hayden didn't have two hundred cents in her account. Even as the city's top neurosurgeon, how did Thomson have that much money just lying around? Did she keep it under her mattress?

"I suggest you take a few days and think about it."

"I'll do it."

Holy crap. Hayden said that.

"What?" Thomson actually sounded surprised. "I really believe you should think about it."

"No. I'll do it."

Thomson might be her least favorite person in the hospital. This might all be absolutely insane. How would they live together? How did you occupy space with someone that you not only didn't know, but didn't even like?

And they were actually going to have to appear to be dating for a month.

And then appear married for a year?

Ew.

"Are you sure?" Thomson's expression was, as usual, indiscernible.

"Yes." In fact, two hundred forty thousand dollars' worth of yes.

"This means pretending you can stand me."

Hayden grimaced. So she really *hadn't* hidden her dislike well at work. Though it was interesting that Thomson had even noticed. "I can manage that, Thomson. I did some drama classes at school."

As if that could help.

Thomson's lips pursed, and Hayden, for a split second, thought she might be suppressing a smile. "And maybe use Samantha. Or, really, Sam."

Thoms—Sam—held her hand out across the table, and Hayden took it. They shook: Sam's hand warm and firm.

"Okay...Sam." Already that sounded too personal.

"Okay, Hayden."

CHAPTER 3

Something cold was on Hayden's nose.

And it smelled like fish.

Cat-food breath.

Hayden opened her eyes and found herself eye-to-eye with Frank. He meowed plaintively in her face, the smell of cat-food breath intensifying dramatically. Foul. That was one word for it. She turned her head so hard her neck cricked. He meowed again, and she sleepily dropped her hand onto his back and moved it in some semblance of petting. He growled lightly and jumped off the bed, padding away. Another meow reached her, this time farther away and, if she wasn't mistaken, from the kitchen, where he'd be standing next to his bowl.

Which was no doubt half-full.

He was such an asshole.

Rubbing sleep from her eyes with one hand, she reached for her phone with the other. Her alarm was due to go off in four minutes. Right on time, Frank.

She had one e-mail from her sister, asking when she was next going home to see their mom. Sighing, she exited out and went on Twitter instead. She could answer that later. After scrolling through boring things for five minutes, she opened her e-mail app again. There'd been another one, but the one from her sister had made her nope out way too quickly.

It was Thomson.

Oh God, what had Hayden agreed to?

Samantha.

Sam.

Sam seemed too light for her. A nickname that didn't quite sit right. There'd been barely anything from her last night—she had no real emotion going on about this. The epitome of cold-ass, no-nonsense surgeon. It had been strange seeing her outside of work. The light in the café had been dimmer, more orange than the blinding fluorescence of the hospital. Although unsure when she'd noticed it, Hayden remembered the woman had a light smattering of freckles over her nose. It had made her look more like a human than she did in the washed-out light and under the mask she plastered on at work.

Well, it wasn't really a mask. It seemed to be her face.

Had Hayden really agreed to get married? Had that been an actual thing?

And, the burning question, why did Thomson—damn it, *Sam* (that was really hard to break)—want to in the first place? Maybe she was going to lure Hayden in and axe-murder her inside her probably fancy-as-hell apartment?

No more axe-murder thoughts. This was getting stupid.

Also, no more late-night TV.

Another drawn-out meow came from the kitchen.

"I'm coming!"

But she didn't move. Instead, she opened the e-mail.

> *Hayden,*
>
> *I feel we should arrange a time and place for the first "date." We don't have to do anything special. It's just so we appear to have spent a month together before signing the papers. I'm aware even a month is quite short to convince people, but it should be sufficient.*
>
> *Also, I feel you agreed too readily. You should really think about this more. How do you know I will pay you? Why have you not asked more questions? You really need to be smarter about this.*
>
> *How is tomorrow night at seven o'clock? Perhaps we can leave from the hospital together, if you're working. Better for appearances.*
>
> *Sam*

There it was, typed out: *Sam*. How strange.

All of this was strange.

Also, patronizing much? Of course Hayden needed to think about this more. Thank you very much, Samantha Thomson. And of course she had questions…like…

Like.

Okay, so maybe Hayden had been blinded by the money. But yes, now her thoughts were going overtime. How could she be sure she would get that money at the end? Could she get a contract?

Would a contract like that hold any legal ground?

Also, could there be a contract? Or would the existence of one prove their marriage a sham?

Maybe it could be more like a prenup? *If (when) the couple divorces, a one-off payment of 200,000 dollars will be made to the innocent party, but no further payments.*

Wait, what if Thomson—Sam—whatever—didn't file for divorce? And left Hayden in some weird limbo land of married to someone she barely knew?

Though after a year, they'd probably know each other.

Hayden shuddered and ignored the plaintive meow that floated into her room again. Maybe they could make a prenup that meant Hayden got a one-off payment as soon as they were married. Was that even legal? Could she ask a lawyer these questions?

So…hypothetically… I wanna marry someone for money?

They'd probably charge two hundred dollars just for her stupid hypothetical question.

This was all too hard. And stupid. But then, money…and money that would come her way soon.

Forty thousand within a month?

Hayden quickly scanned the e-mail again.

Also, better for *what* appearances? If it wasn't to convince green-card people, why did it matter? If they didn't have anything to prove on a legal basis, why were they doing this?

The meow that came from the kitchen sounded like a dying elephant, so Hayden rolled out of her bed and padded through to the kitchen, which took all of five seconds in her micro apartment. She replied to the e-mail, agreeing except to say that she'd need an extra half an hour in case the ER was a mess.

And also to clean up, but Hayden would never admit that to Samantha Thomson. She was going on a "date" with the Ice Queen herself and would not be going out smelling of twelve-hour shift.

All of a sudden, Hayden's hands were clammy. Leave from the hospital? Oh no. The ER would be a gossip pit. Everyone would know. And yeah, okay, that was the point, but that meant this insanity was actually happening.

She couldn't even talk to anyone about it.

Frank head-butted her leg and yowled.

"Okay, okay."

~ ~ ~

"Are you all right?"

Hayden looked up from the chart she was filling out at the edge of the nurses' station. Luce was staring at her.

"What?" Hayden asked.

"Are you okay? You've been spacey all day."

"Have not."

"Have too."

"I'm tired." Hayden stretched out her back, casting an eye over the patients she could see. All were doing okay, and the boy with a broken arm had been wheeled to surgery moments earlier, his parents hovering over the bed and following them. The poor kid was four and had almost been in hysterics. Until the pain medication had set in, and he'd just been plain hilarious. He told stories about a fart monster that scared people by farting the loudest. So much like Hayden's nephew. "Nothing else."

"Okay, if you're sure." Luce's voice was pretty clear on the fact that they didn't believe her. "I'm going to get a coffee. You want one?"

"Please!" Hayden smirked, capping her pen. "I won't offer to come. You need all the time you can get with Coffee Girl."

"She's not on today." Luce's cheeks went red immediately, their skin tone making it a dusky color. "Not that I, you know, know that."

"Well, well, Luce is a stalker. You would never have known."

"I just happened to go by there this morning, that's all."

"Sure, sure. I'll post bail when you get arrested."

"Not funny!"

Luce was already walking away. They really were hopeless with this coffee girl. It was tempting to just give her Luce's number, but Luce would hate that. So would Hayden, so she couldn't really blame them. She froze as she put the folder in its slot.

Over a year of no dating.

Okay, maybe Hayden wasn't a Casanova, but she enjoyed dates and flirting and going out, even if that area of her life hadn't been that active lately. She liked first kisses and first nights wrapped up in sheets.

Over a year with none of that? Or, at least, without the opportunity of that?

Maybe she should rethink this. And not only because of all that, but this would really be turning her life upside down for a year. But then…

Two hundred forty thousand dollars. What she could do with that.

On that thought, she needed to message her sister back. Or suck it up and call.

"Hayden, Neuro will be here in five for that consult."

"Righto." Hayden tried to ignore the way her stomach felt as if it had dropped out of her body. Normally, that comment just filled her with a slight annoyance. But that flop in her stomach? She would really need to get that under control. Would Thomson—damn it, Sam—expect her to be flirty here? Or at least, like, friendly? Would it be too weird? Would Sam actually be *nice* after essentially proposing?

The insane image of Samantha Thomson on one knee and beaming up at her, holding out a hideous diamond ring invaded her mind, and she snorted, clapping her hand over her mouth and hoping no one noticed. The shift coordinator threw her a weird look, but Hayden just pretended she'd coughed.

Grabbing the file for her neuro patient, Hayden shook her head. She needed to calm down. That's what she needed to do. Not imagine strange things that were never going to happen.

Her patient was laid out in her bed, dark skin sallow and her eyes nervous. Hayden touched her hand to hers. Her right eye was partially closed, the same side of her mouth drooping.

"*Hola, María. ¿Cómo te sientes?*" Hayden asked, checking how she was. It was times like this she was grateful her *abuela* ensured she spoke Spanish and kept her connected to her Honduran roots.

"*Estoy…estoy bien.*" María's words were slurred, but her eyes had lit up when Hayden had switched straight to Spanish when she'd first come in two hours ago.

"*Bien—te vamos operar enseguida. ¿Está bien?*"

"*Mi…familia no…está aquí…*"

She'd been worried about her family since she'd arrived. They still weren't there.

"*¿Todavía no están aquí?*" Hayden double-checked with her that they definitely still weren't there.

"No."

Hayden felt terrible for her, but she explained how important it was that María go to surgery as soon as possible and that maybe they could call them before she went.

It was cold comfort to offer a phone call to someone going into surgery if their family didn't arrive in time. A phone call that would do little for María or her family.

"María Villanueva?"

Not letting go of the hand gripping hers, Hayden turned her head to see that the surgical team had arrived. "Yes, this is María."

Sam didn't even look up at the sound of her voice.

"Folder?" Sam asked, and Hayden held it out and Sam scanned it quickly. "Any change?"

"Stable since arrival by emergency flight after diagnosis of a large aneurysm."

"Good."

Sam—finally—walked around the edge of the bed. "I'm Dr. Thomson, the head of neurosurgery. I just need to check your eyes."

Hayden translated in rapid Spanish and Sam blinked at her.

Sam turned back to María. "¿Está bien si miro en tus ojos?"

It was Hayden's turn to stare at her. Her accent was horrendous, and she spoke slowly and translated directly, but still. She knew Spanish?

Sam moved her flashlight quickly, gaze roving over María's face. She did a series of neurological tests, then put her flashlight away.

"Can you translate?" When Hayden agreed, she said, "I have your scans. You're on the emergency list, so your surgery will be within the next hour or so. My intern here will take you through the paperwork and answer any questions you have."

Hayden translated and María's brow furrowed. "Mi familia—"

"Nurse?"

Hayden wrenched her head up. She abhorred being referred to that way. "Yes?"

If Sam saw the anger in her eyes, she didn't react. Her face was as impassive as ever, her gaze steady. "She'll need neurological observations every fifteen minutes rather than thirty now. That scan was worrying."

And she turned and walked away, leaving Hayden wanting to throw something after her and María looking from Hayden to the same twitchy intern as the other day.

The intern stepped forward. "She's a bit scary, ma'am." He started pulling forms out of the folder in his arms, consent forms for the surgery, most likely. "But she's the best you could wish for."

Hayden translated that and, somehow, María's grip on Hayden's hand relaxed.

Maybe she'd misread the twitchy intern.

But seriously? *Nurse?*

~ ~ ~

The next night, showered and wearing black jeans and a white buttoned-up shirt with her favorite black ankle boots, Hayden was still seething. Her e-mail was full of eight drafts she'd started to type out before exiting from the app, huffing. All were filled with the start of some attempt to cancel this plan—not just the dinner, but the entire thing.

But dollar signs appeared behind her eyelids like a cartoon villain, and she couldn't bring herself to hit *send*.

So now she was hanging by the main entrance, throwing a wave to the odd coworker as they walked out, hoping Luce had left already and wouldn't see her.

"Hey, you look fancy."

Which, of course, was far too much to wish for.

"Not really." Hayden tried for casual with a one-shouldered shrug.

"You have your date boots on."

"No, I don't."

"Well, you do." Luce leaned against the wall. "I was with you when you bought them. You tapped the heels together and said, 'There's no place like their bedroom,' and laughed manically."

That was sadly true. Sometimes, Hayden thought her parents shouldn't have let her do drama at school. It had brought out a side to her no one had known had existed.

The thought of her parents as one entity made her stomach roll over.

"They were the first thing I found this morning when I was getting dressed."

"Fine, whatever. Want to get a drink?"

"I, uh, can't. I have plans."

As Hayden had suspected they would, Luce's eyes lit up. "So you do have a hot date."

"No, I—"

"Hayden."

This was a freaking nightmare. Burying her hands in her leather jacket's pockets, Hayden spun on her heel. "Thom—Sam. Hi."

Hayden didn't need to turn around to know that Luce's eyebrows had raised an inch. She could feel the eyeballs glaring into her back. Sam also wasn't in her scrubs but rather dark denim jeans and a loose green shirt. Her collarbones were on show. Hayden hadn't seen her own collarbones so clearly in a while. Not with her habit of enjoying food quite happily and doing little exercise besides walking. It had taken a few years of work on her self-esteem, but she'd ended up comfortable with her extra curves. She was certainly rocking them tonight with her boots.

"Are you ready to go?" Sam asked.

Hayden turned and almost wanted to laugh. Luce was gaping like a fish. They bounced back miraculously, though.

"Hi, Dr. Thomson."

Sam started walking out, and Hayden fell into step with her, avoiding Luce's eye. Within ten steps, she felt her phone vibrate. She ignored it, and they walked across the parking lot. It vibrated again. She would bet her last few dollars this would continue all night.

Luckily, Hayden only planned to order a water and make short work of the night. She had no money to actually do anything more than that and no desire to spend more time with Sam.

Apparently not one for small talk, Sam walked silently next to her. And somehow as they walked, that seething feeling grew. Their shoulders brushed, and the feeling was like electricity, going straight to the ball of anger in Hayden's gut. How would they even manage all of this if Sam couldn't even address her politely in the ER?

"Where are we going?" she bit out.

If Sam heard the anger in her voice, she didn't react. "A bar around the corner. Is that okay with you?"

"Fine."

They walked on in silence. In her pocket, Hayden's mobile vibrated again. And again.

"Are you going to get that?"

Apparently, it vibrated loudly. Hayden pulled it out of her pocket, and she had to stop herself from smirking. Nine messages. She opened them and felt some of that pressure ease in her chest as she almost laughed out loud. Various messages from *what was that about?* to *are you sleeping with Ice Queen?!* to *WHAT THE FREAKING HECK IS GOING ON?* filled her inbox.

Deciding to enrage Luce further, she typed out a *can't talk, busy* and put her phone on meeting mode.

They stopped outside a fairly fancy-looking bar. It even had someone standing out at the front to open the door. Hayden's face fell. Her teeth started biting at her lip. This was the kind of place that didn't give out glasses of water from the tap for free.

This was the kind of place that offered your sparkling water from a spring in a mountain Hayden had never heard of that fairies had blessed on a full moon.

"Uh..."

Sam's eyes were on her. "If you prefer another place, we can go there."

Hayden had ten dollars in her wallet. That stupid chai had been five bucks at the café the other day, and her bus card had needed a refill when it had rained randomly and made walking not an option. A water couldn't be more than a couple of dollars, even at a place like this. And she'd just have one. And hope she'd be fine for the next few days. "No. Here's fine."

But her cheeks were warm. From shame over having to stress about money or still being too angry to meet Sam's eye, Hayden didn't know. The man opened the door, and Hayden followed Sam inside. Jazz music settled over her, and her eyes took a second to adjust. It was brighter than the night outside, but not by much. Small tables decorated the inside, shiny and silver, and booths with black leather lined the walls at the back. It was early for a place like this to be busy on a weekend, but it was already half-full, the murmuring of voices layered in with the sounds of the saxophone that drifted from the speakers.

Hayden, feeling like a sheep, followed Sam over to an empty booth. She slid into one of the seats, the leather supple under her fingers. This was much nicer than the diners and bars Luce and Hayden usually frequented. The clean, polished table didn't even have any water rings on it. She ran her fingers over it. It was as smooth as it looked, gliding under the pads of her fingertips. When she looked up, Sam was watching her, her head cocked. Hayden quickly lifted her hand away and dropped it in her lap.

"Are you going to tell me why you're so angry?" Sam asked.

Hayden swallowed. She'd never been good at hiding how she felt. In Drama, her teacher had loved it and told her that all of her emotions simmered at the surface. He'd said it was a great quality in an actor, since she could access her emotions so easily. Sometimes, she thought it helped her as a nurse. Empathy was always right there. However, it didn't help in other facets of her life. Like this.

But okay. Sam wanted to know? Hayden would tell her. "If this is something we're going to do, you can't treat me like you did yesterday."

Sam's head actually snapped back sharply, as if surprised by the words. Which made Hayden more frustrated. Was it really so surprising?

"How did I treat you?" Sam asked.

"Rudely."

"How so?"

Why was her voice so calm? Hayden sat back against the booth. She opened her mouth to speak just as the waiter appeared at the table.

"Good evening, ladies. How are we this evening?"

"Fine." Sam looked up at him. "I'll have a gin and tonic."

"Of course, ma'am." The waiter turned to Hayden. "And for you?"

"A glass of water, thanks."

He tapped it into his tablet. When he'd left, Sam was watching her again.

"Don't you want something else? It's Saturday night. I assume you don't work tomorrow either?"

Hayden shook her head. "I have tomorrow off. I just want water."

"I'm paying." Sam seemed to have figured it out way too quickly. "This is part of our deal whether we go through with it or not."

"That's—that's not it." Liar. "Really."

"If you insist." Ugh. There it was again—patronizing. "So, how was I rude?"

"You addressed me as *Nurse*."

"You are a nurse."

Hayden opened her mouth and closed it again. She took a deep breath. "You know my name."

"Yes. But at that moment, I wasn't thinking about anything other than that surgery."

"You could still try a little harder. Especially if you want people to believe this could be something?"

Sam was cocking her head again. "Okay."

"Well, I—what?"

"Okay. I'll try to be a touch more, I don't know, warm?"

Did Sam even know *how* to be warm? "Uh, okay. Good."

"Have you been angry about this since yesterday?"

No point in denying it. "Yes."

The waiter appeared again, putting the drinks between them.

"Thank you," Sam said. "We'd also like to order a…?"

Those cool, green eyes bore into her again, and Hayden rolled her eyes. "Another gin and tonic, please."

"Right away." He disappeared again.

"Hayden." Her name sounded foreign on Sam's tongue. Hayden wasn't sure if she liked it or not. "I'm used to having work be only that: work. When I'm thinking about a patient, that's all I think of: their surgery and how I'm going to fix it. The ways I can operate to minimize risk. How to achieve the best outcome for them. Also, how to teach the interns and residents on my service what to do to improve." Her eyes brightened as she spoke about work, something almost excitable that Hayden didn't know could exist there. "But I'll try and be…friendlier. You're right; I have to if this is to be believable in any way."

"Okay." That was all Hayden could really think to say to that. She took a sip of her water for something to do, Sam echoing the motion with her own drink. "How do you know Spanish?"

"It's the most common language in the US after English. I also spent a year volunteering in a hospital in Bolivia and managed to expand the basics I learned in school."

"Oh."

"Are you a native speaker?"

"I'm bilingual, I guess. My grandmother preferred to speak Spanish with us so we would learn."

"Hayden isn't a Spanish name?"

"Dad won the argument of what to call me since my mom chose my sister Sofia's name. My middle name is Alejandra, after my grandmother, María Alejandra."

Her dad had insisted, more than won, apparently. Hayden was the first name of a poet he'd liked. Or so went the story she was told as a child.

"Are you close to your Dad?"

Hayden shifted in her seat. "More or less."

And that was all Hayden wanted to talk about when it came to her family. Sam looked like she was about to ask more but, strangely, didn't.

A silence fell between them. The bar was filling up, the noise level rising. The music was still in the background. Hayden wasn't really one for jazz. She liked lyrics she could sink her teeth into, ones she could belt out and destroy in the shower—better yet, ones she could completely destroy by getting the lyrics *completely* wrong.

"Did you think about the e-mail I sent you?"

Hayden snapped her gaze back to Sam. "What?"

"The e-mail. About the questions."

"You mean your patronizing e-mail?"

A smile played at Sam's lips, and Hayden almost dropped her drink. She actually looked amused.

"It was hardly patronizing."

"Yes, it was." Hayden jutted her chin out. "It was incredibly patronizing."

"And how was I supposed to point out that you were avoiding some of the more obvious questions about our arrangement without being, as you put it, patronizing?"

God she was infuriating. Sam crossed her arms in front of her, putting them on the table, eyebrows raised ever so slightly.

"I don't know." Hayden shrugged. "Maybe give me a few days to actually think about it and process to come up with the questions? It all happened pretty quickly."

"Well?" And she was watching Hayden again, her head tilted to one side.

"Well what?"

"You've had a few days. Do you have your questions?"

Seriously. Infuriating. "Of course I have."

"And?"

If she wasn't careful, Hayden was going to throw a drink in her smug face.

"How do I know you'll pay me the money?"

"Good question."

Hayden had a feeling this was what being on Sam's service would be like. Patronized and painfully poked along a learning curve. No wonder her intern was a jittery mess.

"We can't exactly make a contract that lays out the steps to this plan, highlighting the marriage as fake," Sam stated. "I'm not sure what a lawyer would say to that. We could lay out a simple contract that says that after a period of time, I pay you two hundred thousand. Though I'm not sure how admissible that would be. And if it takes more time, what then? Will you take me to court? How do either of us ensure the other will sign for a divorce?"

She had clearly thought this all out much more than Hayden's panicked nighttime brain had. Not wanting to seem completely stupid, Hayden decided to make the one suggestion she'd thought of. "What about a prenup?"

Something about the way Sam sat back in her chair seemed as if she was satisfied with the suggestion. "Exactly. I think that's the best option. We get a standard prenup, protecting each of our assets and income."

Hayden bit back a huff. Her biggest asset was Frank, and she was pretty certain Sam wouldn't want him.

"However, we put the stipulation in there that at the dissolution of the marriage you receive a one-time payment of two hundred thousand. That way, your interests, and also your assets, are protected, as are mine."

Hayden was chewing her lip again, but she didn't bother stopping herself. She wouldn't even be able to afford a lawyer to look over the prenup. She'd have to read it herself and hope it was valid.

"That seems tight."

"I think so," Sam stated in a way that meant she didn't think, she knew. "We can use this month to ensure this works for both of us and to give time for any more questions. It can also be some time to make it seem like we're dating before going to the courthouse."

To get married. 'Cause, you know, that's what Hayden was agreeing to. Was it hot in here?

"Okay."

"And I will pay for a lawyer of your choosing to look over the prenup."

Well, apparently Sam could afford that. "Okay." Hayden sipped her drink, her teeth protesting at how cold it was. "And I want to know why you're doing this."

"No." Sam straightened, her shirt shifting to cover her collarbones at the motion. "I agreed that you would know eventually, but when I feel the need to tell you. I don't feel that need now."

"Fine."

"Why does it matter?" Sam had an expression on her face Hayden couldn't place.

"Curiosity."

"Killed the cat." Sam ran a finger around the rim of her glass. Apparently, she could get fidgety, even if only slightly, just like the other mere mortals she grudgingly shared this planet with. "Speaking of cats, I'm assuming yours would move in with you."

Moving in. Hayden did her best to shrug off the weird feeling that induced. She'd only lived with a partner once, and that hadn't ended well. "Well, he goes where I go. So, yes."

"Okay. Does he leave the apartment? As my apartment doesn't really have access to the street."

"No. He's a very lazy, happy housecat."

"Happy?"

"Okay, he's a very lazy, hates-everything housecat."

"I can't wait to meet him." Sam's voice was as dry as the gin in her glass, and Hayden bit the inside of her cheek in delight.

"Was that sarcasm?" Completely against her will, Hayden felt a corner of her lips trying to tug up into a smirk.

"Possibly."

"I didn't know you had it in you."

Sam sipped her drink. "There's a lot you don't know."

This was going to be the weirdest year of Hayden's life.

Chapter 4

Someone was hitting Hayden over the head with a banana again and again, and it was making a weirdly wooden noise. Was her head made of wood? Or maybe it was hollow.

Everything went silent.

Hayden yawned.

Nope, there it was again. Something started making the banana noise again, but there was no banana, and this time, she was blinking up at her bedroom ceiling. The noise stopped again.

Hayden rolled over, pulling her pillow over her head. The sheets had wrapped around her legs. As she kicked them out of their prison and dropped them back to the mattress, they bumped into a warm heavy shape. One that gave a grumbling growl.

"Sorry, Frank." Her voice was hoarse, layered in sleep.

He shuffled away from her. That sound happened again. Was that someone knocking at her front door? It was. Insistently too.

"*Why?*"

Hayden was whining to herself, and she didn't even care. It was Sunday morning. She had three glorious days off in front of her, including today. She pulled the pillow tighter over her head. The knocking came *again*, and she flopped onto her back, huffing at the ceiling.

"I'm coming!"

She was going to punch whoever that was in the face. Okay. Maybe not. She was ridiculously nonviolent. But she *was* going to think about it. She rolled out of bed and used the foot of one leg to push down her leggings on the other after they had apparently ridden up during the night. She gave up after a second of weird wiggling. Why was it so bright?

She squinted around the room. Nothing. She grabbed her glasses that she only wore if she was at home off her bedside table; otherwise it was contacts all the way. At least she could see properly now, even if the world was still far too bright.

As she stumbled out of the room, she tripped while trying to get her legging down again. Her little toe ran right into the closet, and a curse word flew out. Her eyes watered as she finally yanked open the front door, her toe throbbing.

"Luce. What the hell?"

Luce peered around her, and Hayden turned her head to look back into her apartment to see what was so interesting. Everything looked normal. She turned back around to scowl.

"Is she in there?" Luce asked.

"Is who in where?"

Luce narrowed their eyes. They had eyeliner on today, the dark brown of their eyes richer in color. "Don't play coy."

Against the doorframe, Hayden spoke though a yawn. "I don't know what you're talking about. If you don't start making the sense, I'm leaving you here and going back to bed."

"Thomson! Is she in there?"

Oh. Right. And ew. "No."

Luce looked weirdly disappointed. "Oh. Were you still asleep?"

Hayden looked pointedly down at herself, her leggings and rumpled sleep shirt speaking for her. No doubt her hair was a flyaway mess on top of her head, spilling out of its bun like a fountain. "No. I was having breakfast with the Queen of England."

"Smart-ass."

"Of course I was asleep. Why are you here so early?"

Luce smirked. "It's twelve o'clock."

"What?"

"Yup. Twelve."

Hayden grimaced. "Oh."

"Can I come in, or do I have to hang out in the hall all day?"

It was tempting to leave them in the hallway. Instead, Hayden stepped back and Luce strode in, collapsing on the sofa in the corner.

"Want a drink or something?" Hayden asked, doing a quick catalogue of what she had to offer. Which was tap water.

"No thanks. Come sit down."

Hayden flopped next to them, pulling a cushion into her lap and hugging it. Rubbing her eyes, she asked, "Now, why are you here?"

"You're kidding me?"

"No."

"You. Went. Out. With. Thomson." Luce pulled a leg under themself and swiveled to face her. "And then ignored my messages."

"Your twelve messages."

"So you saw them."

Oops. "No…"

"Lies."

"I was enjoying teasing you. You made it so easy."

"Hayden…" The last syllable was so drawn out it went on for endless seconds. "Tell me what's going on."

Lying. Hayden detested it. To her core. It left a bad taste that coated her tongue for weeks on end. She had a philosophy: don't lie, because the truth hurts less than finding it out later with the added slap of betrayal. She'd learned that the hard way. Maybe it wasn't a philosophy. That could be the wrong word for it. But it was definitely something to live by.

"Tell me." Luce sounded close to whining now.

"Nothing."

Well, that was an idiotic response. Luce raised one eyebrow—an ability Hayden had always been jealous of; it looked so suave—and watched her.

Nothing else but a solid, judgmental glare.

"Okay, okay, fine." How to lie but not lie? Omission wasn't any better. Something twisted in Hayden's gut. "She just, she asked me to get a drink. I figured why not."

Okay. A lie, kind of. Not even, really. An e-mail *had* been sent saying *let's go to a bar.* Hayden just hadn't added any of the extra information around it. Like that she was probably going to get married to her. For reasons Hayden didn't know, except for her own. And those reasons included a lot of zeros. That even had a number that *wasn't* zero in front of them.

"She what, like, came up and asked you to go for a drink?"

"Well…yeah." It sounded lame, even to Hayden's ears.

"Thomson. Who you really dislike for reasons including, and I quote, 'She's so cold I could ask her to hold my beer in summer to cool it'—" Luce ticked that off on one of their fingers before doing the same to a second "—and, 'She has the bedside manner of a Chihuahua on crack.'" Another finger ticked off. "And, my personal favorite: 'You could pee on her and not get a reaction.'"

Sometimes, Hayden was overdramatic. Obviously, one of those times was, well, every time she'd spoken about Sam in the past. But the woman had rubbed her the wrong way. She still did. And it was easier to vent about Samantha Thomson than the three patients she lost in one day or the crappy health care system she was stuck in, trying to help people and often blocked by red tape.

"Well, all of those assessments were true." Hayden shrugged. "And still are."

"So." Luce poked her in the knee "Why did you go out for a drink with her?"

"Curiosity."

"Curiosity?"

Should she run with that? "Yeah. You know. I was curious as to why she wanted a drink, what she was like."

"So you chose to go out with someone you don't like, rather than with, say, me, who I assume you enjoy spending time with? Or with Owen from Renal, who you share coy little looks with in the hall?"

"I do not share—okay. Fine. But only because he started it."

"So why not go out with him instead? Or Megan from that nightclub who was into you but you said spoke too loud? Or, hell, the guy who fixed your bike that you only ever used once but were glad it broke because you got his number? Or someone you walked past in the street? Why *her*?"

Hayden had opened her mouth to say something, *anything*, when Luce kept going. "Oh my God. Is this one of those sexy things where you, like, hate each other, but it's all filled with eye sex and heat and, really, you just want to tear her clothes off?"

"What? No. No! I was curious. I don't, like, secretly think she's hot or want to—to tear her clothes off. Don't be insane."

Did Hayden think Sam was hot? No. God, no. Well, she wasn't *not* hot. But Hayden had never really thought about it. Mostly, Sam was annoying and rude.

Luce almost looked disappointed. "Oh. I still don't get it, then." They perked up. "Wait. Did you check out her collarbones?"

Hayden blinked. "Uh…"

She had.

Luce's grin could be called evil. "You so did. You always check out a girl's collarbones."

Hayden huffed. "Exactly, I always do it. As for the drink, I was curious. She asked me. I said yes."

"You wore your date boots."

"They were the only ones I had."

Luce flopped back against the sofa. "Fine, whatever. How was it? Awkward? Fun? Filled with flirting you didn't realize was flirting?"

"It was…awkward." That eyebrow was being raised at her again. But now was when Hayden had to convince Luce of this, or at least to start. Otherwise, how would Luce believe any of this later? How would she explain wanting to go out with Sam again? Or, you know, becoming her lawfully wedded wife? Just the thought of that sentence wanted to make Hayden gag. Lawfully wedded wife. *Please.*

It wasn't that Hayden didn't really believe in marriage, it was, well…she didn't believe in marriage.

"It was awkward, but nice. She was…warmer outside of work." Not really. Well, maybe kind of. So, not a lie? There'd been the odd icy, wry comment now and then that could be called funny? Once the shock had died down. "She was funny."

True—*ish.*

"Huh." The eyebrow had calmed down, and now Luce was looking less interrogative. "So you're, like, friends?"

That was safe for now. "Yeah. I suppose."

"Is she gonna be nicer at work?"

"Probably not. I think that's how she works." And, you know, lived.

"Fun." Luce straightened up, peering past Hayden. "Anyway, want to go out for a walk or something? That gallery you like is having a free exhibition. Plus, we can't stay here. Your psycho cat is glaring at me. I think he may rip my face off."

Not wanting to think about the fact that Luce had pointedly said "free," Hayden turned around. Sure enough, Frank was sitting in the doorway to her room, eyes in slits as he focused on Luce, his tail swishing.

"He's just saying hello."

Frank growled.

"Yeah, murderously." Luce scoffed. "I don't think he's ever forgiven me for feeding him when you went to see your family last year. He blamed me for it."

"True. And the exhibition sounds good."

Hayden's heart was thundering in her chest. Lies and half-truths and starting to really step toward getting *married* were making all of this far too real. She stood and scooped up Frank as she walked into her room to change and closed the door behind her. She plopped him on the bed, where he sat gazing at her.

"You should be nice to Luce. They have food when I'm not around."

He turned around and faced the other way, lying down.

"Good chats, Frank."

~ ~ ~

After three days off, Hayden slogged her way through her first day back, which was filled with four patients complaining of chest pain—one of whom just had bad heartburn—two broken bones, a patient who had overdosed, another who had been freaking out on meth, three colds that should have gone to their local doctor—if they had insurance that covered that—and one motorcycle crash.

Somehow, though, she was pinging off the wall when the day was over at around seven in the evening. She'd managed to get everything ready for handover at a decent time and had been the first to slip into the small room with cluttered desks that doctors and nurses alike used to escape the bustle of the ER to do their documentation.

Signing off on the last of her paperwork with a flourish, Hayden bounced on her heels. She hummed under her breath the tune to "Let's Get Down to Business" from *Mulan*, which she had no excuse for watching on her own in her mid-twenties except that it was an awesome film. Frank had certainly liked it.

"Hello."

Her head snapped up. Halfway-in and halfway-out of the room, Sam stood with her hands buried in her lab coat pockets. She had very faint circles under her eyes. Was she tired? Not that Hayden really cared.

"Hey." Hayden capped her pen and kept it in her hand, twirling it around her fingers. "How are you?"

"I'm fine." Sam's jaw twitched once. "And you?"

Like an afterthought. Or like she was listening to a reminder in her head? Hayden *had* told her to try harder.

"I'm fine. Long day."

"Oh." She clearly had no idea how to carry a conversation. "Are you busy?"

Hayden looked around the empty room. "No. Just finished, actually."

"Would you like to get a coffee?"

"Uh—yeah."

"Okay. I need to change. I'll meet you at the entrance."

"Uh—yeah."

"Do you have any other responses?"

Well, that was kind of rude. But there was something about the way Sam's lips twitched, barely noticeable, that made Hayden pause the roll of her eyes she'd been about to give. "Uh—yeah?"

"Funny."

"I'm hilarious, Sam."

"I'll see you in ten minutes."

"Okay."

But she'd already turned and walked away. Just in time for Luce to walk in, sidestepping Sam with a polite nod.

"Are you going out with her again?" Luce asked.

"Uh—yeah?"

"Interesting."

Hayden snapped the folder in front of her shut and slipped it away. "It's really not."

"Oh, I beg to differ."

"You asked out Coffee Girl yet?" Hayden smirked.

"Don't change the subject."

"Don't avoid the question."

Luce grabbed the pen Hayden had started twirling around her fingers again and took the folder they needed. "I'm not avoiding."

"Sure."

"I'm just… Dating's hard."

Well, that was definitely the truth. Hayden sighed, her hip against the desk, and watched Luce open the folder to start making notes.

"Yeah, it is."

Their voice held something, though, and it made Hayden more careful. Luce was purposefully not looking at her, their eyes on the paper, but their pen barely moving. "You know, the whole 'are they interested, are they not? Do they like coffee too, should I kiss them? What flaws are they keeping masterfully hidden? Will they respect my pronouns and understand what non-binary is without making me feel like it's the strangest thing in the world?' That kind of thing. Dating."

Ah. So that was it. Luce's eyes were still fixed on the paper, and Hayden's heart went out to her friend. She knew that Luce had identified as non-binary for several years before they met. And usually they were as confident as people came.

Coming out to their parents, a father who was a third-generation child of Japanese immigrants and a mother who was second, had taken Luce years. Their parents' acceptance had helped their confidence a lot, but sometimes little insecurities sneaked out.

And now this. Coming out constantly could be exhausting, and it was a constant for Hayden. You never came out once, like people seemed to believe. It was every time you met someone, for *any* sexuality that wasn't straight. For Hayden, it was stopping people from calling her a lesbian when she was dating a woman, or straight when dating a man, or getting it completely wrong if the person wasn't either.

But for gender? Hayden couldn't even imagine how constant that must be for Luce.

"Well," Hayden said, hoping she was handling this okay, "if she doesn't respect your pronouns, I'll make sure to order the most complicated coffee order known to humankind every single day for a year."

The corner of Luce's lip quirked up. "Yeah?"

"Totally. And the other thing? If she doesn't understand it, well…her loss. Because you're freaking awesome."

Hayden wrapped her arms around Luce in a tight hug and shook them a little until they laughed.

"Yeah, yeah, okay," Luce said, their cheeks splitting with a grin. "Fine. Go on your date."

Hayden walked toward the door. "It's not a date."

"Sure."

~ ~ ~

"Order something."

"Really, no, it's fine." Hayden said it as authentically as she could. All right, she was starving, but she wasn't going to be someone's kept pet. It was degrading. She was better than that. Better than that, yet her stomach was rumbling.

"Hayden." Every time her name fell from Sam's lips, it seemed like an accident, as if they should both be left blinking at each other in surprise. "We're doing this for appearances' sake, and if we've made a dinner date—" was it Hayden's imagination, or had she hesitated over the word 'date'? "—and only I eat, that will look entirely strange."

The place smelled like heaven. Sam had led the way to a steakhouse a twenty-minute walk from the hospital. It wasn't a classy restaurant, but an honest-to-goodness steak house, complete with (what Hayden hoped was fake) horns on the wall and cow-print seats.

Hayden loved meat. She had zero issues eating it. If she was richer, she'd love to make better choices and choose meat that had come from animals which had trundled freely through green pastures and fed only on pesticide-free grass and got up to whatever happy mischief cows got up to before meeting their end to fill her plate. But sadly, her funds didn't stretch that far. Yet, regardless of this love, she still didn't really understand why people would want to sit in a restaurant adorned with anything and everything to remind them that the thing they were eating was once running around with feelings and moo-type thoughts.

But shit, it smelled good.

"That's true. But who's going to see us?"

Sam shrugged, a gesture that Hayden had never seen her do. It looked far too casual on her. "Most likely? Nobody. But still, possibly someone. Order something."

Hayden grumbled but reached for a menu. She decided upon the cheapest main dish. When she looked up from the plastic menu—which, yes, was covered in happy cow faces (seriously?)—Sam was holding her wine glass and staring at her. She was wearing a white shirt again, something made of material that probably cost more than Hayden's sofa, though she had no idea how much the sofa had cost, actually, as it came with the furnished apartment. The shirt had no buttons and was loose, yet not. Hayden had to admit she looked nice. And that was weird. And her green eyes were boring into her.

"What?" Hayden asked.

"Does anyone else know you have money issues?"

Hayden ran the edge of her nail along the plastic edge of the menu. Being under so much scrutiny was uncomfortable, especially from someone she saw as her superior. Well, that wasn't true. Hayden didn't see any of the doctors like that. And most other surgeons didn't act like it. To her, everyone in the hospital was a team. But it was clear Sam saw herself as superior, and that made Hayden feel like the junior. "I don't—I don't have money issues."

Sam took a sip of her wine.

Hayden bit at her lip. With a sigh, she gave in. "No. Other people don't know. I think my friend does. But we don't talk about it. Is it that obvious?"

"Probably not. But you agreed to this very readily, based on the money." She cocked her head. "Unless you've been holding a secret burning love for me for years."

Hayden barked a laugh. That had not been what she'd expected Sam to say. Sam was actually smiling. Lines appeared around her eyes, deepening, softening her entire face. So those *were* from positive facial expressions. Interesting. "No. It was definitely the money. No offence."

"None taken."

"I tend to not like people to know how broke I am."

The waiter appeared, and they both placed their orders. He was even wearing a cowboy hat that looked like it had been ordered in bulk from the Internet. It was plastic.

This did not seem like Sam's type of place. Had she chosen it especially because Hayden had noticed how expensive the first place had been?

"Can I ask you something?" Sam asked when he'd gone with a "Thankee, gals," in the worst attempt at a southern accent Hayden had ever heard.

"You just did."

Sam shook her head and looked skyward like Hayden's mother used to do, as if asking for strength. "The first question is a usual part of conversation, or so I'm led to believe."

"Fine, yes. Ask away."

"Why are you a nurse and have such money issues? Correct me if I'm wrong, but you were a medical student."

Hayden's mouth went dry. "What?"

"Am I mistaken?"

Hayden's heart was in her throat.

"It was premed. And how did you know that?"

She'd been lucky to find a program that let her shadow a doctor in her first, and only, year of premed.

"I recognize your face. I have since you first started in the ER. You were shadowing a colleague in my old hospital."

Hayden opened her mouth to say something. Then closed it again. Did Sam have a photographic memory?

"I—" she cleared her throat. Her voice was croaky, so she had a sip of water. It felt as if someone had exposed her biggest secret. Which, in a way, Sam had. Or had opened the door that led to something hugely private in her life. A few more steps and Sam would fall right into it all. And if there was anyone she didn't want that happening with, it was Samantha Thomson. "I don't remember you."

"I only helped a little with med students at that time. My hair was longer, and brown, not my natural color."

That deep red was natural? People would kill for that.

"Oh."

And Hayden was being as eloquent as ever. But this was leaving her breathless. Her hands were even clammy. No one knew about this, not in her current life.

"I mean, if you were on your way to study medicine, I assume you had the money for college. And you would be earning a lot more at this point. Or you would be soon. You're still young. Twenty-six?"

"Seven."

Like it mattered. Hayden's mouth was still dry. She sipped her water again.

"I think I've upset you," Sam said.

"No. I, uh, didn't know you knew about that."

"So?"

"I—I'm a nurse. It's a good job."

"Yes. But you could be more than just a nurse, and earning a wage that—"

"*Just* a nurse?"

And that clammy feeling was gone, replaced with heat in her chest. *Just a nurse.* God, doctors, and especially surgeons, with their holier-than-thou attitudes.

Okay. Not fair. This whole just-a-nurse thing wasn't an attitude that doctors expressed often these days.

Yet here was Sam, *pitying* her because she was *just* a nurse. And with no idea what had led to *why*.

"I—"

"I love my job, Thomson."

Sam's brow furrowed.

"Nursing is vicious and hard and *important*," Hayden continued. "I had to study my ass off, still, to become *just* a nurse."

"Of course. It's only, you could have…done more." Sam didn't seem to have anything else to say after that, and Hayden didn't care if she did, because *she* sure had more to say.

Done *more*? Like nursing was less?

"I hold people as they die. I put my hands on their chest and help bring them back to life. I'm the first and last line between incompetent doctors who make big errors sometimes, and I have to know a *shitload* to recognize when that's happening. Nurses have to tell within a second-long window when a patient is deteriorating and intervene while we wait for doctors to get there." Her voice wasn't rising, yet it sure wasn't lowering. But she was *pissed*. How dare Sam? "I miss toilet breaks and lunch breaks, I clean up people who can't do it for themselves, and I hold their loved ones as they sob when there's nothing else we could have done. And you think I could have done *more*? I may not have become a doctor, and I may have been devastated when that didn't happen. But I wouldn't trade my job for anything."

Sam had gone, if possible, much paler than normal. Her freckles stood out so obviously it was impossible to think Hayden hadn't noticed them before. The paleness of her skin made her eyes incredibly green, and that made Hayden even madder, for some unknown reason. She said nothing.

The waiter appeared, putting their food down, and Hayden held Sam's eye. Neither of them even acknowledged him. It smelled divine, yet her stomach felt filled with lead.

"I'm leaving. This is over. All of it."

Hayden stood up. If someone could think so little of her, there was no way she would be able to sit near that person for a year and know that was how they thought.

Let alone freaking marry them. What had she been thinking?

She stood up, her cheeks hot, and left with the feeling of Sam's eyes on her as she walked out.

CHAPTER 5

Hayden woke up still mad.

At work, she was still mad.

She tried not to be mad in the direction of her patients, but it didn't really work. When she woke up, she'd thought there might be *some* kind of apology from Sam, but of course her phone had only had three game request notifications she needed to delete and a photo of Luce's dinner they'd made at home. Which had looked much nicer than the protein bar Hayden had found in the pocket of her jacket and eaten angrily while half-watching TV.

Even while eating a free sandwich her patient had ordered yet couldn't eat since they'd ended up having to fast for an operation, Hayden was *still* mad.

Like, so mad.

Sam had appeared in the ER and had walked past Hayden as if she didn't exist. Again. And, okay, it wasn't like Hayden was exactly being inviting, but was Sam really not going to do or say anything after last night?

Not that Hayden wanted her to. Even for two hundred forty thousand dollars.

That was a *lot* of money though.

No.

She bit into the sandwich and chewed ferociously, staring at the wall of the break room. Another nurse left without saying anything. Most likely, the angry bites and stony silence told him that Hayden really didn't feel like talking.

The door opened and, despite her resolve to give all her attention to the wall, Hayden looked over. Luce closed the door and crossed their arms. Hayden took another bite and met Luce's look.

"Okay. Seriously, Hayden. What is up with you?"

Hayden swallowed her mouthful. "Nothing."

"Oh, totally. I can see that. You're the epitome of calm."

"I am."

"You're so mad you're practically vibrating with it."

"Okay. Yes." Hayden gesticulated with her hands, the tomato filling from her sandwich falling on the ground. Great. Now she'd have to pick that up. "I'm angry."

"What happened?" Luce had their soothing voice on. It always worked.

Hayden took a deep breath and let it out slowly through her nose. "Thomson is an ass."

Luce raised that one stupid eyebrow. "So we're back there?"

"We never really left there."

"Even though you kept going out with her?"

"Two times. Two times is not 'kept.'"

"Okay. Fine. What did she do?" Luce walked over to the coffee machine, switching it on with a wrinkle of their nose. The coffee in the nurses' break room was notoriously sludge-like.

Hayden opened her mouth, then closed it. Tell Luce, or not tell Luce? It wasn't fair to tell the whole story; parts of it weren't hers to tell. Even if she was angry at Sam. But that didn't mean Hayden couldn't open up a little.

"She used the words *just a nurse*."

Mug in hand, still waiting for the pot to fill with stale, gross coffee—even though it was freshly brewed—Luce spun around. "*Excuse* me?"

"Yeah."

"What—but. What?"

"Yeah. That was my reaction."

"But with an epic Hayden-style lecture?"

Hayden smiled begrudgingly. "Yeah."

"Good for you," Luce said sharply. "Why would she say that? Like, even if she thought that way, why would she say it to *you*? A nurse?"

Because she knew Hayden had been on a career path headed toward being a doctor. In pediatrics, if she'd had any say in it. But Luce didn't know that. It involved too many other things, too much else that hit close to something she didn't want to go into with people. Things that would make them give her that pitying look.

Kind of like Sam had last night. And she didn't even know the half of it.

Hayden didn't need pity.

She loved her job. Every word she'd said to Sam was one she meant. Every last one.

Luce was still waiting for an answer.

"She found out I was once in med school. And couldn't understand why I would change that."

"You were?"

"Yeah."

When Hayden didn't offer any more information, Luce, thankfully, didn't push—one of the many reasons Hayden appreciated their friendship. "Okay. And she acted like you lost something huge from that?"

"Yup."

"So, she sucks as much as you thought she did. No loss."

Hayden forced a dry laugh. "Yeah. Exactly. No loss."

Only two hundred forty thousand dollars. And a weird feeling of disappointment bubbling in her stomach that seemed to have nothing to do with the money, but more with the fact that she'd kind of assumed Samantha Thomson didn't think like that.

"You okay?"

Hayden looked up from her hands to deep brown eyes. "Yeah. I'm fine. Thanks. All good with you? Did you ask out Coffee Girl?"

"No. I sat on my couch after cooking dinner and binge-watched TV."

"What series?"

"One with clones. It's epic."

"Should I watch it?"

"Definitely."

"Text me the details, and consider it done." Hayden looked at her watch and heaved a sigh. "Well, my break is over. I've got to get back out there."

"Oh." Luce pouted and poured a cup of the too-thick coffee. "I was hoping you had more time before you finished."

They plopped onto the sofa as Hayden stood up. "No can do, sadly. Too much to do, and I've already had my thirty minutes."

"Sad. Drink tonight?"

No money. "I wish. Can't, sorry."

"Soon?"

"Of course."

"Okay."

Hayden gave an overly cheery wave and walked out, able to feel their gaze on her back.

As soon as she walked back into the ER, she was slammed with the bustle of it all. It was a steadily busy day, and as soon as one bed had cleared, it was filled with someone else. Even with the anger still boiling under her skin, Hayden was able to distract herself by moving seamlessly between patients and mostly shed the shaken feeling.

What did she care what Sam thought, anyway? The loss of so much money was the killer here.

She was thinking exactly that several hours later, typing at a computer to find her patient's blood work results, when a voice interrupted her.

"Can I speak with you?" A pause. "Please."

Hayden didn't even need to look around to know who it was. "I'm busy."

"I know. But you're always busy. I've tried to come up to you multiple times today, but you were always occupied. Now was the only time that seemed appropriate."

Hitting *print* on the blood report, Hayden logged herself out of the system and spun the office chair around. Sam was standing several feet away, hands in her lab coat pockets and looking strangely unsure of herself. She had a little furrow between her brows.

Several expressions in as many days. Who'd have thought?

And she'd been trying to approach Hayden all day? How had Hayden not known that?

"I don't have anything to say," Hayden said.

"That's fine, as I do. Give me five minutes." Sam visibly swallowed, though her expression stayed the same: no hint of anything, except that little crease in the middle of her brow. "Please."

Two *pleases*. Impressive.

"Fine." Hayden stood up. "Five minutes."

Sam nodded and turned, leading the way to one of the treatment rooms filled with medications and dressing equipment. Eyes followed them, and Hayden resisted the urge to frown at the people who were watching without even trying to hide it. Apparently, people had already started to notice they were spending time together. Too bad it was when Hayden had definitely decided against the whole thing.

Sam entered one of the rooms in the far corner that tended to be less frequented. Hayden followed her through and closed the door. A metal table sat in the middle, used for making up antibiotics and other such things, and Sam turned, resting her fingertips on the surface.

Those smudges under her eyes were more prominent.

Hayden crossed her arms and didn't care if she was the image of defensive.

"I'm sorry."

Hayden blinked. But Sam was still there, her eyes boring into her. And she had, apparently, spoken those words.

"What?" Hayden asked.

"I apologized," Sam said. "But I can say it again: I'm sorry."

"Oh."

It didn't look like she was joking. In fact, Sam looked as serious as ever.

"I…" Sam sighed and broke eye contact, looking down at her fingers pressing into the steel. "I didn't mean what I said the way you took it. Though, with reflection, I can see that it sounded like that."

"Oh." Hayden was as eloquent as ever. But this was really not what she'd expected.

"I was simply thinking of the money, for you. Of how you could be in a different situation now, financially. I didn't really understand how you got to be where you are now." She furrowed her brow, still not meeting Hayden's eye. Like this, Sam looked younger. Or maybe it was that she looked different. "I don't like not understanding things. Sometimes I can be abrupt or too pushy when I'm trying to get an answer. I get very…focused on the need to know why or how. And I forget to measure my words."

She still hadn't looked up. But every word sounded thought out. Almost as if she'd mulled on them all night and day.

"Oh." Hayden needed to say something more. "Okay."

"I did not mean to imply that being a nurse was *less*." Sam looked up, and even after the eye contact from before, her eyes were shockingly green. Clear and bright. Sincere. "I should have thought about my wording more. I often make that mistake."

That boiling anger in Hayden was barely even warm now. When had that happened?

"So?" Hayden asked, trying to measure her words more. "What did you mean?"

"In our world, nursing is paid less. Doctors, eventually, make more. We were talking about money. My *just* was in reference to this situation, not the occupation. Without nurses, hospitals would fall apart. Every word you said last night was true. I don't disagree with any of it."

"Oh."

"Do you have any other words?" Sam's lips were quirking up. At the throwback to the comment the day before, maybe. Or perhaps in relief that Hayden wasn't laying into her again.

So Hayden caved. She smiled, finally. "I do. Okay. Thank you for your apology."

"You're welcome." The words were almost stiff, but the smile on her face was less hesitant. "I have a question."

"Yeah?"

"Did you mean it? That the whole thing is off?"

Hayden took in a deep breath. "I did when I said it. But… Now, I don't know."

"Okay."

"Are you still interested?" Hayden asked.

"Yes."

"Maybe I am too."

"Okay." Sam said it as if everything was decided now. "Maybe, if you're interested, we can repeat dinner. Hopefully more successfully this time."

"Does it really matter to be seen out?"

"Yes."

"Do I get an answer as to why yet?"

Sam shook her head. "One day, depending how this—" she waved a hand between them "—goes."

"Fine. Yes. Dinner then. Tonight?"

"I have surgery." Sam buried her hands back in her pockets. "Can you do tomorrow?"

"Okay."

"Good." Sam hesitated on something, her tongue running over her bottom lip. "Hayden. I'm not very good. At being social. I'm awkward. I don't follow cues the way most other people do."

"I've noticed."

Sam dipped her head but held her eye. "Just so you know."

"Okay. Refrain from insulting me, and we'll be fine."

Fine. Enough. Hayden had no idea how this was going to go, really. With the anger completely gone, she felt drained. And curious. Really, now. She did feel curious. Sam was a bit of a mystery, intriguing.

"I'll try." That smile was back, curving up one side of Sam's mouth.

"Well, coming in here alone with a closed door will certainly have gotten noticed."

"What?" Sam looked behind Hayden to the door then back to her face. Her eyes widened, hardly perceptible, but there. "Oh."

Hayden smirked. "Shall we walk out while fixing our shirts?"

"Why would—Hayden!" Sam rolled her eyes, and the reaction was so natural Hayden chuckled. "That's ridiculous."

"Why? Everyone will be thinking it anyway. And that way, we can get that gossip mill really going." She didn't mean it. She was still unsure she wanted to go through with this at all, let alone get *that* rumor going. But still, the half-appalled and half-amused look on Sam's face was worth it.

"I think that's going a little too far."

"We could mess your hair up."

Sam started walking past her to the door, Hayden turning on her heel to follow her out.

"Very funny, Hayden."

"I could rub lipstick on your neck."

"You're not even wearing lipstick."

"Well that'd *really* get them talking, then, wouldn't it?"

Hell must have frozen over, because Sam *laughed*.

CHAPTER 6

Opening her door, Hayden shouldn't have been surprised at who she found. Luce was staring at her, arms crossed.

This was getting tedious.

"All right, you've been out with her, like, six times. And they're just the ones I know about. What's going on?"

With a sigh, Hayden stood aside and let Luce into her apartment. Luce walked through the door briskly, turned on their heel in the middle of the living room, and crossed their arms again. That one talented eyebrow was raised in Hayden's direction as soon as she'd closed the door.

"What do you mean 'What's going on?'"

"What do you think I mean? I mean—" they waved their arms in the air "—I'm in the dark, and I *hate* that."

Hayden smirked. "You're hilarious when you're all worked up."

Now was the point, the time to really move everything forward. To start lying. To not pass this off as curiosity and friends anymore, but to commit to what Hayden and Sam had agreed on and to tell Luce they were dating. It had been two weeks.

Lies sucked.

"Okay. Fine, Luce. I like her."

Well, very mildly true. Okay, barely true. But Hayden didn't *dislike* Sam as much as she had. After being pushed into hatred after their first disastrous dinner, she'd left that behind pretty quickly and slowly eased toward not really minding her. Not that great, but it was something.

Luce's mouth dropped open. "What?"

"I like her." Hayden held their gaze and shrugged. She'd rehearsed this in her head. She could sell it. "I don't really know where it came from or how it happened, but I like her."

"You're kidding me."

"No."

Luce's arms fell to their side. "*You?* Like *Thomson?*"

"Sam's pretty nice, and kind of funny. And, I don't know, we click."

All rehearsed. She'd said it out loud each night to Frank to try and get it to sound natural. Again and again. He'd started to walk away from her whenever she started.

"*Sam?*" Oh God. The incredulous look on Luce's face was making Hayden waver. "What happened to 'Thomson'?"

"That's her name."

"And you *like* Sam?"

"Yeah?"

"You *like* like her? Like, warm, fuzzy feelings?"

"Yeah."

Luce walked backward until the back of their legs hit Hayden's chair. They sat down heavily. "Oh."

Hayden sat on the sofa opposite them. Well, this was going just as swimmingly as she'd figured it would.

"I mean, I can't exactly be surprised." Luce looked exactly that, however. "The last two weeks you've been going out with her a lot."

Which Hayden had hoped everyone had noticed. They'd been getting looks since emerging from that treatment room together, even with their shirts perfectly tucked in and no lipstick in sight.

"I'm surprised you survived two weeks without saying anything." Hayden bit back a smirk.

"I *tried*." Luce fell back heavily into the sofa. "I was hoping you'd spill something."

"And decided to give up *not* asking on a random Wednesday afternoon?"

Luce even managed to look sheepish. "I got bored. Plus, Tasha messaged me and said she'd seen the two of you out and asked if I had any gossip. Which, of course, I wouldn't give her if I had, but I hated that I wasn't even lying when I said no."

"Well, thanks, I guess." Hayden stood up. She needed a distraction from the still-shocked look on Luce's face.

Last week had been payday, so Hayden had actually been to the supermarket that morning. She had vegetables.

"Want a drink?" Hayden could actually ask that and have more to offer than water from the tap. Because she'd been to the supermarket. Had she mentioned that? It had just been so exciting.

"Sure."

"Beer? Juice? Bottle of water? Soft drink?" It was tempting to list the different types of soft drink, if only for the novelty of having a variety to offer, but that would border on weird.

As if knowing what was happening, Luce finally grinned. "Do you have cola?"

"Yup." Hayden stood up. "Ice?"

"Sure."

"Lemon?"

"Why not?"

Hayden took a second in the tiny kitchen to take a breath. By signing up for this, she'd agreed to lie. That was all part of it. Luce wouldn't tell anyone. Hayden knew that. If she told Luce what was going on, they would keep that secret and probably actually help. But Sam had been clear: no one was to know. And really, if Luce knew, Hayden didn't know if she could keep the charade going.

Three ice cubes plonked into the glass, and she squared her shoulders. She could do this. It would all be worth it. Once she had the drinks ready, she sucked in a deep breath and carried the glasses out.

"Thanks." Luce took a sip, then held the glass against their knees. "So you, for real, are interested in her?"

"Yup. Even going for a drink tonight."

And Hayden would pay. This might all be a part of Sam's plan, and therefore included in costs she covered, but it was getting excessive. Hayden liked to look after herself, thank you very much. And, last month excluded, she generally managed. She'd budgeted her ass off for this month.

"Right. Again, okay." Luce took another sip, clearly trying to get their thoughts together. "Okay, fine. You like her. I don't get it, since you really, *really* seemed not to like her before. But okay. Fine."

"Um, thanks." Guilt twinged in Hayden's stomach. And now Luce had to go and be their awesome self.

"So, she good in bed?"

As if she were fifteen, heat flooded Hayden's cheeks. "Luce!"

"Sorry, fine, okay. You're taking it slow." Luce looked wicked, and Hayden narrowed her eyes. "She a good kisser, then?"

"Shut up."

"Why're you so red? Not kissed her yet?"

How was she going to handle this? How was she going to explain not having kissed or slept with someone who, in a week or two, Hayden was going to have to convince Luce she wanted to marry? Not that these things were a requirement. "Of course I have."

"So, why so red? Did you embarrass yourself?"

"You're seriously an ass."

"Yes, I am." They leaned in closer to Hayden. "So?"

Hayden pulled her leg up under herself on the sofa. "So what?"

"*Is* she good in bed?"

Hayden threw a cushion that hit the wall feet away from Luce.

"That was pathetic. I'm so close you could touch me with your foot if you reached out."

Yup. An ass.

~ ~ ~

Hayden chose the bar this time. She and Sam met at seven o'clock at the hospital, making sure that Sam waited inside for Hayden to walk through from the ER locker rooms to meet her. More visibility. More people to see them. Sam was dressed casually in jeans and a flannel shirt that, coupled with her red hair and pale complexion, made Hayden think of a country singer. It was weirdly endearing, although the serious look that was ever present on her face took away from that. They hovered awkwardly near each other, smiling and trying to make it look natural, and then turned to go, the cool air outside washing over them. It felt damp, as if it was about to rain. But the sky looked mostly cloudless, speckled with stars they could barely see, thanks to the city lights.

"Good day?" Hayden asked as they walked toward the bar she had in mind. The wind was cold, and she hunched her shoulders against it.

"Yes. Busy. I had three operations. My intern is…slow. But he's learning."

That guy who had insisted Sam was the best there was. Which was true. But he'd seemed to mean his praise. Maybe Sam was a better teacher than Hayden had anticipated. Though he did always look terrified. Anyone on Sam's service seemed to look like that.

"How were your days off?" The last few times, Sam had seemed a bit more rehearsed in small talk. It was less stilted and random.

"Fine. I spent most of them cleaning my apartment and talking to my cat. I hung out with one of my friends today. You know them, actually. Luce, a nurse in the ER."

"Luce?" Sam's tone made it clear she had no idea who they were. "What does she look like?"

"*They* are of Japanese descent, have dark hair, and have a bright orange stethoscope?" Hayden tried not to stare at Sam to see how receptive she was to the pronoun check.

But it was important to her that someone she was about to spend a lot of time with wasn't transphobic and gross.

"The orange stethoscope is familiar, but I'm afraid I can't really place her—them. I assume you did that so pointedly for a reason?"

So much for subtle. "Uh, yeah, I did. Luce is non-binary and prefers gender-neutral pronouns. *They* and *them.*"

Silence was her answer. They were almost at the bar, and Hayden finally gave in and turned her head. Sam was staring straight ahead, face impassive. There was the tiniest twitch of her brow, though, that made Hayden think she was digesting what had been said.

"Non-binary?" Sam finally asked.

"Yeah. It means you aren't fully one of the binary genders, man or woman. You might be both, or neither, or it might shift around. In a nut shell."

"Oh."

Hayden gave in again and looked. Sam had the exact same expression, and she turned her head, catching Hayden's eye as they walked.

"I haven't heard of that. Okay. So. I'll see if I notice them tomorrow."

Well, that was good, she supposed. Not that respecting someone's pronouns deserved praise, but it was nice that Sam had adapted, even if she hadn't heard of people being non-binary before. It wasn't often Hayden came across someone in the queer community who didn't know *something* about gender identities, though. Maybe Sam wasn't much involved in the community. She did say she wasn't great with socializing.

They were at the bar. Hayden stopped, and Sam copied her, looking at the door with trepidation on her face. No doorman waited to open it. Though, to be fair, they hadn't seemed to go to any places that were like that since the first time. Most had been more low-key.

This place was one frequented by college kids.

The bar was almost entirely made of scratched, cheap timber, with a pool table and a foosball table squeezed into one end. It smelled like beer. It was where bad decisions went to be made. And the best part?

Sam's face when she walked in.

Hayden almost laughed out loud as Sam looked around, muscle clenching in her jaw.

Sam turned to her. "What?"

"Nothing." Hayden was still grinning. "I'll order our drinks. Any requests?"

"I think a red wine."

Hayden shook her head.

"What?"

"I wouldn't drink the wine here."

"Oh." Sam's jaw was still tight, and Hayden was still grinning. This was far too much fun. "A beer?"

"Coming right up."

The bar was mostly empty, and Hayden wove between tables with their beer bottles a few minutes later. She plunked them on the wood—the *thunk* satisfying and cheap—and sat down.

"Good table choice."

"I know."

So she'd chosen it on purpose? Good to know she'd had the same thought as Hayden. "Near the foosball table is always the best choice."

"Near the—?" Sam glanced behind herself. "Oh. No. That wasn't a factor. It was simply the logical choice."

Hayden took a sip of her beer, mulling it over. "How so?"

"It's the closest to the door, the bar, and the bathrooms."

Hayden turned in her chair, eyeing all the points in the room that Sam had mentioned. This table was almost equally as close to all three places.

"Is that how you always choose?" Hayden asked.

"If I can."

"Interesting."

"Why?"

Hayden shrugged, and behind her the door swung open, sending cool air rushing in and voices drifting over. Laughter. "I've just never considered those kinds of reasons when choosing a table. Hence, interesting."

"All right."

Silence drifted over the table. It often did. While the small talk was getting better, they were still finding common ground. Hayden watched Sam look around the bar, every minute twitch of the muscles in her face giving her expression away. It wasn't that she didn't have expressions, like Hayden had thought; it was that she was very good at schooling them. That, or hers were simply more muted. It was Hayden's game, now, to try and guess how she was feeling about something. Sam watched the people who had come in take a seat at the table next to theirs, and something in her cheek flinched.

Hayden failed to hide her smirk. "What?"

Sam snapped her head back to look at Hayden. "It's only—well, why would they sit so close?"

There were five of them, all from the college, from the looks of it, and they were loudly chatting. One of the guys even had a cap on backward. Some of them were flipping their chairs around to straddle them, and there was a strong smell of body spray—"manly" smells from bottles boasting words like *sword* or *rugged terrain* or *shark teeth* or whatever marketers thought men would want to buy. How did they even gender a smell?

"What do you mean?" Hayden asked.

"The place is so empty, and yet they sat at the table that was right next to another that was occupied."

Hayden laughed. "I suppose that is annoying."

"It doesn't bother you?"

"I don't really think about it."

"They're in our space."

"Want to move?"

"It's fine." Sam said it, but Hayden wasn't sure she believed it. "I just don't get why they'd sit there."

"We could glare at them until they leave?"

Sam's lips twitched. "I don't think that's necessary."

"I could talk loudly about my ten cats and how they're my only loved ones."

This time, Sam definitely smiled. "You only have one cat."

"Maybe I tricked you, and I'll have to move in with all ten."

"Seriously?" And Sam's face was so concerned that Hayden laughed loudly.

"No. Just the one cantankerous cat for you to deal with."

"Hm." And now Sam was cocking her head in that way that Hayden guessed meant she was trying to figure her out.

"Yes?" Hayden took a sip of her beer, the bottle damp. "You obviously want to say something, so spit it out."

"I think we've had a couple of weeks. We can't really delay making the decision any longer. I think it should be now."

And with those words, Hayden's palms went clammy. Which was stupid. She'd not wavered, really, since she'd blown up at Sam and her tactless inability to mince her words. "I suppose we should."

They watched each other for a moment, Hayden's heart thumping in her chest.

"So—are we getting married?" Sam asked.

"Will you tell me why?"

"No." Sam said it with a touch less patience this time. "I told you, I would when I was ready. We barely know each other."

To be fair, how could Hayden hold it against her? Hayden had barely scratched the surface as to why she hadn't studied medicine. But that wasn't any of Sam's business. This was Hayden's.

"Fine." Hayden picked at the label on her beer, the glue and wet paper sticking under her thumbnail. "Well, I'm in."

Sam gave a singular nod. "Me too. I think this has come together nicely."

Like they were talking about plans for a lunch, not for marriage. "So?" Hayden prodded.

So? As in *money?* As in when would Hayden see it? That wasn't exactly something she just wanted to burst out with, though.

"If you give me your bank account details, I'll transfer that money tonight as agreed. And I'll give you the other half when we sign papers, which we should talk about when to do."

"And when I move in." Oh, shit. It was happening.

"Yes, that too."

"Okay."

And it got awkward again.

Sam sighed. A real, honest sigh. She leaned forward, her elbows on the table, and some of that straight posture fell away. She barely flinched as the table next to them gave a loud cheer about something. "I say we sign next week. We need to get a marriage license first. And we have to go together. I'm owed time off, so if you let me know what day is convenient for you, I can go then."

"I have next Monday off." Shit. *Marriage license.* Oh, shit. Hayden's heart was still thumping away.

"Okay. I'll apply online. It means less waiting time in the clerk's office."

"Right."

Of course Sam had researched all this. She was serious about it. It was she, after all, who had wanted to do this for reasons unknown. It was she who had taken the time to search out someone who would be appropriate and who had set up meetings and done all the work toward this, unlike Hayden, who had just been scrolling the Internet because she was bored, saw a marriage offer, and thought, "Why not? I'm broke."

"Once we have the marriage license, we have to wait twenty-four hours."

"I start on night shift Tuesday. It's why I have the Monday free. So we could, uh, get married before I start?"

Sam pulled her phone out of her bag, flicking through what Hayden assumed was her planner.

"I'm not free. But I think I can get someone to cover. I covered for Seymour a few weeks ago so he could get his divorce done."

"Seymour as in Seymour from Dermatology?"

Sam didn't even look up from her phone. "The very one."

"He is *such* an ass."

Now Sam looked up. Her eyes held a spark. "He really is."

"He told me once I'd be prettier if I smiled more."

Now Sam had that furrow between her brow. Her version of a scowl? "He said the same to me. And I heard him tell a receptionist she should dress in something 'appealing' if she wanted to get the right attention. He's disgusting."

But Hayden was grinning. Nothing was more fun than word-bashing a misogynist with someone who felt the same way. "Did you hear what happened with his wife?"

At that, Sam dropped her phone back in her bag. "No? I tend to be too busy to be distracted by gossip."

"Well, *some* of us like the distraction." But she wasn't really offended by Sam's comment. Her tone hadn't seemed to mean it as an insult. "Anyway, his wife works in one of the day clinics, and I heard she left him for his sister."

"No?" Was that a subtle note of glee in Sam's voice?

"Yup. Serves the sexist ass right."

"I know I shouldn't find that funny…"

"But it's pretty hilarious."

"It really is." Sam took a sip of her beer, but it didn't smother the smile she still had on her face. It could almost be called wicked.

"Anyway." Hayden took in a deep breath. She could keep this conversation going. Totally. It wasn't at all terrifying. "Marriage. On Tuesday."

"Right. If you're on night shift, what works best for you? To go early so you can go home and sleep, or for you to sleep late and go later?"

"Early." Her sleep would be screwed up whatever way they did it. The joys of night shift. She really was *not* looking forward to it. It might pay marginally better, but her circadian rhythm was worth far more to her than that.

"Okay. We can meet at City Hall at ten. If we get the license as early as possible Monday, that will be twenty-four hours."

Hayden's mouth felt dry, so she took a sip while nodding in the affirmative, the beer fizzing in her mouth and all the way down her throat. It left a bubbling feeling in her stomach.

"And then, uh, I could move in the next day?"

That made even Sam pause. Did she swallow a bit noticeably? "Of course. Won't you be tired?"

"I'll be delirious, but I can pack the Monday and Tuesday and pick it up when I finish Wednesday morning, take it to your place, and sleep all day."

"Will you need a van? I can hire you something."

"I think a taxi will do. There're only a few suitcases and my cat."

Sam looked almost relaxed, elbows on the table. It was strange. "What about your apartment?" She asked as if it had just occurred to her. "Your furniture?"

"All the furniture belongs to the apartment. And, well, I still have two months on my lease. I figured I wouldn't break it and would keep paying until it's up. It's money I would be paying for two months anyway, and that way…"

"If the agreement fails, you have somewhere to go."

"Exactly."

It meant she wouldn't be saving on rent those two months, but the idea of having to rely completely on Sam made Hayden feel panicked, and this way, she had a safety net. She'd be saving on utilities and such, at least. And the money that was coming her way could cover the rent. And so much more.

"So. We're doing this?" Sam asked.

"Looks like. I, uh, started telling my friend about it. A little."

Sam straightened. "Telling h—them—what?"

Hayden smirked. "Relax. Not the plan. Just implying that I—well—that we…that this—" Hayden waved a hand between them "—was something."

"*Something?*" Now Sam was smirking. An actual smirk. It was half-terrifying and half-awesome. "How are you going to sell marriage if you can't even say more than 'something'?"

"Har-har."

Sam looked far too amused. "I thought I would be the one with issue when it came to talking about it. But apparently not. You can't even say the words."

"Yes. It's very funny. I just hate lying."

That took the smirk off Sam's face. "Oh. Well. That's an issue."

"No, it won't be. I can do it," Hayden said, probably much too quickly. "Really, I can." Elbows on the table, she brought herself a lot closer to Sam and looked her right in the eye.

Take whatever is under the surface and use it. Adopt another personality altogether.

She'd won an award at her school for drama for a reason. "I told them we were dating. And that I liked you."

Sam had gone very still.

"I told them you were funny and nice and that we clicked."

Sam sat back in her chair. "Okay, good. And will you be able to tell them next week that we're married?"

Hayden dropped her head on her arms. "Yes." Her voice was muffled. "Yes, I'll do it." She raised her head. Why were Sam's cheeks pink? "I can do it." Hayden gave a nod, as if that could help her affirm it. "We're getting married." She grinned. "And we're so excited."

Sam rolled her eyes and, again, Hayden was struck with how…relaxed it made her look. "Well done."

"Your turn."

"We're getting married." Sam straightened her shoulders, her eyes on Hayden's and looking down at her almost fiercely. Hayden had a sudden understanding of how it would feel to be her underling, and it bordered on horrifying. And a little… empowering. "Yes, we're very happy. It's been building for a while." Her look hardened even more. "Now, stay out of my business."

Hayden burst out laughing, and Sam gave a wry smile.

"Oh, yeah." Hayden pulled her beer closer. "We're utterly convincing."

"We may need to work on this."

"You think?"

CHAPTER 7

"Clear!"

Hayden lifted her hands from the patient's chest and stepped back. The nurse at the defibrillator glanced once around the bed and hit the shock button. Everyone in the room was focused on the monitor, all hoping to no longer see ventricular fibrillation. Hayden's shoulders tensed when she saw the screen return to the chaotic rhythm of before the shock.

"Recommence compressions." The voice of the ER doctor running the code was steady and calm as she stood back and observed everything. "Someone take a new set of ABGs and we need more epi."

Hayden stepped forward, focusing on nothing but the sternum under her hands. She counted aloud for herself and for the anesthetist currently bagging the patient. Not that they'd need it. They'd be as focused as Hayden.

"One hundred. Someone take over."

Luce, who had been on the other side of the bed, stepped up, their knees resting on the edge of the mattress in order to gain leverage. They started compressions, and Hayden looked around, giving her arms a break. The protocol was to always cycle through two to three people giving compressions to ensure the procedure remained effective. Everyone quickly grew tired.

The nurse who had stepped forward to take the blood samples stepped back. "New bloods done."

Someone grabbed them and ran them to the lab for immediate analysis.

"Pause compressions."

Luce paused, hands hovering over the patient's chest. Hayden's gaze was back on the monitor.

"We need to shock again." The doctor's voice came.

The nurse at the machine adjusted the settings according to the instructions the doctor gave, eyes back on the bed. "Clear."

Luce stepped back. The doctor who was still bagging paused and stepped away. With one last sweeping gaze at the team, the nurse pressed the button.

All eyes were glued on the monitor again.

"That's a sinus rhythm."

Even as the doctor said it, Hayden's shoulders were relaxing. Her hands were shaking slightly.

"Good work, everyone." The doctor's eyes were still glued to the monitor, checking oxygen saturation, pulse rate, and blood pressure. "Right, you only need to stay if this is your patient."

Hayden stayed, the code team stepping back. The patient made a noise, fighting at the tube in his throat, his eyelids fluttering.

"*Tranquilo, Señor Gonzalez.*" Hayden's hand fell on top of his. He wasn't fully conscious. Her words were a last hope to calm him while the tube was pulled from his throat.

"Hayden," the ER doctor said, "we're going to transfer him to the cardiac unit. He needs to be monitored."

"No problem."

And she was only an hour into her shift. At least it had ended well. She bustled around for fifteen minutes, following protocols, administering medications, and ensuring he was stable, making sure Mr. Gonzalez remained calm and hooking him up to a portable monitor.

His family wasn't there yet. She confirmed that his fluids were running correctly and his pain medication was sufficient, murmuring words in Spanish to him the entire time. The transfer was quick and easy, Hayden handing over to the nurse in the cardiac unit. She left him in their capable hands and returned to the ER.

Her hands had finally stopped shaking. It always took a while after a code for everyone involved to relax, even with a positive outcome like this one.

"Hayden."

Hayden headed over to a treatment room where Luce's voice had come from. They were restocking the crash cart that had been decimated in the code. It was always left a mess of empty syringes, packets littering the drawers, things half pulled out and discarded.

"Well done," Luce said.

Hayden grabbed the clipboard. She started checking things off as Luce placed them on the cart. "I'm just glad it worked out."

"Didn't he come in for something irrelevant?"

"Yup. Presented to the ER with a broken finger. Crashed randomly."

"Lucky. If he'd been on the street, he wouldn't have made it."

"Fortunate." Hayden checked off a few more things.

"You okay?" Luce paused in their stuffing the bin with empty packets.

"Yeah, on an adrenaline drop now is all."

"Want a coffee?"

Hayden looked at her watch, then pulled out her to-do list. "I have to check on a patient, but after that I could probably take a break. Jan said she'd cover when I wanted one."

Despite the random code, the ER wasn't so busy that morning. Strange for a Sunday.

"Great. Well, I'm finished here. Thanks for your help. I'll check if the code team is covered for me to take my break."

"See you soon."

Hayden left the clipboard on the bench and walked out. Coffee would help. It always helped. She checked on the status of her patients. One had been transferred to the ward while she'd been in the code—bless the nurse who did that for her—and the other two were stable and asleep. The teenager who had broken her leg thinking she could jump down two flights of stairs on her skateboard was more than asleep: the pain medication had knocked her flat; she was out cold while she waited to go to surgery, her parents sitting next to her bed looking half-relieved and half-exasperated. Hayden couldn't blame them. She'd done something similar when she'd been younger, and her parents hadn't known whether to kiss her for being fine or kill her for being stupid.

She'd gotten a bit of a both. Her dad had covered her cast in drawings, designs he'd made up in his head. A week later, he'd gone on one of his business trips.

Back when they'd thought they'd been business trips.

Shaking her head, she mouthed "Thank you" toward Jan. Luce was waiting by the elevators, and together they slipped in right as the doors closed.

"You have fifteen?" Luce asked.

"Yeah. You?"

"Yup."

"Great. That's just enough time to ask out Coffee Girl."

Luce shook their head. "Very funny."

"To kiss her?"

"Har-har."

"Smile at her?"

"I can barely remember how to coordinate my hands to pay her and pick up my coffee, so no, probably not."

"You're hopeless." Hayden nudged them with her shoulder to take any bite out of her tone.

"As if you can talk—oh. Wait." Luce's face lit up. "You aren't so useless. How's Thomson?"

It took everything in Hayden not to flinch and check which doctor was standing at the back of the elevator. She hadn't paid much attention when they'd gotten in. But it wasn't supposed to matter. As far as the world knew, they were dating.

"She's good." That one eyebrow was raised in her direction, and Hayden was glad the doors opened so she could pretend not to notice it as they left the elevator, and also pretend her answer hadn't been weak. She took in a deep breath. Okay. She could do this. "Really good, actually." She hoped it was Oscar-worthy. "We had drinks the other night."

"Oh yeah. Only drinks?"

Hayden gave a demure look, putting on a pretentious voice. "Gentlefolk never spill their secrets."

"So you didn't get any."

"Shut up, Luce. Look, here's your lady love." Hayden smothered a laugh as Luce balked when they walked up to the coffee cart. "Can I wing-woman for you?"

"No!"

"Please? For the love of all that is awesome?"

"No."

Hayden sighed. "Fine. But you have to do the ordering so you'll at least talk to her." She pushed the money into Luce's hand. It was enough for both of them, thank you very much; if she could afford anything, it was the super-cheap hospital coffee. Hayden gave Luce a gentle push in the small of their back toward the cart. With a final grin in their direction, she detoured to one of the tables, sat down, and kept her eye on Luce. She'd almost feel bad, watching them take in a deep breath and wait in the short line. But they really were adorable.

And useless with pretty people.

Luce turned around and narrowed their eyes at her. Hayden got the hint and reverted to her favorite thing when waiting: people watching. Hospitals were great for it. A doctor walked past, muttering to himself, tapping away at a tablet. A woman pushed herself past on a wheelchair, her hair wild around her head. A man sat at a table near her and exclaimed loudly, "Seriously! The baby was nine and a half pounds. Linda's amazing!"

Ow. Nine and a half pounds? Linda was more than amazing; Linda was a damn rock star.

On the other side of her was the twitchy intern who always followed Sam around. He was staring at a tablet, dark smudges under his eyes noticeable even with his brown skin, his lab coat a little too wrinkled, his hair disheveled. The standard intern look.

"Hey—" she paused. It wasn't like she could call him 'twitchy intern.' "Uh, guy."

Thankfully, he looked up at her, bleary for a second, until a hint of recognition crept over his features. "Oh. Hey. Hayden, right?"

Well, now she just felt bad. He knew her name. "Yeah. What was your name? Sorry."

"No problem. I don't think I've ever told you, it's Leon."

"Nice to meet you properly, Leon."

The way of the hospital. Especially when you worked in the ER. You could lose a patient or save a patient with someone, and never really find out who they were as they disappeared off into whichever part of the hospital they'd come from.

"Likewise. How are you this fine Saturday?"

"It's Sunday, Leon."

He gaped, looked down at the tablet in his hands, and back at her. "Really?"

"Really." She tried and failed miserably not to laugh at him. "Seriously."

"Damn it."

"Life of an intern."

He slumped over the table, pulling his coffee toward himself, and stared woefully at her. "It really is."

"It'll get better."

"I'm clinging to that idea."

Hayden quickly glanced at the coffee line. Luce was still one person away from ordering and would hopefully try and chat for a bit. Or smile? Anything. Whatever they did, Hayden had time for the sneaky idea she'd had.

What a perfect time to probe.

"Your attending never let you have a break?"

"Thomson?" He shrugged awkwardly, still sprawled over the small metal table. "She's not known for it. We do more time than anyone else's interns when on her service."

"Sounds rough."

He straightened, his red eyes wide. "What? It's *awesome*. I've learned so much, way more than I do with anyone else in any other specialty."

He looked so sincere. Like a tiny puppy. "Oh?"

"She's hard-assed as hell, don't get me wrong. We're all terrified of her. She made two of us cry our first week. And by us, I mean I was one of them." He gave an unembarrassed smile. "But she pushes us constantly. Everything's a chance to learn with her. I'm just so freaking tired."

And he kept going, as if there was so much to say about Sam.

"There's little room for mistakes, and if you don't know the answer to something, she hands your ass to you, normally with only a look that makes you feel like your skin is peeling off. So yeah, it's rough. Yeah, we're all exhausted. But I wouldn't trade her for anyone else's service when I manage to get on it."

Wow. So Sam was one of the best teachers? Whose interns and residents were so scared of her they cried? Interesting.

Leon gave a huge yawn. "Yesterday. Wait." He slumped back on the table, his chin resting on his arms. "Not yesterday, if today's Sunday. I mean the day before. Was it? Whatever. The other day, I used my husband's cologne as soap. I don't even know why I had it in the shower with me."

Hayden laughed loudly at his sheepish grin. "Really?" she asked.

"Seriously."

"Nice."

"He didn't think so. It wasn't cheap cologne."

His tablet started beeping, and he jumped up as if burned. "Labs are back for a patient." His eyes had lit up. "We think it's a huge tumor. It's *awesome*."

Luckily, no non-medical people were around in that moment to hear him, besides the overly excited new dad who was still on the phone. "Good luck."

He threw her a wave. "Thanks. See you around."

He ran off in time for Luce to sit opposite her and slide a coffee over. "Making friends with the twitchy intern?"

"He's on Sam's service at the moment."

Luce snorted. "*Sam*. Can't get used to that."

Now was a good chance. Hayden took a deep breath. "Well, you better. I—"

"Wait." Luce was smirking. "Were you probing him for information?"

Hayden felt heat creeping up her neck. "No…"

"You're a shit liar. You were."

"I—I was curious."

"That's your word of choice these days." Luce took a sip of their coffee, tossing their head to flick their bangs out of their eyes. "Curiosity killed the cat, you know."

"Stupidest saying ever."

"Yeah, okay, it is. But whatever. What were you curious about?"

Hayden took another deep breath. How do you tell your friend that knows you have a grudge against the idea of marriage, even if they don't know why, that you're getting married? But this was part of it. Luce had to know. And again, it wasn't really a lie. Marriage was on the cards. Just…everything else was a damn dirty lie. "Well, I was curious because…" Hayden's mouth was so dry she thought she wasn't going to be able to get the next words out. "I've made a rash decision. One I feel good about." Lie number one of this conversation. Well, the money made her feel good. After their drinks the other day, Sam had transferred the money immediately. The next day, there the twenty thousand had been: more money in her account than she'd had in a very long time. She'd done nothing with it yet, even though the list of things she needed to pay was endless. But she just liked looking at it there.

"Okay." Luce dragged the end of the word out. "What decision is that?"

"Well, like I said, one I feel good about. And that's why I was talking to the twitchy intern. Because, you know, I feel good about the decision, but was…checking some things." And now she was rambling. Luce had put their cup on the table and was watching her, lips pinched. Hayden tried to smile. She made herself. "So, Sam, uh—" Oh, fucking hell. She was going to throw up all over the table. It took everything in her to keep looking happy. But not maniacally so. That wouldn't help anything. She needed to go for contented. "Sam asked me to marry her. And I, uh—" Luce's mouth was dropping open "—well, I said yes."

Everything went deadly silent. Luce didn't stop gaping.

Still gaping.

Would talking help here? Who cared? She had to say something. This silence was going on for way too long.

Hayden opened her mouth, but before she could, Luce broke the silence. By bursting out laughing.

Hayden watched them double over, cackling madly. Well. Really, what else had she expected? Luce laughed so hard they gripped the edge of the table and the nearby man whose partner had pushed out an oversized baby gawped at them.

"Uh, Luce?"

Still laughing.

Hayden cleared her throat. Nothing changed. "Luce?"

Wiping their eyes, Luce straightened. All Hayden could do was try to not look too sheepish. As suddenly as it started, like a burble, the laughter died away. "Why aren't you laughing?"

"Because I'm not joking."

"I'm sorry, what?" Luce was still breathless from their gale of laughter. "You're getting married to the woman you've always kind of hated and have been seeing casually for only a few weeks?"

"Yeah." If she was going to get through this, she needed to embrace it. "I am."

"No way."

"Yes way."

"Hayden, I..." Luce stopped speaking, their lips pressing together as if trying to trap whatever torrent of words were building there. It lasted all of a split second. "You haven't even slept together."

"Hey! Okay, one: you don't know that."

Luce pointed that powerful one eyebrow at her in disbelief.

"Okay, fine. We haven't yet. But, two: sex is not everything, and I'm actually a bit disappointed in you for implying that it means I can't marry her."

"Hayden." Luce's lips were quirking, as if they couldn't believe they were having this conversation. To be honest, neither could Hayden. "Okay. You're right. That's bullshit. Sex doesn't have to exist or be there for it to be real. I'm wrong on that part. But, well, what I wanted to imply by that, and I did it wrongly, was—" God, Hayden loved Luce. They were so understanding, and Hayden was sitting here, lying to their face "—that this is fast."

"I know it's fast."

Luce visibly relaxed.

"Come on, Luce," Hayden continued. "I'm not an idiot. I know it's fast."

"Okay. Good. I was worried there. But I thought you didn't like marriage?"

"I didn't." She still didn't. "But it... I told you, we clicked. It, it just makes—I don't know—sense."

Judging from the look on Luce's face, it made anything but sense. Which was true. However, Hayden wasn't allowed to say that. Or couldn't she?

"Look, I know it sounds crazy, and insane. And yeah, before you say it, I know those two words mean the same thing. But you know me. I wouldn't do this if I didn't think it was the best thing."

And that was easy to say. Because that was true.

"Okay, look." Luce looked as if they were searching for the right words. "You're the most sensible person I know in a lot of respects, your sarcasm aside. But, Hayden, this…" their gaze turned intense as they lowered their voice, "…This is ridiculous."

"I know it seems that way. But really, I know what I'm doing. This is right. For me. For, for us."

Us. Because marriage meant being part of an us.

And none of those words made the scrunched-up look of concern go away from Luce's face. "I… Like, in no way can I tell you what to do with your life. I'd never presume to, either. But Hayden, this seems way too fast. You two don't even seem…"

"Seem what?"

"You don't even seem like a couple. Or how I've seen you act before, in a couple. I thought you were really friends, and maybe you were into her scary, older-boss vibe."

What to say to that? For some stupid reason, Hayden hadn't thought Luce would look that deeply into it. But the two of them were friends. Close friends. Of course Luce would. If the situation were reversed, Hayden would be saying the same thing. And while she and Sam had tried to appear comfortable with each other, or more so, clearly they hadn't hit the mark.

A watch beeped, and Luce looked down at their wrist.

"We have to go. Break's over. Can we talk more about this later?"

Saving Hayden from trying to over explain this and make even more of a mess of it? Sure. Hayden nodded, and Luce picked up their cup. She followed them to the elevators, a weird silence falling between them.

Well. She'd told her friend. It was getting real.

Considering that tomorrow, she was getting a *marriage license*, it was already real.

Luce didn't look away from the closed doors of the elevator, and Hayden stared at Luce, searching their face for anything.

Just shock. And that weird almost smile that made Hayden realize that Luce didn't believe it.

Shit.

Real was scary.

~ ~ ~

On Hayden's lunch break, instead of eating a proper lunch like she really should have been doing—she was starving and eating a banana faster than was probably healthy—she went to Neuro, hoping Sam would be there. She could be anywhere, really. The neuro ward, in post-op, in surgery, in her office, in consult, on any ward that happened to have a patient who needed a neurosurgeon.

Luck was with her, though, because Sam was there.

She was leaving a patient's room with Leon and an equally twitchy-looking resident, who were both tapping furiously at tablets while Sam's gaze stayed on the patient's notes in her hands. She said something, sidestepping a nurse pushing a medication trolley down the corridor, and both the minions scurried away, heads together. Hayden stood and waited for Sam to look up, which she only did when there were a few yards between them.

Sam halted, holding the notes to her chest. "Good afternoon."

"Hey, Sam."

"Is everything okay? I didn't even know you knew there was a world outside the ER."

"Very funny."

"Sometimes."

"I, uh. I only have a minute. Can you talk?"

Sam tilted her head, eyeing her, before finally saying, "Okay. Wait here a moment."

And she disappeared down the corridor and behind the nurses' station. Hayden propped herself against the wall and crossed her arms, waving at a nurse she very vaguely recognized who rushed past to a patient's room. Sometimes, Hayden came into the wards and marveled at the calm. She wasn't naïve. She knew working on a ward was incredibly busy. Yet still, there was a stark difference between the ER and a ward. Fewer people, fewer voices, less noise, less hectic activity.

But nothing would make Hayden give up the ER. She loved it there.

She watched Sam speak to the coordinator, who wrote down everything she said. Sam buried her hands in her lab coat pockets, like always, and walked down to meet Hayden, who straightened.

"Follow me."

Hayden did. They went up a flight of stairs and through some winding corridors that Hayden had never been in. Offices. She'd never had a need.

They ended up in one of them, which was meticulously neat. The papers and pens on Sam's desk were lined up in perpendicular patterns. The walls were like any office in the hospital probably were: boring white.

Sam sat on the edge of her desk and crossed her arms. "Sit down if you want."

Hayden didn't. She had too much nervous energy. Instead, she stood next to it, keeping a respectable distance between them. "I'm fine here."

"What did you want to talk about?"

Swallowing, Hayden wasn't sure how to answer. She'd suffered through four busy hours after her conversation with Luce, aware at times of Luce's puzzled expression. She'd kept replaying their conversation and the utter disbelief that Sam and Hayden needed to remedy. "Well, I told Luce. My friend."

"Your friend who's non-binary."

"Uh, yes."

"I've been reading about it."

Hayden, who had opened her mouth to launch into the nervous babble she had in her head, snapped it shut. "You have?"

"I realized it was something I knew nothing of, not really. Not enough. So I went home and got on my laptop. After making a mess of our conversation at the first dinner we had, when I pushed too hard about your job, I didn't want to ask you the wrong questions."

"Oh."

Sam had gone home and researched it so she'd understand more? And had purposefully tried not to annoy Hayden?

"It was interesting," Sam said.

"Gender is pretty interesting."

Sam nodded. "Like I said, I hadn't realized. I've noticed you use 'person' a lot, and other words, when other people would have said man or woman. And now I know why."

"Yeah, well, when I met Luce, I knew some things about it. But I've learned a lot the last few years. I'm still learning, though. Always will be, I think."

"So, was there something you needed? I imagine you don't have long."

Hayden's brain stumbled to catch up. "Uh, yeah. Like I said, I told Luce."

"I don't imagine that was an easy conversation."

Hayden gave a bark of a laugh. "Yeah, well, I was trying to convince them I want to get married after a month with someone I never really li—uh, knew." Sam's lip twitched, but she didn't look insulted. Hayden grimaced, but with a smile she hoped was at least charming. "So, convincing them of that isn't easy."

"I'm not surprised. Do you think they'll be understanding?"

"Luce always is. But I think some of the problem is that, well, we're not selling it."

"Selling what?" There was that small furrow in the middle of Sam's brow.

"That we're at a point where we want to get married. Or even, you know, *like* each other."

"Oh."

The room was really quiet, the buzzing of the air conditioner too loud. Hayden swallowed. "So I think we need to be more convincing. At some point."

"You mean, affectionate?" Sam's cheeks had gone a little pink. Not surprising. Hayden's were hot.

"Yeah, basically."

Sam pursed her lips. "That's absurd. In any relationship I've had, I've never been outwardly affectionate. Privacy is fine."

Hayden raised her eyebrows. "Were you trying to convince people, for some super-top-secret reason I don't know, that the relationship was real?"

Sam deflated at that. "No."

"Thought as much."

They stared at each other again.

"So. We need to try to seem more like a, a *real* couple." Sam Thomson, flustered? It would be funnier if Hayden wasn't as well. "Whatever that means."

"Yeah," Hayden said. "Yes. Maybe we can, I don't know, talk about it more next week? Or start next week? After we sign."

Sam took in a deep breath. Because apparently the idea of having to touch Hayden was that terrible. Nice. "Yes. Okay. I'll have to rush Monday and Tuesday due to work, so we could, I don't know, have Luce over for dinner, or go out with them somewhere after work. Once you're settled into my—in the apartment."

This was such a mess. "Yeah. Sounds fine. A rushed wedding. Sounds romantic?" Hayden winked, and Sam gave a short laugh.

"Yes. Very."

"Okay. I'll see you tomorrow. At the clerk's office to get the license."

"See you tomorrow, Hayden."

And Hayden turned and tried not make it obvious she was fleeing the awkwardness.

CHAPTER 8

Night shift might suck, but the assurance of a day off beforehand was always a fun part of it. But this day off was going to be spent packing. Right after Hayden got, you know, a marriage license.

Something she'd never thought she'd need.

The subway was particularly full, being so early on a Monday. But the clerk's office opened at nine, and they wanted to get there as early as they could. They were so in love and eager to tie the knot, after all.

Someone jammed into Hayden's side sneezed, and Hayden wrinkled her nose and angled herself away from them. She was surrounded by sick people all day; she didn't need gross subway-sneeze germs. Looking around the graffitied cabin of the subway line and all the people crammed in next to each other like disgruntled penguins, it wasn't hard to imagine this as ground zero for the next bubonic plague. The person behind her hocked something back so loudly Hayden had to cover a gag.

She hated the subway. She used the bus to get to work, but it would have taken forever to get into the clerk's office. A bus followed by the subway had been the only option.

Closed-in spaces sucked in general, but this was especially bad.

Twenty minutes later, she stumbled into fresh air and weak morning sunshine, and took a deep breath. People bustled past her, focused on getting to wherever they were headed. A definite Monday-morning gloom hung in the air. The traffic was thick on the road, mostly cast in shadow, thanks to the high-rise buildings and skyscrapers lining the streets.

Taking a second to get her bearings, Hayden turned and headed down one of the streets. She only walked for five minutes before she found the building she was after. A few people were milling around outside, waiting for it to open. Sam was one of them.

"Hey." Hayden tried to smile. It was early, and her day off, so "tried" was an appropriate word for it.

"Good morning."

Sam was bundled in a black coat, making her skin seem even paler. Outside of the hospital, she always looked different.

"I brought the papers." Hayden fished around in her bag, groping past her phone and wallet until she found the documents in question. "I spoke with the lawyer I found days ago like you asked me to, and he said they were all locked tight to the specifications I said. So here." Hayden held them out in their plastic sheet and ignored Sam's slight eye twitch as she caught sight of their rumpled state. "One, uh, prenup. The secret to a happy marriage."

"Thank you." Sam tried to smooth out the sheets, and Hayden barely managed not to smirk. "And you ensured the bill would be sent to me?"

"Yeah. Thanks."

"No thanks necessary. This is part of it." Sam tucked the papers into her bag and pulled out another set. "This has the confirmation number to show I applied for us online, so our appointment will be much faster. Thanks for sending your details the other night."

"No problem."

"Your last name was changed years ago?"

"Yeah."

Thankfully, before Sam could ask any more questions, the doors opened. They quickly walked in and stepped up to one of the machines that would give them a number. Someone had managed to get in before them, so Hayden waited, barely able to stop herself from tapping her foot. Sam didn't manage to hide her impatience at all as she pursed her lips and crossed her arms tightly. Their arms brushed, and Hayden wanted to laugh that her reaction to that was to step away from the person she was about to get a marriage license with.

This was all quite ridiculous. Luce was completely right.

In the line next to them, two people had gone through, and still Sam and Hayden were waiting. The man in front of them muttered something, and Hayden realized what the problem could be.

"*¿Quieres que te ayude?*" Hayden stepped up next to him to offer him help.

He turned to her, relief all over his deeply lined face. "*Sí, por favor.*"

She quickly found out what he needed, hit the *back* button on the machine, flipped the language to Spanish, and made sure he was okay navigating.

"*¡Muchas gracias!*"

He headed to the waiting area, and Hayden, trying not to squirm, tapped the button that said *marriage license*, and the computer spat out a piece of paper. Sam grabbed the ticket, and Hayden followed her to the waiting room before sitting down on one of the hard plastic chairs.

"What number did we get?" she asked.

Sam held the ticket up. "Seven."

"That's a low number, and yet I feel like we're going to be surprised at how we'll end up waiting here for hours."

"I hope not." Sam crossed her legs and somehow looked put together even in this weird, plastic environment. Hayden straightened and tried to pretend she did too. "I could only get my shift covered for a few hours and have to work late to make up for it."

"Here's hoping." Hayden chewed her lip, then made herself stop. Calm.

They sat next to each other in silence, Hayden shifting every now and again to ignore the bite of the hard plastic under her butt. The room had filled up, all types of people sitting around, glaring at the screen that announced what number was next and which desk they had to go to. A few couples sat canoodling, one wrapped around each other and giggling.

Most likely there for marriage licenses too, then. One girl sat with her stomach rounded in front of her, a boy sitting next to her. His leg was bouncing up and down, and the girl's face was starkly white. They didn't look old enough to even apply to be married.

"Any good cases lately?" Hayden asked, purely for something to say.

"Actually, we just got a patient with a really rare tumor. We operate this evening."

So Leon had gotten his tumor. "What makes it so rare?"

That conversation kept them going for the next while as it bounced from the current case to some of the cases they'd had over the years.

"So why did you choose neurosurgery?" Hayden ended up asking.

"Our number is on the screen."

Hayden whipped her head around. "Already?"

But Sam was already up and walking toward the desk indicated on the screen. How had the time passed that quickly? Apparently, she enjoyed talking about work outside of the hospital more than she'd realized.

It wasn't until she sat down across from a man with his belly overflowing over his belt that Hayden remembered why they were there.

Right. Marriage certificate.

"Did you apply online?" he asked, his eyes glued to his computer.

"Yes." Sam slid the piece of paper across the desk. "This is our confirmation number."

He took the paper, typed it into the computer, and finally looked at them after one very slow minute. "Identification?"

They both pulled out their photo identification, birth certificates, social security information, and the multitude of other things required and passed them over. He looked them all over, eyes bouncing from the paper in front of him to his computer, comparing the data.

Eventually he gave a nod. "All in order." He hit a button and looked at them again. "The certificate is processing."

It was over so quickly it left Hayden's head spinning.

Something warm dropped on Hayden's knee, and she jumped, trying to cover it up when she realized it was Sam's hand. Her heart in her throat, she looked at Sam, but Sam's attention was on the man.

"Thank you," Sam said. "We're very excited."

Hayden shut her gaping mouth and forced a smile on her face. "Yes. Very."

Sam's hand was so warm it felt like it was going to burn through Hayden's jeans. Was that normal? Heat was crawling out from the spot. Sam's hand was on her knee. *Thomson's* hand was on her knee. Her *hand.*

Hayden's life had officially entered the twilight zone.

The man twisted around, plucked out some paper that had finally emerged from the printer, and slid it over with two pens.

"Please confirm all the information is correct."

Sam left her alarmingly warm hand in place while she looked the paper over and signed at the bottom; Hayden signed it on her line. It was official.

"Congratulations, here's your certificate. You have to wait until five past ten tomorrow morning to proceed."

And with that he turned back to the computer. Sam stood up, her hand dropping away to pick up the certificate he'd slid across, leaving Hayden's leg to be blasted with what now felt like freezing air. Her cheeks were flaming, though. That was enough to make up for it.

They ended up on the street, and Sam's expression was unreadable. "Maybe I should have spoken about the fact that I was going to touch your leg beforehand?"

"What?" Hayden's voice was far too high-pitched. "No. No, no. It was fine." Yup. Too high-pitched and weird. She cleared her throat. "It was fine."

That sounded slightly more normal.

"It was what we spoke about, though, wasn't it?" Sam asked. "Or did I misunderstand?"

"No, you didn't misunderstand." Fewer people were walking on the sidewalks now. In spite of this, they both moved to the side to let anyone who walked past go by. "I was just surprised." Hayden hoped it sounded reassuring.

"I thought it was time we should do something like that. And it didn't matter if it looked awkward, since no one we knew was there. Practice."

"Good thinking. Especially since I made it weird by jumping a foot in the air."

Sam pressed her lips together, but those lines fanned around her eyes, and she looked just that bit more approachable. Hayden had the distinct feeling she was being laughed at. "You did jump spectacularly high."

"Yeah, yeah," Hayden said, as the not-smile on Sam's face turned into a laughing smirk. "I know."

"I really must go. I'll see you tomorrow."

That smile had fallen away, and Hayden felt her own do the same.

Tomorrow.

Their wedding.

Ew.

"Yeah. Tomorrow. Ten at City Hall?"

"Yes." Sam nodded. "Ten. This is it, Hayden. Are you sure?"

The reminder of that money sitting in her account, and how it would double as soon as she signed, made her say, "Totally." The idea of two hundred thousand more made her add, "Yeah, I'm in."

"Okay." Sam started to walk past her. "I'll send my lawyer the prenup this afternoon. I'll send you an e-mail to confirm it's sent. See you tomorrow."

"See you at the wedding."

Sam's laugh was all Hayden heard as she watched her walk away. Her knee still burned, the weirdness of Sam touching her too much, it seemed.

~ ~ ~

"Right. So it wasn't an elaborate joke?"

Hayden took a sip of her coffee and set it on the table, staring at her drink a moment, rather than Luce. "Nope. Sorry."

Luce sucked in a breath. Around them, the café was mostly empty. It was a Monday night, after all, sometime after eight o'clock. It would close soon. But before a night shift, Hayden liked to stay up as late as she could to try and sleep later the next day, or at least be tired enough for a decent nap before she started in the evening. And Luce had messaged her repeatedly to catch up until Hayden had finally relented.

She had promised to chat later, after all. Which had been a stupid thing to do.

"You don't like marriage."

True. "No, I don't." Hayden didn't want to lie even more by pretending that she'd become, completely out of the blue, one of those people that fawned over bridal magazines and thought about what song to play for their first dance. "But, well, it seems right."

"Look, Hayden. That sounds very romantic and…" Luce searched for another word and finished pathetically, "…nice, but it's been a few weeks. How can you possibly know it's right?"

Going for clueless, Hayden shrugged. "I just do. For us. And our circumstances."

"What if you hate living with her? What if she drives you mad because she's one of those people that has to always put the cap back on the toothpaste?"

Hayden wrinkled her nose. "You don't always put the cap back on?"

"Not the point." Luce dropped back against their chair, throwing their hands up. "Seriously. Marriage? Before you even live together? Why not simply live together first?"

It was worse than having this conversation with a parent. Hayden tried to remind herself that Luce cared. Also, Hayden was feeling defensive about telling Luce a big, fat, dirty lie. She took a deep breath.

She was lying anyway. It was time to embrace it.

"Because I want this, Luce. Do you really think I would do this if I didn't have my reasons?" Hayden looked her best friend straight in their big, dark eyes. *Like* was not going to cut it here. "I love her. It's way too fast, and I know that. But I want it. You just have to trust me."

God, that felt like crap. Luce pursed their lips as if having to really think on their words before leaning forward and nodding, their teeth on their bottom lip. "Fine. I'll trust you. It's not my place to push this."

"Thank you." Hayden swallowed. "Really, thank you."

"Okay. So you're getting married." They tried to look interested, and what Hayden assumed was supportive, but instead looked like they were in pain. "Great. When is the happy day?" They took a sip of their tea, and Hayden probably should have planned better timing.

"Tomorrow."

Luce spat their tea so hard it actually sprayed Hayden's face. "Tomorrow?"

"Hey! That's disgusting." Hayden scrubbed at her face with the sleeve of her hoodie. "Seriously, it smells herbal. Gross."

Luce was gawking at her. Their mouth hung open. "Tomorrow?"

Hayden's arm dropped back down to the table. "Yes, tomorrow. At City Hall."

"But... Why?" Luce's eyebrows were bunched together so hard their forehead looked as if it was going to collapse in on itself.

"Because we want to."

"But... What?"

This was a nightmare. Maybe Hayden was going to wake up to find she'd fallen asleep on her sofa the night she'd had trouble sleeping. Maybe she had never found that advertisement Sam had put online.

"Because. Just because. It's what we want. I thought you were being supportive?"

Opening their mouth, most likely to argue vehemently, Luce snapped it shut. "Fine. Tomorrow. Great. That makes *complete* and *utter* sense. I can't think of anything better. Do you have an outfit?"

Narrowing her eyes at the sarcasm that was thick over their words, Hayden shook her head. "Of course not. We're being pretty private and low-key."

"Oh, how extreme and dramatic of me to think you would plan something for this wedding that is logical and that I understand completely. Sorry. Sometimes I overreact."

"You're not funny."

"I'm not remotely trying to be."

"Look, we want to sign the paper and have it done."

"How romantic."

"Since when do you think things have to reach some quota of romance?"

"Fair point. So I'm guessing you're moving in to her place? Or are you guys getting something new—" Luce balked "—together?"

"Why do you assume her place? What about mine?"

Luce raised that one eyebrow at her. The gesture was getting pretty old at this point.

"Yeah, okay, fine. I'm moving into her place. Tomorrow before work."

Hayden couldn't place the look on Luce's face, and for a second, she thought Luce wasn't going to respond. "Hayden?" When they finally spoke, their tone was low. "Are you in some kind of trouble?"

Their eyes were liquid worry. Something bubbled up in Hayden's throat, and the lies she was about to force herself to say had become acrid as they coated her tongue. Other words, ones that would reveal the truth of it all, were building. Breathing too fast, Hayden pressed her lips together in a mockery of a smile and tried to press back casually in her chair. "Luce, of course I'm not. It's nothing like that."

Except that Hayden was so desperate for cash she'd accepted this absurd proposition. "Are you sure?"

Luce was so amazing to even give her a second chance.

Hayden dug deep to make what she was about to say convincing. "I am. Really."

They straightened. "Okay. Good to hear. So, from tomorrow you'll be Mrs. Thomson?"

"What? No? I'm not changing my name. Don't be an idiot."

Changing her surname once had been enough of a pain; she wasn't doing that again. Her current surname meant too much to her. A final up-yours to everything that had happened years ago.

"Aw. Mrs. Dr. Thomson. It has a nice ring to it."

The grin and the lighter tone were making fun of Hayden, but she'd take it.

"Not funny." Even as Hayden said it, she was smiling.

"Yeah it is. You could stay home and bake her cakes."

"If I want to poison her, sure." Hayden was not a baker.

"Oh!" Luce looked absolutely delighted now. "Is that your plan? Marry her, then poison her, and get all her millions when she dies? Is she secretly an heiress?"

Hayden laughed. "Yes. That's absolutely my plan. She's actually got a huge, gigantic trust fund, and I've seduced her, made her marry me, and, when she least suspects it and enough time has passed to avoid suspicion, I'm going to kill her. In the least obvious way ever, like a poisoned cake."

"Or you could push her down the stairs."

"I could hire an assassin."

Luce flicked a rolled up sugar packet at her. "None of these are conspicuous at all. Your plan will go off without a hitch."

"Great. Will you help me hide the body?"

"Hell no."

Hayden pouted. "But why not?"

"Fine. If you split the cash with me."

"What kind of friend are you?"

"The greedy kind."

Hayden threw the packet back at them. "Well, I knew that. Also, Sam would like to have dinner or drinks or something with you at some point."

"Seriously?" Luce's eyes were wide.

"Yeah. Seriously. Me too."

"Uh, okay."

There wasn't much enthusiasm in Luce's words. It was going to be a long year.

~ ~ ~

It turned out that getting married was not a detailed affair.

They waited two hours, chatting on and off about work, and Hayden tried not to chew her lip to shreds. A photographer Sam was paying waited with them. He would act as their witness and take photos to commemorate their romantic day.

Hayden felt like she couldn't breathe.

She'd woken up after late-night bad TV and only four hours sleep. Hopefully, a nap at Sam's later would get her through night shift. The first night of the run was always the worst.

But when she'd woken up, her chest tight, lying there, it had slowly dawned on her what she was doing that day.

Now, two hours into waiting, it was hard to resist the urge to run.

"Can I speak with you?"

And with Sam's words, whatever calm Hayden had managed to bring forth evaporated.

"Uh—sure."

But Sam was already up and walking away from the yawning photographer. Hayden followed, and they wove their way through the many people also waiting—some even in wedding attire. Hayden felt supremely underdressed in her black jeans and white dress shirt. Tucked away from everything, they huddled near a grimy wall.

"Yeah?"

Sam swallowed and glanced around them. Was she nervous too? Or nervous about whatever she was going to ask Hayden?

"Hayden. I was wondering. Would, well…" she took a deep breath. "Would it be okay to kiss, for the photograph after we sign? I've checked the Internet. The entire process is only minutes. And then I can have the photograph?"

Kiss? Like kiss? With lips? And tongue? Hayden's face heated up so fast it was embarrassing. Would there be tongue? "Will you tell me now why you need the proof?"

"No." Sam's voice was sharp. Her gaze flicked upward for a second, and she sucked in a breath before she looked back at Hayden, features minutely softer. "I told you. Not yet."

Hayden eyed her, arms crossed. "Yes. Okay. Of course. This is what we've been talking about. You can kiss me. We can kiss, I mean."

She felt fifteen. Maybe they would count down from three before they did it.

"Okay. And I, uh, I bought these." Sam held her hand out, and sitting in the center were two simple white gold rings. Hayden knew nothing about jewelry, but they seemed well-made. Not cheap, anyway.

"Oh."

"I realize we should have talked about this. There's probably a lot we've not talked about that we should have. But would you be opposed to wearing one?"

They weren't supposed to wear rings at work, but wedding rings were permitted. And it made sense if they wore them, for whatever it was that Sam was trying to achieve. But even the idea made Hayden's skin crawl. This was why she didn't like marriage. Well, it was one of the many reasons. Why did people feel as if they had to wear something to show they were married? Why did they have to prove it? Like they were owned?

"No." Hayden tried to sound as if she meant it. "If it helps all this, no."

"Okay." Sam slipped the rings back in her pocket. "Okay."

"Number twenty-nine," a robotic voice called out.

Was Hayden mistaken, or did Sam tense?

"That's us," Hayden said.

Sam gave a nod. "Let's go."

Sam turned to go, and Hayden reached out and grabbed her hand. She quickly let go again as a thought occurred to her, though the surprise at how soft Sam's hand was echoed in the back of her mind. "Wait."

Sam turned back, shoulders stiff. "Yes?"

Hayden grinned and tried to block out the rising panic. "Let's walk in like we're ecstatic."

"What?" Sam looked at Hayden as if she were making no sense.

"We're doing this for stupid reasons. But you have a photographer, so let's smile and laugh and pretend it's what we want. Pretend I'm Angelina Jolie."

Sam's lips twitched. "I'm not that interested in her."

"Jodie Foster?"

"No. But I wouldn't kick her out of bed."

The words sounded a little stilted, like Sam knew they weren't natural for her to say, but nevertheless, Hayden let out a surprised bark of laughter. "Well, that works," she said.

Sam turned, and Hayden followed, the photographer stepping into line with them.

And so they got married. Both trying not to laugh. With Hayden still unable to breathe properly, but smiling. And maybe they would look like they were happy in the photographs, when really, they were—or, at least, Hayden was—bordering on slightly hysterical.

The Justice of the Peace said some words that hardly registered. It really did only take minutes. Then there were the rings, their fingers trembling as they slid them on. It felt strangely heavy and uncomfortable on Hayden's finger. Then she looked up, and their eyes locked. Her cheeks were burning. Sam was incredibly pale.

"And we're done, ladies. Congratulations," the Justice of the Peace said. With her heartbeat thundering in her ears, Hayden turned to watch as he pushed his stamp down onto several sheets of paper. "Now's the moment, if you want your perfect photo."

Hayden swallowed and looked back at Sam, who seemed to be unable to move, and was staring at her with wide eyes. In her peripheral vision, Hayden saw the photographer raise his camera. Everything seemed too slow and too fast and yet, still, Sam just stood, unmoving.

One kiss. It was nothing. Hayden had had multiple silly kisses, be they laced with alcohol or at the ends of dates that she didn't plan to repeat. She wasn't a teenager. This didn't have to be weird.

So Hayden surged forward, her fingers gripping the lapels of Sam's tailored jacket, and tugged. She pushed up on her tiptoes, and their lips almost crashed together.

Too hard. She'd misjudged it. She felt a puff of air against her cheek where Sam exhaled in surprise and, despite herself, Hayden chuckled against Sam's mouth. The ridiculousness of the situation must have hit Sam, because so did she, her lips curving against Hayden's. Hands rested tensely against her hips, and Hayden tilted her head up, kissing her once more, properly. Chastely, really. Sam's lips were soft, and they moved against Hayden's a little before they both pulled back.

"Okay, sign here, and if your witness could too."

Hayden stepped back, her hands falling away. She tried not to think about the fact that her lips tingled. She'd just kissed Samantha Thomson.

Actually, screw that. She'd just *married* Samantha Thomson.

Whose cheeks were now pink.

The photographer came forward, and Sam was signing on various dotted lines and a pen was in Hayden's fingers.

With her stomach full of butterflies or wriggling worms or something equally strange, Hayden took a deep breath.

She signed on the dotted line.

And that was it.

A giant blur of words, a kiss that lasted two seconds—both of which had been weird—and they were ejected into the overcrowded street, Sam clutching their marriage certificate, and both of them blinking at the shock of it.

Hayden was married.

CHAPTER 9

Sam's apartment building had a doorman.

A very nice doorman who helped Hayden bring up her three giant suitcases, one plastic bag full of cat things, and her growling, angry cat. Sam's building had a *doorman*. If that alone wasn't terrifying, Hayden didn't know what was. She smiled awkwardly at him as he tipped his hat—people did that?—and disappeared into the elevator.

Leaving Hayden in the hallway, to stare at the door in front of her, surrounded by her bags.

Frank growled.

"Same, Frank. Same."

He meowed so loudly that Hayden was surprised someone didn't poke their head out of the opposite apartment and yell at her.

But she couldn't bring herself to open the door.

The key Sam had given her before they'd parted ways at City Hall was in her hand. So that wasn't a problem. The thumb of her left hand was pushing the wedding band that was on her ring finger around and around. It had been on there for a total of two hours, and it had gotten *more* uncomfortable, not less.

Frank yowled.

"All right, all right," Hayden muttered.

She pushed her key in the lock, opened the door, grabbed Frank, and walked inside. Then froze.

Okay. She wasn't stupid. She'd seen the street they'd driven onto. The building. The *doorman*, for crying out loud. The street was full of beautiful trees shedding reddish-brown leaves onto perfectly manicured grass that lined the sidewalks.

Hayden's street was a concrete mess covered with scrawled graffiti tags, featuring a crime rate that was rather alarming. The dog poop that often decorated the sidewalks was the least of its problems.

So, the fact that she was in a different neighborhood was obvious. But the apartment? It looked like something a celebrity bought in the city.

Hayden should have realized. Maybe she was a little stupid. But Sam had to have this kind of money to be able to ask someone to marry her for almost a quarter of a million dollars.

But this apartment was heaven.

She'd walked into an open-plan living area, the kitchen straight ahead and a dark oak dining table taking up space next to it as the area artfully segued into the living room on her left. The biggest sofa she'd ever seen took up most of one wall, long enough for eight people to sprawl over while watching the huge TV. Light flooded the entire space, thanks to the windows lining the entire wall of the living room.

By comparison, Hayden had been living in a dark and murky cave. Was she Gollum? It sure felt that way.

She even had a ring, now.

She slowly put Frank on the ground and quickly dragged her suitcases in, leaving them there once she'd closed the door. She wandered down a hallway on her right. Doors were open, and she saw an office and two guest rooms, one with towels on the bed.

The bedroom was bigger than her living room.

There was even an en suite bathroom in the *guest* room. With a *bath*.

But where did Sam sleep?

Hayden walked down the corridor's highly polished floors, back to the living area. That space was bigger than her entire apartment. No wonder Sam could pay someone to marry her.

Because wow.

The kitchen was full of sparkling countertops and gadgets Hayden didn't even recognize. One countertop held a piece of paper. She picked it up.

> Hayden,
>
> There is a spare bathroom at the end of the hall I thought you
> could put your cat's litter in. The room I thought you would
> prefer has towels on the bed, but feel free to change to the
> other. However, it doesn't have a private bathroom. Not that it
> matters. It will just be you using the other down the hall.

"Do you not use the bathroom, Sam?"

She went back to the note.

Please help yourself to anything in the refrigerator and pantry.

I'll most likely see you at the hospital tonight, as I'm working later than normal.

Sam.

"What, no *love to my darling wife?*" Hayden put the note down. Then she noticed it: along the opposite wall in the living room, obscured from view when she'd walked in, was a small white staircase.

So that's where Sam slept.

She jumped when Frank's angry meow reached her. She walked over to his carrier and opened it. He didn't budge. She kneeled down and looked straight inside.

"Frank. I know you hate moving. But this apartment is *way* nicer than where we were before. There's so much room for you to run in. And frolic. Because, you know, you're such a frolicker." All she could see were huge yellow eyes and backward-facing ears. Damn, was he mad. "Come out?"

He glowered at her.

"Okay. Well. I'll leave the door open, and you come out when you're ready. Okay?"

He shuffled around so his behind was facing her and stared at the back of his carrier.

"Have it your way."

He'd come out eventually. She walked to the living room. It had carpet. Plush and thick. And really white. Hayden was going to destroy something in this apartment so fast simply by being herself.

She looked back to the staircase. The note hadn't said *not* to go there.

She put her foot on the first step, took a deep breath, and, feeling like a snoop, walked up as quietly as she could. Her head appeared inside a loft bedroom. She looked around quickly, eyes wide. It was stunning. The bed was huge, with a heavy wooden base and headboard. The space stretched forever, a door on the left leading to what was most likely a bathroom. Another close to Hayden possibly opened into a walk-in closet.

It was stunning, filled with light. She quickly snapped her gaping mouth shut and turned and went back downstairs.

It felt way too intrusive, like that space was completely Sam's.

At the bottom of the stairs, she flopped onto the sofa.

How was this place even real?

Frank was still in his carrier, miles away, near the door. Only his butt was visible.

"Coming out yet?"

He didn't move.

"Cool."

She needed to take her things to that room. And set up the litter and Frank's food and water bowl. She needed to nap for her shift that evening.

But for now, she was going to sit and stare around this apartment that was apparently a work of art, her thumb spinning that ridiculous wedding band around and around her finger.

~ ~ ~

"What the hell is that?"

Hayden's head snapped up, wondering if a spider had fallen on her head or something. She tugged her scrub top over her head, emerging from it with her hair in static all over. She was in such a rush she banged her elbow on the cold metal of her locker.

"Luce…" She rubbed her elbow and let the word drift off. The bruise for the week was already blooming, for sure.

Luce was standing in front of her, arms crossed. "What is that on your *finger*?"

Hayden had shut her locker door, which was stupid as that put her hand up on display. So, of course, Luce completely took advantage and grabbed it, not even that gently. Hayden let them tug her hand in front of their face; she even wriggled her fingers.

"Hayden." Their eyes were glued on the ring. So much for hoping no one would *really* notice. "Is this shit for real?"

"Nope. I won it in an arcade game and thought, 'You know what? I'm going to wear this just to mess with Luce.'"

"Funny." Luce was still gripping Hayden's hand. "You really are a comedian." Luce's gaze was back on the ring. "So you did it? You got married?"

Hayden took her hand back and straightened her shirt, trying to appear calm and normal about it all. But wait.

Shouldn't she be happy? And excited? The fake version of her, anyway? About her fake marriage?

This was exhausting.

She grinned and put her stethoscope around her neck, holding on to each end with a hand. "Yeah. We did. This morning."

"Oh."

"Oh?"

"I still kind of thought it was a joke."

"Nope." Hayden shook her head. "No joke."

"Oh. Okay. *Congratulations?*"

And why was Hayden miffed about the lack of genuineness inflected in that single word about her fake marriage? "Gee, thanks. Sound *less* sincere."

"Look, I'm trying. I'm still surprised. And, I won't lie, confused. But if it really is what you want, then I do mean it. Congratulations."

"Thanks."

"So, you're actually, honestly married?"

"Yup. I can show you the marriage certificate if you want. Wait." She grimaced. "No I can't. Sam has it. But I can later?"

Luce inclined against the lockers, their hands in their pockets. "The ring's sold me, to be honest. I'm still processing, is all."

Luce was processing? *Luce* had to process? Hayden's *brain* was about to explode. "Me too, I won't lie. Like I told you, I know it's fast." Hayden kept her fingers wrapped around either end of her stethoscope, like a safety net. That ring still felt so noticeable. How long until it wouldn't anymore? "But it's what I wanted."

The twenty thousand Sam had told her she'd transferred that afternoon was why. Not that Hayden could say that.

"Good." Luce took a deep breath and smiled. Genuinely. And that made Hayden pause. If this was Luce, Hayden would be giving them an even harder time, especially given her feelings about marriage. But even without that—if her friend told her they were marrying someone they'd never seemed to really like, after a few weeks of dating them, Hayden would not have stayed as calm. There'd be more than spat-out tea.

"Thank you, Luce." Hayden finally let go of her stethoscope and squeezed Luce's upper arm. "I appreciate it."

"Yeah, yeah." Their tone was gentler, though. "Just know I'm around, okay?"

That band on her finger felt heavy as she squeezed Luce's arm briefly before letting her hand fall. "I know."

"Hayden."

Hayden jumped and turned. Sam was standing there, still in scrubs, with no lab coat. She must have come straight from surgery. She had a surgical cap still on. Not one of the hospital-issued ones, but a personalized one. It was green with rainbows all over it.

"Hey, Sam."

Oh, this was uncomfortable. No one else was around to diffuse this. The locker room was empty. Hayden had arrived super early for her shift with the idea of eating in the cafeteria beforehand. She'd slept too late to want to risk figuring out Sam's monster kitchen. That was a lie; she'd woken up groggy, cranky, and not wanting to cook.

But now it was only Sam, Luce, and Hayden.

So uncomfortable.

"Hi, Dr. Thomson."

"Hello, Luce."

Sam had remembered their name. That was a good step.

"Nice scrub cap." Luce had their evil smile playing at their lips.

Sam stared straight at them. "Thank you."

"It's a lot more colorful than I would have expected."

Sam looked unsure as to why Luce was saying that. Hayden wanted to slap her friend upside the head.

"Well," Sam said, "I had surgery on a six-year-old today. I did a lot of reading years ago on how to deal with small children. Colors and patterns appeal to them. It makes the surgery easier."

"Oh." Luce's shit-eating grin was gone. Good. "That makes sense."

What *didn't* Sam look up to support what she did? Hayden had thought her addiction to googling every little thing that crossed her mind was bad, but it seemed Sam was far worse than she.

Sam gave a singular nod and didn't even acknowledge that. She lifted her hand to push a tendril of hair back behind her ear and under her cap, and the ring on her finger glinted in the light. They were wearing matching wedding bands.

This was so weird.

Also, why was she wearing a wedding band in surgery? Maybe she'd put it back on after. They were supposed to be passing as happy about their decision. People who just got married probably loved to wear their rings.

Had Sam fielded questions about it? Surely she had. Hopefully, Sam handled it with more finesse than Hayden had with Luce. It would be easier with someone who was more of a colleague than a friend. Hopefully.

"So. I have to finish up with some patients." Luce looked between the two of them and sidled away. "See you."

"See you at handover," Hayden said.

"Good night." Sam didn't even look at Luce, instead keeping her eyes trained on Hayden, who gave back a weak smile.

"Oh!" Luce exclaimed.

Now Sam did turn around to look at Luce.

Hayden wanted to sink into the floor. "Yeah?"

But Luce wasn't looking at Hayden. They were looking at Sam, slightly friendlier than before. But there was something in their eye, a narrowing, or a shadow. Something mistrustful.

"Congratulations, Sam. So nice to hear about this wedding."

Hayden closed her eyes and thought about praying. To whom, she didn't know. The second she'd had any say in it, she'd stopped going to church with her mom and Abuela, who still chastised her for it—and her sister, apparently, who Hayden really needed to call.

Abuela would chastise her for marrying for reasons other than love too. But she didn't need to know.

Hayden still had her eyes closed, searching for strength, when Sam said, "Thank you."

She opened her eyes, but Sam was still fixed on Luce, who still looked…odd. Pleasant, really, but something *not* pleasant too.

"We should go out for drinks to celebrate." Luce's smile grew. "Get to know each other."

Oh, this was awful.

Sam nodded. "Yes. Sounds acceptable."

Acceptable? Nice one, Sam. Hayden sighed, but neither paid attention to her.

"Great. We'll organize something."

And Luce walked out, not looking back at Hayden, most likely because they knew Hayden was glaring at them. The door swished closed, and Sam and Hayden were alone. Sam turned around, and Hayden gave a wave. "Hi."

Sam gave her a strange look. "Hello?"

Hayden wasn't going to have time to get food at this rate, and she still needed to finish getting changed. She started undoing the buttons on her jeans. "Did you need to talk?"

"I wanted to ask you something."

Hayden rolled her eyes inwardly at herself. She'd been about to pull her pants down with her shoes still on. Smacking her elbow was enough for one evening, surely; she didn't need to fall on her ass too. She dug her toes into the heel and kicked one off, followed by the other and started shimmying her pants down her hips. When she looked up, Sam had turned the other way. Hayden snorted. Because her legs were so hideous, right? Well, she really did need to shave them. Still hilarious.

Though if someone walked in on Hayden's newlywed-*wife* avoiding watching her change, it was going to look pretty ridiculous.

"What's up?" If Hayden squinted, she could see the backs of Sam's ears were red. Even more hilarious. Everyone changed pretty openly in the locker room. Not Sam, apparently.

"I was wondering when you were going to tell Luce. Though I see you have. So my next question was when you were telling your family."

Scrub pants now on and one foot in her work shoes, Hayden stopped dead. Her family? The joy of this was she didn't need to do that. Lying to Luce was eating her alive. Lying to her family? No.

"And also, well, where they lived and if I'll meet them," Sam continued. "I realized we hadn't really talked about that."

Which had been stupid. What else would come up that they hadn't thought of?

She had to tell her family? That was part of the deal? They were in another state. She'd assumed it wouldn't matter. Why did it feel like all the air had disappeared from the room?

When Hayden didn't answer, Sam turned around, her eyebrows bunching together. Hayden stood, one foot half in her shoe, frozen.

"What's wrong?" Sam asked.

"My family?"

"Yes. Your family."

Hayden cleared her throat and sat down on the bench nearby. She pushed her foot into her shoe completely and started doing up the laces. "I didn't think I'd need to tell them?"

"You didn't think you'd need to tell your family you were married when we're trying to pass this off as real?" Sam had lowered her voice by the end of her question, even though they were completely alone.

"Well…yeah." That sounded as stupid as Hayden felt now. "But do they really need to know?" She rested her elbows on her knees, her one shoeless foot growing cold against the floor.

Sam was still looking confused. "If we need to be convincing, yes."

"But we *can* be convincing. To everybody else. Why does it matter if they know?"

"Hayden, I thought you understood. The people in our lives would have to know."

"Well, does your family know?"

Sam flushed. "That's beside the point."

"So I have to tell mine and you don't?" That was entirely unfair.

"For the purpose of this marriage, and what I'm aiming for, no, they don't need to know."

"What are you aiming for?"

Sam's flush deepened, and her hands disappeared into her scrub-top pockets. "That's unimportant."

"I think it's very important."

Sam's nostrils actually flared. Hayden could see from where she was sitting. It was kind of terrifying. "You agreed to this. Our agreement was that it had to appear legitimate. Whether my family knows or not has no bearing on that."

Hayden felt heat crawling up her neck; it always did when she was angry. "So I turn my life upside down and you don't?"

That was why Hayden was being compensated. She knew that. But she couldn't let it go.

"You think this isn't doing just that?" The words almost hissed out, and Hayden flinched backward from the emotion in them. Sam looked as if she was about to say more, but she snapped her mouth shut. She looked upward for a moment, before looking back at Hayden. "What I do doesn't matter. If you don't wish to follow through on the stipulations of our agreement, we have a big problem."

They did. The money. They signed that day. How had they not talked about this?

They'd both simply assumed.

What was that stupid saying?

But regardless, Hayden was pissed. She pushed her cold foot into the other shoe and did it up. "Well, clearly we do. I don't get why my family has to know."

"Because the deal was that. They need to know, in case this is looked into."

"By *who?*" Hayden stood up, and the last word exploded out of her mouth. Abuela would tell her she was flaring up too quickly. In that moment, she didn't care. "If it's not for a green card, I don't understand why they have to know."

"That's not my issue." Sam's voice was deadly calm, and Hayden hated that. "We had an agreement. Part of that agreement was I don't need to explain my reasons to you. And that we convince the people we need to."

Damn it, that was true. Hayden took a deep breath in through her nose. It didn't help. She was still mad. And that didn't make any real sense, but she was.

"I have to go and eat something." Hayden needed to leave, and that was as good an excuse as any. "I have a twelve-hour shift ahead of me."

She walked past Sam, managing not to brush her shoulder.

The door swished shut a second time, this time behind her, and Hayden stomped up the stairs to the cafeteria, out of breath by the second landing.

Sam's piercing green eyes didn't leave her mind. They'd stayed cool and calm, even as color rose in her cheeks. Even as Hayden had bit at her, she still stayed composed and spoken logically.

How infuriating.

CHAPTER 10

Hayden smelled like twelve-hour shift.

And she really wanted a shower.

Five hours into her night, she'd ended up with *three* separate types of bodily fluids covering her from *one* patient. She'd had to shower and change, but still, all she wanted was another shower. One that reached scary levels of hot. And there needed to be steam. And shampoo.

And then bed.

Oh, bed.

She greeted the doorman—how did she live somewhere with a *doorman*—and would have taken the stairs, but Sam's apartment was on the top floor, and Hayden was succumbing to exhaustion, the kind that itched behind her eyes and left them heavy-lidded and threatening to close at any point against her will. The elevator seemed to take forever, and she let her eyes close, the humming sound the elevator made almost dropping her into a trance.

At least Sam would have left for work by now. And Hayden could avoid her successfully until at *least* tonight at the hospital. Most likely for a few days, what with the night shift. Hayden hated conflict, but she hated the awkward "hi" after it more.

Also, maybe she'd overreacted. Maybe. A little.

Perhaps.

Still mad about the entire thing, though.

Despite the big, well-lit, open apartment she was about to enter, she had a weird pang in her stomach, one like homesickness. She wanted to go somewhere familiar after the oddity that was getting *married* and moving into a new house and that strange argument and Luce's weird looks, not to mention the longest night shift ever. But Frank would never forgive her, and she felt bad leaving him in a strange place after only being there with him for a few hours.

Also, if Sam wasn't there, she could pretend she was some rich person in her fancy apartment for a few hours. And that bed had been amazing. As the elevator doors opened, Hayden actually let out a groan at the thought of falling face-first on the bed and passing out; after a shower, of course.

She opened her eyes and almost fell over at the fact that Sam, framed by the elevator doors, was standing there and staring at her. Also, she looked far too amused.

"That was an interesting sound."

Was Sam smirking? She was smirking.

"I thought of the bed I was about to fall into."

"Ah. Long shift?"

Hayden nodded and stepped through the doors. They slid shut after her, and Sam made no attempt to stop them. "I don't know if I'm more excited about the shower or the bed."

Sam's nose wrinkled slightly. "What's that in your hair?"

"Don't ask."

Sam was still staring at a spot near her ear. "It looks like—"

"It probably is."

"Charming."

"No. It's not charming." All Hayden wanted was to sleep. "Shouldn't you be at work?"

For some reason, her bluntness didn't faze Sam in the least. "I have a conference today. It starts at nine."

"Lucky you."

Storming away from Sam into the apartment seemed unfair. But on second thought, screw that. She turned and fished her key out of her bag, slipping it into the lock and walking in. She glanced around—Frank was nowhere to be seen. Most likely he was on her bed, where she'd left him when she'd gone to work in the evening, his tail swishing angrily.

She went to the kitchen and put her bag on the table. When she turned around, she bit back a sigh. Sam had followed her in.

"We should talk," she said.

Hayden didn't think she could even stand up for much longer, let alone make words. But Sam was only a few feet away, didn't seem to be going anywhere, and was blocking the exit from the kitchen, one hand resting on the countertop. How did she look so put together first thing in the morning? She was wearing a black, tailored suit jacket, and Hayden felt as if she'd been hit by a truck that had left behind questionable goo in her hair.

"Okay." Hayden sighed and waved her hand vaguely in the air. "Talk."

"Are you going to act like a child the entire time?" Sam cocked her head.

"Yes."

"That's helpful, thank you."

Hayden closed her eyes, took in a deep breath, and tried to ignore the way her anger was flaring up again, hot in her blood. "Okay. I'm tired. Extremely. And I'm still pretty pissed off."

Sam nodded once at that but didn't say anything.

"So, sorry. I'll try and not act like a child."

"Okay." Sam seemed to consider her words for a second. "I didn't want to make you angry. That was not my intention. I was genuinely surprised *you* were shocked. I thought we had an understanding."

"So did I. I don't get why my family has to know."

"But if this was about making people believe it was real, why would you think they *shouldn't* know?"

Hayden's mouth fell open to snap something back, but nothing came out. Damn. "Okay," she finally gave in. "Good point. I guess I figured if everyone in the hospital knew, including my best friend, and we had the marriage certificate, why would my family have to?"

"Because." Sam broke eye contact, looking somewhere over Hayden's shoulder. "It has to be as convincing as possible."

"Why?"

The eye contact was back, and more intense. "I don't have to tell you that. Our agreement was clear."

"I don't see why I have to turn my life upside down to that extent without an explanation as to why you don't have to."

"You have no idea what I am doing with my life. And actually, you have to do it because that's what you agreed to, Hayden. This is not a surprise."

"Yes, yes. Okay. You keep saying that. But can you see why I'm mad?"

"Not really, no."

That heat was creeping up her neck again, and she didn't feel so tired at the flare of it. "Seriously?"

"No." Sam was so damn calm. It wasn't fair. Hayden felt ready to fall into a heap in hysterical, overtired tears. "I don't see. I'm sorry for that, but I don't understand. We made a deal. That was your part of the bargain." Her brow creased, as if she was genuinely lost from that point on.

Sucking in a deep breath didn't help much. "Yes. We made a deal; that was my part. I did misunderstand how deep it had to go. I should have understood that from the start, or maybe we should have talked about this all in a lot more detail." That ring on her finger was like an anchor dragging her hand toward the floor. Crossing her arms didn't help the sensation. "Logically, that is all true. I made a deal. But I'm still kind of pissed. Do you get that?"

Sam eyed her, lips pursed as if she were measuring her words. "I don't get it, I'm sorry." But her tone had lost its condescending edge and sounded sincere, if a bit lost. "I don't because the expectations were clear." She held up a hand as Hayden opened her mouth, and Hayden closed it. "But I can see you are upset. I acknowledge that."

"Okay." Hayden sighed. More would be too much to ask for, probably. "Okay."

What else was there to say? She was still kind of pissed off. But Sam did seem to be trying. She was a conundrum, really.

"So, do we have an understanding?" Sam asked.

"I guess so. I have to tell my family. Your family apparently doesn't need to know." That part could have held a very bitter edge. Possibly.

"As per the agreement, yes."

"Yes, okay, I get it, Madame Logic." Hayden flagged against the bench top, rubbing her eyes. "Aren't you going to be late?"

Sam checked her watch. "I'll make it right on time." But she pursed her lips at the reminder. Right on time was probably still late in Sam's world. She straightened her bag on her shoulder. "Are we—are we okay?"

Hayden, who had pushed herself off the counter, paused. She'd stepped closer to Sam and was surprised at the sincere gaze that was on her. The question sounded strange coming from her. Finally, Hayden's shoulders slumped. "We're fine."

"Good." She turned and walked toward the door. "Sleep well."

And with that comment, Sam closed the door behind her, and Hayden heard the elevator door open and close. She resisted the urge to throw her bag after her. It would only hit the door and spill its contents everywhere, anyway. Then Hayden would have to do something hideous like bend and pick things up.

What had Hayden gotten herself into? She was really going to have to tell her family—her sister, her abuela, and her nephew.

The lie was spreading, and it left her sick. They would benefit from this too, though. Hayden would have more money to send them. But a giant lie was what had set their lives on a doomed course years ago, one that had shattered everything from under them.

But really, could this one do any harm?

Everything was starting to feel fuzzy around the edges. She climbed into the shower as soon as the water was hot, steam billowing out from behind the glass door in waves. It was like heaven, and she stood under it, wavering for longer than she meant to, her fingertips pruned when she finally climbed out. She pulled on an oversized shirt and underwear, tugged the heavy curtains over the window, set her alarm, and crawled under her covers.

She groaned again. Loudly. It felt so damn good. The bed was warm. The blanket was thick.

She had to tell her family.

But that was future Hayden's problem. Current Hayden's eyelids were filled with lead. When she felt a thump at the end of the bed and heard the padding of tiny paws, she didn't open her eyes as she pulled the blanket up off herself and held it up until she heard scurrying. Frank's warmth pressed into her stomach in a tight ball. She dropped the blanket back down and curled around him. His purring was barely muffled.

Sleep was like a wave, tugging her deeper until it was all she knew.

~ ~ ~

Four shifts of night shift always flew by.

All she did was work, go home, sleep, wake up like the dead, eat cereal at five in the afternoon, go to work, go home, maybe have a beer at nine in the morning, because, for Hayden, it wasn't really morning. Then it was sleep, repeat. The shifts were always busy; the staff were always bordering on loopy, but interesting things always happened.

The bonus? Hayden didn't really see Sam. She was gone by the time Hayden arrived home, and Hayden was heading to work by the time Sam was leaving it. She saw her once when Sam was called for a consult and Sam had obviously stayed late.

That was interesting.

"So, you're really married to her?" Tasha asked, her eyebrows so high up her head Hayden thought they might launch into space.

"Yup." Hayden said it happily and kept checking lab results on the computer. She'd better look happy—no, ecstatic. That was what she was going for.

"I heard. And I saw the ring on your finger. I mean, I knew you'd been seeing each other outside of work. People were talking about it. And one night I saw the two of you looking cozy in a bar. But married?"

Choosing bars near the hospital had paid off.

"Yup," Hayden said. "Married. Lawfully wedded and all that." She glanced up. "And yes, I know it's fast. When it's right, it's right, you know?"

She'd practiced that one in the mirror. Perfected it, really.

Tasha's smile was a little uncertain. "Yeah, I guess so. Well, congratulations."

"Thanks."

It was one of many such congratulations she'd received, all with that tone that said the person couldn't really believe they were actually saying it. The ring had been eyed, and not long after someone from surgery had come down and whispered something to someone else, which meant Hayden had made herself look giddy and joyful, and eventually someone brave finally asked, and *wham*. It had spread faster than news about a new flu.

Everyone was clearly skeptical. Most didn't really care. They weren't overly involved, and Hayden knew from experience that to them it was merely an interesting bit of gossip that they moved on from quickly when they heard something new. Hayden and her super-fast wedding got replaced as soon as the director of the hospital was charged with fraud. Luce kind of eyed her between shift changes, but neither of them really saw each other much when one of them was on night shift. Mostly they sent stupid messages and humorously captioned photos back and forth. Night shift sucked them in, and all anyone could do was buckle down until it was over.

Which Hayden was so ready for, as was Tasha, if the bags under her eyes were any indication.

"Actually, I'm due for my break. I've called for a consult, so if Neuro turns up, I'm sure you won't mind taking it." Tasha winked. "There're unused beds everywhere."

Hayden wrinkled her nose. "Ew, Tasha. This isn't a medical drama on TV."

"Well, just saying it's been done before."

"Well, it won't be this time. It's two in the morning. The Neuro consult won't be Sam."

Tasha gave her a weird look. "She's the on call tonight."

Shit. How had Hayden not known that? Oh, right. The avoidance. "Oh! Yeah. I assumed she'd send a pleb."

"Right. Anyway. It's for a patient in bed four. MVA, looks like a bad concussion. Has had a scan and needs the review." Tasha updated Hayden in more detail and gave a quick overview on her other patients in case they needed anything while she took her break.

"No problem."

"Enjoy your honey." Tasha flounced away.

Of course, Sam took over twenty minutes to arrive. She walked up to the nurses' station, scrub cap on and no lab coat. It was another decorated one, this time light blue and covered in tiny stethoscopes.

Sam was such a nerd.

"Hello," she said. She put her elbows on the nurses' station, and Hayden looked up at her from the other side.

"Hi." Hayden glanced around. No one was really paying attention, but you never knew. They smiled at each other. Sam's eyes softened with the gesture. She was pale, smudges under her eyes. It was always so obvious when she was tired. "I didn't know you were on tonight." She kept her voice low.

"It was an emergency cover." Sam smothered a yawn. "I was *not* prepared for it."

"Clearly."

"Did someone need a consult?"

"Yeah, my coworker. Here's the folder. Car accident." Hayden updated her on the status, making sure to tell her everything Tasha had said. She pulled up the scan on the computer, and Sam came around the nurses' station to stand behind her and look at the image.

"Hm."

And then Sam was leaning forward, her hand planted on the desk next to the mouse, her fingers against Hayden's. Sam's head was next to Hayden's and her chest against Hayden's shoulder blade.

Softness. And a very subtle perfume. Or was that a subtle soap?

Sam's cheek was almost against Hayden's ear.

She was too tired to comprehend this.

"Hayden," Sam murmured. "Someone, who I assume knows you, is watching us. Blonde hair. Nurse."

"That's Tasha. It's her patient whose scan we're looking at." Hayden kept her own voice low.

"She was watching us. I thought this was appropriate. Am I wrong?"

"No." Hayden cleared her throat. "No. This is… This is what married people would do."

Okay, so it had been a few months since Hayden had…well. Or maybe more than a few months? And when Sam turned her head a touch, her lips brushed Hayden's hair as she spoke into her ear.

"Then you need to relax."

Goose bumps erupted down Hayden's back. This was weird and uncomfortable as hell.

Hayden took a deep breath and tried to make her shoulders loosen. The movement pushed her back further against Sam's chest.

This was utterly ridiculous. She'd sit with Luce like this. Or most other people in the ER. Okay, there would always be fewer lips near ears and chests pushing against her shoulder blades. But this was just like being affectionate with a friend, right?

She forced her lips up and turned her head back toward Sam. Their eyes ended up inches apart. "Better?"

Acting. She could act. That was all any of this had ever been.

"Much." Sam's eyes were vibrant in the fluorescent light of the ER. It was never dark here, no matter the time of day or night. "Now, have a look at the scan." Hayden turned back to her, her ear brushing Sam's cheek. "What do you see?"

Hayden moved the mouse, flipping through the images. "A bleed."

"Good. Do you think it needs surgery?"

Hayden didn't feel like she was being patronized. But she did feel as if she was being tested. She wasn't a neurosurgeon or a radiographer. She narrowed her eyes, concentrating on the image, flicking through the fine slices. "Yes?"

"Is that a question or an answer?"

"An answer. She needs surgery."

"That she does." Sam straightened, and cold air swirled around Hayden's neck. "That nurse is the patient's?" Hayden nodded, not trusting her voice for some reason. "I'll see you at home."

And Sam walked away to Tasha, who really had been skulking near a treatment room and watching them.

So yeah, night shift was a weird world.

By the end of her fourth shift, Hayden was looking forward to being back in the land of the living. She'd read the studies. She knew night shift workers plain didn't function as well as other people. But it was part and parcel of the job, and there was always the relief to look forward to when it was over.

Like right now.

She threw herself into the shower and into the comfort of her bed. Sadly, she set her alarm for only a few hours from now, the idea being that she'd make herself get up after a nap so that, hopefully, she'd sleep kind of normally that night; but getting up after only a few hours always hurt.

Really, this was how she'd gotten into this mess—being wide awake at a ridiculous time, thanks to night shift, and stumbling across Sam's ad.

She quickly grabbed her phone and sent her sister a message. Phone away, she dropped her head back to her pillow. Maybe she could sleep forever. That was her last thought before her alarm was ringing what seemed like two minutes later. The backs of her eyelids were surely layered with sandpaper. Blearily, almost knocking her phone off the nightstand, she pulled it in front of her face.

She'd been asleep for four hours.

"Ugh." She threw herself backward onto the bed, nestling among the pillows with a thump. Almost immediately, her eyes drifted shut again.

With strength that deserved a medal, she opened them and sat up.

She felt hungover. Kicking her blankets off, she frowned and looked around. No Frank. He'd abandoned her.

She pulled her glasses on, and the room came into better focus.

But where was he? He barely left her room, except to find his food and litter tray. She quickly pulled on some sweatpants and a hoodie, as well as a thick pair of socks. It was only one p.m. Eight hours until it was an appropriate time to go back to sleep. God, this sucked.

She needed coffee.

Running her fingers along the wall of the corridor, Hayden walked down and emerged into the living space and jumped.

Sam was sitting on the giant sofa.

No, Sam was sitting on the giant sofa with Frank next to her, curled in the fold of her knees. Hayden felt her mouth drop open. Sam looked up from her book.

"Good afternoon."

Everything was blurry, even with her glasses on. "Uh, hi."

"How are you feeling?"

"Like the dead."

"You don't want to sleep more?" Sam asked.

Hayden shook her head. "I want to sleep tonight."

"Ah. I can sleep anytime, anywhere."

Narrowing her eyes, Hayden walked into the kitchen. "Rub it in." She paused and frowned at her cat. "And you—since when do you like people?"

Sam looked down at him, her hand rubbing the top of his head. Frank even tilted his chin up for Sam to rub under it. Hayden could hear his purring from across the giant room.

"Does he not normally like people?" Sam asked.

"I think he only barely tolerates me. I've hardly ever seen him like that."

His face was smug. Stupid cat. In fact, they were both far too self-satisfied. "Aren't you supposed to be working?" Hayden snarked.

"I have the day off." Sam continued to scratch Frank's head. "You know what shift work is like."

Did she ever. Hayden cocked her head at the coffee machine that was covered in more buttons than the defibrillator at the hospital. There were knobs. And levers. And compartments. Did it have a manual?

And then Sam was next to her. Hayden jumped.

"Would you like me to make you a coffee?"

"It's okay. I can, uh…make one."

"Okay." Sam turned to leave.

Hayden spun so fast loose hair whipped her in the eye. "No, wait." Sam was supposed to follow Hayden's response with "are you sure?" so that Hayden could politely acquiesce to her ministrations, wasn't she? "I changed my mind." She tried to look both sheepish and useless. "Could you? Please? I have no idea how this works."

Sam turned back right away. "Okay."

Hayden stood tugging on the ends of her sleeves in the middle of the huge kitchen, as Sam pulled out cream and milk and coffee from the fridge. When she turned around and Hayden was still standing there, she raised her eyebrows.

"Go sit down. You look like you're about to fall over."

"Thanks. I'll ignore the part where you implied I look like shit."

As she walked to the living room, Hayden heard Sam sigh. She fell down on the sofa next to her cat, who looked at her as if she was a bad replacement. Nice.

"That's not what I said." Sam's voice filtered over from the kitchen area.

Hayden didn't bother to answer as her eyes drifted closed again. Blindly, she rubbed circles on Frank's head. He didn't purr as loudly as he had before. Bastard.

"How do you take your coffee?"

"Tiny dash of milk, no sugar."

Sounds wafted from the kitchen: the grinder for the beans, something that sounded like it heated up milk. She could almost be in a café. Except that here was warm and comfortable, and no terrible people were around her.

Just awkward Sam and Hayden's traitor of a cat.

"Here you go." The quiet words tugged her out of an almost sleep, and Hayden sat up. She went to rub her eyes but instead hit her glasses. Sam, standing over her with a coffee, failed to hide a smile.

"Thanks." Hayden took the coffee and had a sip. It was splendid. She sighed contentedly. Loudly too.

"You're very vocal with your enjoyment of things, you know."

Hayden chuckled as she took another sip. "I've been told."

She almost choked the second she realized what she'd said, warmth flooding her cheeks. She turned to look at Sam, who had sat at the other end of the giant sofa. Her cheeks were red, but she looked thoroughly amused, her eyes dancing.

"Is that so?" Sam asked.

"Can we pretend I didn't say that?"

"No." Sam's lips were twitching.

"Please?"

"No."

Hayden sighed and lay back against the sofa. "That's very cruel."

They settled into silence, Hayden taking sips and trying to wake up properly, Sam with her laptop and tapping away at the keys. It was strange to sit there in Sam's house, and it was even stranger to sit there with her in it. Her ring glinted as she typed. Hayden's clinked against the porcelain of her cup as she took a sip.

Her tired brain hurt. This situation was so bizarre. Also, the silence wasn't awkward, even after their weird non-argument days ago.

"Did the money transfer okay?"

Hayden rolled her head to look at Sam. "Hm?"

"The money I transferred through the day we signed?"

"Oh. Yeah. I checked and forgot to confirm with you, what with the craziness of night shift. Thanks."

"Good."

Hayden closed her eyes, and Frank's purring slowed down as he fell asleep, warm against her leg. It wouldn't be long before she joined him.

"Your coffee's spilling over the edge."

Hayden opened her eyes and looked down at the coffee she gripped against her chest. Sam was right; it was about to tip everywhere. She took a sip, and another immediately after.

"Good coffee. Thank you."

"You're welcome." Sam cleared her throat, and Hayden looked at her. She didn't take her gaze off the screen. "Are you doing anything tonight?"

"I was going to meet Luce at seven for a drink, then crawl into bed and hopefully sleep for twelve hours."

"Do you sleep okay after night shift?"

"The first night, yeah. The second and third, not really. I end up scrolling my phone in the early hours."

"Is that how you found my ad?" Something about Sam's tone made it seem she was joking.

"Yeah, actually."

Sam looked up sharply. "Oh?"

"Yeah. I thought it was a joke."

Sam glanced down at the ring on her finger and back up. "And now you're here."

"Yup." The eye contact went on until Hayden finally broke it and looked at her coffee. "I'm still kind of mad," she admitted.

"I know." Sam was back to tapping at her keyboard, no reproach in her tone.

"Sam?"

Sam looked up, her fingers pausing.

Hayden sighed. "Want to come with me to the café to meet Luce properly? We should really get it over with."

Sam's expression didn't change, but she did swallow noticeably. "Okay. Though I have to be somewhere and will finish up after seven. I can meet you both there?"

That was good. Hayden could warn Luce to not be weird.

"Sounds fine. I'll send you the location of where we're going."

"Okay."

Sam snapped her laptop shut and put it on the coffee table. "I have to go. I'll see you then?"

"Yeah."

Sam grabbed her bag and disappeared out the door. Quick exit indeed. She didn't strike Hayden as one for long goodbyes. Or, apparently, any goodbye at all. So Hayden grabbed her phone, which was flashing with a reply from her sister.

They were going to video-call in ten minutes. Hayden took a deep breath. She could do this. She quickly drained her coffee and rinsed the cup out in the kitchen before placing it in the sink. Frank sprawled out on his back on the sofa, watching her from across the room.

"Maybe your issue was that you always knew you deserved a higher standard of living," she told him.

As if in agreement, he wriggled onto his back and closed his eyes.

Hayden rolled her own and went to brush her teeth and wash her face, hoping the cold water would wake her up. She avoided the mirror. She already knew she looked like hell; she didn't need to confirm it.

With her laptop in hand, she sat on the sofa. Her sister was already online. She pressed the *call* button, and the familiar music filled the room. Frank's ear twitched, but other than that, he didn't move. The image of herself on the laptop was at a hideous upward angle. She now had a thousand chins. Hayden couldn't even care less. She did nestle back into the couch a bit more, leaving her legs up on the sofa and putting the laptop on her knees. She looked less terrifying now, but wow, her eyes were really red-rimmed.

The music cut off, and her sister's image filled the screen. She was a darker-haired version of Hayden; her eyes the same chocolate color and skin the same dark brown. There were exactly twelve months between them, and sometimes they bounced back and forth between acting like the younger sister and the older sister. Technically, it was her sister who was older.

"Hayds." Her voice was tinny through the speakers, but still the sound sent familiarity warming all over her.

"Sofia. Hey."

Sofia was managing to look both really pleased to see her and pissed off at the same time. "It's been a while."

"I know. Sorry. I've been really busy."

"So have I."

"I know you have." Hayden felt the frustration that had flared up with ease. "You know I know that."

That pissed-off expression that Hayden knew was a mirror of her own when she used it faded. "Fine, whatever. Let's move on from that. How's work?"

"Busy. Hectic." Hayden half shrugged. "I love it, though."

"And your stupid cat?"

Hayden tilted the laptop so the camera fell on her laid-out, lazy, round cat. "He's fine, as you can see."

"He looks relaxed."

The camera was back on her in time to catch the roll of her eyes. "He is. *¿Y mi sobrino?* Is Javi there?"

"He's got soccer this afternoon."

Hayden chuckled, liking the idea of her four-year-old nephew playing soccer far too much. "Soccer? At his age? How much soccer do they actually play?"

"At the last match, three kids sat down and started playing some weird clapping game, and two ran headfirst into each other. The rest picked up the ball and ran around with it in their hands."

Hayden laughed, Frank twitching next to her. "I'd love to see that."

"If you came and visited, you could."

And there it was. "I know, Sofe. I do."

"Hayds, Mom and Javi ask for you all the time."

The mention of her mother made Hayden's stomach flip with guilt. And Javi. She never saw enough of him, and last time, he'd gone from toddler-slash-baby to little boy. Who knew that happened after four? "I'm sorry. The last year has been a real balancing act, trying to send enough money and manage here too."

Plus, Hayden doubted her mom really asked for her that much.

"You know you could be living here. That would cut costs."

Hayden's jaw clench. And give up even more? Including her feeling of independence? "You know I wouldn't cope."

Sofia huffed. "True, fine. But you do need to visit."

"Well. That's kind of why I called."

Sofia perked up, her face brighter. "You're coming?"

"I don't have anything planned yet, but I want to. I'll have to get leave from work."

She waved her hand in the air, dismissing that. "Yeah, yeah. Semantics. But you're coming?"

"Yeah. But I have to tell you something first."

Sofia's eyes immediately narrowed. Her sister knew her too well. "You have your guilty face on."

"I do not!"

"You do."

Hayden huffed. "Look, I wanted to tell you and Abuela together. Is she there?"

"Yeah, I just didn't tell her I was calling you so we could chat first."

"Good plan. Could you call her in?"

Sofia turned. "Abuela!"

"Or you know, scream."

"Shut up. You know she's half deaf."

Hayden's felt dry-mouthed all of a sudden. This was going to suck. She really didn't want to lie to her family. Avoid them, fine. Blame them for things out of their control sometimes, sure. Get frustrated as hell by them, completely.

But lie? No. She wasn't *him*.

"*¿Qué?*"

The old woman's voice reached her, and Hayden couldn't help but grin. "Abuela!"

Her grandmother's face appeared on the screen, hovering over Sofia's shoulder. She lit up after she was done squinting at the laptop, her eyes bright and sharp.

"Alejandra." Abuela's voice was warm like syrup coating her insides and leaving her comforted.

"Abuela, are you ever going to call me Hayden?"

She never would, but it was almost a habit to ask now.

Abuela pushed at Sofia's shoulders until Sofia rolled her eyes and stood up. She sat in the other chair right next to the one she'd vacated, that Abuela deemed too uncomfortable, and Abuela sat down in the comfortable one. Her lined face was still bright as she squinted at Hayden, intense.

"Why? Your name is Alejandra in the middle. Just because that *gringo* gave you that name does not mean I must use it."

That, and Abuela loved that Hayden's middle name was a tribute to her.

Hayden couldn't even be mad. It would never change. "Fine, fine. Y *¿cómo te va?*"

"You know I am practicing the English now. I teached you—"

"Taught," Sofia and Hayden chorused.

She didn't even miss a beat. "...taught you Spanish, now it is *mi turno*."

"Your turn."

"That." She waved a hand in the air. "And we are fine here, the same. *Como siempre*. And how are you? Why you never call?"

Sofia was smirking, and Hayden sighed. "I'm sorry. I've been busy. Work's been non-stop."

"She said she's coming to visit," Sofia added.

Abuela's face lit up. "Good. This will make your *mamá* very happy."

"Where is she?" Hayden had been avoiding the question.

"She's got swimming this afternoon," Sofia said.

"Oh. Good." Hayden smiled. "Is she liking it?"

"Loves it some days." Abuela flicked her glasses from the top of her head onto her nose and finally stopped squinting. They weren't allowed to suggest she use them. She'd only had them a year, and she thought they made her look old. "When you come?"

"I'm not sure yet, but soon."

She waggled a finger at the screen. "Until you have a ticket, I don't believe you. Always 'I'm coming, I'm coming,' and then *nada*."

Sofia was smirking again. "She also said she had something to talk to us about."

Both stared at her through the screen. Hayden's pulse was too quick, nausea bubbling in her belly.

"Well…"

How did she say this? Just spit it out? Ease them in?

Not tell them?

Sam's raised eyebrows entered her head, and she sighed. That wasn't an option.

She pushed a piece of hair behind her ear, fallen loose from the sloppy bun piled on the top of her head.

"*¿Qué es eso?*" Abuela's voice was sharp. That voice had struck fear in her as a child. Hayden froze, exactly like she had back then too.

"*¿Qué?*" she asked. "What is what, Abuela?"

Her grandmother's eyes were like a laser beam; the camera's stupid perspective made it hard to know what it was focused on.

"On your finger. What is that?"

Hayden's eyes widened. As did Sofia's. Both gazes were now focused on her hand. She held it out in front of her face, fingers spread. The damn ring.

"*Mierda.*" Sofia blurted out. "What is that?"

This was bad, because Abuela didn't even admonish Sofia for swearing.

"Uh, well. That's what I wanted to tell you."

That sick feeling in Hayden's stomach hadn't gone away. She would have to lie as little as possible. That's how she would get through this.

No mientan a su familia. Nunca. Abuela had said it, once, years ago, her eyes fierce as she'd put a hand on each of her teary granddaughters' shoulders. *You don't lie to your family. Ever.*

Hayden wasn't naïve. Of course you did sometimes. White lies and all that. But big lies? No. Lies in general wrapped you up, and you tugged at one thread and then another, and the whole thing fell apart.

So she'd lather it in enough truth.

"I got married." Hayden said it like ripping off a Band-Aid. Which was exactly how it felt.

Abuela and Sofia went silent. Sofia's mouth hung open for several seconds.

"Married?" Abuela asked. At Hayden's nod, she shook her head. "*¿Estás casada?*" It was as if she needed it in Spanish to believe it.

"Yes." Beaming beatifically was asking way too much of her tired brain, but Hayden at least tried.

"You?" Sofia asked. "You got married? You think marriage is a useless institution with zero use in today's society."

"I never said that."

"In fact, that's exactly what you said. Word for word."

"*Nieta*, you are married—*¿en serio?*"

"*Sí*. Really, I'm married." And Hayden said it with conviction.

"And without your family?" Even the terrible speakers couldn't hide the tone in Abuela's voice.

"Abuela, no. It wasn't like that. It was a small thing for us. There wasn't a ceremony."

Actual tears were in Abuela's eyes, and Sofia put an arm over her shoulder. "Seriously, Hayden?" Sofia sounded alarmed. "You're actually married?"

"Yes. I am."

"Why we not know him?" Abuela asked. "Or her? This person? Why?"

"It's new. And it was fast." True. All very true. "It was a bit of a whim." Also true.

"You do not marry with someone on, on this...whim, *cariño*."

"Abuela, I know. But I'm really happy." She thought of the money, and smiled harder.

Sofia and Abuela peered at their screen.

"I think she means it, Abuela." Sofia still sounded shocked. "Like, she looks happy."

Abuela sniffed. "She does. Tell us about this person. I cannot believe you married with them without us."

Hayden swallowed. "Well, her name is Sam. She's a surgeon."

"A surgeon?" Abuela asked. "Can she fix my varicose veins?"

Hayden chuckled. "She's not that kind of surgeon. She's a neurosurgeon."

Her eyes lit up. "Can she fix—"

"No, Abuela."

The question her abuela was about to ask was no use. Sofia looked away quickly, and Hayden wished that she could give her a hug.

"Well... How we know she is good for you? Alejandra, what if she is bad person, and you no know because you're blinded with the lust?"

Hayden burst out laughing, and even Sofia snorted. "Well, you'll meet her. When I come." That was a random, fast decision. But Sam got her in this damn mess, and if Sam was going to get out of having to tell her own family and deal with this, she could deal with Hayden's repercussions instead. She grinned at the idea and hoped her family assumed it was because she was just so deliriously happy. "She wants to meet you all."

Okay, that was her first real lie. But at least it was a funny one.

"When?"

"Soon, Abuela."

"Hayden." Sofia sounded so serious the smile melted off Hayden's face. "You're actually *married?*"

"Yeah."

"Well." Sofia seemed lost for an appropriate reaction. "She must be amazing to have got you to agree to that."

Abuela narrowed her eyes. "She better be."

What a mess.

CHAPTER 11

After the video call from hell, Hayden fell asleep on the couch for thirty minutes while watching a show on her laptop. She woke up with a startled look at the time, ran to the shower, and rushed through waking herself up enough to meet Luce at the café on time.

Luce and Sam.

On her way out the door, Hayden pulled on her leather jacket, wrapped a scarf around her neck—it was really starting to get cold—and paused at the kitchen counter, shoving her phone in her bag. She eyed Frank, curled up on the sofa still.

"You all right there? Need anything, Frank? A mani-pedi? Massage?"

He opened one eye. Then closed it.

"I'll get right on that."

She hiked her bag onto her shoulder and sucked in a breath. Okay. Social time. Luce *and* Sam. It would be…great. Not at all awkward. When it was over, Hayden would come home and sleep forever. Tomorrow, she had all day to lie around in her bed and do absolutely nothing. She might even binge-watch something. And make pizza.

No. She'd get *delivery* pizza.

She really shouldn't get stupid with her money, but she could splurge, just this once.

This was all still too weird and scary, and Hayden couldn't quite shake the feeling that it was all going to explode one day and she'd have to give the money back. It didn't seem likely—how would Sam demand it back? Why would she? This money was for the parts of the agreement Hayden had followed through on. So it was hers.

But it still seemed too good to be true.

Hayden opened the door and pulled it closed behind her. When she turned around, she came face-to-face with a guy standing at the opposite apartment doing the same, his hand still on the door handle.

Something about him was familiar. A common feeling after all the faces she saw coming in and out of the hospital.

She smiled, mostly at the irony of their mirrored position. He seemed young, early twenties, maybe even younger. He had floppy blond hair that made her think younger. Rather than smile back, he cocked his head.

"Hi," she said.

He looked her up and down and turned fully from his door. He slipped his hands into his gray coat's pockets. "Hello."

His voice was cool.

Talk about friendly neighbors. Hayden decided this wasn't worth hanging around for and reached over to press the call button for the elevator. She really should take the stairs, but she was exhausted. And it was going to be winter soon. She needed the few extra pounds to keep warm.

He was still staring at her. "Are you new?"

"Just moved in about four days ago."

His eyes widened. The elevator rumbled behind her, and she wished it would hurry up. He was acting kind of weird, wasn't he?

"Strange we haven't run into each other, then," he said.

Finally, the elevator pinged. "I've been on night shift, so keeping pretty irregular hours."

"You work at the hospital?"

He followed her into the elevator and leaned against one wall, appraising her. He had the look of someone very well-cared for—neat clothes, neat haircut.

"Uh, what do you mean 'the' hospital? There are a lot in this city."

"Oh, I meant the same one as Sam. You're living with her, right?"

The neighbor and Sam were friends? Or at least close enough that he knew which specific hospital she worked at. This would be someone to play it up to. "Yeah, we work together. It's how we met."

"That sounds like you're dating."

He was smiling now, a dimple popping in his left cheek. He had a charming air around him. He must slay in bars.

Hayden winked at him. "More than that. We just got married."

That was still so, so strange to say.

His eyebrows raised, the smile disappearing for a second before it appeared again. "Really?"

"Yeah."

The doors opened, and Hayden breathed a sigh of relief. She slipped out, and he walked behind her, both of them greeting the doorman on the way out. On the street, the light was muted, the sky a dark gray. It was already getting dark. Wind lifted up Hayden's scarf and her hair. She hunched her shoulders against the shock of cool air. The guy's face was already kissed a little pink from it.

"Well." Those dimples popped again. He looked like a cheeky kid. Now his age was even harder to place. "Congratulations."

"Thanks... What was your name?"

Already walking a step backward to head down the street, he said, "Jon. Short for Jonathon, though no one calls me that."

"Well, Jon, it was nice to meet you. I'm Hayden. Alejandra to my grandmother, but no one else."

"Cute." He winked and turned completely before disappearing into the masses walking down the sidewalk.

Maybe he *was* a friendly neighbor.

The bus ride was short, and Hayden managed to slip through the door of the café right on time. Inside was buzzing with warmth, and some kind of folk music was playing over the speakers. The staff moved between tables, bringing out coffees and teas and clearing empty spots. Hayden loved this place. The chairs were all mismatched; a mix of old-school armchairs and sofas. Different colored cushions were scattered over each one. It had an eclectic, comfortable atmosphere.

A quick glance located Luce, sitting in a corner, holding their e-reader. Hayden wove through the tables and flopped into the worn red armchair opposite Luce.

"Hey, stranger." Luce slipped their e-reader into their bag. "So you survived night shift? You look, uh, great."

"The word you're looking for is 'crap,' Luce. I look like crap."

"Well, I was never gonna *say* it. Still as gorgeous as ever, though." They thought they were so charming. "So, how's married life?"

"Luce..."

"What?" They pouted. "Genuine question."

"Your smirk says otherwise."

"There's no smirk."

"There really, really is." Hayden acknowledged the waitress who approached them, her pad already open and pen in hand. "Hi," she said. "One shot espresso, thanks."

Luce wrinkled their nose at the order. "Gross." They turned to the waitress. "Mocha frappe with extra syrup, please."

It was Hayden's turn to wrinkle her nose. "Gross."

"Anything else?"

Hayden shook her head. "Not for me. Though someone else will be joining us in thirty minutes or so."

The waitress disappeared, and Luce was staring at her. "They are?"

Hayden cleared her throat, and she flicked her thumb along the band on her finger again. She needed to stop that, even though it had replaced the gnawing the inside of her cheek habit nicely. "Uh, yeah. I asked Sam if she wanted to join us. You said you wanted to get to know her."

"I suppose I did."

"Did you mean it?"

"What? Of course. It's just... Won't it be awkward?"

"Not if you behave."

"Me? Whatever do you mean?" Luce even tried to flutter their lashes innocently.

"You look like you have something in your eye."

"I do. It's insult at your insinuation."

"You're a drama quee—kin—uh, drama quing?"

Luce's eyes lit up. "I love that."

"Excellent. Henceforth, *quing* is the gender-neutral term for royalty. I may have read it online, but we can pretend I came up with it."

"Great. But, back on track, I am not a drama quing."

"You really are."

"Well, awfully sorry if your shotgun wedding has brought out my more dramatic side."

Their coffees appeared in front of them, and they both threw a thankful expression at the waitress.

"It's not a shotgun wedding." Hayden reached for her tiny espresso glass, stirring it slowly with a spoon in the hopes it would cool faster. She needed it to get through the next two hours until she could fall into bed.

"Isn't it?" Luce sat straighter. "Are you pregnant?"

Hayden didn't know if they were being serious. "No."

"Right. You have to have had sex for that."

Instantly, her cheeks warmed. "Still going with that theory?"

"Well, I haven't seen your legs for a while in the change rooms, but last I saw they weren't the smooth you go for when you're getting lucky."

"Well, now they are."

More lies. And, damn it, now she was going to have to shave them all the time. Far too much effort.

"Well, I assumed you've shagged now. Done it at the hospital yet?"

"No. Seriously, Tasha insinuated that the other night. Who has sex in a hospital?"

Luce paused with their glass halfway to their mouth. "Uh—everyone?"

"Who? Who is everyone?"

"Like, everyone. The amount of affairs going on there is scary."

"I think you're thinking of TV shows. Who has *time* to have sex at the hospital?"

Luce sipped their drink, shrugging while they swallowed. "Look, it happens."

Wait. "Have *you* had sex at the hospital?"

And suddenly Luce couldn't look at her.

A slow smile crawled over Hayden's lips. "Holy shit. You have. Haven't you?"

"Well, it was just once."

"Once?"

"Okay, twice."

Hayden stared at them, and even though they weren't looking at her, she knew they could feel it.

"Fine!" Luce looked at her. A blush wasn't always obvious on their skin, but it was right now. "Multiple times. But with one person." They held up one finger. "One. So. That's the same as once."

"It's really not." A laugh rippled out of her. "This is hilarious. Who? Oh! Coffee Girl? Have you two already hooked up? Did you go on a date? Is she nice? And you've *already* slept together multiple times at work?"

Luce put a hand up in the air in front of them. "Whoa. Slow down. It was a couple of years ago, with the radiographer I was dating."

Hayden fell back against her chair. "Oh. Still interesting, though not as exciting."

"As much as I appreciate your investment in my sex life, that's creepy. And no, I have not hooked up with Coffee Girl."

"But you have gone out?"

Luce couldn't control their delight. "Yeah, I wanted to tell you, but you're all newly married and were sucked into the hole of night shift."

"I am *never* too busy for you to tell me these things. Or anything."

"I wanted to tell you in person."

"When did you go out? Where did you go? Who asked who? Wait, who am I kidding? As *if* you asked her."

"Hey." Luce glared at her. "I might have."

"Did you?"

The glare fell away. "No."

"Thought not."

"She asked me. We went to dinner at the little Thai place near my house."

"I *love* that Thai place."

"I know, right? So we went there. It was nice."

Hayden narrowed her eyes. "That's it? It was *nice*? You got a story of marriage from me, and I get *nice*?"

"Well, I'll never top that story."

"Luce," Hayden whined. "How was it? What did you think of her?"

Hayden didn't want to ask "did she misgender you? Do I need to go after her with itching powder?" but really that was where she was going with this.

There was something coy about the look on Luce's face. "It *was* nice though. We talked a lot, and she kind of noticed me flinch when she used the wrong pronoun and asked. So I explained I was assigned female at birth, but I'm non-binary, and she was really open about it and interested."

"That's good."

"Yeah."

"And...?"

"Get your head out of the gutter."

"You've been talking about *my* sex life."

"And you still haven't told me anything."

Hayden pouted. "It's private."

"I'm pretty sure you telling me about how flexible that girl was that you went home with months ago was private too?" Luce looked smug. "Or how that guy liked it when—"

"Yeah, okay. I get your point. But come on. Give me details?"

"We're going out again."

That made Hayden sit up and take a true interest. "You are? That's awesome. When?"

"In a couple of nights."

"Aw. Are you in *lurve*?"

Luce snorted. "Not all of us move that quickly."

Ouch. But fair. "Hey." Hayden pretended to be insulted anyway. "That was unnecessary."

"Was it, though?"

"Yes."

"Come on. You got married after a month. I've heard you go on rants that last hours about how stupid marriage is."

Hayden took a cautious sip of her still-hot espresso. She closed her eyes in bliss and quickly opened them again as she felt them get heavy. "Well, I was mistaken."

Marriage was stupid. But not if it got you enough money to sort your life out. And more.

"Well—"

"Hello."

They both swiveled their heads. Sam was standing next to them. She looked windswept, her long bangs that normally sat over her right eye blown every which way. Her hands were in her pockets. Hayden shook herself and came back to the moment. Right. Married.

Convincing Luce.

"Hey." Hayden nudged the chair between Luce and Hayden. "Have a seat. How are you?"

Sam pulled her coat off and hung it over the back of her chair. She was wearing a light-green scarf that she kept on, and that made her eyes incredibly vivid. Hayden knew, because when she sat down, Sam turned those eyes straight on her.

"I'm good. How are you feeling?" Sam's hand landed on her knee, and Hayden's entire body started to tense. With a breath, she relaxed. "Did you give in and fall asleep?"

Warmth was pricking up her spine. Must be embarrassment from the fact that, yes, she did pass out on the sofa. "Maybe."

"I'm not surprised. You barely slept." She turned to Luce, keeping her hand on Hayden's leg. Hayden adjusted so she could sit comfortably and have her leg where it looked natural for Sam to do that. The movement pushed her leg into Sam's.

So much body heat being shared.

So much weirdness.

Luce was looking at Sam's hand.

"Hi, Luce. How are you?"

Luce met Sam's eye. "I'm great. Unlike someone, I wasn't stuck on night shift for four days in a row."

"Come on," Hayden protested. "I'm going strong."

"You blinked while sipping your coffee before and almost didn't open your eyes again." Damn. Hayden had thought she'd hidden that well. Luce looked back to Sam. "How are you? Did you work today?"

They were being so civil. While teasing Hayden. Great.

Sam shook her head. "I had a day off."

"Lucky you."

No one had anything more to say, and thankfully the waitress appeared before it could get too awkward. Sam ordered a green tea and as the waitress walked away, caught Hayden's fake gag.

"What?"

"Hayden has an aversion to herbal teas." Luce looked at Sam with a benign smile. "As her wife, you'd think you'd know that?"

The hand on Hayden's knee squeezed.

Sam tilted her head. Hayden looked between the two of them. "I do know that. I thought something else was wrong."

Luce cracked a grin, super friendly again. Suspiciously so. "Sure. So tell me, you two—" Luce looked from one of them to the other "—how did this delightful thing happen? Who asked who? Where were you?"

Hayden felt the blood drain out of her face. How had they not thought of a story for this? How had it not occurred to them that someone would ask this?

"Uh—"

Sam's hand squeezed her knee again. "I asked her."

"Oh?" Luce quirked one eyebrow. Seriously, Hayden needed to learn to do that. It conveyed so much. Like amusement and disbelief. And maybe some scorn. "That's nice. Why?"

"Excuse me?"

That hand was squeezing even harder. But Sam looked calm as anything.

Luce was grinning benignly still, as if they were really interested and not testing them. This was exactly what Hayden had meant when she'd told them to behave. "I'm just curious what made you want to ask that so quickly. You don't strike me as the spontaneous type."

"It seemed right." Sam's grip hadn't faltered. "But I don't really feel the need to justify anything." Her tone was still light, relaxed.

"Oh, I'm not asking for justification. I'm just a real romantic at heart. I'd *love* to know this story."

Hayden sighed. Luce was not going to give this up. Romantic at heart. As if.

"Well." The hesitation in Sam's voice wasn't going to sell it. "We were walking from the hospital, through a park." Hayden watched as Luce fixed their eyes on Sam, intent. "It was cold, but not like today. One of those nights without clouds, the sky really clear, for the city. For some reason, the stars were easier to see." Hayden wasn't watching Luce anymore. She watched Sam's eyes soften, her voice gaining some strength. "And Hayden looked up at the sky, and everything was so still and dark, and the light was silver in her hair. She looked stunning. And I asked."

Hayden's chest felt weird. Sam was selling it. They *had* walked together through the park one night, cutting through it to reach a bar. It had been strange, to see the stars so well in the city. Sam had said so. Hayden remembered, because it had seemed unusually poetic to come from her.

It was much easier to weave a lie from a real experience. That must have been why Sam chose that night.

"So you *can* be spontaneous?" Luce asked.

Sam gave an awkward, one-shouldered shrug. "I have my moments."

"So why so fast? Couldn't wait?"

Luce was being an ass. They had a look of pure mischief in their eye.

Hayden realized she needed to join in. "You know I don't like marriage and weddings. Well, we wanted to do it, but without any of the fuss and madness. So why wait when we didn't have anything to plan?"

Sam gave a nod.

Luce's face gave the impression that they could think of a lot of reasons to wait. Hayden leveled a look at her friend and hoped they'd finally back off.

"So, are you having a honeymoon?"

Nope. No such luck.

That hand on her knee almost hurt now.

"We haven't thought about it. Nothing has been traditional thus far. Why change that?"

Luce held Sam's eye. What a time to get their challenging hat on. They grinned slowly. "You don't think your lovely new bride deserves a holiday?"

Hayden was going to kill them. Maybe Sam would help her hide the body. Judging by the iron grip on her knee, probably.

"Bride? Calm down, Luce."

Luce winked at Hayden. "Fine, wife."

Hayden sighed. "Okay. Anyway. Let's move on."

"Okay." Luce's eyes lit up. "So, Sam, has Hayden met your family?"

Hayden almost dropped her head on the table.

~ ~ ~

Entering the apartment together after the world's most awkward coffee meet-up made everything even more awkward. It was weirdly intimate. The apartment was dark when Sam pushed the door open and she flicked on a few light switches next to the door, washing the living space and kitchen in light. She'd put on the dimmer ones, which meant Hayden wasn't left blinded. There were a lot of switches next to the door, and Hayden still had to flick through all of them before getting the right ones.

They stood at the entrance, and Hayden almost wanted to shuffle her feet. Sam cleared her throat and turned on her heel, walking to the kitchen. She started putting the kettle on, opening cupboards and getting a cup and a teabag.

She paused, the packet in her hand after she'd unwrapped the tea bag. She looked at Hayden, still standing by the front door. "Would you like a tea? It's herbal."

Hayden made a face. "No. Thank you."

Sam went back to pottering.

It was weirdly domestic.

Finally, Hayden hung up her coat and put her bag on the countertop. Sam poured hot water into her cup, the steam rising. Hayden slipped onto a barstool opposite her. When Sam focused on something, that thing seemed to get all her attention. Hayden rested her chin in her hand and watched Sam wrap her hand around the warm ceramic. Only then did her eyes make contact with Hayden's again.

"Just, uh, so you know," Hayden said. "Like Luce pointed out, I really hate herbal tea. One of those things a wife would know."

"Oh, of course they did say that." Sam wrapped her other hand around the cup, too. "That is helpful. What else do you hate?" Sam was watching her as if she expected a written list she could memorize.

"Uh, not much. People chewing with their mouths open. The subway, it's a germ fest. Spaghetti from a tin—it's not natural."

"That's an easy list to remember."

"What about you?"

Taking a sip, Sam seemed to ponder the question. "Pineapple on pizza." Well at least that would mean they'd never have to share pizza. "Incompetency. Bad table manners."

"See? We're a wife match. I hate people who chew with their mouths open, and you hate bad table manners."

"Yes, I'm sure that will be one to tell the grandchildren."

Hands held up, Hayden grinned. "Whoa, whoa. Were they in the fine print?"

"Yes. Right next to the part in which you signed over your spleen."

"Who needs one of those, anyway?"

Hayden was chuckling, and Sam gave a small laugh. A bubble of sound, like she didn't make it often.

"We really didn't plan this well, did we?" Sam asked.

"Nope."

"I thought I'd considered most things." She clicked her tongue, as if disappointed in herself. She blew along the surface of the herbal abomination in her cup, lips rounded. The motion made Hayden think of a kiss, and she blinked at the weird thought. "I was wrong."

Hayden shrugged. "I don't think this was something we could ever really have prepared for. Not everything, anyway."

"Still. More so than we did."

"Mm." Something occurred to Hayden, a way to maybe find out more information. "One month was a very short time frame to make it convincing."

Distracted, Sam hummed. "Yes, well, I wanted to get it done, and I'd been trying to find someone appropriate for a while."

"Why the rush?" Would she get more information?

"No, Hayden."

"Can't blame a girl for trying." Hayden's head felt heavy in her hand.

"Your friend is..."

"An ass."

Sam actually smirked. A real one. It changed her face, making her look younger, more playful for a split second. "Not the word I would have chosen, but yes. An ass."

"I'm sorry. They're... It's more about being protective. They really don't understand this."

"Had you really always hated marriage?"

Hayden nodded, an uncomfortable thing to do, considering her head was in her hand. "Still do."

"May I ask why?"

"Long story."

"Okay."

No pushing. Just like that. No "come on" or anything else many other people would have given her.

"Thanks."

Sam's brow furrowed over the rim of her cup as she took a sip. "Thanks? Why?"

"For not pushing."

"You're giving me the same courtesy. Mostly."

Hayden's cheeks warmed. Oh. "Well, not really. Sorry. I will now."

"I'd appreciate that."

Steam was still rising from the cup in Sam's hands. Wisps of it floated up. It was a little hypnotizing.

"I have to tell you something."

Sam's eyes immediately narrowed. "What did you do?"

Hayden sat up. "Hey! How do you know I did anything?"

"Your tone. Those words."

Fair enough. "I told my family."

Sam put the cup down, though she kept her fingers wrapped around it. "Thank you."

"And, uh, there's something else."

The narrowed eyes were back. "What?"

"They were obviously surprised. They also knew that I hated marriage. My abuela was pretty upset she wasn't included." She still kind of felt gleeful that she'd dragged Sam down with her. "So I told them you wanted to come with me when I go and visit, so you could get to know them."

"You what?"

"Said we'd visit."

Sam went very still. "When?"

"I didn't say a date."

But it would have to be soon. They'd need to get it over with and convince her family that she was okay and that—oh. Hayden felt the blood drain from her face. They'd have to convince her family.

And they'd be staying in her family's house.

"Did you finally catch up?" Sam asked.

Hayden's mouth was hanging open. "Maybe I didn't really think this through."

"You think?"

"Well, we were never going to get away with you *not* meeting them." Hayden felt like dropping her head down. "If we have to have people *convinced*, like you keep saying, you would have to meet them at least once."

"I thought I'd maybe have lunch with them. Not skip off to stay in their house, where we'd be under constant scrutiny."

Ugh. Hayden really hadn't thought this through.

"Sam, my family would never have let it go if we didn't visit. And you said you needed them on board."

"Why couldn't they visit here? We could have put them up in a hotel?"

Hayden stared at her. "Who puts family in a hotel?"

Sam stared right back. "Who doesn't?"

Well. That was weird. Her family may have been a lot to handle, for many reasons, and she might ignore them every now and again to try and get some breathing room. But make them stay in a hotel? "Uh, me?"

Sam went, if possible, paler. "Does that mean staying in a hotel there is completely out of the question?"

"Of course."

They stared at each other again.

A loud meow made them turn to look near the corridor. Frank sat, glaring from one to the other. When neither of them moved, he yowled again.

"Is he dying?" Sam asked.

Hayden snorted. "He thinks he is. Most likely his food bowl is only half-full, which means he has to panic. Ignore him."

Sam took a sip of her tea. "Well, then. Which state is your family in?"

"Florida."

The cup hit the counter.

"Yeah, I know."

"I have to go to Florida?"

Hayden grimaced.

"Florida?"

"Yes."

"Hayden."

"I know."

Sam squared her shoulders. "Okay. Fine. Florida. We visit your family." She swallowed. "I can't wait."

"There's that dry wit again."

"It's all I can manage. Did you do this to get back at me?"

Hayden waggled her hand in the air. "A little, yeah. But you have to admit, it makes sense. You wanted them convinced."

Sam sighed. "Yes. True." Her gaze swept Hayden's face. "You look ready to fall asleep right here."

"I kind of am." Hayden slipped off the stool. "I'm off to bed. Want to plan this in the next few days?"

"Yes. Fine."

Hayden started toward the corridor and scooped up Frank. He put a paw on her face and glared her straight in the eye. She knew that look: food or death.

"Hayden?"

She turned around. Sam's hip was against the counter, cup back in her hand.

"Yeah?"

"We should start letting each other know our work schedules. The other day, a nurse asked me when you were on next, and I pretended to receive a call to get away because I had no idea."

Hayden smothered her grin in Frank's neck. "You faked a call?"

"Mhm."

"That's hilarious."

"Yes, it was all very funny. I'll put my rotation on the fridge. Can you do the same?"

"Sure," she said, yawning into Frank's fur. He twisted his head around to look at her, affronted. "Okay."

"Good night."

"Night, Sam."

CHAPTER 12

"So, when you coming?"

Hayden got off the bus a stop early. She'd be on this call for a while, and she knew how much it sucked listening to someone else's phone conversation on public transportation. The wind swirled around her neck, and she hunched her shoulders, kicking herself for forgetting her scarf in her locker. She held the phone to her ear and sidestepped someone whose gaze was glued to the ground.

"Abuela, soon. I promise."

"Yes, but when? We talked weeks ago."

Hayden was grinning in spite of herself. "Sam and I were talking yesterday. We think we can both get a weekend off in a couple of weeks."

"Sorry, you said one weekend? *¿Un fin de semana? Solito.*"

"Yes."

"We don't see you in months and months, and you come for one weekend? Three nights is *nada*?"

Hayden winced. "Probably two."

Silence on the phone. Hayden took a left at the next block and glanced around. Was she walking the right way to Sam's house? Her house? Their house? Whatever. Her gaze fell on a tiny magazine stand that was run by a happy guy with the biggest beard she'd ever seen. Yes, right way. She was still getting used to this. This fancy-ass area was still a bit of a mystery, even after a month.

"Abuela."

"Two nights?"

"It's really hard to get time off at work at the moment."

Which was true.

"You get married to someone we no know and then only come visit with us two nights?"

"Abuela. I'm sorry. I'll try come for longer next time."

Without Sam. More than two nights in a house they had to pretend to be *very* married in? No, thank you. A weekend was stupid enough. The shine of her getting back at Sam and dragging her down with her had faded quickly, and it had left Hayden with gnawing anxiety.

Abuela huffed. "I will believe that when I see it."

"How's *Mamà*?"

A pause. "She is the same. No better, no worse." Abuela's voice had changed; it was softer. It always was when she spoke about her daughter. Hayden's heart tripped over in her chest. "She will love to see you when you come, I'm sure."

"Good." Hayden's throat seemed to have closed over; a prickling crawling up the inside of it. "Okay."

"You are okay?"

"Yes, yes." Hayden swallowed hard and kept her voice as normal as she could. "I'm fine."

"Tell me more about this Sam."

Hayden laughed, dodging a guy on a bike who shouldn't even be on the sidewalk. "I told you everything."

"If that is all that you know and have to say about your wife, I am worried."

"Fine, fine. What do you want to know?" Her fingers were getting cold holding her phone, but she was enjoying her abuela's voice. Even if the topic wasn't fun.

"Everything."

"That's a lot of things."

Abuela clucked her tongue. "Always too smart, you are. Tell me how you met."

"At work."

"That is it? All I get? 'At work'?"

Hayden paused at a red light, looking up past the buildings at the gray sky. It would be winter soon. Rain and storms were going to start any day. The wind had already picked up. Snow would start not long after. She hated snow. Slushy and cold and horrible. Everything got icy and slippery.

"Well, that's where we met." The little person turned green, and Hayden crossed with the crowd she'd been waiting with.

Abuela sighed as if she was the hardest done-by person on the planet. "Fine. I will just question this Sam when she arrive to here."

"Arrives here," Hayden corrected, recognizing the park she was walking past. Almost home. It was going to be warm there.

"Yes. That. Arrives here. I will write a list of everything I want to know."

Hayden groaned. "Awesome."

"It will be. You wait. And your sister too. And Javi. He does not believe us that you married without telling us."

Hayden could have groaned aloud. One more person to add lies to. A four-year-old who believed everything she said. Great. "It's because it wasn't a wedding, Abuela. It was something for us at City Hall."

Abuela sniffed. "Whatever. Now go, I have to make empanadas. Your mamá asked me for them."

"*¿Con pollo?*"

"*Sí. Con pollo.*"

Hayden almost pouted. She missed Abuela's cooking. And her mother's. "*¿Y qué más?*"

"No. I am not telling you all the amazing food I will cook. You are in my—my black books?"

"Your bad books?" Hayden laughed.

"*Sí. Eso.* My bad book."

"Where'd you learn that?"

"A book. And it's true."

"But you still love me, right?"

Her front door was approaching.

"*Sí, cariño. Te quiero.* Always." But Hayden heard the mildly infuriated tone laced through it. Ah, the sound of her adolescence.

Hayden grinned. "I'll call you when I know the dates."

"*Un beso. Adiós.*"

"*Adiós.*"

She hung up and slipped her phone in her pocket. Well, that hadn't gone too badly. As she approached the door, the doorman opened it. She grinned at him.

"Hi."

"Hello," he replied.

Hayden slowed down before walking in, pausing next to him. "I'm Hayden." She held out a hand. "What was your name? I pass you every day; it's weird not knowing it."

He kept one hand on the door handle and shook her hand with the other. His smile was the kindest Hayden had ever seen.

"I am Nicolas." He had a voice that deep and smooth, a slight accent on his tongue. "It's nice to meet you."

"You too. You don't stand out here all the time, do you? It's freezing."

He chuckled. "No, I stand inside most of the time."

"Good." She gave him a wave. "I'll see you around, Nicolas. Have a good day."

"You too."

Hayden scampered inside, heading toward the stairs. She could do this. For a second, she hovered at the bottom, staring up at them. She told her patients to get light exercise all the time. But the elevator would be so much easier.

Sighing, she started walking up, the sound of her feet bouncing off the walls of the stairwell.

Halfway up, she paused, breathing hard. Her legs were small. That was why. She took the second half more slowly. When she pushed open the door and wandered down to her apartment, she paused at the door, her hand buried in her bag to find her keys. As she rummaged, voices floated out from the other side of the door.

Fairly loud voices.

"—the hell?"

"Do you really think I haven't planned this out?" That was Sam's voice, as unaffected as ever. Hayden could just imagine her standing straight-backed, right near the door, her eyebrows high.

"Sam, I really don't think you have." Surprisingly, that voice, a male voice, was one Hayden knew too, she was sure. "You didn't need to do this for me." The man barely sounded mad, more tired.

Jon! It was Jon, from the opposite apartment. Wow, they really were friends, to be hanging out in Sam's apartment. From what Hayden had seen, Sam didn't really hang out with *anyone*. And she seemed perfectly content with that.

"I did need to do this. No one else was going to."

What did Sam need to do for Jon that no one else would? Hayden should really announce her presence. Listening was rude.

She stepped closer and turned her ear to the door.

"Of course no one else would do *this*. *This* is an idiotic idea."

"Why?"

"You'll lose them too! For no reason."

"For no reason?" Sam's voice had gone an extra layer of cold, obvious even through the thick wooden door. "You think what they've put you through is no reason? Or that they would have done the same to me in the end was no reason?"

"That's not what I said. And like you care that they would have done the same to you. You've shown that just by going through with all this."

"Well, that's true." Sam actually sounded *amused*. Wow. "But I—you weren't supposed to find out about this."

So they were clearly talking about the marriage. Was Jon in love with Sam? No. That was stupid. That made no sense given what they were saying. But then why would Sam care if Jon knew?

What the hell?

"How would I not have found out?" he asked.

"Well, obviously, you would have. I was hoping it would be near the end."

"You had a big reveal planned, didn't you?" He sounded smug. Was he *teasing* her? This was so strange.

"No." Hayden could practically hear the roll of Sam's eyes.

"I still think this is a bad idea. There's no need."

"There is, and you know it."

He sighed, and the door handle turned. Hayden flew backward, heat rushing to her face and her fingers trembling. She shoved a hand in her bag as if she was searching for her keys, but when the door opened, she was pretty sure that she looked like a deer caught in headlights.

Sam and Jon blinked at her. His hand held the edge of the door as he held it open, a slow, easy grin rolling over his lips.

"Why, hello," he said.

Sam just stared at her.

"H…hey." Hayden tried to smile and hoped it didn't look shaky. "How are you two?"

They side-eyed each other and looked back at Hayden.

"I'm well," Sam's voice was measured. "How was your day?"

"Good. It's freezing out."

Jon's hand ran down the door and fell away. He stepped forward, still grinning. "Pretty cold in here too." He winked and walked past Hayden.

Sam gave a huff of irritation, but something like affection was on her face. "Go home," she said.

"Already there," he called out, his key in the door, and Hayden turned in time to see him vanish behind it. "Bye, lovebirds."

When the door snicked shut, Hayden turned back to look at Sam. Sam shook her head, and walked back inside. Hayden followed her straight to the kitchen, dropping her bag on the counter.

"So." Sam grabbed a bottle of water from the fridge. "How much did you hear?"

"Not much." Hayden spoke too quickly.

Sam uncapped the water and didn't take her gaze off Hayden.

"Okay, a little, but I didn't understand much."

Maybe they *were* lovers.

"That was my brother."

Or maybe they—wait.

"What?"

"Jonathon is my brother."

"Oh." Not lovers, then. "*Oh.*"

Also, he said no one called him Jonathon.

"What?" Sam asked.

"That explains why he seemed familiar. You actually do look alike."

"Yes, he mentioned that you had met. That's how he knew we were married."

Or he would have seen her ring. Hayden couldn't help but notice it constantly, like now, as she took a sip of her water.

"I didn't know I wasn't supposed to tell him."

"I know. How could you?"

"He seemed more amused than anything."

"Yes, well. It's complicated."

Hayden desperately wanted to know why but had said she'd stop pushing that. So she bit her tongue, literally. "Does he, uh, know it's not real?"

Sam sighed, the water bottle going onto the counter. "Yes." As Hayden's eyes widened, she waved a hand. "He won't tell anyone. It won't be an issue."

"But—"

"It won't be."

"Okay." There were a thousand ways it could be, in Hayden's eyes. But that wasn't exactly Hayden's problem. "So, you have a brother?"

"Yes. A very infuriating one. Do you want a bottle of water?"

"Thanks."

Sam fished another from the fridge and handed it over.

Hayden added, "An infuriating brother, but one you like." The affection in her tone had been unmistakable.

Sam seemed to consider her words for a moment, her thumb running idly over the rim of her bottle. "Yes. I do."

That reaction was practically a love poem from Sam. "How old is he?"

"How old do you think he is?"

"I can't figure it out." Hayden's hips dug into the counters as she leaned forward on her elbows, the marble cold under them.

"No one ever can. It's how he gets into so much trouble. Or got, anyway."

"So, by that, I'm guess he's younger than I would think."

Sam shrugged, a smile playing at the corners of her mouth. She clearly wasn't going to help.

"Hm." Hayden flicked the cap of her bottle under her finger, following it with her eyes as it skittered across the counter. "Well you said 'got,' so maybe he's over twenty-one now, but he used to get into bars as a minor because he could look older?"

Sam half-shrugged again.

"You're not helping at all. I'm going to say twenty-one."

"Bingo."

Hayden fist-pumped. "Right on the first guess. He looks older at times, then he grins and he looks like he's a—"

"A cheeky five-year-old."

"Exactly."

Sam sighed. "That's him in a nutshell. He's charming and cheeky and gets into all sorts of trouble."

"And you help him out of it?"

"He's my brother."

So Sam had a soft spot. "There's a big age gap between you two."

"Yes, thank you for pointing that out. It's never occurred to me."

Hayden snickered. "Sorry."

"You're not at all. And yes, over twenty years. My parents were indeed shocked about him."

"I like him."

Hayden had just decided that.

"Good. Because he's apparently back, so be warned: he drops in from time to time."

"Has he always lived next door?"

Sam hesitated. "No. I rented it for him. It's a place he knows he can always go to."

How loaded was Sam? To have both apartments? "That's…nice of you."

"I don't know about that." Her brow was furrowed, her thumb still running over the rim of her bottle.

"Did you not expect him to be here? Where has he been?"

Sam didn't look up from her bottle. "College. Interstate. But it seems he dropped out."

Interesting.

"Why?"

"Who knows with him?"

Hayden felt as if she'd peeled back a layer of this secret business and instead of finding a clue buried underneath, found there were more layers than she'd realized.

But Hayden knew when someone didn't want to be pushed. And now was that time. Sam wasn't so difficult to figure out, after all. Hayden turned around, bottle in hand, to go sit on the sofa and stopped in her tracks. She shook her head.

No, she wasn't imagining things.

Opposite her, looking her right in the eye, was Frank. His yellow eyes looked smug. And to be fair, he had every right to be: He was in one of those hammock things that were at the top of those giant cat trees Hayden had always eyed when buying cat food for him but never even bothered looking at closely; they were super expensive. This one was so big the hammock thing was in the middle, not the top. The top almost touched the ceiling. Frank stretched and rolled onto his back, his legs in the air.

"Where the hell did that come from?" Hayden turned on her heel.

"I bought it," Sam said simply.

Hayden looked again. It was huge. Really huge. It had ladders and platforms and boxes to sleep in. And it was next to the sofa. Like Frank was the king himself.

She looked at Sam again. "You bought my cat *that*?"

The green of Sam's eyes sparked, a cheekiness that mirrored her brother's. "I thought it was better than him sleeping on the sofa."

Well, that was a total lie. Sam hadn't cared he was on the sofa. In fact, the other day, Hayden had caught her picking him up and putting him next to her on it while she read.

Hayden was slowly grinning. "You bought it for him because you thought he'd like it."

"Don't be ridiculous."

Sam picked up her bottle and headed for the stairs.

"You did!"

"No," she called back without even turning around as she disappeared.

Hayden turned back to Frank. One foot twitched. He'd apparently fallen asleep in the last few seconds.

"You're getting far too spoiled."

But she couldn't shake the feeling of just how *nice* that had been of Sam.

~ ~ ~

"So, two weeks?"

"Does that work for you?"

A muscle twitched in Sam's cheek. "Yes."

"Sure?"

"I said yes."

Hayden held up her hands. "Okay, okay. So you have it off?"

"I checked the three dates you suggested today, and it was the most suitable." Sam made a face at the to-go coffee cup in front of her. "I know this is the best in the hospital, but it really isn't that great."

Hayden smothered a smile, despite her stomach rolling over. They were spending their coffee break discussing the trip to see Hayden's family. They'd both secured the weekend off. The plane tickets would be booked that evening. It was happening.

Joy.

And while discussing it, they were having a coffee together, commiserating over their workplace's bad coffee. Like happy work wives should.

"Don't let Luce hear you say that."

"Why?" Sam looked up from it sharply.

"Because they're coming this way, and their girlfriend made it."

Sam sighed. "Great."

Luce and Sam were still learning to like each other. It was funny to watch, as long as Luce wasn't picking at their relationship and looking for holes. In their fake relationship.

Keeping this from her best friend still felt awful.

Hayden smiled at Luce when they appeared next to the table. "Hey."

"Hey." Luce turned to Sam. "Good morning."

Sam didn't even smile. "Good morning."

Awesome. Not at all uncomfortable or weird.

"Why don't you join us?" Hayden asked.

Luce seemed to consider it for a moment. "Okay." They slipped into a seat. "Clemmie is going on break in a second, so she may come over. Is that okay?"

"Clemmie?" Hayden was stumped for second. "Oh! The barista." She grinned wickedly. "So we're naming her now, properly? That's the second time. That means it's serious."

Luce squirmed. "No."

"Oh, please. It does too."

"Naming her?" Sam interjected. "What on earth?"

It was Luce's turn to light up, turning to Sam. And Hayden knew exactly why. They were about to dump Hayden in it. "If you name them, you get attached." Luce looked far too delighted to be imparting this knowledge. "So we use nicknames to distance ourselves. A while back, Hayden here used 'The Salesman' for six months before finally using his name when she admitted they were dating."

Oh, Hayden wanted to throw things at Luce. So badly. Sam turned to her, eyebrows raised.

"Really?"

"It's stupid." It was hard not to wince at her own behavior. "And shows my emotional intelligence."

"Uh, hello."

They all turned to see Clemmie, awkwardly hovering at their table. Luce's face went all enamored at the sight of her, the look not one Hayden was used to seeing on her friend. It was kind of adorable.

"Hi." Luce pulled a chair close, and Clemmie sat down in it. "This is Hayden." They hesitated for a second. "And this is Sam."

Clemmie gave a little wave. "Hi. I recognize you both."

"Nice to meet you." Hayden tried to sound friendlier than Luce had been with Sam. Which was not difficult.

"Hello," Sam said.

"So," Luce turned to them both, "what were you guys talking about before I interrupted earlier?"

And Sam dropped her in it, as if it were a new game for her and Luce to play together. "We've got a weekend off in two weeks to go and see Hayden's family."

Luce's eyes widened, and their mouth fell open right before they grinned at Hayden. "Seriously?"

Hayden sighed. "Yes. We're staying with them for two nights."

She didn't know it was possible to crack up so hard that you could nearly fall off your chair, but Luce managed it. Clemmie just watched, bemused.

Chapter 13

A little under three hours.

That's all it would take to get to Miami.

Sam closed her eyes on the takeoff, her lips a tight line and her face pale.

"Don't like flying?"

She didn't give an answer. Once they'd leveled off, the white of her knuckles slowly flooded with pink again and she opened her eyes, taking slow breaths.

"What?" Sam asked when she caught sight of Hayden's barely concealed amusement.

"You're not a big flier, are you?"

"No."

"Okay."

Hayden bit down a smirk and looked out the window. She really enjoyed flying—watching the land unfold underneath her, catching a view of things she'd most likely never see any other way. Fields and other patches of color splattered over the ground once the city was left behind. She could stare at it all for ages, especially when the sun was coming up, all blazing orange, like this morning.

"I'm fine, once we're in the air." Was Sam actually offering more information without prodding? That was new. Though another glance at her face showed her color hadn't completely returned. Maybe it made her feel better just to talk.

"That's good. And it's a fairly short flight."

"Not short enough."

Hayden smirked and looked out the window again. Yeah, really not a flier.

Sam squeezed out of her seat next to Hayden and pulled out her laptop. Apparently, like always, she had an article to finish. Or read. For some people, this aspect of medicine—the constant call to learn, to innovate—was the joy of it all. For others it was the bane. Sam seemed to be in the former group. Hayden had always heard good things about the lectures and presentations she'd given, and she'd even been to one a few years ago, as part of her Continuing Medical Education hours. It was good. Intense, with a lot of information thrown at the audience, but good. She'd walked away with a headache, but she'd learned a hell of a lot.

When the drink cart came around, Sam asked for a straight whiskey so fast Hayden actually did laugh.

So Sam said, "We'll be with your family in less than three hours."

Hayden's smile fell away, and she ordered the same. And she didn't even like whiskey.

The flight attendant chuckled. "A weekend with the in-laws?"

She directed the question at Sam. Which was hilarious. Then Hayden remembered they were wearing those obvious rings, and what Sam had just said. After a split second, Sam nodded once, smiling benignly.

"First time meeting them, in fact."

The flight attendant gave a sympathetic tut. "Ouch. Well, good luck."

"Thank you." Sam tipped her drink toward her, and Hayden waited until the woman was engaged with the next passenger before she whispered something.

"Was that you being social?"

"Sometimes I can fake it." Sam rested back against her seat, spinning her plastic cup on the tray in front of her.

"Is it really faking it if you're doing a good job at it?"

Sam rolled her head to look at her. Her hair was mussed, as if she'd gotten out of bed without doing much to it. It made her look less put together, but in a good way. They'd needed to wake up hours before sunrise to make their flight. "Mostly, yes. I really don't see the point of small talk."

Sam was kind of fascinating. And infuriating. And still kind of rude sometimes. And she really didn't get a lot of what came out of Hayden's mouth. But her way of viewing the world was fascinating.

"Okay." Hayden took a sip of her drink and tried not to choke at the taste. Sam went back to her laptop.

This was going to be the weirdest weekend ever. And they were going to have to be a convincing couple. Hayden had lost all smug feelings about making Sam suffer too, and it was only now sinking in how complicated she'd made it by saying they were both going. Yes, they would have had to meet her family at the same time eventually to convince them. But staying in their *house*? And so soon?

And Hayden still hadn't filled Sam in on everything she needed to know. But the thought of doing it made her mouth go dry. It felt like cracking her chest open and exposing something of herself. Something Hayden had tried hard not to do with anyone, especially her fake wife that she was still learning to get along with, let alone *like* enough to share her private life with.

Luce didn't even know the entire story.

At this point, Hayden wasn't sure how much she could share without Sam guessing the rest. Or without having to expose the rest herself.

But they would be there soon, and Sam needed a heads up before they were literally there.

With a deep breath, she turned to Sam. Who was tapping away at her laptop.

"Sam?"

She tapped a few more keys then turned her head, her fingers staying on the keyboard. "Yes?"

"It's... Can I tell you something? That I think, maybe, you need to know?"

"This sounds extremely serious."

Hayden's pulse was thundering in her ears. "It's not. Really. I mean, it's not fun. But it's not a big deal."

Sam closed her laptop and turned in her chair. Hayden's voice was almost a whisper, and, luckily, no one was in the seat next to Sam. But it still felt strange to be having this conversation here, of all places. Surrounded by people and breathing in gross recycled air. It felt like the air vents were going to suck up her secrets and spit them out for everyone to sort through.

"Does it concern this weekend?"

"Yes." Hayden swallowed. Yeah. Dry mouth. Like she had any other time she'd thought of bringing this up before being stuck on a plane and getting closer and closer to Miami. She took a sip of the whiskey, but mid-sip thought better and drank it all back, the ice hitting her top lip. When she put the glass down, Sam could not have looked more confused.

"And you thought you'd wait until right before we land to tell me this thing that makes you drink whiskey like a teenager taking their first ever shot?"

"Apparently?"

"You like to avoid issues, don't you?"

Hayden held the cup just for something to cling to. "Hey, we're spotlighting one issue today, not two."

"Continue."

"I just... My mom has early onset Alzheimer's."

Sam pressed her lips together. She looked like she did at work when she'd shared difficult news with a patient and they freaked out. Apparently that face was her figuring out what the hell was appropriate to say.

"I'm sorry," she finally managed. And she nailed it.

Hayden swallowed. "Thank you. She lives with my sister, grandmother, and nephew. He's four. Javi. You might like him." Sam's face sang a different tune, and Hayden tried to picture her interacting with a kid. It was hard. "But, yeah. Uh. That's all. I just thought you should know before we get there."

"Okay." Sam sat back against her seat, but didn't move to open her laptop. She stared straight ahead at the back of the chair in front of her.

Hayden sighed. "You can ask questions."

Sam turned back to face her. "How old is she?"

That always caused a stab in Hayden's chest. Because her mother was too young to have to deal with this. "Fifty-five."

"When did she first show symptoms?"

Hayden broke eye contact with eyes too intense, instead watching her cup as she flicked her nail over the rim. "At first we thought she was busy. Distracted, you know? She worked a lot; she always had, but especially the two or so years before. My dad had left and wasn't doing anything to help us. I finally convinced her to go to the doctor, and that led to a whole round of tests. She was diagnosed at forty-seven."

"So you were nineteen? Twenty?"

"Almost twenty." The burn of Sam's gaze was like a red-hot brand, but Hayden couldn't bring herself to look up. Sam would connect the dots. She was too quick with these things not to.

"Around when you dropped out of premed."

Hayden winced. There it was, the slap of truth. "Yes. I found out right after you saw me when I was shadowing a doctor."

"Did you have to give up college to go home?"

Hayden let out a shaky breath. "I didn't *have* to. But my sister, Sofia, was pregnant. And my grandmother was looking after my grandfather. He had Alzheimer's too. He died four years ago."

"So you went home?"

"I did. She didn't need constant care then, and I worked and looked after her for a year."

When Hayden finally looked up, Sam's face was full of questions. She asked the most basic one. "But why didn't you go back to medicine?"

There it was. Hayden had never spoken about it. Why bother? It was what it was, even if it sucked. "She had no health insurance. There were a lot of tests, medications, doctor's visits. The money my parents had put away for my college degree went toward that. My sister had used her money earlier. She hadn't wanted to study. She'd gone on a trip for a year, backpacking. It's, uh, complicated."

"Why did your father allow you to spend your college money on that?"

"Because he's an asshole."

Sam clearly had no idea how to respond to that. "Oh."

"He cut us all out of his life. For reasons. Disappeared. He'd been fairly well off, and I had a pretty great childhood. Our college funds were in our names, and the house stayed with Mom, but he took his money with him and got out of paying anything else because, well…because. With no alimony agreement, she lost her insurance. Her new job didn't provide it, and she couldn't afford it."

"Charming."

Hayden huffed a laugh. "It wasn't, actually. But, well, that's it. We could have sold the house, but we wanted Mom in familiar surroundings. It was the house I grew up in." Plus, it had seemed like a final slap to all of them.

"I had a little money left, and rather than use it all, I combined it with a scholarship I could get to become a nurse, which would mean I'd have money to send home to help them all out. My sister lost the baby, and she moved in to live with Mom. She worked her ass off, like I did while I studied, to have some money for her. Then Abuela moved in too. I go back sometimes, but mostly I work a lot try to make sure they have enough money for meds and anything else they need."

Because over eight years of med school and who knew how many more years until she actually earned any decent money would have left them all struggling. Because even with the little bit of money she had to pay for school and the scholarship she'd gotten, she'd still been forced to take out terrible student loans whose repayments still ate up much of her monthly budget.

"I'm sorry, Hayden."

Hayden shrugged. "Thanks. We've all made peace with it now. Mom is just floating in the middle stage of the disease. She's mostly happy, really. Well, usually. Calm. But she wanders a lot. It's a waiting game, really."

"Were you close with your mother?"

"Yes. We were always a close family. Now?" Hayden chewed on the inside of her cheek, not bothering to stop herself. "Now, it's hard. My sister wants me to live in Miami to help more. Abuela just wants me to visit more at this point."

"But you have a very secure job. And you gave up your career to help already."

"I guess. I also pay for an assistant to come three days a week and to stay one night a week. My sister works, so it gives her and my abuela a break too."

"But your sister wants you to do more?"

Hayden hesitated. "Maybe I'm selfish. But this is what works for me."

Sam looked her straight in the eye. "I don't think you're selfish. Not at all."

For some reason, Hayden's cheeks warmed. "Thanks. That actually helps."

Without further ado, Sam turned back to her laptop, her hands falling back to the keys and resuming typing without hesitation.

Well, that could have gone worse.

Maybe Sam didn't know everything about Hayden's dad, but that didn't matter anyway.

Now, at least, she knew what she was getting into.

~ ~ ~

"Hayds!"

Her sister's arms were around her before Hayden had even registered she was there. She smelled the same. Like home. Like Sofia.

"Sofe. Hey."

She squeezed tighter. "I'm so glad you're here."

Hayden gave a squeeze back and pulled away. She squatted on the ground, throwing her arms out. "Javi."

The little boy poked his head around his mother's legs, before ducking back behind them.

Hayden sighed dramatically. "I thought I saw Javi, but he's disappeared." She sighed again. "Sofia, did you not even bring your terror of a child here to see me?"

His head popped back around, his hair a wild mop of dark brown curls and dimples in his chubby cheeks. "I'm not a terror!"

Hayden threw her hand over her heart and pretended to fall backward on the cold airport floor. "Where did you come from?"

He giggled wildly. "I'm magic."

"You must be. You appeared out of nowhere." She held her arms out again. "Do I get a hug?"

He bolted into her arms, and this time, she really did fall backward, landing on her behind. She couldn't have cared less, though. He gave her a full-body hug, his arms and legs wrapping around her. Hayden buried her face in his neck, breathing him in—a combination of grass, child, and kiddie shampoo.

"Who's that?"

His voice was next to her ear, and Hayden turned awkwardly. Sam was standing a few feet back between two carry-on suitcases. Hayden released Javi, who stepped back and was against Sofia's legs again in an instant.

"That's Sam."

Heaving herself off the ground, Hayden made herself smile. Sofia was watching her, amused.

Hayden stepped back and held out a hand. To Sam's credit, she barely missed a beat. Her left hand, warm and smooth, slid into Hayden's, their fingers interlocked. Hayden tugged gently so that she was standing with her side against Hayden's. This felt more intimate than their strange wedding-day kiss, more so than a hand on her knee or her chest brushing into Hayden's back. Especially under the scrutiny of Sofia's watchful eye. Javi gazed at them, his fingers wrapped around the hem of Sofia's shirt. She was probably imagining it, but she swore she could feel Sam's ring digging into her finger.

"Sofia, Javi, this is Sam. My wife. Sam, this is my sister and nephew."

"I'm a terror." Javi beamed.

Sam looked unsure, as Hayden snorted. She stepped forward, their hands still linked, and held her right hand out to Sofia. "It's a pleasure to meet you."

Sofia took her hand, a smile on her lips. But her eyes narrowed; something not entirely friendly. If Hayden didn't know her sister so well, she'd fall for the smile and miss the look in her eyes. But Sofia had had the same look on her face when she'd said in front of their mom once that she forgave Hayden for breaking her soccer cleats. The next day, Hayden had found mud in the bottom of her bed.

"You too, Sam."

Javi stared up at her. "Tía Hayden told me that she thinks marriage is stupid."

The hand in hers squeezed tighter.

Sofia cackled.

Hayden laughed. "I did say that, yeah."

He turned that earnest gaze on Hayden. "You did. On the 'puter when we talked."

Hayden swallowed. She didn't want to lie to Javi. He was at an age where he believed what you told him. She hadn't even meant to say that in front of him, but she hadn't known he was in the room when she'd been talking to Sofia. "It seemed like the best idea for us."

"Oh. Okay. Can we get ice cream before home?"

If only her entire family would be as easily convinced as a distractible four-year-old. The walk out to the car bordered on awkward, but it was always going to. When they got there, Javi shrieked as soon as Sofia went to lift him into his car seat. She quickly dropped her hands.

"Javi, what the—what?"

He crossed his arms. "I want Sam to put me in."

Sam, who had walked around the other side of the car to get in, slowly appeared back around. "Excuse me?"

Javi kept his arms crossed and turned to stare at her. "I want you to buckle me in."

"Uh—" Sam was rarely wordless. Huh. Hayden did nothing to help, just tried to smother her smirk and walked around the car, sliding into the back seat so she could sit next to Javi—and also watch this unfold.

"Can you? Please?"

His lisped *s* was pretty adorable when he threw in the puppy-dog eyes. Sofia hovered, most likely not wanting her kid to be a nuisance but looking as entertained as Hayden felt.

"Okay," Sam said, and he turned back to clamber into the car, grinning at Hayden. Kids were so weird.

He settled himself into the car seat and looked expectantly at Sam, who ducked into the car and tugged at the straps, looking at the entire thing as if she had no idea what to do with it all. This from the woman who could fix brains.

Javi wriggled his arms under the arm straps. "These parts go here."

"Right."

He pointed a pudgy finger at the two clips on the ends that needed to be pushed together and at the piece that would then be clipped in between his legs. The front door slammed as Sofia got into the driver's seat, and Hayden flicked her gaze to the front. She was watching from the rearview mirror, her eyes squinting as she suppressed a chuckle.

"These bits all go together. Like a puzzle."

The *z* was more a lisped *s* than anything. He always made Hayden *aww* internally, but Sam looked like she'd been given an incredibly important mission. She picked the two pieces up and tried to press them together, but as she tried to push that into the piece between his legs, it all fell apart. Hayden bit back laughter as it happened again three times. Eventually, she guffawed, and the dirty look Sam shot her should have been enough to make her shut up, but it only made her laugh harder.

"Sam." Sam looked at Javi, her face a foot away from his sincere expression. "You don't know what you're doing, doesn't you?"

Sam rolled her eyes, but a smile crinkled the corners around them. "I really don't. I've never done this before."

His eyes widened. "Never?"

"No. Never."

"You can learn. Tía Hayden did."

Sam looked at her. "Maybe Hayden could help me?"

"But you're doing so well on your own," Hayden said.

Sam's eyes narrowed further, so Hayden slipped her hands between Sam's and the buckle. Sam pulled her hand away and watched as Hayden quickly snapped the pieces in. She gave a tug on the straps over his shoulder and gave Javi a thumbs-up.

"All good?"

"Yup." He gave a thumbs-up of his own.

Sam closed the door and hovered between joining them in the back and sitting in the front. Hayden pointed through the window to the front seat, and she obeyed. Sofia started the car.

Within five minutes, they were headed toward the city, the airport fading behind them.

"Look, Tía. Planes." Javi had his entire hand smooshed onto the glass of his window.

She dipped her head level with his to stare out where he was indicating. "Wow. How many?"

"Many. Many, many." He turned his head, his hand still on the glass and his eyes huge. "Maybe a thousand."

"Wow. That's a lot. Where do you think they're going?"

"New York." He said it as if he was sure. Hayden could hear Sam and Sofia talking in the front, but her attention was on Javi. He changed so much every time she visited.

"New York? Why there?"

"That's where you live. So where else?"

Interesting logic.

He kept her entertained like that the entire drive. It was forty minutes to their house, and the city sprawled around them the whole way. Occasionally, she tried to prod the two in front into conversation, but their interactions were stilted and strange.

When they entered their neighborhood, Hayden asked, "Is Abuela with Mom?"

"Yeah. Mom wasn't having a good day, so we thought it better to have a quiet house for a couple of hours."

Which meant Javi had been loud. He patted her hand. "Grandma got cranky, but Abuela made it all better."

"Grandma is your mother?" Sam asked.

"Yeah." Sofia nodded as she turned the wheel. "To save confusion, *Grandma* is for our mom and *Abuela* is for, well, Abuela."

Hayden asked Javi, "What did Abuela do to make it better?"

"Singed."

"Sang."

"She sang."

Hayden throat got a little tight. "Yeah, that does always help your grandma."

He hummed an answer, kicking his legs as he stared out the window. "Sam!"

Sam turned in her seat quickly, visibly startled at his sudden shout. "Yes?"

"We're almost home. Did you know?"

She shook her head. "No. I've never been there before, so I couldn't know."

"That's okay. I can tell you the stuff you don't know. Like the bath sometimes has monsters."

"Monsters?"

"Yup."

"Monsters aren't real."

Sam with kids was Hayden's latest favorite thing.

Javi threw up his hands. "Abuela says that too! But they do. I saw it."

"Where?"

He pushed forward as much as his seat allowed, which wasn't much. His voice lowered. "I told you. In the bath."

Sam eyed him. "The bath?"

He nodded, dead serious. "Yup."

"Can you show me them?"

"No. Only kids see them. You're old."

Hayden bit her cheek to stop from laughing, but Sam said, "Fair enough."

Luckily, they had pulled into their driveway. Hayden swallowed as she unclipped Javi and held her door open as he clambered over the backseat to follow her out. The house was still the same. Sam stepped out of her seat and stood next to her, closing her door.

"Nice house."

"Come on." Javi grabbed Hayden's hand. "Let's go."

He dragged them around the back of the car to pull out their carry-on cases, groaning at how slow they were. Sofia held open the door to the house, and Javi led the charge with thundering steps.

"Abuela!" he shouted. "Hayden and Sam are here." He disappeared into the kitchen, and Sofia closed the door behind them.

"Just leave your case here," she told Sam. "We'll put them in your room later."

She walked down the hall and left Hayden and Sam staring at each other.

"Hayden." Sam's lips pursed as she seemed to think out her next words. "Are we sharing a room?"

Hayden, her mouth open, nodded.

"Why is it we keep not thinking of these things?" Sam asked. "We're intelligent women. Yet these things just keep escaping us."

It was true. They were kind of stupid. Maybe Hayden could sleep on the floor in the room. She wasn't too old for that.

Wait, that would be ridiculous. She'd shared beds with people before. It didn't have to be a big deal.

Before Hayden could respond, Abuela was walking down the corridor toward them. "Alejandra! *Por fin.* You are here."

Even though Hayden had explained to Sam about Abuela calling her Alejandra, she still blinked in surprise at the name. Abuela had yet to even look at Sam.

She walked straight up to Hayden, her hands cupping her cheeks. She was a foot shorter than Hayden, which was impressive, since Hayden wasn't exactly tall in the first place. Even as Hayden grinned, her cheeks all pudge in Abuela's hands, her heart was in her throat.

"Why you so skinny?"

Hayden rolled her eyes, her hands resting on Abuela's forearms. Her skin was like paper under her fingers, yet she was warm and full of wiry muscle. An ox of a woman hidden in a tiny package. "I've gained weight, Abuela."

"No. I no believe it."

Well, it was true. "At least I have a few days of your cooking?"

Those sharp, dark eyes zeroed in on her, and Hayden almost ran away, but her face was still smooshed in Abuela's hands. Why had she gone there?

"Yes. A few days. More like barely three days. Two and a half." She turned her head so sharply that Hayden was left blinking down at her ear. Hayden turned too, hands still on her cheeks. Sam stood, her gaze caught on Abuela's. "So. You are the…wife of my granddaughter?"

"I am."

"And you could not make her come for more time? We are just meeting, and you don't wish staying more with us?"

Sam's mouth actually gaped. It was barely perceptible, but Hayden caught it and grinned again. Abuela's hands finally fell away. Hayden kept a hand on her arm, though, wanting that physical connection. She also wanted to remind Abuela to take it easy on Sam, despite the amusement it gave her to watch the two of them together.

"We have work," Sam said.

Abuela waved a hand in the air. "Work. You cannot live your life working. What about family? And friends? And my granddaughter?"

Sam looked at Hayden with an expression that said *help me*, and Hayden thought about rescuing her. She did. Really. For a fleeting second.

Apparently seeing no assistance forthcoming, Sam turned back to Abuela. "We work together?"

"Hm." Abuela stepped into Sam's space, squinting up at her. She flicked the glasses on top of her head onto her face. "Well, *es guapa*."

"Thanks," Sam said.

Being called pretty by a glaring old lady didn't even make Sam go red.

"You speak Spanish?"

Sam clearly had no idea what to do about any of this. "A little."

"Good. I want my other great-grandchildren to speak Spanish too."

What? Great-grandchildren? Something twisted in Hayden's gut. Abuela could never know this was all a lie.

"But yes. She's pretty, Alejandra. You didn't tell me she was an older woman?" Abuela glanced at Hayden and back to Sam, whose nostrils had flared. Hayden's stomach hurt from holding in her laughter. "Very good. Means she has a good head on her shoulders. Sometimes you need someone to pull you back to earth."

"Hey!" Hayden glared at Abuela, who grinned wickedly at Sam, even throwing in a wink. Sam responded with a hesitant smile.

"I am not happy with you still, Samantha. But we will see." Abuela turned and walked down the corridor. "Come, Alejandra," she called over her shoulder. "Your mamá is in the kitchen. She is having a bad day."

That made the grin that had been back on Hayden's face slide. Meanwhile, Sam was glaring at her.

"That was not enjoyable," she said.

"Oh, it was for me."

"Bad day?" Sam asked pointedly.

Hayden sighed, turning to walk down the corridor and follow the amazing smell coming from the kitchen. Lunch was going to be good. Hayden walked into the kitchen and took a deep breath, trying to relax. Javi was standing on a chair at the counter, piling food on a plate. He liked to help but wasn't good at it. Sofia was sitting at the table, and next to her, with a search-a-word in her hand, was Hayden's mother.

"Mamá." It was always good to see her. Even when it was hard, it was good to see her.

Her mother glanced up at her. No recognition flashed over her features; that rarely happened anymore. She had some lucid days, and on those days, her memory came in and out. Hayden walked to the table and sat next to her mother. "Hey."

Her mother gave a jolty smile. "Hello."

"It's me, Mamá. Hayden."

"Ah, yes." Her mother was still staring, as if desperately searching for a way to recognize the face in front of her. The search-a-word was mostly randomly circled letters. A lump swelled in Hayden's throat so fast she had to work hard to push it back down. "Hayden. Yes."

"Your daughter."

Little reminders, no pushing. The more you pushed, the more panicked she would become.

"Yes." She looked to Sofia. "But I don't think I have a daughter?"

Sofia patted her hand. "It's okay."

"Oh. Good." She looked down at her book. "Can I keep doing this? Then later I have to go meet my husband."

"Of course. But first, Mamá." She looked up again, something of the name registering even as she said she didn't have children. "This is Sam." Hayden turned in her seat, and Sam walked forward, her hand on Hayden's shoulder. They'd agreed on more touches for the weekend. It was finally not so strange, now. "Sam, this is my mom, Paola."

"Hello, Paola."

Hayden's mom might not know she recognized Hayden. But she was always more nervous with people who were genuinely new. She looked from Sofia to Sam again, her gaze jittery. "Hello. I have to finish so I can meet my husband soon."

She focused on the book in front of her and started circling letters, her shoulders relaxing after a few moments.

"She's calm still. Most of the time. Well, less and less."

When Sofia spoke, that lump in Hayden's throat still made it hard for her to swallow.

Sofia gave her a small smile. "The new medications have made her mellow. She's happy enough."

"Good." Hayden licked her lips. That first year had been heartbreaking. She'd watched her capable mother, aware of what was happening to her, lose herself, her memories, her personality. She had been scared and nervous all the time. Now that the disease had advanced, it was worse in so many ways, and yet better in others. She couldn't be alone, though. She wandered, tried to cook in the middle of the night.

The hand on her shoulder squeezed and Hayden couldn't look at Sam, else that lump would break and her eyes might leak.

"So!" Hayden stood up, and Sam's hand fell away. "What's for lunch?"

She turned around and grabbed Sam's hand, tugging her to the counter, opposite Javi and Abuela, who was putting various chopped vegetables in bowls. Hayden's eyes swept over the counter.

"Are we having *pollo con tajadas*?"

Javi nodded at her. "Yup."

"And salad," Abuela said, stirring the pot on the stove that smelled like heaven probably did.

Javi made a face. "And salad."

"Well, we need it," Hayden said. "Gotta stay strong."

"You two put your stuff in the room." Abuela shooed them with her hand. "When you finish, lunch."

"*Gracias, Abuela.*"

Abuela waved a hand in the air, her eyes on the pot, and Hayden led the way out and upstairs toward her old room. When she'd lived here for that year, she'd cleared all her stuff out, and now it was mostly like a guest room with a big bed. That they'd share. Or, again, Hayden could sleep on the floor? But that seemed stupid.

Sam followed her quietly. Hayden walked up the steps that led to the second floor, taking the first door on the left. She put her suitcase down and looked around. The bed was all made up in a dark cover, the walls still the same white they had been before. She'd left a few photos around, mostly of her and her sister when they were younger. Some were of her mom and Abuela, and one or two of her school friends she mostly liked posts of on social media and not much else these days.

The door closed behind her, and Hayden looked at Sam, who was staring at the bed with an indiscernible expression. Hayden looked back at it too.

Well. This was going to be interesting.

CHAPTER 14

Abuela managed to keep her cool until dinner that night.

They had all had lunch, and after, Javi had dragged Hayden outside to play soccer. Her mom had sat on the back step and watched them, and Sam had sat next to her. Hayden hadn't caught what Sam spoke to her about, but whenever Hayden looked over, Sam's lips had been moving. Hayden's mom had calmly listened. At one point, as Hayden had pretended to fall over while trying to stop Javi from carrying the soccer ball to his 'goal' (a tree), her mom had stood up, her hands wrenching in front of her. Hayden had paused, ready to go to her if needed, but Sam had hesitantly put a hand on her mother's forearm.

"It's done." Hayden had heard Sam say the words as Javi took a breath between cheering his own success. She didn't hear anything else but watched as her mother sat down, still looking stressed until, eventually, her shoulders relaxed.

At seven, they went out to dinner, a tradition on the first night when Hayden was home.

All day, Hayden hadn't been able to get rid of the ball of anxiety in her stomach— Sam knowing about her mother, lying to her family.

It all felt rotten.

The restaurant was the same one they visited whenever Hayden came home, a small Vietnamese place with amazing service and delicious food. It had been her mom's favorite place years and years ago. It was a pity, but Hayden's mom couldn't tolerate restaurants anymore. The noise and new people left her confused and agitated for days. So she had stayed at home with the assistant, and with Javi.

"Samantha."

Hayden looked up from her plate. Sam had been 'Samantha' all day, and not once had Sam corrected Abuela, which in itself was enough for Hayden to smirk into her food.

"Where did you meet Alejandra?"

Hayden could feel Sam looking at her and kept her eyes firmly on the chopsticks she was using to grab some noodles. Sam had wanted Hayden's family to know they were married? Well, welcome to the reality of that.

Across from Hayden, Sofia fixed her gaze on Sam, her shoulder brushing Abuela's. Their eyes were twins of each other as they gave Sam all their attention.

"I met her at work," Sam said finally.

Hayden winced internally for her but happily chewed on another mouthful of noodles. Did she really think that would suffice?

Sure enough, Abuela's eyes narrowed and Sofia pursed her lips, her entertainment completely unhidden as she reached for one of the rolls on her plate.

"At work. That is the story?"

"Well, yes."

Hayden had never heard Sam sound as unsure as she had all day today.

Abuela looked at Hayden, who tried to look innocent, then back to Sam, whose shoulder brushed Hayden's.

"That is not romantic. Where is the story?" Her eyes narrowed even more, the creases in her brow deepening. "Where is the love? Alejandra." The smirk on Hayden's face finally fell when those sharp eyes flicked to her. Sofia buried her amusement in her glass. "Why you marry this girl? This is not love."

Hayden took a deep breath. "Maybe we're shy with the story, Abuela?"

That gaze didn't move from her face. "Shy? Why? I ask for the story. I expect more than we meet at work. Did you meet with…with bad situation?"

"What? No!" Hayden sighed. Now Abuela thought she and Sam had had some kind of raging affair or something. So Hayden finally looked at Sam and let her hand fall on Sam's knee. The posture was obvious for her sister and for Abuela, even if they couldn't see what her hand was doing. "Honey," she addressed Sam, "I know you're normally reserved about these things…"

Sam's green eyes were only a foot from her own, filled with panic.

"But just tell the story."

For a second, Hayden thought Sam was only going to stare at her. Hayden smiled, trying for reassuring and yet tightening her grip on the warm knee under her hand. In the back of her mind, it ticked over that this didn't really feel awkward anymore. Good.

Finally, Sam turned to Abuela. "We *did* meet at work. I was called to a consult, a patient who had presented to the ER with left-sided weakness and memory loss. It was a rush, but one thing I really took away from the consult, and the subsequent hurry of getting the patient to surgery, was the nurse who was looking after him. How she responded to everything efficiently and had everything I needed without asking.

The last thing I saw when I followed the patient as he was wheeled to the OR was her gaze watching us go."

Hayden swallowed. Sam looked so sincere. And, actually, that *was* the first time they'd met, excluding Sam seeing her back when she was in premed.

She was surprised Sam had remembered it. Hayden hadn't been long out of school, and it was her first real brush with Sam. She'd found her rude and closed off. Maybe it was all efficiency. Maybe Hayden had always read Sam wrong. Or she hadn't, but she hadn't seen the full picture.

When Hayden made herself stop gazing at Sam's face, Abuela still looked unconvinced, but Sofia tilted her head as if really taking Sam in for the first time.

"And then?" Abuela asked.

Hayden squeezed Sam's knee again; more a rub, her fingers brushing the jeans under them. She'd meant to pull away but figured it was more natural to leave them there.

"And then we were colleagues. Kind of friends," Hayden added. That was a stretch— well, a full-blown lie. What was the saying from that British show? In for a penny... "But something clicked," she continued, "and we started dating. And Sam asked, and I said yes."

Sam, her cheeks a very faint red, recounted the story of her supposed proposal. As she spoke, Abuela's face still didn't really change. Sofia's stayed intrigued. Hayden took in a breath and let it out slowly. They were lying already, and they needed to sell it. Even if just to make Hayden's life easier over the next however many months. As Sam finished, talking about the stars and the way Hayden had looked under them, Hayden slowly moved her body closer, making sure she was smiling like she was lovestruck; pulling in deep from that well that was apparently always there. When she pressed her lips to the softness of Sam's cheek, Sam's speech hitched subtly before she kept speaking. Perfect. Hayden made sure to press her smile into it, the warm skin under her lips warming even further in the few seconds she lingered there, pulling away as Sam finished the story. She left an arm draped over Sam's chair, her eyes still on her. Sam met Abuela's eye, and Hayden turned her head, making sure her shoulders stayed relaxed.

"And I said yes," Hayden chimed in. "I know it was fast, and I always said I didn't believe in marriage."

"Not always." Abuela's face was not as easy to read now, but at least she wasn't glaring at them both like they'd denied her the epic romance of the year.

"Well, almost." Hayden looked from Sofia to Abuela. "But that's why it was quiet and no big deal. Because it was what we wanted."

Her lips still felt too warm.

"Well." Sofia held up a glass, lips curved up, something genuine in her action that made Hayden feel a little better. "To you two. May you stay happy."

Sam relaxed back into Hayden. They all raised their glasses, clinking them together, and Hayden took a long sip. The fizz of the champagne Sam had ordered bubbled over her tongue.

"*Felicidades.*" Abuela even managed to make her congratulations sound sincere.

"*Gracias, Abuela.*"

"Thank you." Sam took an even longer sip of her drink than Hayden, and on impulse, Hayden turned her head toward her properly as she lowered the glass. She pressed her lips over the corner of Sam's. Sam went very tense for a second, and Hayden felt a loosening as she relaxed and turned, dipping her head to kiss Hayden properly. Sam's lips tasted of champagne and surprise, especially as Hayden deepened the kiss lightly. It was the quick kind of kiss a newly-married couple would press on each other's lips in front of family at a toast in their honor. But even as she pulled back, Sam's eyes fluttering open to meet hers, the softness of Sam's lips lingered on her own. For a second, the buzz of the restaurant died away. The green of Sam's eyes was almost unnoticeable, her pupils dilated in the dim restaurant.

The affection was getting easier, now that they were more comfortable with each other. Maybe that was all she could feel in the gaze that felt heavy on her face. Hayden could feel Sam's breath washing over her lips, and Hayden swallowed as that look slipped away.

They pulled apart. Hayden didn't have to fake the coy dip of her head at the delight on her family's faces. Her family was loud, and they never had qualms about doling out hugs and kisses in front of each other. When they resumed their meal, Abuela had calmed down with her questions. Mostly.

"What your family do, Samantha?" she asked.

Well, that was an interesting one. Hayden munched on her food and turned, watching her.

"Finance."

That wasn't interesting enough for Abuela to want to prod at. Which was a pity, because while Hayden wasn't allowed to ask about family, Abuela could probably get away with it.

"You have sisters? Brothers?"

"A brother. He's much younger than I am and a bit of an idiot."

"Brothers always are," Abuela said. "I have four. They are all idiots."

Sofia snorted. "Even Tío Juan?"

"*Especially* Tío Juan."

"Tío Juan is Abuela's brother," Hayden said to Sam. "He could murder someone, and she'd still adore him."

"No. He is an idiot," Abuela repeated.

Her grandmother's lie prompted a shared look of amusement between Hayden and Sofia.

"When we meet your family?" Abuela's eagle eye was back on Sam.

Another interesting question.

"They're based in New York and don't really travel. Perhaps when you come to visit?"

That was incredibly clever. As if Hayden's family could afford to go there, especially with Hayden's mother.

Abuela huffed. "Family living everywhere in this country makes the life hard."

When the bill came, Hayden breathed a sigh of relief. They'd made it through dinner, even if her lips were tingling from the spicy sauce. Sam insisted on paying, to everyone's protests, and Sofia drove them home. Abuela was suspiciously quiet. It was bordering on late, so when they got in, Javi was already asleep. The assistant, a friendly guy called Abdul, met them at the door.

"Everything okay?" Sofia asked him.

He gave a nod. "She fell asleep after her evening meds, like normal. She's upstairs still. I checked on her five minutes ago. She was really agitated before the meds, though."

"What about?" Hayden asked.

"She was insisting that she had work. I tried to distract her, but it didn't do much. She kept trying to leave. So I hope it's okay, but Javi and I went for a walk with her, in the hope it would help."

"That's more than fine," Sofia said. "How was Javi?"

"Javi wanted six stories. We compromised on two."

Hayden laughed. "You're less of a sucker than me. I give in."

He winked. "Okay, I may have lied, and he really got all six."

He waved goodbye and closed the door behind him, leaving Sofia, Sam and Hayden in the entrance. Abuela had disappeared to the kitchen. She never went to sleep without tea.

"Samantha!" Her voice boomed down the hallway.

Sam jumped, and Sofia and Hayden chuckled. "Ah, yes?"

"Come. Have tea. It will help you sleep."

With a pleading look at both of them, Sam took a step toward the kitchen.

Sofia held up her hands. "Don't look at us. She asked for you." She grinned. "You joined this family willingly."

Sam threw Hayden one more look and walked to the kitchen.

Hayden pulled off her coat and hung it by the door on the stand, taking Sofia's when she handed it over. Turning back, Hayden paused. Sofia was appraising her.

"What?"

"You've been avoiding being alone with me all day."

"Have not."

She totally had.

"Hayds." Sofia pushed her shoulder, and Hayden was warm inside at the familiar, frustrated gesture. "I'm not going to lecture you."

Maybe that was partly why she'd avoided being along with her sister. And also because Hayden didn't want to lie more than she had to.

"Okay, sorry. I should have given you the benefit of the doubt." Hayden missed her sister at times, but she was also relieved to be away from the pressure that came from this house—from the eyes always judging her, from the woman sleeping upstairs, from the grandmother that wanted her to live her life but also thought a little less of her for disappearing.

"But marriage?" Here it comes. "After Dad?"

"Yeah, I know. People change."

Hayden hadn't, but Sofia didn't need to know that.

Sofia was still eyeing her. "Well, fine. She seems—"

"Mami!"

The insistent child's voice floated down the stairs, and Sofia winced. "Talk more tomorrow?"

"Yeah." Hayden couldn't think of anything worse than *that* conversation. "Of course."

"Great. Can you check on Mom while I check on Javi?"

Ice filled Hayden's stomach, even as she said, "Yeah. Of course."

"Mami!"

"¡*Voy!*" Sofia called "Coming."

She led the way upstairs, and Hayden paused at the room her mother and Abuela shared. Abuela was an incredibly light sleeper. And considering Hayden's mother had disappeared once before at night, it was necessary she shared a room with someone who could wake up at the slightest noise. One day, it would all fall apart around them, and they'd need to start talking about putting her mother in full-time care. They'd danced around the topic a lot but had never really committed to it.

None of them were ready for that. Especially while they could still manage. Especially while Abuela was so opposed to the idea.

She pushed the door open quietly and padded in, the light from the hall flooding the space just enough to light up the bed against one wall. Her mom was curled up in the middle of the mattress, and Hayden's stomach ached at how she looked the most like her mother when she slept. Her mom's face was smoothed out from the agitation and confusion it often wore, no sign of the anger that often boiled over: a side effect of the fear.

Anything could make her mom panic with no warning. An idea would implant in her mind, and sidetracking her was hard. She'd want to cook for a gathering she thought she had the next day, or she'd think she needed to check something that wasn't actually in the oven. She'd want to shop at four in the morning or would wake up sobbing and hysterical, with no idea where she was, a child again but unable to recognize the mother bending over her who'd aged too much to be the version Paola remembered.

It was all so hard to be around.

That lump was back in Hayden's throat, and she remembered how Sam had soothed her mother on the step, how her mother had simply sat back down next to her.

Hayden turned and walked out, her hand on the door handle she'd tugged on to close the door. Sam stood on the landing, a cup of tea in her hand.

"Your grandmother made me promise to make you drink this."

Hayden, still a little shaky from the flood of thoughts, held out her hand.

"Thank you." The mug was hot, as were Sam's fingers as they brushed against Hayden's. There was something strange about standing here with emotion crawling up her throat and Sam considering her with a careful eye in her childhood home with her mother asleep behind her, her mind lost. Hayden suddenly wanted to crawl out of her own skin to escape this feeling she couldn't name.

"You're welcome. I didn't think I should say no to her."

The small laugh Hayden gave eased a little of the tightness in her chest. "Yeah, you learn fast."

The footsteps on the stairs made Sam turn, and Abuela emerged. "She is sleeping?"

"Yes. She's out."

"Good. Since her new medicine, she is sleeping better at night. Though sometimes…"

"What?"

"She still wake up at three or four. Wanting to go walking or pick you girls up from school."

That tightness was back in Hayden's chest. "Oh." She was never good at talking about this.

Abuela threw her hands up. "This is the life. I need to sleep, cariño. I used the bathroom downstairs, so this one is free. Samantha, good night."

"Good night."

Abuela walked up and kissed both of Hayden's cheeks, her cheek soft and fragile against Hayden's own.

"Buenas noches, Abuela."

"Hasta mañana."

And she disappeared into the room behind Hayden, leaving Sam and Hayden alone again, the cup in Hayden's hand slowly burning her skin.

"Do you want a shower?" Hayden asked.

"I'd prefer to wait until the morning." Sam hesitated. "If that's okay?"

"Sure. Well, I'm going to shower. I'll, uh…see you in a bit."

Hayden grabbed her things from her suitcase while Sam hovered in the hall. Toiletries. Pajamas. Underwear. In the hall, she heard Sofia murmur a good night to Sam and call good night to Hayden.

She slipped out the door, holding her things against her chest, her cup still in one hand. Sam had her phone out, back against the wall, most likely trying not to look awkward.

"Night, Sofe."

"See you in the morning. Be warned Javi might run in." Sofia winked as she walked down the hall.

Hayden made herself chuckle but avoided Sam's eyes as she headed for the bathroom, even as she took Hayden's cup for her. The room heated up as she turned the shower on right away, wanting to have a while to decompress. It wasn't until steam was billowing out of the shower, the mirror fogging over, that she stepped under the spray, hair in a pile on top of her head. It was so strange being back in this house. After being in her mom's room, her fingers had started to feel cold, that uncomfortable feeling she always had when facing the truth of all this squirming in her stomach as the cold spread. Being home was like being hit with a truth bomb.

Her mom. Her sister. Abuela. Javi, who saw the world so simply.

Sam being a part of it all.

It had felt weirdly normal today to let Sam rest her hand on her shoulder and press close at dinner. Hayden wasn't someone to sensationalize a kiss, but it was strange that it had been so simple to do. Being in Sam's space was starting to feel…normal. Which was good for their charade. But it was strange to think that the two of them were actually at a point of comfort with each other.

And Hayden's lips were still tingling. It had reached a point where she couldn't blame the spice from dinner. Her fingertips no longer felt cold, warmth was spreading through her body.

Sam had really soft skin. And soft lips. And she had huffed against Hayden in her slight surprise, before she'd kissed her back.

Clearly, it had been far too long since Hayden had kissed anyone. The squirming feeling in her stomach had eased, and a pool of warmth had settled there in its place. Her eyes fluttered closed, and she leaned against the wall, running her fingers against her lips ever so gently, down her cheek, down her neck. She found herself imagining it was someone else's skin under her sensitive fingertips.

It had been months—months and months—since she'd touched someone else in any way that wasn't platonic. As her fingers ran against her breast and over her nipple, her lips parting at the touch, images from that last time danced in her mind: a woman with blonde hair and fair skin. They'd met through Luce and after a few dates, had fallen into bed. She'd moaned so loudly that Hayden had smiled against the dip where her hip met her stomach.

She slid her hand between her own legs and bit her lip, remembering how the woman had dug her nails into Hayden's skin when she'd first touched her. The sound of her own breath echoed in the room, the steam hopefully muffling the sound. The last of the tension that had swept over her had now dissipated completely.

It didn't surprise her when she came undone against her own hand minutes later, that it had been fair skin and red hair instead in her mind at the end. She stood under the spray a minute longer, her lip hurting where she'd bitten it to keep herself quiet, amused at the entire episode.

Maybe it wasn't surprising, but if thinking of Sam had made her come, it really had been far too long. And the frustrating thing was this was about all she could do about it. No way could she could risk going out and meeting anyone. It could blow the entire charade if anyone that shouldn't see saw it. And she'd never really enjoyed one-night stands. She liked going out, dating, taking a bit of time.

Feeling better, with her mind half-asleep, Hayden got out and dried off, dressing quickly. She tiptoed down the now-quiet hallway and opened the door, her legs only a little wobbly. Sam was sitting in bed, her knees drawn up under the blankets. Sleep was clamoring at Hayden's eyes, and she decided to embrace it. People shared beds all the time without it being a thing. The surprise earlier today had knocked them for a second, but only because they were idiots who didn't think ahead about things. All she wanted to do was sleep after the day she'd had anyway, and the shower had done nothing to stave off her sleepiness. For…reasons.

To embrace her newfound desire to not make it weird, Hayden flopped face-first next to Sam, her face hitting the pillow with a soft thump. When she finally rolled her head around to look up at Sam with one eye, Sam was doing the thing with her lips that meant she was trying not to smile.

"Tired?" Sam asked.

Hayden nodded, feeling her hair frizz around her ears. "Aren't you?"

"I am. But I like to read something before I sleep." She held her phone against her knees, but her attention was on Hayden.

"I sometimes do, normally after night shift when I can't sleep. Not tonight. Tonight, I'll sleep like a baby."

She closed her eyes, almost as if on cue. Wriggling and refusing to lift her head up, she kicked the blanket down bit by bit from under her, rolling and lifting her hips to get it all the way down to her feet so she could kick it up without having to sit up. When it was finally almost at her hips, she reached backward blindly and pulled it over herself. Satisfied with its position on her body, she nestled more into her pillow. She opened that eye again. Sam was now smirking openly.

"What?" Hayden asked.

"That was interesting to watch."

"It was the easiest way."

"Was it, Hayden?"

She closed her eyes again. "Mhm."

She heard Sam give something like a laugh and then only the very subtle sound of her thumb tapping at her screen.

Had Hayden thought about that thumb, a little, in the shower? About where it could be touching her?

Well, now she felt too hot.

This was awkward. Abort that thought process completely.

"Are you okay?"

Hayden's eye flew open. The other was still mashed into her pillow. "Why?" Was her heart speeding up? Could Sam read thoughts?

No. Of course she couldn't.

But what if she could?

"I imagine today hasn't been easy. You seem very private about these things at home. And I've been here, in that space. And you've been having to pretend to like me."

That was surprisingly on point for Sam. Had she been searching "why is my friend mildly panicking after sharing a big secret" on the Internet?

"It's been weird. I won't lie. But Sam..." Her shoulders relaxed into the bed more, the truth of what she was saying easier than the lies. "I don't have to pretend to like you."

Silence. Then, "Oh."

"I think—" Hayden lowered her voice as if about to offer up a big secret and laced some ironic humor into her words "—I think we may be becoming friends."

Pink bloomed over Sam's cheeks. "Oh."

"And normally, you're the eloquent one."

"Well, we did acknowledge you don't like me when we started this."

Had Sam been preoccupied with that? "True. But sometimes I have been known to make harsh judgments. You're...okay, I guess."

Sam rolled her eyes, and for the first time, Hayden saw that warmth in them that she'd seen when Sam had rolled her eyes at her brother. "Well," Sam said, "high praise. Thank you."

"Anytime. So, are we?"

"What?"

Sam's warmth radiated from under the blanket. The bed was comfortable. Her pillow was plump. Again, her eyes drifted shut.

"You know, friends?" Hayden asked.

Silence buzzed around them, and Hayden resisted the urge to open her eyes and look at Sam to see if she displayed any emotion that would give her feelings away. Of course, she might have gone back to her phone, freaked out by all the talk of feelings.

"I think we are, Hayden."

Hayden kept her eyes closed, but she let those words worm into her, and sleep pulled her under.

She woke up hours later to the sound of footsteps.

CHAPTER 15

Hayden sat up, shrouded in darkness.

Those had definitely been footsteps. Down the stairs. Why would that wake her up? People went for water all the time. Or maybe Sofia couldn't sleep. Or Javi was sneaking downstairs to watch early morning kids' shows. He worked the remotes better than Hayden could ever hope to do.

The next generation was going to rule the world.

Groping for her phone, she glanced over where Sam was a lump under the blanket, the top of her head sticking out. Her breathing, slow and steady, filled the room. She was as far over as she could be. Hayden was surprised she hadn't fallen out of the bed completely.

Finally, her fingers brushed her phone and she grabbed it, checking the time. The screen was way too bright. She squinted, then finally managed to focus. Just after three a.m. Definitely not Javi walking downstairs.

She lay back down. It must have been Sofia. Or Abuela.

Or her mother.

Suddenly, she was wide awake.

Taking in a deep breath, Hayden got out of bed, her toes hitting the cold floor. She stumbled around, using her phone as a light, hoping she didn't wake Sam. Her suitcase was still flung open in the corner of the room, Sam's next to it, neatly zipped up. Hayden really needed to at least try and keep her stuff together. Or not. She fished out a pair of socks and her hoodie and opened the door as quietly as possible, slipping into the hall. The light was left on there in case Javi needed the bathroom or for her mom if she did wander. Luckily, Hayden's pajama pants had huge pockets. She dropped her phone into one and tugged on the hoodie and socks. It was Florida, so it wasn't exactly *cold*, but it was comfortable. The whole house was silent; that moment in the true early hours of the morning when it felt as if the entire world had gone still.

She heard a noise downstairs, and that bubble burst.

She walked down the stairs as quietly as she could. At the bottom, she looked around. No lights were on down here. Everything was encased in long shadows thrown by the light filtering down the stairs. She turned left and headed for the kitchen. It was even darker in there, and Hayden squinted. Someone was moving around. Her eyes adjusted further.

Her mother was in the kitchen.

"Mamá?"

The shadow froze, and Hayden flicked the light on, the sight in front of her making her stomach go cold. Her mother was squinting at her, wild-haired. She was in a summer dress, back to front.

It would be comical if not so sad.

"Who are you?" Her mother's eyes were as wild as her hair.

"I'm Hayden."

"I don't know you."

Hayden swallowed, holding her hands up, placating. "I'm your daughter."

"I don't have a daughter." She narrowed her eyes. "What's your name?"

"Hayden." Repetition. All the time. A constant. "My name is Hayden."

"I need to go." Her mother's eyes were narrowed slits now, eyeing her. "I'm not supposed to be here. I'm supposed to meet Bradly."

Hayden's stomach dropped. "Dad—Bradly—isn't here." She kept her voice calm.

"Well, obviously. That's why I need to go. I'm supposed to meet him. At four."

"In the afternoon?"

"Yes. Yes." Her mother's voice was impatient, and she shivered, wrapping her arms around herself. It was too cold for that dress. Maybe not to Hayden, who was used to much colder, but for her mother... "When else?"

"Look out the window, M—Paola."

For a second, Hayden thought she was too suspicious to do so. She was watching Hayden as if she was afraid Hayden was going to launch herself over the counter and attack. Hayden tried to remember that, for her mother, she really was an unknown right now—or always, these days.

Finally, though, Paola did turn her head, looking outside at the dark yard. She turned back, her brow knitted.

"What time is it? And who are you?"

"I'm Hayden. It's about three in the morning."

"I'm supposed to be meeting my husband."

Hayden dealt with this fairly regularly at the hospital. But with her mother, it had never been the same. Little words tugged at her, left her unraveled. Like those ones.

"Well, not at three a.m."

"I suppose not."

Hayden stepped forward, and her mother stepped back. "Who are you?"

"I'm Hayden."

Something, a shadow, flitted over her mother's face. "Why are you in my house? I don't know you. Get out."

Her voice was rising. Hayden needed to calm her down. Her pulse was raising, something tight in her chest making it difficult to breathe.

Who was *Hayden*? But she could remember her father? That asshole? It was unfair to be angry about it; it wasn't her mother's fault. But it still stung irrationally. This entire thing was unfair. Her mother had been brave and quick and intelligent. Independent.

"Paola, I—"

"How do you know my name? I don't know you."

"You're okay. You're safe here."

Her mother darted to the door that led to the yard. But she was uncoordinated now she thought she was in her twenties, yet she was in her fifties, with advancing Alzheimer's. She stumbled. Hayden jumped forward and around the counter, but not fast enough. Her mother's head collided with the door with a crack that made Hayden's blood run cold. The cry her mother gave was pitiful. She didn't fall: her hands flattened against the door to steady herself. Hayden reached for her mother, but as soon as her fingers closed around her arms, her mother pushed backward, throwing her arm over her head in a blind hit, and Hayden felt the elbow collide with her mouth, her head snapping back.

"Don't touch me!"

"Mamá." Hayden went to reach for her again, but her mother's hand gripped at the wall to hold herself up. Something metallic-tasting was in Hayden's mouth. She dropped her hands when her mother drew in a sharp breath, her look wild.

Blood was dripping down her mother's eye and cheek from a gash on her forehead. A bruise seemed to already be blooming, noticeable even on her dark skin. Hayden scanned her, mentally checking the injury. Superficial, mostly. The crack had been loud. Could she be concussed? Hayden needed to get closer to manage that. "Let me help you. You're bleeding."

Her mother swiped a hand at her face and examined it. She looked down at the red smears there and blanched. "No. I have to go. I have, I have somewhere to be."

She was definitely dazed. But she had been before.

"Is everything okay?"

Hayden spun around. Sam was standing in the doorway, straight-shouldered and tall, even in a wrinkled T-shirt and pajama pants.

Hayden shook her head. "No. She—she tripped, trying to leave."

Sam didn't try to step closer, and Hayden quickly checked on her mother. She was cowering against the door, bloodstained hand held in front of her face.

"You're bleeding too."

Hayden licked her lip, that metallic tang hitting her taste buds. She'd thought her mom had barely touched her. "Oh," was all Hayden said. She turned back to her mother. "Mamá—Paola."

Her mother flinched away. It could have been another slap all over again. She stepped back, hoping it would make her feel better.

"Paola?" Sam was beside her. Hayden's mom shrank back again.

"Who are you?" she asked sharply. "What do you want?"

"My name's Dr. Thomson."

"Doctor?"

Hayden stepped away, until she was around the counter and by the door. Her hands were shaking.

"Yes. I'm here to have a look at your head. Do you know what happened?" Sam had the voice on that she used at the hospital. Hayden hadn't heard this exact version, though. It was softer.

Hayden's mother looked back down at her hand, then back at Sam, who stayed a few feet away. "Remember? No. I—No."

"That's okay. You've hit your head. Do you mind if I take a look?"

Her eyes were less wild as she looked around, her gaze landing on Hayden. "Who is that?"

"That's my nurse."

"Oh. Well, then."

Sam stepped a bit closer, and Hayden's mother didn't flinch. "Can I take a look?"

"What has happened?" The whispered voice behind Hayden made her jump. Abuela's hand held her upper arm, the touch grounding her.

"She was down here, insisting she had to meet Dad." Hayden watched as her mother let Sam lead her around the counter to sit at the table. As she walked past the doorway, she eyed the two of them standing there. Hayden tried to make herself smile and not look threatening when all she wanted to do was walk out the door.

She didn't know if Abuela did the same. She couldn't take her eyes off her mother. "She got scared when she didn't know who I was. She tried to run for the back door and tripped and hit her head. When I tried to help her get her balance, she hit me, accidentally, really."

Sam was murmuring to Hayden's mother, trying to get her to follow her finger. But it had been a while since her mother had followed the simplest instructions. She either forgot what she was doing or couldn't understand what was expected of her. Abuela's fingers tugged on her chin, and Hayden acquiesced, turning her head and finally locking eyes with her. Abuela's gaze roamed her face.

"She has split your lip," she whispered. Her thumb grazed Hayden's bottom lip.

"It really was an accident."

"She hit me once, some months ago. Normally we can calm her before she gets that...that *agitada*." Abuela sighed. "I get worried about Javi."

Hayden didn't know what to say to that. Abuela's fingers, achingly gentle, were still on her chin. Hot shame pooled in Hayden's throat. She should have been able to calm her mother down, to do what Sam was doing just now. "Me too."

"I did not wake up." Abuela sighed, her hand finally falling away from Hayden's chin. "I always wake up."

"Maybe she was very quiet."

"I think it was the champagne." She tutted at herself. "No more."

Hayden swallowed and looked back. Sam was covering her mother's eye with one hand, pulling it away quickly, a makeshift way to check her pupil response without a flashlight.

"Is she okay?" Hayden asked. Her voice was raspy after whispering to Abuela, combined with sleep and emotion.

Sam looked over. "She's fine."

Hayden felt her entire body go loose. "Good."

"It could use a stitch or two, but Steri-Strips will be okay too."

"We must to go to the hospital?" Abuela asked.

They'd had to a couple of times before. It often led to the need for sedation. The situation was too confusing and involved pain and lights and new people.

"I always have some first aid things in my suitcase." Sam had her eyes back on Hayden's mother. "Hayden, can you get it? There are some strips and creams."

Wordlessly, Hayden turned and headed for the stairs. Her lip was starting to sting. Actually, it was hurting a lot. But she could deal with that later. As quietly as she could, she walked into their room—weird thought—and squatted in front of Sam's suitcase. Hayden's fingers were trembling a bit. That was embarrassing. She'd dealt with far worse in the hospital.

Her own suitcase was spilling its contents, and she shoved a few things back on top to make it appear neater, which didn't do much. She unzipped Sam's and flipped it open. So much organization greeted her that she almost had to squint. It was as if her suitcase was sectioned, and Hayden poked into the neatly stacked clothes just to check a divider wasn't deftly separating them all. Nope. Wow. The inside pocket of the suitcase held a zipped bag with a list taped neatly on the front. It listed all the things you'd normally find in a first aid kit, plus a few extras. Written next to each item was a number indicating how many of each should be in there.

This went beyond simply being organized. This was utter nerd.

Which Hayden wasn't complaining about right now.

Hayden zipped it open and pulled out a sterile pack of Steri-Strips, gauze, some numbing cream, and some antiseptic. She zipped it closed and was tempted to drop it on top of the neatly ordered contents of the case and leave it open, purely to enjoy a bit of destruction. It was all just so perfect. Instead, she replaced the little bag and zipped the case closed.

Upstairs was still quiet as she tiptoed back down to the ground floor. Thankfully, Javi and Sofia hadn't woken up. Hayden swallowed at the thought of the conversation she was going to have to have with her sister tomorrow night. Tonight? It was technically morning.

Before this, she already hadn't been looking forward to such a conversation. But now? How often had this getting up in the middle of the night stuff been happening? For how long had her mother been this aggressive in her confusion? Was this a one-off? It was the first time Hayden had seen her like that, but Abuela hadn't seemed surprised.

In the kitchen, Abuela was pouring steaming hot water into four mugs. Her mother was sitting at the table still, and Sam was beside her. She appeared calm.

"My head hurts," she said.

"You had an accident." Keeping her voice low, Hayden handed the things to Sam. She sat down. "But you're okay."

Her mother furrowed her brow, then winced. Someone had cleaned up her face. The cut wasn't too bad. Sam was right: one or two stitches would do, and the Steri-Strips should work fine. But the skin around it was raised. A lump was forming.

"But what happened?" she asked.

"You slipped." Sam turned to face her. "I'm a doctor. Can I look at your head?"

Paola nodded, and Sam reached up. Her mother pulled back. "That hurts!"

"You hit your head," Sam said.

"It does hurt."

"It would. I'm just going to have a look."

Hayden jumped as a cup was put in front of her. Abuela touched her shoulder. "You go to bed, Alejandra."

"Who are you?" Hayden's mother was staring at Abuela. "Where am I?"

"At home." Sam was using some gauze to smear cream over the cut. "I'm a doctor." Every time she said it, Hayden's mother relaxed. "My head hurts."

Sam hummed. "It'll be okay."

"I need to meet my husband." Her mother's eyes were flicking between them all, even as Sam smoothed down the strips over the cut. "I'm going to be late."

"It's three in the morning." Sam pulled her hands away, and Hayden's mother stared at her. "But maybe if you go to sleep now, the time to meet him will come sooner."

"But I need to meet him."

"Look out the window." Sam indicated it with her hand, and Hayden's mother turned.

"It's dark."

"So maybe it's time to go to bed until it's time to meet him."

"No, I need to go."

Hayden took in a deep breath. "What about watching some television until he comes?"

"He's coming here?" Her eyes were sharp as she turned to stare at Hayden.

"Yeah. So why not watch some TV until then?"

"Oh. Okay." She stood up, unsteady as always.

Abuela held her hand out, and Hayden's mother took it. The sight made Hayden's stomach ache.

"You two go sleep. I cannot, not after this." Abuela looked at them both. "Take your tea. Thank you, Samantha."

Real gratitude deepened in Abuela's eyes, and Sam shifted. "You're welcome."

Abuela led Hayden's mother around the table and through the door that connected the kitchen to the living room. After a second, the sounds of the television filtered through. Hayden pressed her lips together, her eyes burning. But that made her lip sting more. Her tea was cooling on the table in front of her. The steam was faint now. She should have offered to go in Abuela's stead. To sit with her mother. That was what she had flown here for. She could have at least offered.

"Hayden—"

Sam's voice was still soft, softer than it usually was, but Hayden was standing up already. She took her tea and walked around the counter, dumping the contents into the sink. Without looking at Sam, she tried to smile but imagined it looked pretty gruesome. It felt it.

"Don't tell Abuela." She'd meant it to sound lighthearted, but instead it came out choked. "Thanks for your help. You're really good with her."

Hayden left the room, walking quickly back upstairs to the bathroom. She closed the door behind her as quietly as possible and fell back against the wood. Her reflection stared straight back at her. Her lip was definitely split. Not terribly, but blood was smeared at the corner of her mouth. It was swollen too.

It hurt. And would probably do so even more in the morning, when it became more swollen. Hayden dropped her head back against the door, closing her eyes. Could she have stopped that from happening? The few minutes in which it had all occurred were a blur now. She always handled confused patients so well in the ER. Hayden sighed and was horrified when it turned into a weird, sobbing hiccough. She clapped her hand over her mouth, ignoring the burning sting. This was not happening. She did not cry in the bathroom. Crying was for in bed. Or in the shower, maybe. But she did not cry about this. None of this was her mother's fault; she couldn't help it. Hayden squeezed her eyes shut and swallowed heavily, hoping it would push that lump in her throat away. She took in a long, deep breath. When she blew it out, it came out shaky. She did it a few more times until it sounded steady.

Only then did she open her eyes.

She told herself again this was not her mother's fault. The woman downstairs wasn't even really her mother, not anymore.

She watched her own reflection's eyes widen at that sudden horrible thought. And pushed it away. She couldn't think that.

There was an unobtrusive knock on the door.

"Hayden?" Sam's voice whispered.

For a second, she thought about fobbing her off. But Sam had been dragged into this. Okay, maybe she'd half dragged herself into it. But she deserved to be acknowledged after dealing with Hayden's family drama.

She pushed off the door and opened it. Sam blinked, as if surprised to be face-to-face with Hayden. Like she hadn't really expected to be invited into her space.

"Hi." Sam held up the plastic container in her hand, in which some ice cubes floated in water, gauze soaking in it. "I thought we could try and stop your lip from swelling. I brought something for the pain too."

"Thanks." Apparently Hayden hadn't swallowed that lump down completely, because her voice came out hoarse. She stepped to the side, and Sam hesitated for a moment before walking in. Hayden closed the door behind her. "I don't want to wake up Javi or Sofia."

Sam put the container down on the hand basin. "Come here."

Hayden stayed near the door, feeling raw and exposed, arms crossed over her chest. "I can do it."

"Are you really that stubbornly independent?"

"And you're not?" That was childish. Sam's expression showed she thought so too. The silence carried on until Hayden dropped her arms. "Sorry." She stepped forward and turned sideways to face Sam, her hip digging into the basin.

Sam didn't acknowledge that. Instead, she placed her fingers under Hayden's chin. Applying a little pressure, she tilted Hayden's face toward the light, her gaze intent on Hayden's lip. They were a few feet away from where Hayden had been, just hours before, thinking of those hands. Heat crept into Hayden's cheek.

"It's split, but not too badly, though it's swollen a lot since you were in the kitchen." Sam's voice was low, clearly conscious of not waking anyone else up.

Her thumb brushed the edge of Hayden's bottom lip. It was so gentle, and Hayden felt so fragile after everything, that she thought she felt something crack open in her chest. The urge to let herself give in to the sobs building inside her welled up, and Hayden clenched her jaw to push it down.

Without removing her right hand, Sam pulled out a piece of the gauze and dabbed at Hayden's chin, cleaning up some of the blood. It was shockingly cold, the kind that brought relief. She dropped that piece in the sink and took another, this time holding it against her lip. Relief spread through Hayden's mouth. For the first time since Sam had touched Hayden, her gaze flicked upward. This near, with a mere foot between them and Sam's hand cradling her face, it felt too intimate, too close. Hayden's fingers clenched against her own T-shirt, the urge to pull Sam toward her so intense. She wanted to drop her forehead against Sam's chest, to cling to something, anyone that could drive out this painful throb in her stomach, this feeling of rejection or grief or whatever was crawling along her skin.

Sam broke the eye contact as she glanced back to Hayden's lip. Finally, Hayden took in a breath.

"How does it look?" she murmured.

"It'll be fine." Sam's voice had a catch in it, and her gaze stayed on Hayden's lip after that. She changed out the gauze for new ones, fresh and cold. "I'll leave you with that one and go clean these ones up." Her hand fell away, and Hayden felt the loss immediately, her own coming up to hold the gauze against her lip.

"I can clean them up."

Sam shook her head as she put the dirty gauze in the container and picked it up. "No, you take the pill and go to sleep. It'll only take a second."

And she left. Hayden stood for a moment, aching for something she didn't have a word for. Eventually, she dropped the gauze in the trash can and took the pill Sam had left for her, cupping her hand under the faucet to rinse and spit a few times before finally swallowing it. Her lip didn't look much better, but she seemed less creepy without the red around her mouth. Her eyes were weirdly bright and Hayden turned, not wanting to stare at herself anymore.

Sam wasn't back in the bedroom, and Hayden got into the bed, pulling the blankets up and curling onto her side. That exposed feeling wouldn't go away, so she tugged the blankets up more until they were almost over her head. It was at least ten minutes later that Hayden heard the door open. She didn't move, pretending to be asleep. The light clicked off, and the bed dipped as Sam got in it.

"Hayden." Hayden didn't answer. "Hayden, I know you're awake."

"How?" Hayden whispered back.

"Well I didn't really, but now I do."

"Smart-ass."

"Are—are you okay?"

The words felt ready to fall apart in the air.

"I'm fine." Hayden had to be fine. "Though I hope my lip makes me look badass."

It sounded weak, even to her.

"Is everything a joke to you?" Sam didn't sound accusatory, more inquisitive.

The words were too big, though, in the darkness of the room, with no way for Hayden to deflect them with a grin. They pressed down on her and felt as if they were flying away from her, all at the same time.

"Hayden." She'd never heard her name said so often. "You're shaking. I can feel it."

And maybe she was a little. There was a shuffling sound, and a warm hand brushed over her hip before falling against it more firmly. Nothing more. And Hayden wasn't sure if she could have handled anything more, anyway. But strangely, it was enough to feel like something was being slid back together. Bit by bit, she felt herself relax, the trembling she hadn't even really noticed fading until she was still.

It was with the warmth on her hip that she finally fell asleep, the throbbing in her lip dissipating along with the one behind her ribs.

CHAPTER 16

Hayden woke up comfortable. And with a sore mouth. It took a moment, as she ran her tongue over her puffy lip, to remember the night before.

She kept her eyes closed at the memory.

Why was she so warm?

An arm was draped over her waist. Hayden's eyes shot open. The dim light spilling in from the curtains was enough to make her slam her eyes closed. Someone was lying along her back. *Sam* was lying along her back. Bit by bit, Hayden's brain was starting to catch up. She relaxed—Sam had been so thoughtful the night before.

Did Sam pity her?

The idea of that was enough to make Hayden want to hide. It was why she didn't share this side of her life. She'd had enough pity thanks to her father. Feeling people's eyes on her, feeling bad for her, always left a bad taste in her mouth.

But then Sam had cupped her chin, her hand soothing Hayden's lip with that cold gauze, and Hayden hadn't seen anything resembling pity.

Soft air was puffing against her neck, steady and slow. It felt nice, like her frazzled brain was being soothed.

The second Hayden shifted, Sam woke up like a ninja, her hands flailing. Instantly, she was half sitting up, as if prepared to take out bad guys. Hayden rolled partially onto her back as Sam looked blearily around and down at Hayden, pressed into Sam's hip.

"Morning." Hayden didn't dare smirk, what with her lip and all.

Sam's hair was sticking up all on one side, the other completely flat. Her cheeks were flushed, and she still looked half-asleep, even after her weird adrenaline-filled startle. She glanced down at their bodies next to each other and flushed even more. "Sorry. You woke me up at some point and seemed upset. This helped."

Well, that was embarrassing. Hayden's cheeks burned. "Oh. Thanks."

Sam shuffled so she was back on her own side of the bed, the space between them cooling rapidly, and Hayden had the weird swooping in her belly she got when she missed someone.

"It's okay." She wasn't looking at Hayden, though. "How are you?"

"I'm fine. I'm sorry about last night."

Then Sam did make eye contact, her eyes vibrantly green. "Why?"

The question made Hayden half-shrug and push up so she was sitting against the headboard. She drew her knees up to her chest, linking her fingers around them. "Because it was…"

"A lot?"

Hayden nodded.

"You know I'm a neurosurgeon? I've seen much worse things than that."

"Yeah, but that's for work."

"Yes, it is. But you don't have to be sorry." She paused. "I think you handled it very well."

That wasn't true. Hayden's stomach filled with lead at the thought. "I really didn't. I made it worse. I know you've seen that, and more, before, but so have I. I deal with worse every day. I should have de-escalated it."

"None of those patients were your mother."

And that was what made all the difference. Something froze in her every time something like that happened. As if all her training and knowledge flew out the window, and she was left unarmed and hurting and completely unsure of what to do. She *should* know how to deal with her mother's behavior. Of all her family, she should be the best at it.

"True," Hayden said anyway as she picked at some lint on the blanket. "I still hate that you saw it."

"Why?"

How did she put it into words? That this was Hayden's secret, her burden. She didn't need someone feeling sorry for her. Especially someone who understood the repercussions of this disease as thoroughly as Sam would. "I don't…I don't want…"

"You don't want pity."

Hayden cleared her throat. "How did you know that?"

"Because I wouldn't either. And I don't pity you. I—" Sam looked incredibly awkward, her gaze flitting away before settling somewhere over Hayden's shoulder. "I admire you for doing what you do for your family. For everything you've told me."

"Oh."

They were both silent for a minute. Hayden heard the water running down the corridor. Sam admired *her*? Hayden? When all Hayden felt was that she was making a mess of everything with her family?

"Still." Hayden swallowed and looked at her knees. "I should be doing more."

"Why?" The question was sharp, and Hayden looked up.

"Because she's my mother. I should be here."

"That's absurd." Sam's gaze didn't waver.

Hayden straightened. "Well, it's not. Of course I feel I should do more. I live so far away, and I've left the rest of my family to deal with all of this."

"And what was the alternative? All of your family giving up everything? Would your mother have wanted that?"

That made Hayden pause. All her mother had ever wanted was for Hayden to go to college like she'd wanted and get the job she'd dreamed of. How long ago did all that seem? But Hayden had forgotten all of that. She'd only thought, really, of what her family wanted. Of their expectations, and her expectations of herself.

"I—I don't think she'd have wanted me to leave all the responsibility with my family, though."

"How is it all with them? How much money do you send them each month?"

"I—" A lot. Hayden sent them a lot. "That's not the point."

"Who pays for the assistant who is here several times a week?"

"Well, me." Hayden hated someone using logic on her.

"Who helps to keep paying the mortgage on this house?"

"How did you know I was doing that?"

"I didn't until now. I assumed. Who pays the bills?"

"I don't pay all of them. My sister works part-time."

"And has a child."

"I—"

"Hayden, some people help with time. Some with time invested to make money. One isn't worth more, when you consider what each provides."

Hayden swallowed again, more heavily this time. Sam's knee was very close to Hayden's toes under the blanket. Had it always been there? Now she'd noticed, she couldn't *un*-notice. Which was absurd, because minutes ago their whole bodies had been pressed together.

The door flew open, and Javi stood in his Superman pajamas with his hands on his hips. A cape was even attached.

"You've been sleeping for *hours!*" he exclaimed.

Hayden grinned. "Hours and hours?"

"Yes!"

"So were you," Sam said.

Javi opened his mouth, then closed it. Finally, he said, "But now I'm awake."

"So we have to be?" Sam asked.

"Yeah."

Sam almost looked confused. "Oh."

"Come on. It's breakfast time. And Grandma has a lump on her head. What happened to your lip?" Javi was evaluating her mouth.

"Uh—I hurt it." Hayden didn't know how much Sofia told him.

"Did Grandma do it?" His little voice had dropped lower, his dark eyes all warm worry. He crept farther into the room.

"It was an accident, Javi."

He finally crawled onto the bed. "She hurt Abuela one time. And Mami." He was almost whispering, his small brow knitted together. "It's always an accident." His lisp made everything sound almost sweet. Hayden dropped her knees and held her arms out, and he clambered into her lap, straddling her, gaze still on her lip. "Does it hurt?"

Hayden smiled and it stung. A lot. "Nope. Well, a bit."

"There's blood." He sounded aghast. Blood was serious. Once he'd cut his foot and hadn't noticed until someone asked him what happened. He'd looked down and started screaming, hysterical.

"It's fine. Just a little."

He put his hands on either side of her face, surprisingly gentle. Hayden could feel Sam's eyes on her. "Mami kisses things better real good. Want me to ask her?"

"That'd be great, thanks."

"Or Sam can kiss it better." He turned his head, his hands still on Hayden's cheeks. "That's your job, right?"

Hayden was grinning, the sting in her lip be damned. She turned her head, huffing a laugh at Sam's raised eyebrows. A weird tingling started in her stomach at the memory that last night Hayden had thought, for a short second, about kissing Sam in the bathroom, even with no one present to put on a show for. Hayden was always needy when emotional.

"Yeah, Sam." Hayden had to tone down her grin; it was hurting too much now. "Isn't that your job?"

"You're hilarious."

"What's that?" Javi asked.

"It means funny."

Javi looked at Hayden again. "You are pretty funny."

"Thanks, Javi. At least *you* said it like you mean it."

"I want to watch TV now." As he always did, he announced it like it was the most important thing they would hear all day.

"Did Mami say you could?"

He seemed to find the sleeve of her shirt very interesting, his small fingers hooking into the material as he stared at it. "Yes."

"Hm. Really?"

"Yes."

"*Really*, really?"

He liked to lie sometimes. He was just useless at it. Sofia liked to joke that he got that from Hayden. A smile was slowly curling up his lips. "Yes."

"I don't think so." And as punishment, she tickled him, catching him unawares and getting her fingers under his arms. Throwing himself backward over her legs, he squealed. Warmth spread throughout her chest at the sound of his laughter, high and gutsy and completely unrestrained. He'd broken the serious atmosphere that had overtaken them, and they eventually untangled themselves from the blanket, and Sam headed for a shower.

When Hayden walked into the kitchen, Abuela was standing over the stove and Sofia was at the table, a cup of coffee on the table in front of her. The smell of it was all in the room, and Hayden instantly headed to the over to make herself one, Javi following her.

"Morning."

Sofia looked up. "Morning." A shadow crossed her face. "How's your lip? Abuela told me what happened."

"It's fine. I iced it and took a pill."

"Sam didn't do her job." Javi stood on the footstool kept in the kitchen for him, eyes hardly coming up over the edge of the countertop as he spoke to his mother.

"What job was that?" Sofia asked.

"She didn't kiss it better. It's her job."

Sofia chuckled. "I'm sure she did last night."

Javi looked up at Hayden, who was next to him and pouring beautiful, hot coffee into a mug. "Did she?"

"You bet." Hayden kept her eyes down, adding a splash of milk. "That's why it barely hurts now."

"Good. Can I have more cereal?"

"You had a very big bowl already." Abuela stepped up beside Javi, her arm reaching behind his head so that her hand lay comfortingly on Hayden's back. "How can you want more?"

"I'm growing."

Javi absorbed everything around him. Everything they said would be spewed out at them later, often in some context that didn't really fit.

"*Sí, verdad.*" Abuela sounded completely amused. "*¡Okay! Más cereales para tí.*"

His eyes lit up at being told he could have more, and he ran to get his bowl, ducking under Abuela's arm.

"Where's Mom?" Hayden asked, stirring her coffee.

"Sleeping in her chair."

Hayden looked down at Abuela. Short and small and never changing. "Did you get much sleep?"

Bags sat under her eyes. "She go to sleep after two hours. I slept in there with her. You can go sit with her?"

Hayden shook her head, looking back down at her coffee. "I'll let her sleep."

"Hm. *Sí*, okay."

There was the sound of something spilling all over the floor, and both Hayden and Abuela turned in time to see Javi standing, holding a box of cereal over his bowl, wide-eyed and surrounded by cereal all over the floor.

"Oops."

~ ~ ~

Hayden took Javi to his soccer game with Sam. They watched him head-butt the ground by accident and bounce back up with grass in his hair, laughing wildly.

"This is like watching rabbits on speed play soccer." Sam's voice was deadpan, and Hayden laughed so hard she snorted. Sam looked sideways at her, a half smile playing on her lips.

They left the game with no idea who had won; none of the kids seemed to really care. Three of them had started a dance competition in the middle of the field halfway through, and two had sat in the corner of the goal throwing sticks at each other.

They took Javi for ice cream, and Hayden watched Sam, constantly amused. It seemed like Sam was never sure what to do with Javi, how to take his blunt honesty and weird views of the world. But he responded to that. When she answered like she would to an adult, he only asked more questions and sat closer and closer to her, his sticky fingers playing with a bracelet around her wrist or plucking at the strap of her bag. Hayden listened to them chatter—or rather, let Javi chatter at Sam—and let everything from last night ebb away. Her mother had still been sleeping when they'd left, and Hayden was trying to shake the nerves that had settled over her at the thought of seeing her again. It was absurd, because her mother wouldn't remember any of it at all.

When they got home, it was late afternoon and Javi was crashing. They ushered him inside, and Hayden's elbows brushed with Sam's as she helped Javi take his coat off. It was weirdly domestic. Sofia came down the stairs, rubbing Javi's back when he rammed into her for a hug.

"Don't you three all look cute."

"We're an absolute picture." Hayden hung their coats up. "Javi scored a goal."

"I did!"

Sofia grinned down at him. "Awesome. Why do you have a green forehead?"

"I face-planted. Tía Hayden told me that word."

Sofia brushed her fingers over his hair, picking out bits of grass Hayden had left there because it looked funny. "It's a pretty good word for some of the stuff you do."

"Can I watch TV?"

Sofia recovered quickly. "All right. Just for an hour."

"Someone help me cook! *Por favor!*" Abuela's voice came from the kitchen as Sofia took Javi upstairs to her room where she had a television.

Hayden looked at Sam. "Coming?"

Sam followed her down the hallway. Right before the door, fingers brushed hers and Hayden glanced down as they entwined their hands together. Right.

Swallowing, Hayden looked forward again. This whole intensely faking it thing was getting exhausting. She was looking forward to getting back to New York and being able to just *be* in their own space.

Yet, at the same time, the comfort was nice.

The kitchen was warm, and vegetables littered the counter, all types of colors. The smell of cooking beef hit her, making Hayden's mouth water. Her mother sat at the table, her book of puzzles in hand.

"*Buenas tardes, Abuela.*"

"*Mis amores.* How was Javi and his game?" Abuela walked over to them, an apron on and a spoon covered in some kind of sauce in her hand.

"It was…interesting?"

Abuela cackled. "This is the word. One time, one little girl just laid down and slept. Right there."

"But he seems to like it."

"We will see. He is distracted—" she waved the spoon around in the air from place to place, sauce flying off "—all the time."

"You said you needed help?" Hayden asked.

"Yes. Come." She walked back around the counter.

Hayden hovered a second. "Hi, Mamá."

Her mother didn't look up, and Hayden felt Sam side-eye her.

"Paola?" Sam tried.

Her mother looked up.

"Hello."

She didn't say a word, but went back to her puzzles. A definite bruise had bloomed on her forehead, the white of the Steri-Strips stark against her skin. Hayden, giving up, went to stand with Abuela.

"Can I help?" Sam asked.

"No. Sit." Abuela slid a cup of tea across to the opposite side of the counter, and Sam sat on a barstool there.

"Thank you."

For a while, they puttered in the kitchen, chopping and slicing, adding flavors and spices to pots of food. Mostly it was quiet except for the sound of chopping knives on wood or bubbling from a pot. The smell of beef got stronger and wove with the smell of the sauce. Occasionally, Abuela hummed a song, and whenever she did, Hayden's mother would look up and eye her, sometimes smiling blankly. Eventually, she stood up.

"I have to go for a walk."

Hayden paused, a tomato in her hand. "Where to, Paola?"

"I have to do the shopping. My girls get home from school soon. I need to have it done so I can fix their snack."

Hayden smiled softly. "They'll like that."

Hayden's mother's look was back to fragile. It would have broken Hayden's heart if she let it. "They love their afternoon snack."

A lump had swelled in Hayden's throat. "They do."

She couldn't do this. She should offer to take her outside and walk with her. She knew that. That's why she was here, really. For Javi and her sister and Abuela to get a break. But also for her mother, who wouldn't even remember she'd been here. Hayden had a sudden longing in her stomach for New York—for Luce and Frank and work. For a life she'd buried herself in to keep her distracted from the one she was losing here.

"I need my bag." Her mother started walking around the table, not as unsteady as the night before. "I need to go to the supermarket now. And then my mother is coming over for dinner."

Abuela hummed. "What are you cooking?"

"Beef. She loves beef."

Hayden couldn't look at Sam. She went back to the tomato, dicing it to join the bowl she was slowly filling.

"I'll go with her," Sam said.

Hayden looked up at Sam. "You don't have to do that."

"You're cooking." Though she had a look in her eyes that made Hayden think Sam was offering for more reasons than that. "I don't mind."

Hayden looked back down, guilt flaring in her stomach.

"You are sure, Samantha?"

"Completely. Where's the supermarket?"

Abuela gave her directions, adding, "Let her shop. It will help. She likes to go, and sometimes it's easier than trying to convince her not to. There is money in her bag."

Sam turned to Paola, who was wringing her hands. "Can I come with you? I have some things I need to buy."

"If you must. I don't have much time, though."

"That's fine."

And Sam followed Hayden's mother out, trying to convince her to put a jacket on.

"I like her." Abuela's eyes followed Sam. "She is good."

Hayden nodded, grabbing another tomato. "She is."

Hayden was starting to get that.

~ ~ ~

By the time they sat down to dinner, which Hayden's mother refused to eat, it was dark outside. The meal was good, as it always was, and that longing in Hayden's stomach for New York was melded with the one of missing things from here, even as she experienced them. Sam sat close at the table, their shoulders rubbing and knees together at random times.

A show for everyone. The happy, newly-married couple. When Sofia was watching them, eyes hard over her glass, Sam dropped a kiss under Hayden's ear, soft and barely there and leaving that ache behind that had hit her the night before in the bathroom.

It didn't go away.

After everyone had passed over their empty plates to Hayden, Abuela took Javi to the bath. Hayden started washing the dishes with Sam, and as they finished, Sofia came in from the living room where she'd been with their mother.

"Hayds? Can I speak to you?"

Hayden looked to Sam.

"You go," Sam said. "I'll finish up."

"Are you sure?"

"It's almost done."

So, with that ache still in her chest, Hayden kissed her lips. She pulled away quickly, her cheeks warm, but Sam looked as she always did, calm. Hayden ignored the way her body wanted to move into the kiss more, to press along the length of Sam.

This weekend had *really* made Hayden needy.

Hayden followed Sofia out the back, sitting next to her on the porch swing that Hayden had spent hours in as a teenager, reading and sleeping after lunch. Outside was cooler than the warm kitchen, the air brushing along her arms, leaving goose bumps behind. When she shivered, Sofia grabbed the blanket left thrown over the back and threw it on top of both of them. Hayden shuffled closer, their shoulders rubbing. She could have breathed a sigh of relief for contact that wasn't wrapped up in confusion or layers of pretense. To be able to enjoy it without questioning all the consequences. They linked arms, and, with her foot, Hayden made the swing rock. The backyard was cast in shadows, the tree Sofia had fallen out of when they were small rustling in the breeze.

They used to sit like this in between their teenage bickering. The day after her father had left behind three broken people, they'd sat almost all night and tried to ignore the sobs in the house their mother futilely tried to hide.

That memory, among many, was one of the reasons Hayden avoided coming back.

"You wanted to talk?" she murmured.

"Are you okay?"

Hayden dropped her head on Sofia's shoulder. "I'm fine."

"How's your lip?"

"Sore."

"She doesn't mean it."

"I *know* that, Sofe."

Sofia sighed. "I know you know. Sorry. I didn't mean it like that."

They were already about to flare up at each other; it was biting at their words. A sharp edge.

"I know. I know, sorry too. Of course you didn't." Hayden tugged the arm that was through hers closer. "Sofia, we might need to talk about other solutions soon." Hayden felt her suck in a breath. "It's not fair to you all."

"We're not ready for that. We don't need to yet."

"But—"

"Hayden, you don't know. You're not *here*. You can't come once every six months and say this stuff."

Hayden straightened up, angling her body to look at her sister, trying not to let the anger that always jumped up so quickly take over. "Maybe that's why I can say it. Because I'm fresh eyes."

And soon, Hayden would have money to pay for all of that.

The look on Sofia's face was almost anguished. "You get a few days' window. We know, Hayds. We know her and what it's like. What she's like. But she really has been better with the new meds, and you and I both know that once she's in a home, she's going to go downhill so much faster."

Hayden didn't know if she could say it; she could barely think it. But maybe that was the kindest thing for all of them. It left her sick at the thought. And she pushed it down, away, because what kind of daughter thought that?

"Maybe we need to talk about it in a few months, then?" Hayden said instead.

"Will you answer my calls?"

Hayden managed to resist the urge to squirm, though she did look away, back into the yard. "Yes."

"Because I've tried to call to talk about this stuff, if something new has happened, or after a particularly bad morning."

"Why don't you tell me when I call you back?"

"Sometimes it's days later! And by then, other things have happened, and it's easier to just move on from it."

"Okay." Hayden looked at her sister again. "Okay. I'll try harder."

"Thank you. You know—you know I do know how much you do?"

Hayden swallowed and shrugged.

"I do." Sofia looked so earnest. "I do know. I know you gave up your career and you send so much money and make it possible for us to care for Mamá from home, like we all wanted. I know I volunteered to come in then."

"Thank you." Hayden's voice was tight. "I'm so glad you wanted to do it, because I don't think I could have. And I know Steven left you, and I know you're raising Javi alone and do so much for Mamá."

Sofia wrapped her arms around her, and Hayden wound hers around her sister's back, hugging her tight, their chins tucked into each other's shoulders. They stayed that way, close and hugging and unable to say anymore. When Sofia pulled back, her eyes were glistening in the low light washing in from the kitchen window behind them.

"So, Sam."

Hayden gave a strangled laugh and swiped at her eyes. "Yeah, Sam."

The lies. She didn't want them infecting this moment.

"She's nice."

"She is."

"She's older than you."

Hayden gasped and threw her hand over her heart. "No? Is she?"

Sofia rolled her eyes. "Okay, that was stupid. I still don't get why you married her, though."

"It made sense at the time."

"And now?"

"Still makes sense."

"Okay. Good. Does she know about Dad?"

Hayden sighed and sat back against the swing seat, moving them back and forth with her foot again. "No. Not everything. Telling her all about this was hard enough."

Sofia looked at her strangely. "But she's your wife. Shouldn't you be sharing that stuff with her naturally?"

"You and I both know that sharing stuff takes time."

"True. But I still think Steven and I could have been okay if we'd talked more."

"I still don't like him for leaving you."

"We were unhappy, Hayden. Before Mamá, even. Before Javi."

"Okay." Hayden threw up her hands. It really wasn't her job to argue that. But she could still not like the man for leaving her sister. Sofia was awesome—also infuriating, but only Hayden was allowed to think that. "At least he's a great dad."

"Exactly. He let me have Javi this weekend because you were coming, even though it was his turn."

"That was...nice of him, I suppose."

Sofia chuckled, the sound finally easing some of the residual tension in the air. "From you, that's high praise for him."

"It's all he's getting. Tell him thanks, though. I've missed Javi."

"He misses you."

They rocked in silence again, arms tight together. A cricket started somewhere in the corner of the yard.

"Mami!"

Sofia sighed, standing up and dropping the blanket back over Hayden. "Duty calls." She turned, her arms crossed. "In a few months, let's talk. Abuela is still coming around to the whole thing."

"Okay. And I'll answer the phone."

"Good."

"Mami!"

Sofia groaned and walked inside.

It wasn't any cooler, but Hayden pulled the blanket tighter over her legs, something comforting in it. She pushed hard once with her foot, then pulled her leg up so she could sit cross-legged.

She stayed there for a while, in her childhood backyard, awash in the last few days. Tomorrow, they were flying out early, and she could fall back into work, see Luce, and tease them about Clemmie. She could cuddle Frank, if he'd let her. He would be cranky for days about being left with only Sam's cleaner dropping by to feed him. She should also go around to her old apartment and make a token check-in. The lease would be up soon.

The screen door opened, and Hayden turned, expecting Abuela, but instead Sam stood there in oversized clothes. She'd never looked so...soft. Even outside of work she dressed with a sense of style Hayden herself had never mastered. But here, in old jeans and a light sweater that looked well-worn, she seemed homey.

"Hey," Hayden said.

"Hi."

"Want to sit?"

Sam hesitated. Finally, she stepped forward. "Okay."

Hayden held the edge of the blanket up and put her feet back on the ground. The air was so cold, and when Sam sat next to her, heat flooded Hayden's side. She dropped the blanket back over them and started rocking the swing like before.

"Your grandmother is very nice."

"She is."

"I think she thinks I'm starving."

"She likes to feed people. Like all grandparents."

Sam was strangely silent at that, her expression bordering on cold.

"Are you okay, Sam?"

"Yes, fine. How's your lip?" As she turned to face Hayden, her gaze dropped to Hayden's mouth, her face close.

Hayden swallowed heavily. This was ridiculous. She needed to get back to New York where everything made sense.

"It's okay. Feels less swollen."

"Good." Sam was still staring at her lip.

"Does it look worse?"

"Just sore." Her voice was low. Was that concern? Sam looked back out to the yard, and Hayden let herself watch her.

"Are you really okay?"

"I am." She cleared her throat. "Your grandmother told me something I don't know if you wanted me to know."

Hayden sighed and looked back out at the yard. "About my dad?"

"Yes."

"When?"

"Yesterday when she made me tea, after we arrived."

That was fast, even for Abuela. "She would have thought you knew already."

"I don't think she told me all of it. Mostly that he walked out on you all when you were sixteen. Is that why Luce joked about you hating marriage?"

Hayden shrugged, their shoulders rubbing. "I know it sounds immature, but I just… I don't see the point of it."

"Except for money."

Hayden snorted and turned to stare at Sam, who had a crinkling around her eyes. "Oh, you're funny again."

"As I said, sometimes I am."

"I think you're funnier than I realized."

Sam bumped her shoulder against Hayden's. "Good."

They were silent for a second, rocking slowly. "Dad left us behind when I was sixteen because Mamá found out he'd had an entire secret life. He had another family, another wife."

Hayden could swear Sam inhaled sharply through her nose. She couldn't look at her though, not when talking about this.

"Hayden…" Her voice cracked as she trailed off.

"He was never away on business trips like he told us. He was with *them*."

The memory was like acid in her chest, a burning pain, full of shame and anger and betrayal. Even now, she still felt overwhelmed by protectiveness for her mom, who'd been left behind, humiliated, and devastated.

"I didn't know."

"No one does. I don't talk about it. It was… Everything was a mess for a long time. Their marriage had never been legally valid, because he'd married the other woman first. He let Mom keep the house but just…left. Because I was over sixteen, he didn't even have to pay child support anymore."

"And you all never knew?"

Hayden turned so fast she hurt her neck, anger biting at her throat. "Of course not."

"I was only asking, Hayden."

With a deep breath, Hayden said, "Sorry." One day, Hayden would learn to take a breath *before* reacting.

"It's okay."

"It's just… It sounds like a bad TV soap opera story."

"A telenovela."

Hayden gave a laugh with no real mirth. "Yeah. Thanks, Dad." She pushed the swing again with her foot. "I have three half siblings out there, somewhere."

"Would you ever…"

"No."

The cricket started up again, a sound rooted in her childhood that she found herself missing in the city, at strange times, normally as sleep claimed her when all she could hear was traffic.

"Is that why you changed your last name?"

"Yes. I didn't want anything that linked me to him. I feel more connected to Pérez, anyway."

"But he gave you Hayden?"

Hayden sighed, the night wrapping around them tighter out here, their voices low and this conversation too intimate to feel entirely comfortable. But Sam's shoulder was warm, and that cricket didn't stop. "Yeah. But mom liked it too, plus it felt like *mine*. Everyone called me it. Besides, it was the last name I wanted gone. The name he had with his *other* family."

Sam just hummed, and the swing rocked.

"I need to forgive him."

For a second, Hayden thought Sam wasn't going to answer. But she said, after a long pause, "Sometimes parents don't deserve your forgiveness. But you need to do it for yourself."

"He left her brokenhearted."

"Not just her."

Well, that was true. "He had a secret other family our entire lives. And then left us behind to be with them."

Sam turned to stare her right in the eye, her look frank and bare in the night. "It doesn't mean the childhood you remember wasn't real."

Heat crawled along Hayden's neck. "He made it not real. He was never working away, everything was a lie. And then when he had to make a choice, he chose them."

"I'm sorry."

Hayden rocked them more, the swing creaking. "I want to be back in New York."

"Tomorrow."

On a whim, Hayden dropped her head on Sam's shoulder. Maybe it wasn't the smartest idea for their increasingly weird relationship, but it was hard to care right then. Sam tensed for a split second, before, ever so slowly, relaxing. And Hayden rocked them, letting the sound it made settle over everything else.

CHAPTER 17

"Did your grandmother give her the third degree?"

Luce looked far too delighted at the idea. Biting back a smile—not literally, because her lip still hurt—Hayden sank into her chair near the coffee cart.

"If you must know, yes."

Luce paused mid-sip. "Oh, I wish I'd seen that. It would have been magical."

"You barely know Abuela."

"I've spoken to her a few times when you were on a video call. It's enough to get a taste, believe me."

"True."

"I love that woman. She's pure spunk."

"That she is. Now, Luce." Hayden sounded evilly delighted, she knew, but she'd waited all morning to ask this. "What is that?"

Luce scrunched their brow. "What?"

"That mark on your neck." Hayden's grin was hurting her but she didn't care.

"Nothing." Luc's hand went straight to their collar and tugged. "Absolutely nothing."

"Really? Nothing?" Hayden worked hard to keep her voice low. "Because I saw it this morning in the locker room, and I realized you didn't message me the entire weekend. That never happens."

"To be honest Hayden, I'm insulted you didn't realize that until then." Luce scrunched down in their chair.

"You are not. Don't try to change the subject. You're covered in hickeys."

It felt so good, after the weekend with her family, to be laughing. Even if it hurt her lip. To be teasing a friend. For everything to feel easy again. She had to try really hard to not feel bad that this was why she couldn't live among that complicated home life. Her year with her fading mother had proven that.

"Hayden." Their voice was muffled in their cup. "They aren't hickeys. They're... um..."

"You don't even have anything prepared to defend yourself with. You totally had a sexed-up weekend." This was so much fun. "You were in bed all weekend and didn't even *think* about sending me a message to tease me about taking my wife home." Hayden's eyes widened. "The sex must have been *mind-blowing*."

Luce, pink in their cheeks, finally cracked a grin, their cup on the table. "If you must know… It really was."

Hayden held her hand up for a high five. "Awesome to hear."

"You're so gross." But Luce high-fived her over their coffees anyway.

"No. I'm just genuinely really happy for you."

And she was. Though something strange was in her stomach at the way Luce was looking now—happy. Besotted.

"Well, thanks. I really like her."

"So, what happened to going slow?"

"Oh, shut up, Hayden. We'd been on, like, five dates."

Hayden laughed, hands held up. "Your words about what you wanted, not mine."

"You're one to talk, *Mrs.* Married-In-A-Month."

"Touché."

The teasing atmosphere settled and Luce cocked their head. "Hayds?"

"Yeah?"

"Are you going to tell me what really happened to your lip?"

Hayden's heart skipped over, and she grabbed her cup. Anything to do with her hands. "I did tell you. I swear. It was no big deal."

"No, you told me that. That it was no big deal. Not what actually happened."

Thumb running along the rim of her cup, Hayden finally said, "I mentioned my mom wasn't well?" At Luce's nod, Hayden took in a deep breath before continuing. "It was an accident, I promise. And it was to do with that."

Hayden had spent so many years dancing around the topic of her mother. Never lying, but never telling the story either.

Luce's face was immediately filled with concern. "Are you okay?"

"I am. Promise."

"I thought that…"

"Sam?" Luce shrugged, and Hayden leaned over to squeeze their arm. "You're an awesome friend. No. Never. She was actually really amazing."

"Yeah?" Surprise elongated Luce's vowels. Hayden couldn't blame them.

"Yeah. I think this weekend would have been a lot harder without her."

And it was weird to not have to lie about that. Nice, but weird.

"I'm really glad to hear that." Luce smiled, wide and sincere. "Look at us. All happy and stuff."

"It's gross."

"It so is."

"Where's Clemmie?" Hayden asked Luce.

Luce took a sip of their coffee and sat back, sprawling in their chair.

"She's off today. She's at her photography class."

"She's a photography student?" That was pretty cool.

"Yeah, she's actually really good. I saw some of her work on the weekend."

Hayden smirked. "I bet you did."

Luce narrowed their eyes. "How old are you, exactly?"

"Get a good view of her work? Up close and *personal*?"

"Seriously? So are you fourteen now?"

"Fifteen." Hayden sipped her coffee. It burned her tongue, and she quickly put her cup back down. "Ow. Burning."

It was Luce's turn to smirk. "Karma."

"No, it wasn't. Anyway, tell me more. Does she exhibit? Use film? Digital? Does she do portraiture?"

"I had no idea you knew so much about photography."

"I literally used every phrase related to it that I know besides 'selfie.'" Hayden grinned sheepishly, taking a more cautious sip.

Luce snorted. "I should've known. She does this thing where she alters the photos into kind of these fantasy worlds. Like she immerses the real with fantasy?"

"Isn't there a name for that?"

"Probably?" Luce was avoiding Hayden's eye.

"Did she tell you that name?"

"I think so? Maybe she was only wearing my old T-shirt, and I was distracted."

Hayden laughed, loudly from her belly. "Well, it sounds interesting. Maybe if she does an exhibit I can come?"

"You totally should. And, you know, bring Thomson. Your wife."

"Thanks."

"Did I hear my name?"

Hayden swiveled her head and grinned when she saw Sam standing near them, her hands in her lab coat pockets. No scrub cap today. Pens in her breast pocket. It must have been a consultation day with no surgery; she'd hate that. Sam seemed to prefer emergencies and days with back-to-back surgeries. It made for less patient interaction.

"You did." Luce smiled, though less warmly than Hayden had. Still, it was something. "My, uh, friend, may have a photography show on soon, and if I go, I was just saying you two should come along."

"Okay. I like photography."

Hayden managed to stop the surprised *you do?* from escaping her mouth. "Great. We can all go." Hayden paused. "Do you have a break now?"

"No." Sam indicated with her head to the coffee cart. "I was able to find time to get a coffee to take back to the consult with me."

Hayden eyed her. "Have you had lunch?"

"Yes."

"You're lying."

Sam was very interested in watching the coffee cart. "No."

"You won't even look at me."

She should have known better than to say that. Sam simply looked her straight in the eye. "Satisfied?"

"No. I bet you just ate a candy bar."

Sam said nothing. One point to Hayden.

"Knew it."

"I'll take a sandwich away with me too. Happy now?"

"Yes. I find that acceptable."

Sam rolled her eyes upward. "Highlight of my day. I was going to bring something home for dinner. Will you want some?"

"Sounds great."

"There's my coffee. Bye, Luce." She cleared her throat almost awkwardly. "Uh, you should really come over for dinner soon, with your friend."

Sam left, and Hayden picked her coffee back up, watching Sam grab her coffee and walk away, a sandwich in her hand. Good. When she turned back, Luce was giving her a *look*.

"What?" Hayden asked.

"You two are really domestic."

Had they been? Wow, they kind of had.

"Well," Hayden cleared her throat and tried to hide her own surprise. "We *are* married."

"You look really happy. That smile when you saw her?"

Hayden felt supremely uncomfortable and couldn't even really say why.

"Well," Hayden's thumb flicked at the ring on her finger, pressing against the smooth band and moving it around, "I am."

"Good," Luce said, though something still wasn't entirely right about the look in their eye. "I'm glad."

It was a relief to disappear from that hairy eyeball and back to her shift. It had been hard saying goodbye to her family the day before, but a relief to get on the plane and head back to her life. But the evening back home in the apartment had been strange. With no audience to cater for, it was as if Hayden and Sam fell out of step and didn't know how to be with each other anymore. Sam had disappeared in the late afternoon, and only then had Hayden relaxed, flopping on the sofa to watch television with Frank glaring at her from the other end.

Yet, back at the hospital with Luce watching, they seemed to pick it right back up again.

That night, after eating take-out on the couch, Sam disappeared for the evening. When Hayden heard her come back when she was already in bed, she resisted the urge to get up and ask her what she'd been up to. Had she seen her brother? Her mysterious family?

Instead she rolled onto her side and tried to pretend that the two nights of having someone in bed with her hadn't shown her how much she'd missed it.

~ ~ ~

Cold bit at Hayden's ears as she ducked into the building and walked as fast as she could up the stairs. By the time she reached her door, she was warm but huffing. It was the price she paid to stop feeling so cold. Her shift had gone quickly, but she was still glad to be going home. After a week back home, Frank would finally have forgiven her for being away, and she could have a long, hot shower. And eat something. Sam had appeared mid-shift and said she was bringing home Thai for dinner, and Hayden's mouth flooded with saliva at the thought. She only had another day shift before she somehow went back onto night shift, and she was going to enjoy feeling like part of the living while she could.

She walked through the door and stopped dead. She blinked too, but that didn't help. Despite all her efforts, Jon was still standing in the kitchen, smiling at her from over the fridge door.

"Hey," he said.

"Uh, hi."

She kept staring at him as he pulled out a beer and popped it open, closing the door after he did so. He turned and saw she hadn't moved.

"Everything okay?" he asked.

"Well, you're in my home?"

"My sister's home."

"Okay. But I live here." Hayden finally closed the door behind her and walked through, dropping her bag on the counter. She sat down on one of the barstools opposite him.

"You do. But it's my sister's place, and I..." he paused while he fished a hand into his pocket and pulled out a set of keys, jangling them in front of her "...have these."

He grinned again, and Hayden was slapped with how much he could be a blond-haired, jovial version of his sister. Their eyes were the same bright green. How had she not twigged right away?

"Well, shouldn't you give a warning?" She glanced at his beer. "Also, isn't it rude to take a beer—one of mine, by the way, as if your sister has such good taste in beer—and not offer your sister-in-law one?"

He winked and slid his over, which he hadn't sipped from yet. She scooped it up, rescuing it before it fell off the edge, and he grabbed another from the fridge as he said, "*Fake* sister-in-law."

"Not on paper."

"True." He popped his beer open and stared at her candidly.

Hayden took a swig and let him stare. Yeah, he really *was* like his sister. He had that same even look, intense and difficult to pluck apart. Except there was something lighter about him in the set of his shoulders, a glint in his eye Sam didn't quite have. Was it youth? He was twenty-one, after all. Or was it personality? He was obviously a bit of a joker, someone who liked to pull easy laughter out of people. Before, Hayden would have said Sam was the absolute opposite of that. However, now she knew it was that she was dry—witty in a way that was easy to miss. That she didn't show to just anyone.

Hayden got to see it.

At that thought, she almost wanted to squirm under his gaze.

"So. What are you doing with yourself, Jon?"

"Bit of this, bit of that. By the way, your cat hates me."

"He tends to do that."

"So why do you look so delighted?"

Hayden shrugged. "Actually, he loves Sam. It's weird. He used to only like me—well, conditionally. But I guess it's good to know that he's not just abandoning me for anyone that walks through the door."

"So you're happy to hear I got hissed at?"

"Completely."

Jon raised his beer. "I like you. You're a little evil."

"Why, thank you."

"Sam had a cat, years ago. A tiny little thing. She was really sweet."

"What happened?"

"Her shit ex-girlfriend moved out and took her with her. I think Sam was more devastated about the cat than the breakup."

Hayden laughed as she sipped her beer, the liquid fizzing into her stomach. She put her elbows on the cold countertop. It was like getting a glimpse through someone else's window, to get facts like this about Sam. Sneaky glimpses she really loved but shouldn't. "I get that. No question, I'd be more upset if someone took Frank than if they left me."

Movement from the corner of her eye caught her attention. Frank was walking in from the corridor, eyes narrowed at Jon, who narrowed his own right back.

"Really? You'd be more upset?" he asked Hayden with a final scowl at Frank. "I can't really see why."

"Well, he's not like that with me." Hayden made a kissy noise at Frank. "Come here."

He turned his gaze on her for a second. Hayden made the kissing noise again. His ear twitched, and Hayden thought she'd won. That was short lived, as he turned away and stalked back down the hallway. She sighed and looked back at Jon, who was biting back a laugh.

"Yeah, he seems great," he said.

"Shut up."

He laughed loudly, and Hayden took another sip, grinning.

"So," he said, "you fake-married my sister."

"Yup."

"And I'm the only one who knows it's all a sham?"

Hayden sighed. "Yup."

He cocked his head, so much like his sister that Hayden wondered if he'd learned that from her or if it was all genetics. "That bother you?"

"I hate lying to everyone," she said.

"Couldn't you let them all in on it?"

"That'd eventually ruin it. One person knows, who tells someone, and so on."

He nodded, thoughtful. "Yeah. You normally an honest person?"

"I think it's the easiest way to be in the long run. Aren't you?"

There was nothing joking about his expression now. He sipped his beer slowly. "I learned the value of lies young. My entire family did. It's *not* lying that screwed everything up."

What was that supposed to mean? Hayden leaned forward so far she almost fell off her chair. His expression had darkened. Something clouded the look in his eye. He looked sad, Hayden realized. Sad and small and young. "Wanna talk about it?"

"You really don't know?"

"I—well, no."

"Huh." His nail flicked over the label on his beer, but his eyes stayed trained on her. "I mean, my sister is *really* good at the keeping-everything-close-to-her-chest thing. I thought I was good? But I still thought she would have given you something."

"Not a thing." Hayden felt a weird, guilty leap of excitement in her stomach. She shouldn't be prying. At all. Sam had made it clear she would tell Hayden more when she was ready. But Jon seemed a part of it, and if he *wanted* to tell Hayden something, surely that was his choice?

"She still hasn't forgiven herself, then."

"What?" Hayden kind of blurted it out in her eagerness at getting any kind of information.

"Oh, just—nothing." And with that he shook his shaggy head. "Wouldn't want to bore you. Besides, I'm with you—the truth is far better in the long run."

The door opened, and they both turned. Sam stood in the doorway, looking from one to the other. She had two plastic bags of to-go containers in her hand. It smelled divine.

"Jonathon." The level gaze that made Sam's interns melt landed on Jon. "I thought I told you to call from now on. I don't live alone."

Hayden swung her head to eye him, and he shrugged.

"I must've misunderstood. Besides, Hayden doesn't mind."

"You two certainly look cozy." Sam closed the door and walked over to the kitchen, placing her bag on the floor next to the counter and two plastic bags of food across from Hayden. "Which didn't take long."

Hayden tried to ignore the way her heart was going too fast. What had Sam not forgiven herself about? It was so hard not to pry for more. So instead, she said, "Well, you stole my cat, so I thought I'd steal your brother."

Jon, fork in hand, stepped up to the bags and pulled out one of the containers. "Never worry, dear sister. You brought food, so my affections are securely in your favor." He pulled the lid off, and Sam smacked his hand as he dug his fork in.

"That's supposed to be for Hayden and me."

He pouted. "But you have so much."

"I didn't know what she liked."

So she'd bought enough to feed five people? That was hilarious. And kind of cute.

"Well, you'd think that would be a question you asked someone before you married them."

Hayden laughed, and Jon threw her a wink, shoveling his fork into his mouth while Sam pulled out plates and more cutlery.

"At least use a plate, you heathen." Sam pushed one along to him, and he ignored it, opening his mouth to chew sloppily.

"Why?" he asked.

"You were raised better than that." Sam tugged the containers over and started opening them, pushing them into the middle with a spoon so Hayden could put food on her plate.

"Was I, though?" he asked. His tone was light, but still held a note of seriousness Hayden didn't understand.

Sam clearly understood, because she caught his eye and even gave him a wry smile. "When it comes to your table manners, yes."

This was clearly a conversation Hayden couldn't really take part in, so instead she piled some pad thai onto her plate and squeezed lemon over it. With her shirtsleeves rolled up, Sam took the same container and added some to her own plate. She stood in the kitchen, across from Hayden and next to her much younger brother, eating right there, the picture of domesticity. Her cheeks were pink, probably from the outside air, and Hayden felt something lunge low in her belly. She took a huge forkful of noodles, hoping swallowing them would bury whatever that was.

Jon rested his hip against the counter, still eating from the container. "Anyone want some of this?"

"After you've massacred it and pushed your saliva-covered fork through it?" Sam asked.

Hayden raised her fork. "I'll take some."

"Clearly you two are a friendship made in heaven." Sam twirled her fork on her plate, elegant even with that simple motion. She had delicate, slender wrists, with muscles that stood out on her forearms. Surgeon arms. Delicate hands. Strength that could surprise a person.

Every time she spoke to her brother, affection layered her tone. Something softened in her eyes. The lines around them showed more as she tried to hide exasperated smiles. It was nice to watch, as if Hayden was witnessing something private and a little breakable.

Jon winked at Hayden and slid the container over, rummaging for another container. He opened it and breathed it in. "Mm. Chicken."

Hayden stole a few forkfuls of what he'd been eating onto her plate. Sam watched her. "You're encouraging him."

"I'm doing no such thing," Hayden said, and all of that softness was directed at her. Another swoop-like feeling, low in her stomach, and Hayden swallowed, looking away to go back to her food.

Jon cleared his throat. "You two sure you're not really married?"

Sam huffed a laugh. "We've only been acting like it far too much."

Hayden made herself smile. "Clearly," she said. Yet it had a weird aftertaste, as if she hadn't really meant it.

Eventually, Frank reappeared, and Hayden scooped him up into her lap while she sat on the stool. He sat, rumbling a purr, his eyes closed as she scratched his head. She shot both Jon and Sam a haughty look over the counter.

Sam swallowed, something glinting in her eyes, a smile playing at her lips. "He slept on my bed last night."

Hayden gasped, aghast. "No?"

"He did." Smugness played on her own face now. "All night."

Hayden stared down at Frank, his eyes still closed, his purr loud. "You traitor."

Jon snorted, and Sam laughed, the sound low and wrapping around them all.

CHAPTER 18

A month later and stumbling home from her third night shift in a row, Hayden paused at the door with her key in the lock.

Would it be there again?

Maybe it wouldn't.

She tried to quell the hope that swirled in her.

She turned the key and walked in, pausing in the kitchen.

There it was, in the oven.

Pizza.

Hayden all but salivated.

Each morning she'd stumbled in from night shift thus far, she'd come home to something ready to eat. The first morning had been pasta: rich and creamy and filling. The second, a baked potato topped with chili.

And now, pizza.

Hayden did a happy wiggle and turned the oven on, wanting nothing more than to hug Sam. Food often had that effect on her. Sam knew what days Hayden was working the night shift, and Hayden knew when to expect to run into her if she was on call, thanks to the rosters they put up on the fridge each week.

But really, they weren't important, as they talked to each other about their shifts now. Over food at the counter, sometimes with Jon, or on the sofa at the end of a long day. Sometimes they talked about shifts and sometimes Sam asked about Hayden's family. Sometimes Hayden wasn't really sure what they talked about.

Hayden didn't ask about Sam's family, even as the questions about Jon's revelations burned away at her, desperate to be asked.

And this new tradition of food was one she could get behind.

With the timer set for ten minutes, Hayden went for a shower.

Under the hot spray, she breathed in the chemical smell of her face wash and lathered it in her hair, scrubbing it in. It took five seconds of that to realize what she'd done, and she sighed, feeling dramatic as overtired tears welled. She washed the face wash out of her hair, used shampoo instead, and then put in the conditioner. Once she'd applied face wash to her actual face, she washed everything off, sighed again, and stood under the spray for a moment to collect her strength.

Her brain was so useless on night shift. It was as if she concentrated so hard at work that as soon as she got home, her brain gave up on her and melted.

But who cared? Maybe she'd discovered the best way to wash hair.

She got out and pulled on comfy, warm clothes, tugging on socks. Even in the well-heated apartment, it was obvious the temperature had really fallen outside.

Bleary-eyed, Hayden went back to the kitchen and paused. Sam was there, a coffee in hand, put-together and smelling like she, too, was freshly showered.

"Hey." Hayden smiled genuinely, half-asleep.

"Good morning. Or night." Sam looked up. She was dressed up: a tailored jacket over a work shirt. It hugged her waist and Hayden had the urge to slip her hand under it and run it over the soft shirt, feeling the line of her waist, the dip above her hip.

Her fingers actually reached out to do it and she pulled them back against her leg. That would have been weird.

"Not in the hospital today?" Hayden asked.

Sam shook her head. "I'm participating in a lecture for a neuro conference, on short notice. Also, I turned your pizza off."

"Thanks. And thanks for making it."

"It's no problem. I remember my internship. And residency." Sam gave an unimpressed look, as close as she'd probably get to a grimace, and took a sip of her coffee. "It wasn't nice. I also found these." She held something up.

Hayden squinted at Sam. Her glasses were foggy. "My keys?"

"They were next to the milk in the fridge."

"What?"

"Your keys were in the fridge."

"I don't even remember opening the fridge."

"I'll leave them here on the counter." Sam looked far too amused.

"Thanks." Hayden pulled the pizza out onto a plate and grabbed a knife and fork. She sat down across from Sam, who was still smirking. "What?"

"Keys in the fridge? Really?"

"Hey. I washed my hair with face wash this morning. Keys in the fridge is nothing."

Sam was now definitely chuckling at her. "Really?"

"Yup. I'm just glad it wasn't toothpaste."

"How could you wash your hair with toothpaste?"

"Because it was in the shower." Hayden started hacking at the pizza with the cutlery. It smelled like melted cheese and tomato sauce. Heaven.

"Why?"

Hayden paused with a forkful of pizza on the way to her mouth. "Because I brush my teeth in the shower?"

"You brush your teeth in the *shower*?" Sam sounded horrified.

"As my wife, that's probably something you should know."

"If I'd known that, I would never have married you."

Hayden chewed happily and swallowed. So much cheese. "Lucky for me you didn't know, then. Now you're stuck with me, for better or worse."

"I'm clearly the lucky one."

"Clearly."

Sam's eyes were alight, laughing, and Hayden grinned at her sleepily. It struck her that she really didn't want Sam to go to work, that having her there was comfortable, nice. She wished, then, that she could ask her to skip the conference and hang out. She wanted her to be there when she woke up.

Sam looked down and away, and stepped back to rinse her coffee cup.

Turning back around, she gave Hayden a nod. "I may see you at the hospital tonight if I get called in."

She didn't move, as if she didn't want to go anywhere either.

"Good luck with your thing today," Hayden said.

"Thank you." And Sam finally walked out.

The door closed behind her, leaving a silence that was heavy in the kitchen. It was tempting to stand up and go call her back.

Instead, Hayden dropped the knife and fork on her plate and picked up the pizza with her hand, making quick work of it. That was probably the first time she'd ever used cutlery for pizza. Once done, deliciously full, she headed to her room to brush her teeth—not in the shower, since she'd done that already—and crawl into her bed. Frank was a blob under the blankets, already there and waiting.

~ ~ ~

"Pause compressions, we need to check the rhythm."

Hayden stepped back from the bed; everyone did. All of their focus returned to the monitor. Asystole, flat line. Still.

"Resume compressions."

So she did. On autopilot, Hayden pushed down a third of the depth of the chest at the usual rhythm. In her head, she sang *another one bites the dust*, a morbid joke, but it really did help to keep the correct number of beats. After a minute, she called, "Switch."

Luce stepped up to the other side of the bed and took over. Hayden stood back, gaze sweeping the scene. The bed was littered with plastic wrappers from sterile syringes, needles, and other such things. The body on the bed stayed inert. He could have been anyone: graying hair, medium build.

They'd been going for thirty minutes.

"I'm going to call it."

Luce dropped their arms, and they and Hayden shared a look over the bed. It had been a rough night—patients beyond their help on arrival, an underage drinker who was in ICU, and now this.

"Time of death, 0213."

And with that, some people disappeared, and others stayed to help. They detached the machines, unclipped cables and cords, pulled out IVs and intubation tubes—anything that would make seeing the body harder for the family.

Nothing would make it easier, though.

When it was all cleaned up, Hayden looked at Luce. "Need anything else?"

They gave a shake of their head. "No. Thanks. The doctor is telling the family."

"Coffee?"

"You have time?"

"Yeah."

"I'd love one."

Hayden double checked with the coordinator that she was okay to duck out, washed her hands, and made her way up the stairs to the cafeteria. No coffee cart at this time, just sludge. Maybe she could get them both some chocolate. Hayden hated shifts like this. It was never an easy job, but sometimes it got under your skin. She walked slowly up the steps, her feet echoing. Night was such a strange time in a hospital. Parts of it, like the operating rooms, the ER and intensive care, operated like any other time. Other parts shut down completely and became a ghost town, while wards entered a twilight zone.

The cafeteria had one lonely man behind the till. He cracked his gum and beamed, the lines in his face so deep it was like someone could disappear into them. "What'll it be, hon?"

"Two coffees and these two giant chocolate bars."

"One of those nights?"

Hayden nodded.

"Coming right up."

"Make it three?"

Hayden turned at the voice, smiling easily. "You got called in?"

"No," Sam said deadpan. "I just like to hang out here in the middle of the night."

"Oh, you're funny. Very funny."

She was in scrubs and a scrub hat, the bright green one that looked like a children's coloring book had thrown up on it. She was bright-eyed, almost bouncing on her heels. Almost. Sam didn't do that. But she did look...enthusiastic. "I got called in. It's an emergency, I haven't even seen her. They're prepping her now."

"So, some caffeine before you disappear into surgery?"

"Exactly. It should be a long one."

"Anything interesting?"

"Three-year-old girl hit by a car."

"In the early hours of the morning?"

"They'd been returning from a trip. The details are unclear. She has a severe bleed."

"Well, she's lucky she has you."

Red bloomed on Sam's cheeks, obvious under the harsh lights. Hayden found herself wondering what patterns her freckles would make if she ever got long enough to trace her gaze over them. "She should be fine."

"Sorry to interrupt the flirting session, ladies. But I have your coffee."

Hayden turned so fast she hit her hand on the counter. Pain flared, and she shook it. "We're not flirting."

He scoffed. "I'm sixty-two years old. I know flirting when I see it."

Sam picked up one of the coffees. She oozed confidence, while Hayden felt like an uncoordinated fool.

"We're married." Sam held up her hand, ring catching the light. "Not flirting."

He grinned, those lines somehow even deeper. "Well, it's still flirting. And so it should be. I flirt with my wife every chance I get."

Hayden finally snapped herself out of her weird reaction. She jammed the two chocolate bars into her pockets, as well as her staff scrip card, and picked up the coffees. "Well, we'll make sure to keep at it."

"You do that." And he actually winked at her.

Hayden followed Sam, who paused at the elevators, hitting the *up* button. The doors opened instantly.

"Nice recovery, Hayden."

Humor laced her words, and Hayden kept walking for the stairwell door. "Oh, shut up, Sam."

But Hayden went back to her shift feeling lighter than before. She walked past the beds that held her patients, her gaze sweeping over them. All was fine. The nurse who had been keeping an eye on them while she was having a quick break gave Hayden a reassuring nod.

"Why are you smiling?" Luce asked.

Hayden handed them the coffee over the nurses' station desk and rested on her elbows, her fingers warming as she clung to her cup.

"I just saw Sam."

"She got called in?"

"Yeah—a kid who was hit by a car."

Luce looked up from the computer they were clicking through. "Oh, her. She came in before my patient coded. She was a mess. I think you were busy dealing with the family that was causing issues earlier, and you missed the entire thing."

Hayden winced. Yes, that was most likely exactly where she'd been. It had been a long thirty minutes. "Yeah, I imagine so. Was she in bad shape?"

Luce's eyes were back on the screen, most likely flicking through blood results. "She was, yeah. But I'm sure it's nothing your superstar wife can't fix."

"Obviously."

~ ~ ~

Hayden's shift hadn't gotten much better. But it did end. And it was with a skip in her step that she flounced up to the front of her building.

Nicolas came out of the alcove and greeted her. "You're skipping, yet you look exhausted."

"I'm a little delirious, Nic. But now I get three days off work."

"Good to hear." He pulled the door open, and she walked past him. "Enjoy your sleep."

"Soon I'll think you're trying to tell me I look terrible," she called over her shoulder. She had a bag with some groceries in one arm and decided that justified the elevator. In the apartment, Frank was sitting on the back of the couch, staring out the window.

"Morning, Frank."

He turned around but didn't offer much else. Hayden quickly put the milk and other things away and stopped at the counter. Sam's bag was on the sofa. She was home. Hayden walked into the living room and glanced up the stairs.

"Sam?"

She didn't want to shout, in case she was asleep. But if she was awake, maybe Hayden could offer to make eggs to say thanks for the food every morning.

No one answered.

"Sam?"

Nothing. Hayden gave up and walked over to Frank, kneeling on the sofa next to him and looking out. The gauzy curtains were easy to see through. With her elbows on the back of the sofa, she nuzzled Frank with her chin and grinned when he gave a hearty purr.

She paused. Was that a balcony they had?

Had Hayden lived there for months and completely missed a *balcony*? How had she done that?

The curtains hung to the ground. Hayden stepped off the sofa and walked over, tugging them aside.

There was a door.

It was like discovering Narnia. Glad she hadn't taken off her coat, she tugged the door open and stepped outside. It was so high. The street was lined with morning sunlight. It was after nine o'clock, and cars were moving down the road. People were bustling down the sidewalks. This street was amazing. The trees were shedding golden brown leaves all over it, their branches almost completely bare now. In that light, it looked like some kind of dedication to fall.

She looked right, to where the balcony ran along the length of the living room wall, then down, and almost screamed.

Sam was sitting on the floor, back against the window.

Hayden put her hand over her chest. "Sam. Shit, you scared me. I thought you were asleep in your room."

For a moment, Sam's lips pressed together in a straight line. "No. Not asleep."

Why was Sam not making use of the comfortable, ornate chairs decorating the balcony? Hayden could now make out Frank's silhouette, above Sam's head. So that's what he'd been looking at.

Hayden crossed her arms, about to ask why she was on the ground. But Sam's red-rimmed eyes became more obvious, and Hayden sniffed the air. Cigarettes.

"Have you been smoking?" she asked.

Sam's hand was next to her leg, hidden from Hayden's view. She lifted it up. Smoke rose up almost lazily from the cigarette she held, practically invisible in this light. Hayden sat next to her, their hips and sides together.

"I haven't smoked any of it."

An ashtray was sitting next to her with several squashed, only partly-burned cigarettes, ash strewn in the bottom.

"No?"

Sam shook her head. "No. I quit fifteen years ago. I just needed…something."

Her voice was flat, and Hayden looked at her. The back of her head was against the glass as she looked up at the sky, patches visible among the tall apartment buildings. She was starkly pale, the green of her eyes vivid and alive. They were the green of spring, while her hair matched the fall leaves.

Like Sam herself. A contrast Hayden couldn't really figure out.

"You okay?"

Sam swallowed and didn't look at her. She nodded. Her eyes glistened, and she shook her head. "No."

"Your patient?"

"She died. On the table."

Hayden sucked in a breath. Kids were always hard. Always. Sometimes you did what you constantly did and pushed past. Sometimes you couldn't.

"I'm sorry. What happened?"

Sam blindly put out the cigarette and dropped her hand on her knee, her fingers tapping at it. She still didn't look at Hayden. "She was awake when I got there. Just. Her eyelids were fluttering, and she was crying. I talked to her while the anesthetist put her under, her mother stroking her hand until she was asleep. Then I looked that woman in the eye and told her I'd do everything that I could." Sam turned her head, looking at Hayden, and the shock of her eye contact, the depth of it, was like a slap. "I lied to her."

"No. Sam, you didn't lie. That's what we say. And we mean it. You did your best."

"I knew. I saw the scan right before I scrubbed. I knew she would die. I mean, it was something that we would always operate on, it was the only chance. But I had a feeling… The damage was so extensive…"

"But you still did your best?"

"Of course I did!" Sam spat the words out, and Hayden didn't even flinch, just met her eye and let her heat transfuse through where their bodies touched. Sam licked her bottom lip. "I'm sorry."

"Don't be. I get it. Some patients stick with you."

"She was so very small."

Hayden hesitated, the urge running down her limbs to do something, *anything*, to comfort. Finally, she dropped her hand over Sam's on her knee, and when Sam didn't pull away, she squeezed gently. Sam turned her hand around, and their fingers laced together. It was cold outside, despite the sunlight and blue sky, and a few minutes ago, Hayden would have loved to be in bed and sleeping, but right then, there, in that moment, she wouldn't have wanted to be anywhere else.

"What was yours?" Sam's voice sliced through the quiet of the rumbling street below and their steady breathing.

"My what?"

"Your worst."

Oh. Her worst patient loss. Dredging up those memories was never fun, or easy.

"Two years ago, we had a thirteen-year-old come in with anaphylaxis. We tried to resuscitate. But we failed. We lost him so quickly." Hayden took a deep breath. "I'll never forget the way his parents screamed his name."

Sam's hand, in her own, tightened. "This mother blamed me."

"You know it wasn't your fault."

"I do. And I also know it will help her to have someone to blame."

They sat there for an hour, the day starting around them for everyone else while their night came to a close.

Hayden's phone began chiming, and she started, digging it out of her pocket with her free hand. It was her abuela.

"Sorry," Hayden said.

"No. Take it."

Sam went to stand up, but Hayden tugged her back down. "Want to join? It's not weird if you do. I mean, they kind of expect it? It would be weirder if they never see you."

"Okay."

Hayden quickly answered the call and accepted the video request. Abuela's face came on. Javi was sitting in her lap, his face lit up.

"Tía! And Sam!" He flapped his hand enthusiastically at them. "Hi."

"Hey, Javi." Hayden waved her hand, now free from Sam's.

Sam wiggled her fingers at the screen, her head pressed against Hayden's ear so they could both be on the screen. "Hello, Javi."

"Alejandra. You look exhausted." Abuela squinted at them. "You also, Samantha. Why?"

"We had night shift, Abuela. Well, Sam was on call and had to go in."

"They work you both too much." Abuela clicked her tongue.

Hayden thought it better to skirt the issue of work. "Javi, shouldn't you be at school?"

He shook his head, wilting into Abuela dramatically and pouting. "I can't go. I'm sick."

"What happened?" Hayden asked.

"I vomited. In Mami's bed."

Hayden bit down a laugh. "That's pretty gross."

He nodded solemnly.

"You feeling better?"

"Yup. And I get a whole day with Abuela. We made up a superhero name for me."

"You did?" Hayden loved her nephew. "What is it?"

"Yes." Abuela sighed. "Tell her your superhero name."

"Danger Fart!"

Sam snorted and burst into laughter. The sound made Hayden gape at her at first, then she joined in. Through her phone speaker, she could hear Javi cackling.

Chapter 19

"Sam. What is that?"

Hayden couldn't look away from the living room wall under the stairs that led up to Sam's room. She closed her eyes. Opened them again. Stared some more. The photo was still there.

"Hm?" Sam's voice came from the kitchen.

Hayden finally spun around. Frank wove around her feet, and she scooped him up, holding him to her chest. "That. What is that?"

Sam finally looked up from the counter where she was busy chopping tomatoes. They were fresh ones, organic and plump, and the smell of them filled the room. Hayden was getting spoiled living in this house. To be fair, she had some money now, more than she'd ever really had. That forty thousand still sat there, though, untouched.

"That," Sam said, her eyes doing that slightly squinty thing they did when she was amused, "is a photo."

Hayden huffed, scratching Frank under the chin. "Yes. It is a photo. But where did it come from?"

"It's been there two days."

"I—what?"

"Two days, Hayden."

Hayden spun on her heel and stared at it again. "Two days?"

"You're really not very observant. I was waiting for this reaction."

"You had a photo of us kissing on the wall for two days and I missed it?" Frank squeaked, and Hayden loosened her grip. He struggled, and she let him jump down. He stalked off somewhere toward his ridiculous cat tree, where he would, she was sure, stare at them all judgmentally from his hammock.

"I put it up, knowing your friends were coming tonight. It came about a month ago. Around when you were hiding your keys in the fridge."

The photo was huge. And beautifully shot. It was candid, the two of them kissing in City Hall, smiles on their lips. It looked real. The photographer had captured it at the perfect moment. You couldn't tell that they were laughing out of awkwardness, at the pure insanity of the situation.

They looked like two fools in love.

"I like that it's in black and white," Hayden said.

"Mm. He did a good job. There's another on the TV cabinet."

Hayden spun on her heel again. "There is?"

Sam chuckled. "There is."

Hayden walked over to the television, picking up the much smaller framed photo. This one was color. Sam's cheeks were flushed. Hayden was biting her lip as she slipped a ring on Sam's finger. She barely remembered doing that. The entire thing had passed in an anxiety-ridden blur. The photo was finely enhanced. He really had done a good job.

"So this is the subtle 'look at us we're genuinely married' touch?" Hayden put the photo down and walked over to sit on one of the barstools, watching Sam add balsamic with a flick of her wrist to the salad she'd prepared.

"It is. Do you think it works?"

"It does." Hayden quickly stole a piece of cucumber and dodged Sam's hand that moved to slap it away. She popped it in her mouth, victorious. "Jon will think it's hilarious."

"Yes, well, as I've mentioned before, Jon is an idiot."

"He's your brother. What does that say about you?"

Sam pushed the salad bowl further away, out of Hayden's reach as she tried for another piece. Hayden pouted, and Sam tugged it back over with a sigh for Hayden to snag a piece of carrot. She bit into it happily.

"It says nothing about me. We're two very different people. He's over twenty years younger, for a start."

"Age means nothing."

Sam's eyes shot upward to meet Hayden's gaze for an intense second. It was a loaded look, one Hayden hadn't meant to induce, nor did she fully understand. But it was true. Age wasn't important. After a slow blink, Sam went back to pulling out plates and cutlery.

"Yes, well, if it means nothing, then Jon and I are dramatically different simply due to personality."

"Can I ask something?"

Sam placed the four plates on the counter in front of herself, her hands resting on them as she gave Hayden her full attention. "Go ahead."

Hayden swallowed. "If it's out of bounds, just let me know." She had been really good about not pushing for answers. She'd promised. And breaking a promise was like lying in Hayden's book. You don't break promises. She still hadn't pried for more about that mysterious comment from Jon. "But the age gap is pretty big?"

Sam ran her thumb over the curved edge of one of the plates. "That's not a question."

Hayden almost threw something at her. God, she could be really infuriating. "You know what I mean."

And Sam did, because her lips were quirking up. "My mother had me when she was twenty. I was an only child, and I don't think they planned on more. Jon was an utter surprise they announced when I was twenty-one."

"Do you feel like a sister to him?"

"I was so busy with studying and, later, my residency." She seemed to consider her next words. "I tried, though, to be there for him, because I knew what it was like to grow up with them." She had a distant look in her eye, her thumb still moving back and forth against the china, and it made Hayden hold her breath. There was an achingly brittle moment growing between them. "But I suppose I felt like an aunt. A sister too. In some ways, maybe even his mother." She laughed so softly Hayden thought for a second she'd imagined it. "He once packed a bag and left the house. He was five. They called the police, and when they found him walking down the street with his *Ninja Turtles* backpack, he announced to them he was moving to the hospital to live with his sister."

Hayden grinned. "He loved you."

"He idolized me. He realized I was human, eventually." Something, a shadow, flitted over the green of Sam's eye. "But he's everything I have."

"And—and your parents?"

Sam cocked her head and took in a deep breath, her tongue running over her bottom lip, considering something, maybe. "They—"

The buzzer interrupted her, and Hayden had never wanted to kill someone more. Sam straightened her shoulders and gave Hayden a wry smile before padding over to the intercom.

"Let them up, Nicolas. Thank you."

"Are you ready for this?" Hayden asked.

"No."

Hayden laughed. "Me neither. Dinner with Luce and their girlfriend."

"Do I call Luce Clemmie's *partner*?"

"Yeah, that one's fine. But Luce isn't the biggest fan of it. They prefer *boo*."

"Seriously?"

"Yup."

Sam sighed. "Right. Luce is Clemmie's...*boo*."

"Nah, I'm just messing with you. Though Luce doesn't mind *boo*. Datefriend is fine."

Sam grabbed a pen from the table near the entrance and threw it at her. Hayden ducked, laughing. A knock sounded at the door, and Sam sent over a final frown before tugging it open.

"Hey!" Luce's cheery voice carried through, and Hayden slid out of her chair and walked over to greet them both like a married couple probably should. Whatever that meant. She plastered a smile on her face.

Clemmie gave a wave. "Hi."

Hayden slid close to Sam, slipping a hand around her waist. It was natural now. Something they did in other's company easily. "Hey, humans."

Luce held up a bottle of wine. "We bring wine, since Sam insisted we didn't need to bring anything."

Sam reached out and took it. "Thank you."

Everyone shuffled inside and did the dance of showing where coats went and getting everyone in. Luce was looking around the apartment, letting out a low whistle, their hand still entwined with Clemmie's.

"Nice place, you two."

Hayden slipped into the kitchen to get out of having to feel awkward about accepting compliments about an apartment she had nothing to do with nor would be living in after they were divorced. She started opening the bottle of wine, listening to Sam tell them about the apartment.

"Do you want a tour?" Sam asked.

"Yes, please." Luce was far too eager. They were clearly interested in seeing how the two of them lived. Luckily, Hayden had smooshed everything she owned into her closet, and her room was looking like a guest room again, her toiletries all hidden away just in case. Sam had even taken Hayden's jacket upstairs and dropped it on her bed, and had left a pair of Hayden's shoes on the floor.

Maybe there was even a photo of them up there?

Luce set off down the hall after Sam like it was a covert mission, shooting Hayden a thumbs-up as they did so. Clemmie shoved them gently in the back and mouthed "sorry" at Hayden.

She liked Clemmie.

Luce was an ass.

By the time they were back, Hayden had four glasses poured and was setting the table. Her hands were clammy as she put the salad in the center. It was strange to be putting on such a show. But they'd finally bitten the bullet and picked a day, after offering so many times for Luce and Clemmie to come around for dinner. That date turned out to be the four-month anniversary of their wedding, which they'd decided to mention at dinner. It was the kind of thing they *should* draw attention to.

Hayden sighed. Being married was hard work.

Across the room, in his hammock, Frank blinked at her and Hayden poked her tongue out at him.

"Thanks for the wine," Clemmie said, picking up her glass.

"You bought it." Content that the table looked good enough, Hayden met them all over at the kitchen counter. "So, thank you."

Sam took a long sip of hers, and Hayden tried not to smirk. Instead, she sidled close until they were side by side. Opposite them, Luce put their elbows on the counter, and Clemmie settled close to them.

"What's for dinner?" Luce asked.

"Hayden made *baleada*."

"Sounds delicious," Clemmie said. "What is it?"

"It's like a taco, but Honduran style. My abuela's recipe, though hers are always better. Luce mentioned you're vegetarian?" At Clemmie's nod, Hayden continued, "Great. They're with beans."

"Thanks."

"I really love the apartment." Luce straightened and picked up their glass. They walked away, and Hayden closed her eyes for a second when she saw them walking straight for the photo on the wall. "And I *love* this photo."

"Thank you." Sam's voice sounded so genuine, and Hayden opened her eyes. Luce had their back to them all, staring at the photo.

They tilted their head. "You look really happy."

"My favorite is the one on the TV." Sam took a sip of wine, and when Hayden turned to look at her, Sam's gaze quickly flicked to Luce.

Was it her favorite? Well, it could be her favorite without it meaning anything intense. It was a really nice photo. Clemmie walked to the television and picked it up, Luce standing next to her. They tucked their chin on her shoulder, both of them looking down at the photo. They matched, standing there. Their posture folded around each other. Clemmie relaxed back into Luce, and the sight was adorable. Which worked well, because when Luce looked up at her, Hayden must have been smiling.

"Is it your favorite too?"

Hayden shook her head. "No. I like the one on the wall." Sam's eyes were back on her now; Hayden could feel it. But she kept her gaze on Luce. "I like that we're smiling. It's not serious or overly…*wedding-y*."

Luce grinned at her, and Clemmie looked up too, the photo still in her hands. Shaking their head, Luce said, "I still can't believe *you* got married and didn't invite anyone. Namely me."

"Leave them alone, Luce. They're happy. You can tell from the photos they didn't want a traditional wedding anyway."

Yup. Hayden really liked Clemmie.

Hayden stuck her tongue out at Luce. Sam slipped her arm around Hayden's waist, and Hayden was tight against her, her hand over Sam's on her hip. Their wedding bands would be right next to each other. "Yeah, Luce." Hayden rubbed it in. "Leave us alone."

Sam's weight against her was comfortable.

They eventually sat down, food dished up and Frank still glaring at them from his cat tree.

"How is good ol' Frank settling in, Hayds?" Luce asked.

"Oh, he's in heaven."

"He loves me." Sam reached for her wine. "And Hayden's jealous."

"I am not!"

Luce cackled. "Oh, they who protest too much."

Hayden grumbled, stabbing at her food. "I'm not protesting too much."

Clemmie grinned at her over the table. "You kind of are. You went high-pitched."

Hayden narrowed her eyes, making sure it looked playful. "Just as I was starting to truly like you."

Too quickly, considering Hayden would rather not do this at all, Sam nudged Hayden with her shoulder. Hayden looked at her with raised eyebrows. Sam lifted her own and looked pointedly at Luce and Clemmie. Oh. She wanted to do the "yay, we've made four months" thing. Her eyes were really green tonight. Their faces were close at the table, and the freckles over her nose looked charming. Hayden had drunk too much wine.

"Are you two having a married eye conversation?" Luce asked.

Hayden whipped her head around. Luce and Clemmie were watching them, amused.

"No," Hayden said.

"A little," Sam said.

"Okay, fine, yes." Hayden reached for her glass. "We just wanted to say that, well—" Hayden slid her arm around the back of Sam's chair. "We've been married for four months today. Thanks for being here."

Hayden turned her head, and she was eye to eye with Sam, their noses almost brushing. Sam smiled, and Hayden echoed it without thinking. She closed the gap, their lips grazing before Hayden kissed her properly. When Sam's lips moved, ever so slightly, Hayden deepened the kiss, their lips parting. Losing herself, Hayden hummed, quietly. It was more indulgent than usual, lingering. Something tingled from her lips and down her spine, pooling in her stomach. Sam pulled back and turned to Luce and Clemmie, leaving Hayden with warmth in her belly and wondering how Sam acted so easily.

And also wondering when she'd become really, really attracted to Sam.

When Sam had turned back to the others, it had left Hayden with the image of Sam's ear, and she wanted to move right into her space and brush her lips right under it, against the softness of her neck. And not because Luce was watching and they needed to put on a show. And not because it had been a long time and Hayden felt lonely—or was hurting, or was emotional.

She really wanted to kiss Sam the *person*. Not Sam her fake wife.

"Aw! Here, here!"

Her mouth dry, almost breathless, Hayden turned to face her friends, cheeks overheating. She raised her glass with them, and they all clinked them together. Her arm was still over Sam's chair, and Sam leaned lightly into her side. Hayden's head spun, that low heat in her stomach giving off a throb.

Well. This was new.

~ ~ ~

The next morning, Hayden lay in bed, looking unseeingly up at the ceiling, her legs twisted in the blankets. She would wait until Sam had left for work to get up. Hayden had the day off and was really grateful for that.

Until it left her alone in the house with her thoughts.

She wasn't so grateful anymore.

How long had she been attracted to Sam? She'd been ignoring it since they'd got back from Florida, hadn't she?

Had brushed it off.

Hayden was an idiot.

She took in a deep breath and blew it out slowly. But that didn't help the weird, hopped-up nerves in her stomach. It was as if discovering this attraction had turned Hayden into some kind of turned-on teenager.

She contemplated a run. That could help. Burn off some of this energy ticking in her bloodstream. Or she could get up and eat breakfast, go for a walk to find a café that looked nice to sit in, and call her sister.

That sounded like a better idea.

Hayden sat up and went to stand, one foot still wrapped in the sheet and she tripped her way out of it, slamming her knee into the bedside table.

"Shit! Ow!"

Frank ran out from under her bed, pelting away, his fat little belly jiggling.

"Frank! Come back." Cursing, Hayden rubbed her knee.

She had a quick shower, figuring her hair could survive a third day without washing it. She'd do it tonight. Probably. She pulled on layers. Christmas was only three weeks away, and it looked like red and green had thrown up all over the city. Luce and she were sending constant photos back and forth of the most outlandish decorations. Luce had thus far won, with a caption that read "an elf took too many drugs and then exploded in here."

When her toast was ready and she had a coffee in hand, Hayden stared at Frank as he slept in his tree and mulled her predicament over.

So. She was attracted to her wife. That would be considered a good thing to most people. This was not an everyday situation, however.

Well, a crush was nothing. Wait. Not even a crush, an attraction. She was an adult. She could deal with this, even if the entire thing was embarrassing. No doubt Sam saw her as a means to some kind of end Hayden still didn't understand. Even if they were kind of close now—friends, really—she probably looked at Hayden like some kind of childish cousin.

She saw her brother as really young. Hayden was only six years older.

Taking a too-big bite of her toast, her gaze fell to the picture on the wall. It set off an ache low in her belly. Yup. Just attraction. Not a crush. That would be silly.

Why? How had this happened? Sam was rude and arrogant and had no bedside manner.

But she was also stunning and witty and calmed Hayden's mother down when Hayden was left flailing. She cupped Hayden's chin as if Hayden was something breakable when her lip was split and aching. She cried over patients she failed. She put up with her joker of a younger brother with an affectionate roll of her eyes.

She had eyes so green they could have been digitally altered and freckles that Hayden wanted to memorize, to trace her fingers over and figure out all they ways they could come back together. In the photo, Hayden could see the fanning of laugh lines around Sam's eyes, a sight that set affection roiling in her gut.

This could not end well.

Hayden grabbed her phone off the counter and started typing a message to Luce. Then stopped.

She was panicking, and she couldn't even talk to her best friend about it.

Or her sister.

She couldn't speak about it because, according to them, of *course* Hayden was attracted to Sam. This wasn't new. She had no one to have a freak-out at. Everyone thought they were happily married.

Except Jon.

Hayden considered that option, her phone held against her chest.

Jon knew the truth. And Sam clearly trusted him to keep a secret; he was the only person who knew.

But Jon was also Sam's brother.

Okay, so over the last month especially, Hayden had hung out with him a bit. He appeared for a beer on the sofa some nights, often when Sam wasn't even there. She liked him. He was what she imagined any younger brother would be like: a bit of an idiot, but nice enough. And he was clearly protective of Sam.

So, no. No telling Jon, then.

Hayden's phone buzzed in her hand, and she squealed and dropped it.

Frank didn't even move.

Clucking her tongue at herself, she scooped it off the floor. No cracks. Lucky. She opened a message from Sam. She rarely ever sent messages. She kind of hated her phone. She had to be attached to it for work.

Can we talk about Christmas when I get home this evening?

Hayden sent an affirmative.

Christmas? What about it? Sam already knew Hayden was working. She'd managed to get last year off, which meant this year was definitely a no go. Sam was working too, as far as Hayden knew.

They'd be kind of spending Christmas together.

Maybe with some eggnog and Christmas lights, glowing from the tree neither of them had bothered talking about putting up. Mistletoe.

No. No romantic, kissy thoughts.

No thoughts of *if we just drink enough wine...* No. None of that.

This was a business deal. One for money. She'd given up her lease officially ages ago. She couldn't make a mess of this now. She needed the apartment for the next however long this went for. She needed the cash. This deal had to work out.

And then with the money, she'd figure out what the heck to do. How would she explain to her family she'd come into some money to really set their mother up? Or, more importantly, divorced a woman they now all liked and Hayden had convinced them she was deeply in love with?

Hayden's head was hurting.

She put her dishes away and grabbed her coat, wrapping a scarf around her neck and adding gloves for good measure.

The air outside was bitingly cold, wind whipping her hair around her head where it spilled out from under her beanie. Her cheeks and nose lost feeling quickly, yet she walked around for an hour, her feet pounding the pavement and her thoughts clashing wildly in her head. She needed to get rid of this idea. Maybe if she could say it to someone she'd realize how insane it was, and she could laugh about it and move on. Hayden and *Sam*. It made no sense. Hayden needed a date. Or to get out and flirt with someone.

Except that wasn't what she wanted to do, at all. She wanted to fall into Sam, to lose herself in those kisses they occasionally shared. To pull back those layers Hayden was getting a glimpse of and see what else lurked beneath. To find out what made her sigh, and moan. She wanted to know what made her laugh as much as Hayden's nephew calling himself "Danger Fart" did.

Because over the last several months, Hayden had learned so much, but it had only left her wanting more. She had learned so much, but also so little all at the same time.

Hayden stopped at a small café. The blast of warmth quickly had her stripping her layers off. She ordered a coffee and slipped into a seat by a window, away from anyone else. She called Sofia and tried not to sound like she wildly wanted to sleep with the woman she'd fake married and introduced to them all as her real wife.

Talking to her sister was nice.

Hayden had been trying harder to answer her calls and call her sometimes. And over the last few weeks, they'd talked about a home. About eventually moving her mother somewhere more secure. She'd started trying to wander more and more. Abuela was getting worried.

Their concern left a knot of worry in Hayden's throat.

But at least they were talking about it.

They were all worried about how to pay for it. There was talk of selling the house and using that money, and Hayden continuing to pay what she was already contributing. Even with that, though, the care they could afford was on the lower scale. And if they sold the house, Abuela and Sofia and Javi still needed somewhere to live.

Hayden would be able to afford somewhere amazing for her mother soon. And with the forty in her account, they could look at moving her in that somewhere amazing whenever they needed to.

If only Abuela and Sofia would agree.

"Okay. I get it, Hayden. We'll talk more later. And how's Sam?"

The question alone made Hayden's breath hitch. "She's fine. Good. Christmas discussions are happening."

"Oh, great. Are you both working?" Sofia sounded muffled. Probably trying to cook while she talked. She was always doing several things at once, whereas if Hayden attempted that, she'd just hurt herself.

"Yeah, we are. She wants to talk about it tonight."

"Will you be with her family, then? What are they like?"

"They're—" a complete unknown "—fine. Her brother is nice. He's twenty-one, so, you know, young. But I get along with him pretty well."

"That's a big age gap."

"Mm. Accident, I think."

"I imagine. Still, that'll be fun."

"Are you all having the normal Christmas?"

"Yeah. Low fuss. Mass with Abuela. Javi's written his list."

"He was so funny last year, yelling in the morning about how the reindeer had eaten the carrots we gnawed on before going to bed at one a.m."

Sofia chuckled. "I'd forgotten that. I have the photo of you doing it, with wine in your other hand and scraping your teeth down the carrot to make it look authentic. I'll just have to send that to Sam."

"Why do you do these things to me?"

"Because I love you."

"Lies."

"Well, I do. We'll miss you this year." The joking tone faded to a more serious one.

Something clenched in Hayden's stomach. She did love Christmas with her family. "I will too. You know how it is at the hospital. I had the holidays off last year, so this year was impossible."

"Yeah, well, you can still look forward to Abuela trying to convince you that you just didn't ask for the time hard enough."

"Can't wait. Now tell me about Javi's present requests so I can send him something awesome."

Hayden lost herself in conversation with her sister, trying and failing to forget everything else.

~ ~ ~

Hayden was in her sweats on the sofa with Frank that evening, watching reruns of an old comedy show, when Sam came through the door. She was wan, clearly tired. Luce and Clemmie had left quite late the night before.

"Hey," Hayden called from the sofa.

"Hi." Sam smiled, and Hayden's stomach lurched. Her plan to not let this get to her was already failing.

"How was work?" she asked.

"Long. I had an eight-hour surgery with Reeves."

That wouldn't have been pleasant. "That resident who talks nonstop?"

"That one, yes." Sam put her bag on the counter and opened the fridge, pulling out a bottle of water. "He was finally quiet around the three-hour mark."

"You mean you glared him into silence around the three-hour mark."

"I did no such thing."

"Oh please." Hayden tucked her legs under herself, and Sam walked over, sitting close, her hand falling to Frank's neck to stroke him. He purred. "You can't not be aware of how powerful your glare is."

"I don't know what you're talking about."

"Then why are you smirking?"

"I don't smirk. Nor do I glare."

"You do both, and you know it." Hayden dropped her head against the back of the sofa. "There's some pasta on the stove, if you're hungry."

Sam cocked her head, something soft in the curve of her lips, and Hayden wanted to fall into the look in her eye. "Thank you. How was your day?"

Oh, you know, just ruminating on how badly I want to kiss you.

Or how badly she wanted to push Sam back against the sofa and bite at her neck until Sam groaned her name. "Fine." Her voice squeaked, so Hayden cleared her throat. "Fine. Relaxing. I didn't have any obligations today, so I went for a walk, called my sister."

"How was that?"

"Good. She's coming around to the idea that Mom will have to go into a home. Slowly. It's Abuela who's fighting it."

"She thinks she's the best thing for her daughter."

Sam looked at her as if she hadn't just dropped a huge truth bomb. "Yeah. Exactly." Hayden took in a deep breath, because Sam being understanding right now was not helping the whole...attraction thing. "Plus, you know, her idea is that no one looks after your family better than you do. To her, admitting Mom elsewhere is like being selfish. Family belongs with family." Hayden swallowed. She didn't want to talk about this anymore. "You wanted to talk about Christmas?"

And now it was Sam who was looking everywhere *but* at Hayden. "Yes."

Hayden waited. And waited. "You know that involves words?"

That glare was leveled on her. "Yes, thank you. I'm aware how conversation works." Sam sighed. "My family is having a dinner. Christmas Eve. I know we should both finish work around seven-thirty. They'll have dinner at eight-thirty. Will you join me?"

"Uh, me? As in wife-me? Or friend-me?"

"Wife-you. I think it's time we tell them."

"We? As in us? Tell them together?"

Why did Sam want to tell them now, so randomly? And together? Something like hope fluttered in Hayden's stomach.

"Yes. We. As in us."

"And their reaction will be...?"

Sam was smiling. It could be called wicked, if not for the flicker of doubt Hayden could see in her eyes. "They won't like it."

Hayden squashed that rising hope quickly. She was being stupid. She'd always known this was all part of some plan of Sam's.

"Okay, so am I finally finding out what's going on?"

Sam visibly swallowed and broke eye contact again, watching Frank as he purred and lifted his chin for her to pat him more. Hayden had the urge to run her hand through Sam's hair, to let it rest on the back of her neck until she looked up so Hayden could brush their lips together.

What would it be like, to kiss her with intention on her mouth?

"Soon."

Hayden sighed. "Surely I need to know *before* we go in there."

"That's true."

The buzzer rang at the door. Hayden jumped. "Seriously? Every time you're opening up?"

Sam chuckled and jumped up too quickly, clearly happy to get away with it. "I can feel you glaring," she said as she walked away.

Hayden stubbornly relaxed her face. "I'm not glaring."

Sam ignored her and opened the door. "Jon. You actually used the buzzer and didn't just let yourself in. How novel."

"Sam. Hi." He didn't step in, so Hayden couldn't see him. His voice sounded tight. "Can we talk? I just, I can't believe them."

"Who?"

"Who do you think?" Hayden was clearly not meant to be witnessing this. "Mom and Dad."

"Okay, Jon—"

"I just, I even went over there. To try and talk to them again?"

"Jon." Sam's voice was soothing in a way that Hayden had only heard that night Hayden's mother had accidentally hit her. "You know there was no point in doing that. But listen, Hay—"

"I know." His voice cracked, something broken. Should Hayden make it obvious she was here? "But with Christmas, I thought… I didn't really think they'd cut me out completely, you know? They made the cleaner tell me to leave."

"They what?" Hayden asked, incredulous.

Sam closed her eyes for a second, took a deep breath, and opened them. Jon stepped through the door, wide-eyed. He swallowed, pale, like Sam often got.

"I thought you were alone."

CHAPTER 20

"Jon, your parents did what?"

Hayden knew there were parents that could be that horrible. Her father was a great example. But what Sam and Jon's parents had done sounded so callous—to not even talk to your child? To send the cleaner?

Jon's gaze flicked from Hayden to Sam.

"Well," he grimaced, "I hope you were planning on telling her soon?"

Sam closed her eyes for a second, hand still on the door handle. When she opened them again, she looked calm, though her lips were a tight line. "I was going to soon, yes," she finally said.

"Good." He still looked pale, his joking dimples long gone. "Sorry, though."

"It's fine. You're upset."

"Um—I'm right here." Hayden gave a wave, and they both looked at her again.

Jon looked back to Sam. "Do you want me here for this?"

The fact that he didn't leave made Hayden wonder just how upset he was. He looked shaken. While he could normally manage to look more mature, now he seemed small and young.

Sam must have seen it too. "Stay," she said to Jon, and Hayden relaxed.

"You sure?" he asked, hovering in the doorway.

"Grab a drink, if you want." Sam stepped away from the door, opening it wider to let him in.

He walked through to the kitchen, and Sam rubbed her hand over her eyes, pushing the door closed as she did so. This all seemed like a family thing, and Hayden felt as if she was imposing. As if she was butting her way into something that was none of her business. For a moment, she thought about going to her room and giving them space.

For a moment.

"What the hell is going on?" Hayden blurted out.

Sam considered her briefly, then walked over to sit at the end of the sofa.

"Does anyone want a beer?" Jon asked from the kitchen.

"I won't say no," Hayden said.

"Sam?"

"Please."

He walked two over, already opened.

"Thanks."

With a nod, he went back to the kitchen, pulled out another beer and twisted it open. The swig he took was a long one, and Hayden mimicked him, as did Sam. They all lowered their bottles and gazed around at each other. Finally, Jon leaned against the fridge. He looked small. Every now and again, he flicked his thumbnail at the label. Hayden crossed her legs and pulled Frank into them. He meowed-slash-whined once, and settled into a ball in her lap.

"My family is...difficult," Sam said. From the kitchen, Jon snorted. Sam shot him a small, wry smile. "Perhaps that's putting it mildly."

His expression agreed.

"Am I finally about to find out what's going on?" Hayden asked.

"Seems like," Jon said. "And also find out why I'm against the entire thing." He raised his beer bottle to Hayden. "Nothing against you, personally. I think you're great."

Hayden scratched Frank under the chin. "You can't help but love me."

"If you two are done?" Sam said. When she again had Hayden's attention, she continued, "At Christmas last year, Jon was outed."

"Outed? For being gay? Like celebrities are grossly outed by mass media?"

"Just like that." Jon stepped forward so he was leaning against the counter. The space was so big, he seemed ages away. Maybe he needed the distance for this conversation. "Except without the fame. And apparently without the fortune." He gave a laugh, though the joke was lost on Hayden.

Sam put her elbows on her knees. "Yes, very funny, Jon." The moment reminded Hayden that Sam was so much older and didn't feel like only a sister to him. Her feelings about him were all wrapped up with a mother's concern. "Our parents had him followed, as they suspected him of being gay, though I don't know why. Some private investigator had photos of Jon in a club and later in a car."

Bile rose in Hayden's throat.

"Yay, privacy," Jon said, his voice flat, dead. Hayden wanted to get up and hug him. Why hadn't they just asked him if he was gay?

"It exploded at Christmas; they threw him out at dinner." Sam's voice was tight, wrought with anger.

"They waited for Christmas?" Hayden asked him. "Seriously?"

His thumb was flicking at the label with more vigor now, his brow furrowed. "There's nothing they like more than staging a good show." Bitterness coated his words. He sighed, and his brow relaxed, though his thumb kept flicking. "They waited until I got home on college break—"

"How old were you?"

"It was last year. So, twenty." He picked part of the label off completely. "I had really only just kind of, I don't know, accepted that I was gay. I knew my parents couldn't know. We knew what they thought of being gay."

"They were always so openly homophobic?"

Jon gave a mirthless laugh, but it was Sam who spoke. "They donate money to every Republican supporting every anti-gay movement—especially those that wish to promote conversion therapy. We grew up hearing about our gay uncle and how he was depraved. They compared him to things that I won't bother going into now. There were rants about the good ol' days."

Hayden felt something sick twist in her stomach. Imagine growing up in that? Hayden had grown up in a family who loved her. She'd come out young, and they'd pulled her close and hugged her. It had taken Abuela a while to understand. The idea of a man in Hayden's life being a sure thing was something she'd clung to. She hadn't been able to understand why she'd 'choose' a harder life. But they'd spoken about it, and she'd made an effort and now dressed in rainbow colors for Pride every year.

How lucky she'd been.

This story seemed like one from the fifties. Not from today. How naïve of Hayden.

"I had no plans to come out to them," Jon said. "There was an...understanding that my uncle should have been discreet. Buried it. Married a woman anyway. I thought I could just—I don't know. Hide it. Sam had."

"Your family doesn't know you're gay?" Hayden asked her.

"A lesbian. And no. I was always discreet. Also, I was focused on my career. It was never the most important thing to me." Sam took a sip of her beer. It was a strange image, her drinking from the bottle. Like she wasn't quite comfortable doing it. All those neat lines in her. Her posture. The carefully-monitored expressions.

Were these the results of growing up in such a controlled environment, or was it just Sam? There probably wasn't a distinction. She itched to pull Sam closer and tug at her to get to know her better. An ache swelled in Hayden's throat at the thought of it.

Hayden tore her gaze away and back to Jon, who was watching her thoughtfully. Heat crept into her cheeks. "So they just..." she really couldn't comprehend this "...told you to go?"

"There was a discussion first." A muscle twitched in his cheek, and Sam breathed harshly through her nose. "But yes, I was told to leave. My mother wouldn't even look at me. I'd never seen her..." he swallowed "...her face so twisted? Like she felt sick at the sight of me. Dad—" he all but spat out the word "—had a lot to say. Finally, he threw me out, literally, and told me not to come back unless I could prove my depravity was over."

Depravity. Charming. That sick feeling was back.

"I'm so sorry, Jon."

He gave a half-hearted shrug, as if it could shrug off the pain lacing his expression. Even his attempt at a smile failed miserably. "It is what it is."

"Were you there?" Hayden asked Sam.

Sam opened her mouth and closed it. She hesitated over her words. Not used to seeing Sam flounder, Hayden leaned forward, squishing Frank, who didn't even seem to notice. Her fingers itched to rest on Sam's knee, or to offer something small, anything, to help.

"I was there."

"And your parents wouldn't listen to you?"

Sam watched Hayden pat Frank. "I tried to reason with them at first. I didn't really do enough."

"You did what you could." Jon's voice was low.

Her eyes flashed, and she looked over at her brother, cheeks flushed. "I did no such thing. And you know it."

An old hurt etched over his face as he looked back at his bottle.

"I just, I watched them throw you out, Jon. I watched and I said nothing. I've never been more ashamed of myself. Ever."

Silence rang in Hayden's ears, and Sam swallowed visibly. Jon was picking at the sticker on his bottle again. There'd be no label left soon.

"When Father told me to stay out of it, I—I just stopped speaking." Her voice was thick, and Hayden wanted to reach over and twine their fingers together. To soothe the edge on her brow. "They said hideous things, and it was like I'd lost my voice. I spent...years keeping that part of myself locked away from them. And I watched you stripped bare, exposed to them against your will—it was my worst nightmare playing out in front of me. But instead of me, it was you—and that was even worse." The words rang, for a minute, almost solid in the air. "And I just couldn't get myself to say anything."

Jon looked up, finally. "You did try. Harder than I think you realize. But there was no point. They were never going to change their mind. They're assholes."

Sam licked her lips, then sighed. "I know they're assholes."

The word, on Sam's tongue, almost made Hayden laugh hysterically. This was all so heavy.

Sam looked at Hayden. "I *know* they're assholes. But they're also our parents. And I may not like them, at times. But I also—well, they're my parents. They weren't cold, callous people. They could be distant, but they encouraged us and were there—at the thought of disappointing them, after years of doing nothing but trying to do the exact opposite, I froze." She sucked in a breath. "I let Jon down."

"You didn't." The protectiveness in those two words made Hayden want to pull Jon close. All they both did was speak of trying to protect each other, when both were hurting.

"I did, and it's okay if you say that. I watched our father take you by the scruff and half heave you out the door. I listened to the things they called you, and called me by extension, and I didn't say a word. I had always thought, maybe, if it was one of us, their children…" Sam swallowed heavily again and cut herself off. "We didn't eat much. I left as early as I could, and I walked around for hours. I tried to call Jon, but his phone was off."

"I maybe threw my phone in the river." He shrugged. "Which was not a smart move. I'd just been completely cut off and had no way of getting a new one."

Sam had turned to stare out the window, as if it made baring herself easier. "After a few hours, I was numb with cold. I wanted to go back, to tell them I'm a lesbian. I wanted to scream it at them at that point. But it was late, and instead I went home."

"You went home with a stupid idea bubbling in your brain." Jon walked over and sat on the floor near them, resting his elbows on the coffee table.

Sam turned to look back at them. "It's not a stupid idea."

"It really, really is."

"You wanted to get married to make a point to them?" Hayden asked. It made so much sense. Marry a woman. Make her homophobic asshole parents angry.

"It started like that," Sam said. "I woke up in the morning, and that was my idea, to find a girlfriend and either come out to them, or let them discover it themselves, another salacious drama for them to use as an excuse to turn away their daughter. I don't need them, financially. It wouldn't affect me the way it affected Jon."

"How did it affect you more?" Hayden asked.

"They cut me off completely." His voice was monotone. "They stopped paying for college. I tried to finish this year, since it was paid for, but there seemed no point— there was no way I'd be able to finish the degree."

"You're an idiot," Sam said.

He shrugged. "With our family's financial background, I'm not eligible for any scholarships."

"He was due for his trust fund, a small amount, in the scheme of things, at twenty-one. They liquidated it. They stopped paying for college. They stopped paying his rent. They cut him off completely." Sam looked at Hayden. "You have to understand that I realize we sound spoiled." She raised her voice, as if mimicking someone. "Mommy and Daddy stopped paying for him." Her voice dropped back to normal. "But they always had. They abruptly left him with literally nothing and didn't care what happened to him as a result."

The air had left Hayden's lungs. Her gaze flicked to Jon, staring adamantly at his beer bottle, and to Sam. How could parents do that?

She had no understanding of the type of money they were talking about. "But surely you had some cash?" she asked him.

"It was all tied into their money. When they froze the funds they usually gave me, I had a couple of hundred in my account. But that was it."

"So you married me to make them angry?" Hayden asked Sam. She was subject-hopping, she knew. But her brain was all over the place.

Jon snorted, and Hayden whipped her head around to look at him, but he was still appraising his half-full beer.

"In part," Sam said.

"But that means you'll lose them too." Not that Hayden saw that as a huge loss at this point. But it wasn't up to her to say they were both better off with or without parents like theirs. Who was she to make that judgment? It had turned out that she was better off without her own father, but his rejection hurt every day, if she let herself think about it.

"Exactly!" Jon exploded. "Exactly, Sam. You'll lose them too. Why do that when you don't need to? Why put yourself through that?"

His cheeks were flushed, and his eyes were bright, intent on Sam.

"You know why," Sam said, her own gaze steady on his.

"It's bullshit. You could still have them."

"I don't *want* them. The fact that they could do that to you—that's not parenting. This closet they've forced us into isn't living. I. Don't. Want. Them."

"That's easy for you to say when you haven't lost them." Jon's voice broke on the last word, and Hayden almost did get up and hug him. Sam didn't move, though, and Jon didn't make any indication he wanted that. His eyes were glistening, though. A little boy lost. "I thought they couldn't have meant it, that after a year, they'd be ready to talk." He swallowed, his voice thick with tears that weren't falling. "They wouldn't even let me in the front door. Dad walked past, and he wouldn't even *look* at me."

"I'm aware of the consequences," Sam said. "And I'm willing to accept them."

"For what?" Jon asked. "I don't need the money."

Money. Ah. So they were getting somewhere. "Money?"

They both snapped their heads to look at her, as if they'd forgotten she was there. "Yes," Sam said. "Money."

"You get money for marrying me? A woman? Even though your family are homophobes?"

Jon laughed, the sound real and rich, even with his cheeks still washed out. "You have a way with words."

"Yes, very." Sam's words were dry. "The money we came into—well, I came into, at twenty-one, was to set us up. I bought this apartment and invested the rest. However, most of our inheritance is in a fund set up by our grandparents."

"Who were even more old-fashioned than our parents," Jon chimed in.

"Extremely." Sam gave a nod. "Which is hard to imagine. The trust funds have several stipulations. One," she held up a finger, "we must have a college degree."

"Well, look at that, I'm out already," Jon said.

"If you let me pay—"

"No," he interrupted Sam without hesitation.

She sighed, a second finger going up. "The second is that we're over thirty."

"Well, obviously I'm not there yet. But number one stops me, even when I am thirty."

Sam shot him a look, and he pretended to zip his lip and throw the key away. Sam continued, her third finger up, her elbow resting on her knee. "The third is that we're married. Good, old-fashioned family values. If we don't meet these stipulations, no money."

She blinked at Hayden, and Hayden blinked right back. "Oh." She cleared her throat. "So you married me for money."

"Essentially, yes. But not for me. I don't need it."

So why, then? Hayden glanced at Jon, who was now *glowering* at Sam. "Oh! For Jon."

Jon threw up his hands, his beer sloshing. "Yes, for me. She's going to get herself cut off from our family, completely, to get me money."

"Jon. That's not the only reason. I was going to go there that morning and tell them. Or get a girlfriend and destroy them slowly."

Whoa. Sam had some malice in her tone. Was it from anger at her parents for hurting her brother or from finally wanting to be herself without worrying about her parents? Or was it all tied up together?

"It was going to happen anyway," Sam continued, "but then I remembered the inheritance. Our parents talked about it often enough—the expectations we were to meet, the degree we needed, the responsible lives, the marriage we had to have. They even paraded around potential candidates."

"They did that?" Hayden asked.

Jon actually laughed. "Oh, we had so many awkward dinners with other 'suitable' families over with age-appropriate suitors." He made exaggerated air quotes.

Sam pulled a leg up under herself. "Remember the girl who had actually been to finishing school?"

Jon grinned. "They literally arranged for her to come over after my high school graduation. I remember even more the brother they brought over for you. Not surprised you remember the sister."

Sam actually returned his grin, her eyes lit up, and Hayden had a weird stab of jealousy she decided to ignore.

"So you two just checked out each other's dates?" she asked.

"All the time," they said in unison.

"Or the older sister, if she had one," Sam added.

"That's actually hilarious."

"It was." Jon said. "As soon as these candidates left, hints that were as subtle as a hammer would start about 'setting up our futures.'"

"The inheritance," Sam said simply.

"Which I don't need," Jon ground out.

"To get you your college education, Jon. To get you some stability. It's why I needed this marriage to happen so fast. I thought the sooner I received the money, the sooner you could get back into college. That maybe you wouldn't have to miss any at all." Sam moved forward, meeting his glower head-on. "You have fifty dollars in your account, and you won't take money from me. You've just dropped out of school and can't find work that actually pays you anything livable. This will help set you up. I don't need it."

"I don't want your money!"

"But you need it."

He snapped his mouth shut and looked away.

Hayden's thoughts were racing, bouncing off each other. Sam had needed this so fast for a reason. Her thoughts ground to a halt as something occurred to her.

Hayden raised her hand and waited until they both looked at her. "Uh, sorry. But if they're so homophobic, how is you being married to a woman legitimate?"

Sam crossed her arms. "It was stipulated by my grandparents, who passed away years ago before same-sex marriage was legal. The stipulation is *marriage*. It doesn't say what kind of marriage. And my parents can't alter that. It's not in their legal rights to do so."

Hayden's mind was whirring. "So, why the charade? Why pretend we're married for months? You have the paper. Why not just do it?"

Sam ignored Jon's glare. "They could try and complicate it. Hire someone to sift through everything, try to prove the marriage is a lie. I doubt it could affect anything anyway, but I wanted to ensure they couldn't slow it down or possibly expose it."

"Okay." Hayden's brain was whirring way too fast. "Okay."

"You still don't need to do this," Jon chimed in again. Hayden had the feeling he'd said that a lot to Sam over the last several months.

"I know I don't," Sam shot back. "I was going to tell them anyway. I spent all my life making sure they were happy, making sure that I met their expectations. I never wanted to disappoint them. You know how that feels. But I couldn't let them kick you out and hate you and then praise me and say they love me, when that was all a lie. So if I was going to do it anyway, why not do this too?"

"I still don't need the money."

"No. Maybe you don't. Maybe you could try for a scholarship or put yourself in debt or get a job that barely pays you." Sam's tone showed what she thought of that idea. "But this money is there, and it's rightfully ours, and if I'm going to lose them anyway, I may as well get something out of it."

Sam was blazing, her cheeks slashed with red and her eyes fierce. She looked stunning, and in that moment, more than ever, Hayden was reminded that she was doing all of this for her brother, for money. Not for Hayden. Hayden was a means to an end.

But wow, did Sam look hot.

"Right," Jon said. "Yeah. I guess so." He tilted his chin up, meeting that fiery, protective blaze in Sam's eye. "I just don't want to be the reason you feel like I do right now."

Hayden's breath caught at the vulnerability in his voice, and Sam's face softened.

"You wouldn't be the reason. They're the reason. And this is my choice. I can come out to them and lose them and everything else. Or I can come out to them and gain some money to get you on your feet. Either way, I lose them. But I'm coming out to them regardless." She clenched her jaw. "They set you up for everything, then stripped it away. You were sleeping on friends' sofas."

He sighed, but a smile was creeping up his face. "They're going to *hate* that you get the money for marrying a woman."

"Why do you think I made sure it was a woman and not a man?" The smile on Sam's face was one Hayden had never seen before, but it had a familiar edge. It was like Jon's—playful and confident. It suited her. "It's true, Jon, we may not have them after this." Sam paused, then said, "But you have me."

He tried to smother his surprised look with a smirk, but it was more a smile. "I think that's the most emotional thing you've ever said."

"Yes. Well." Sam picked off imaginary lint from her pants. "Don't tell anyone."

"I heard it too." Hayden raised her hand again.

Sam side-eyed Jon. "Maybe we'll have to kill her."

Jon laughed. "I think you'll have to. She witnessed the softie deep down inside you."

"There is no such thing." Actual disgust was thick in Sam's voice.

Yet, Sam was giving up her parents because her brother needed her. She was sacrificing something that was clearly important to her, since she'd stuck with it for over forty years, because she couldn't stand the way her brother suffered.

Samantha Thomson was a softie. Well, deep down. Like, deep, *deep* down.

"Do they know you're seeing him?" Hayden asked.

"They do. But we don't talk about it."

"Our family?" Jon asked. "Not talk? Never."

Sam's upbringing was sounding more and more like something Hayden herself could never imagine. Hayden had grown up in a house full of yelling with her sister, and pounding up and down stairs, and being whoever they were, as loudly as they could be.

"So, Christmas is…?" Hayden needed clarification.

"Christmas is when I will tell them. Do you still want to be there?"

Her eyes, green and deep, were impossible to look away from, let alone say no to.

"Of course."

~ ~ ~

Later, when Jon had finally peeled himself off the floor after several more beers, Hayden padded out from the shower, her hair still damp. The couple of beers she'd consumed had left her head fuzzy. Frank was nowhere to be seen; he was probably upstairs on Sam's bed.

At least *he* got to be on Sam's bed.

Hayden's cheeks burned at that errant thought. Now was not the night for that.

The living room was empty, and Hayden grabbed the beer bottles off the coffee table, the remains sloshing in the bottoms, and dumped them in the recycling. No light filtered down the stairs, no sounds of someone from up there. But that could mean that Sam was asleep. It had been a weird, emotion-filled evening, after all.

In fact, Hayden would never have thought Sam could spill her thoughts like that. Looking back on it now, she almost felt guilty for having witnessed it.

No wonder she'd waited to tell Hayden. She'd bared herself completely.

Would she have disclosed so much to anyone? Or did Hayden get that much information because they were friends? Would someone else have been told to stand with Sam at the Christmas dinner and act the loving spouse because she wanted to get money and left it at that?

Would they have been told about the shame that had eaten Sam alive for the last year?

Hayden pressed her palms into the cool granite of the kitchen counter. A shadow moved on the balcony.

For a moment, Hayden hovered in the kitchen, unsure what to do. Go out there and see if Sam needed someone nearby? Or had she gone out there to be alone? Hayden went back to her room, and emerged back in the living room with her coat tugged on over her sweater and pajama pants. Hopping on one foot, she tugged her socks up over the bottom of her pants, almost falling over but catching herself with a hand on the wall.

She looked ridiculous. A mirror wasn't even necessary to tell her that. But it was going to be damn cold outside.

The door slid open smoothly, barely making a sound. Hayden slid it closed behind her and crossed her arms, her fingers in her armpits. The cold was like a slap, biting at her cheeks, and creeping into any open space in her clothes. The light from inside washed over the balcony in a faint, golden glow. Sam was leaning against the rail, a tumbler glass of something in her hand. Her breath fanned out in front of her, a white mist that drifted away into nothing in the still night. Below, cars passed, the sound muffled.

Sam gave no indication of wanting Hayden there, but she gave no sign of irritation either. She just stared out over the street, her lids heavy. Her profile was going to be locked in Hayden's brain forever—that strong nose, her cheek kissed pink by the frigid air, lips dark from the same. A scarf was wrapped around her neck, her hair fanned out over her forehead and down against her ears. It was mussed; it had started to grow out.

Stunning. Hayden almost breathed the word, an ache deep in her stomach at the thought.

She looked absolutely stunning.

"Do you want me to go?" In the silence of the night, in the moment, Hayden had no option but to whisper.

A second stretched on forever, until Sam gave the tiniest shake of her head, her gaze still on the outside world.

Hayden walked over, mimicking Sam's pose, her elbows on the rail, a barely perceivable gap between their arms. Gloves would be heaven. But Sam shifted, barely perceptible, so that they were closer together as she took a slow sip of her drink and didn't move, and Hayden wouldn't have gone to get those gloves for any promise of warmth. Her fingers trembled and she clenched her hands into fists. It wasn't from the cold.

Sam was breathing softly next to her, and Hayden could make out the sweet scent of whiskey. Sam shifted her weight again, and their shoulders and hips were flush, an entire side of their bodies sharing heat.

The flutter in Hayden's stomach sped up. She turned her head to watch the planes of Sam's face, the slope of her cheek. Closing that gap would be so simple, to run her lips over Sam's jawline, up over her cheekbones. Her eyes were that slash of green in white snow, something fragile forcing its way into the world.

When had Hayden turned poetic about a pretty woman? She swallowed. "Are you okay?"

Sam didn't turn to look at her, and Hayden was actually relieved she didn't, because she didn't know if she could stop herself from surging forward and kissing her.

Why hadn't Hayden let herself enjoy those few times they'd kissed for show? Or had she, and just not thought about it?

"Yes," Sam breathed.

"I don't believe you."

The corner of Sam's mouth twitched up. "I am."

"Okay."

Hayden thought they'd drop it and turned to look back over the street. The air was foggy down below, the light from the streetlights glazed.

"I'm not used to sharing like that." Sam hesitated over her words, and Hayden turned back to look at her. Even as she didn't want Sam to meet her eyes, something in her longed for her to turn and actually do so at the same time.

"Have you talked about it at all? Since last Christmas?"

Sam shook her head and raised her glass, taking another sip. Ice clinked as she did so. Why she needed ice, Hayden had no idea. The air would keep it cool enough. Sam's bottom lip shone from the liquid when she lowered the glass and Hayden wanted to suck on it, to trace her tongue over the softness.

"Not even with Jon?"

"No. We—he finally showed up days later. I said sorry, but that was all. We moved on." Sam twirled her wrist, the ice clinking in the glass again. "We don't really talk about things, in my family."

Hayden had gotten that idea. "So you've just lived with that shame you felt?"

Sam sucked in a breath and gave a nod. "I deserved it."

"No, no you didn't." Hayden spoke in a rush of words. "Sam, no."

"I did. I wouldn't normally have spoken so much tonight. But I—I wanted Jon to know."

Had Sam spent the entire last year punishing herself for what had happened? Hayden thought she might have.

"I think he knows," Hayden said. "I think Jon knows you more than anyone."

"You may be right." Hayden watched the bob of Sam's throat as she swallowed. "But I don't think you would have done anything like watch your family throw your sister out."

Hayden sucked in a slow breath. "No. Maybe not. But I've done other things."

Sam's gaze was still so steadily not on her and Hayden ached, then, for that green to be focused on her, caution be damned. "Like avoiding your mother completely?"

The words were like a slap, even with a soft tone.

"I—" Hayden gritted her teeth, at a loss after that.

"I noticed, even before what happened that night, that you avoid being alone with her. Or avoid her in general. It's subtle. You have good excuses—Javi, helping your grandmother. But I noticed."

No judgment was in Sam's voice, but shame burned Hayden's cheeks all the same. She wanted to deny it, but what slipped out was, "It's too hard. To see her like that. I watched her decline for a year, and I think it just took it all out of me." Sam took another sip, and Hayden wanted to take the glass and finish off the last of the amber liquid. Her neck was starting to twinge, but she didn't want to look away from Sam. "I hate seeing her like that."

"I completely understand. But you still do what you can for her. I let my brother get tossed into the cold for the crime of something I was equally guilty for."

"It's not a crime," Hayden hissed.

Sam nodded, and there was nothing bitter about it. "In my family, it's the greatest there is. There are people in jail for fraud in my family, people who have done completely reprehensible things in the name of making money and covering up their tracks. Affairs and bribery and worse. But being gay?" Sam clicked her tongue. "And I stood by and watched them reject him."

Her voice cracked, and Hayden wanted to pull Sam into her. Sam had said that again and again, and Hayden imagined she lay awake at night playing that scene in her parents' house over and over in her mind, the shame coursing through her veins, leaving her heated and sick.

"I don't apologize for my actions, Hayden. My choices are my own. But that?"

Sam stopped speaking and Hayden turned further to face her, one elbow left on the railing and her body almost against Sam's.

"Everyone makes mistakes, Sam."

Finally, Sam turned, her eyes alight with tears that weren't falling. Her gaze flicked to Hayden's lips, once, before it went back to her eyes, and Hayden thought the bottom may have dropped from her world. "I don't."

And Sam surged forward, all warmth and whiskey-tinged breath. The arm not hindered by the glass slipped under Hayden's coat, fingers digging into her back and her face hot in the crook of Hayden's neck. All Hayden could do was wrap her arms around her and pull her closer, wondering as she did when Sam had last hugged someone. Her nails were sharp, even through the sweater, and the answer could only be: far too long.

Hayden didn't know what surprised her more. The fact that she had genuinely thought Sam had been going to kiss her, or the desperate need with which Sam actually hugged her.

Hayden hugged her back and didn't let her go until Sam pulled away, minutes or hours later, Hayden had no idea, with her cheeks dry. She slipped back inside without a word, and Hayden stayed out in the cold, her thoughts a mess.

Chapter 21

So. It wasn't just an attraction.

It was officially a crush.

A week of trying to ignore it didn't ease anything. Long showers alone with her own hand didn't. Cold showers didn't. Trying to pretend she didn't actually care did nothing.

None of it helped.

Hayden was, it turned out, a little besotted.

Even at work, watching Sam's brisk manner with patients didn't do anything. Hayden purposefully stuck around when she needed Sam for a consult and couldn't even get overly annoyed by her terrible bedside manner. Now Hayden saw her as efficient and just a bit, well, useless with patients.

An amazing surgeon.

Maybe that was why she managed to be such an amazing surgeon. She focused on the facts and the case and relied on the team to do the rest.

She operated with cold efficiency.

And saved more lives than most.

"You're staring at your wife with moon eyes."

Hayden jumped, moving her chin off her hand and straightening up from the nurses' station desk. She rounded on Luce, who was looking utterly delighted, and managed to knock a piece of the tacky decorative tinsel off the desk. Picking it up gave her the perfect excuse to not look at her smirking friend. "I am not."

"You really, really were. Like, I expected a breeze to waft through and wave your hair gently around while violins started up."

Bright red tinsel back in place, Hayden jammed her hands in her pockets. "Stop exaggerating. I have to set up some antibiotics. Come with?"

Luce followed her through to the treatment room. They both started getting their equipment together, syringes and needles and vials in hand. Luce spread out their medication chart and Hayden started mixing an antibiotic.

"I'm really not mooning," she said after a while.

Well, only a bit.

Luce snorted like Hayden was ridiculous. "You're still so smitten with her."

Hayden ducked her head. Still? Try newly. But she couldn't talk to Luce about that. Which was insanely frustrating. And, also, sad. Their friendship had been suffering . In between work, new relationships, and Hayden's guilt from all the lies about her said relationship, a small divide had grown.

Hayden really was going to explode soon if she didn't get to talk about this. She was a talker. Not a keep-it-all-close-to-your-chest type at all. She wanted to sit over a coffee, or to sprawl over a bar top, and whine and have Luce pat her head a little.

But that wasn't an option, and it sucked.

All Hayden could do was try not to let Sam catch her mooning. Because after the hug that had left Hayden both swooning and aching for the woman, all she could conclude was that Sam was really, really not into her.

It wasn't that Hayden thought she was only the way to screw over Sam's parents for Sam anymore. No way Sam would open up like that to just anyone. Especially not someone she was doing business with. They were friends. They'd agreed on that, long ago in Hayden's bed in her family home. And that had definitely grown over the last few months.

But that was all.

Hayden quickly checked Luce's antibiotic and fluid order, and they both headed out to their respective patients. Hayden got swept up in a patient who came in after a nasty fall and another who presented from an aged care home with sudden onset confusion.

"Classic urinary tract infection," Hayden murmured to Luce as she walked past them on her way to grab some supplies. "Bet you."

She fist-pumped when the dipstick lit up and proved her right. She sent off a sample and let the ER doctor know.

It was hours later that Sam appeared again, followed by Leon, the still-twitchy-but-a-little-less-so intern. Hayden finished dressing a patient's hand, which they'd sliced open while disagreeing with a tape dispenser while wrapping Christmas presents.

She was already pulling her pen out of her pocket when she dropped the chart down onto the nurses' station and flipped it open to start filling it out. There was no need to look around and see what Sam was doing. None at all. Why would Hayden feel the need to do that?

"Hey."

The word whispered over her neck, low and gravelly, and Hayden jumped, even though she knew who it was. She swallowed, smiling at Sam, whose front grazed Hayden's side. Because they were married. And while they never made out in the hospital or anything, they still kept up the subtle touches.

Keeping up appearances was slowly killing Hayden.

"Hi. I didn't know you were down here." Lies. Hayden just spoke lies all the time lately, apparently.

Sam put a file down next to Hayden's clipboard. "I've been in and out all day. You've seemed busy?"

Hayden turned so they weren't as close together but were facing each other properly. A week had gone by since they'd been anywhere near this close, except for at work when they ran into each other for show.

"Yeah, it's been busy."

As usual, Sam was looking at her steadily, and Hayden wanted to squirm away from it. "You've barely been home." At least her voice dropped low; Sam was aware of the ears that were always listening in a hospital.

"I—" And what could she say? She hadn't. When work was over, Hayden went out for food or a drink with whoever was finishing the shift with her, or Luce, when they weren't with Clemmie. It was always late when she got home, and she had been quickly sliding into her room. "You know how it is, the lead-up to Christmas. Social things."

"Okay." It sounded measured. "Is everything all right?" The words were mannered, as if she'd practiced them. And that wouldn't have surprised Hayden, if Sam did run the words over again and again in her mind to make sure she said them right. Or to know if she wanted to say them at all.

The idea of it made affection bloom in her chest. Hayden smiled widely, making sure her teeth showed. It was probably too much, but there was no turning back now. "Oh yeah. Everything is fine. Why wouldn't it be?"

Maybe because Hayden was being driven a little mad with a desire to kiss Sam, to touch her, all the time, and had been avoiding her since. That glimpse of her on the balcony had left Hayden flush with feelings and desires and nowhere to direct them. Months were left of this and she couldn't mess it up.

Not when she'd promised Sam.

And the money, she supposed.

The money had been the last thing on her mind recently.

"I don't know," Sam replied. "I don't know why it wouldn't be. That's why I asked."

Damn Sam and her logic. Right. Hayden had to get her act together. Especially with Christmas in three days and the show they were going to have to put on. Or rather, the show Hayden was going to have to watch. "Sorry. I've just been distracted with—with family and stuff."

Lies again. Hayden was going to be sick with them all soon.

Sam's brow furrowed. "Is everything okay? With your mom?"

Apparently Sam was not going to make this easy. "Yeah." She nodded for emphasis. "Everything is completely fine. I've just been thinking, you know, what to do. About Mom and everything."

"Okay." Sam shifted her feet. "Did you want to have dinner tonight? I thought we could go out. My treat."

And she smiled, so genuinely that Hayden's stomach actually fluttered. "Sounds great."

"Okay. We can discuss Christmas."

"Good plan. I have some questions."

"Such as?"

"You know, what do I wear? How are we acting? What's the plan? Those types."

"Such simple questions?"

Hayden chuckled. "Exactly."

"Hayden!" They both turned rapidly to the coordinator on a phone down at the other end of the desk. She looked harried. "Pileup on the bridge, first patient en route, you're on."

"Got it." Hayden turned back to Sam. "I gotta—"

"Go." Sam picked her file back up and held it against her chest. "I'll meet you after work?"

"Sounds like a plan." And Hayden kept that smile on her face as she turned and walked away.

All right. Operation Get Her Act Together and Stop Creepily Mooning After Her Fake Wife was on. She could be Sam's friend. Supportive and caring.

~ ~ ~

Christmas Eve started with a deathly quiet ER.

Never a good sign.

Luce tiptoed up to Hayden where she was restocking shelves in a treatment room, nothing else to do outside. "Hayden," they whispered.

Hayden looked up from her half-empty box of bandages. "Yeah?" she stage-whispered back.

"There's nothing going on." Luce kept whispering.

"Well...yeah?"

"Like, nothing. I have one old lady with a broken hip who's all settled with pain relief and is waiting for the OR. My other patient just got transferred."

"At least you have patients. They decided to use me as manual labor today." Hayden stuffed as many bandages as would fit onto the shelf, stood up, and shuffled the box against the wall with her foot. "But I still don't get why we're whispering?"

"You're superstitious."

"What?"

"Well, you believe that if I say it's quiet, every—"

"Luce!"

Luce snorted. "See?"

"You can't just—you're not allowed to say—"

Tasha walked past the door.

"Tasha!" Hayden called out. "Luce just said the 'Q' word."

Tasha stopped dead. "No? They wouldn't?" She leveled a look at Luce. "You wouldn't?"

"They did."

Luce looked from one to the other, scowling, perhaps comprehending they were in too deep.

"They totally did," Hayden said.

"When everything goes to shit, I'm coming after you." Tasha held two fingers up to her own eyes then pointed them at Luce and walked away.

Luce leveled the scowl at her. "Snitch."

Hayden crossed her arms smugly. "You're the one who said the word."

"The word has no power."

"You don't know that." Hayden wasn't really mad. Okay. Maybe a little mad. That word was a hideous curse, even if she didn't usually believe in this stuff. "So did you just come to annoy me?"

Luce fiddled with the bandages Hayden had haphazardly stuffed onto the shelf, their long fingers plucking at plastic packets and rearranging them into a less perilous pile. "Not just that, no."

"What's up?"

"What are you doing for Christmas?"

That was a random question, flung out of nowhere. "Uh, working. Like you. You know that?"

Luce huffed, bending over to grab a few more packets from the box now that their organization had made some more room. "I mean for tonight."

Oh. "Uh, I have dinner. With Sam's family."

Luce kept stacking. "You sound nervous."

"I kind of am. I, well, haven't really met them?"

Within the shelf, Luce's hands stilled. They turned their head. "Seriously? You guys have been together—and, well, married—for, what, five months now?"

"A little more, even."

"How have you not met them?"

"I don't know. They're not close. I've met her brother. You'd like him. He's a smart-ass."

"He sounds great already." Luce went back to the bandages. "So, are you nervous?"

Yes. Though, at least Hayden didn't have to act when it came to Sam anymore. But that was the issue. She found herself freezing up now, like in the beginning, worried she'd give too much away, when that was the idea all along. "Not really. It'll be fine. What are you doing?"

Luce swallowed visibly. "I'm meeting Clemmie's family. And then tomorrow she's coming for dinner with mine."

"Really?"

Luce wouldn't look at her. "Yeah."

"Is this the meeting-the-parents?"

Luce looked at her, all fragile. "Yeah."

"Luce! That's a big deal."

"You're doing the same!"

Hayden laughed. "Yeah, but we're already married. You guys are dating, and you're meeting them, and it's cute—"

"Yeah, yeah. I'm nervous enough."

Luce almost looked gray. "Luce, it'll be awesome. They'll love you. They can't not."

"This is a big deal, isn't it?"

"Yeah. But in an awesome way. Think, a few months ago we were laughing at our inability to even say hi to a woman."

"And now you're married, and I'm meeting the 'rents of this amazing woman."

Hayden nodded, her breath catching. She held up her hand, and Luce rolled their eyes and slapped their own hand against it.

"Celebrating?"

They both turned to the door and Hayden let the smitten smile curve her lips up at the sight of Sam there, hands buried in her lab coat.

"Just enjoying our own awesomeness," Luce said.

"That's…" Hayden imagined Sam wanted to say *strange* "…nice. Is it me, or is it utterly quiet down here?"

Luce chortled, and Hayden held up her hands. "Okay! You two, that's officially a double whammy. Whatever happens now is on the two of you."

She was met with smirks from the two of them.

"Hayden." Sam spoke like she would to a child. "Speaking the word 'quiet' has no relation to the influx of patients."

A phone rang out in the ER. Another started. Then another. It was a cacophony of them. Someone shouted down the hall.

Hayden crossed her arms.

"My partner is having a baby!" was screamed out from somewhere nearby.

Luce and Sam looked at each other, and Hayden glowered at them both.

"Well." Luce bit their lip. "That was oddly timed."

"I maintain it has nothing to do with my saying it was quiet." Sam didn't even sound remotely regretful.

An emergency bell went off, and Sam stood aside as Luce and Hayden rushed past her.

"You two both suck," Hayden called over her shoulder.

CHAPTER 22

"You grew up *here?*"

"Yes."

Hayden gaped up at the townhouse. "But, like, *here*. In all of this?"

"Yes."

"Really?"

"Yes."

It was huge. And domineering. Looming over the street. Maybe looming wasn't the right word—too dramatic and scary sounding. It was painted a rich reddish color, the outside completely renovated but maintained in an old-fashioned style.

The taxi pulled away behind them.

"They own the entire building?"

"Yes."

"Oh."

"Breathe, Hayden."

Hayden took in a deep breath and turned to look at Sam. She had a woolen hat pulled low over her ears, her cheeks ruddy with cold. Auburn bangs peeked out over her eyes. She looked adorable. Though she would probably hate that descriptor.

"What?" Sam asked.

She went for it. "You look adorable." Sam rolled her eyes, and Hayden snickered. "Knew you'd hate that." Smother it in humor, and Hayden could say what she was thinking. She mentally high-fived herself.

"We could always pretend work was inundated and that we couldn't make it." Sam's face was inscrutable as she looked back at the house, but even in the glow of streetlights, Hayden could see how she swallowed heavily.

"To be fair," Hayden said, "that did happen. We were lucky to get out on time. Which, by the way, I maintain is your and Luce's fault."

"*Quiet* is not a cursed word, Hayden." Sam paused. "Though I will admit the timing tonight was…interesting."

"Interesting because you cursed us."

"Sure."

Hayden laughed. "Was that sarcasm?"

"You tell me."

They faded into silence, and Hayden rocked on her heels. "So, are we going in?"

Sam was still looking up at her family's house.

Hayden touched Sam's elbow, and Sam continued looking up. "Hey. We don't *have* to do this."

The look on her face hardened; a subtle clench of her jaw. "Yes, we do."

And she walked up the front path, Hayden on her heels. "Hey, Sam?"

"Yes?"

"Why don't they ever come to your house?"

"They never really did. But now that they know Jon comes by regularly, they refuse."

Well, lovely. And that certainly didn't make Hayden dread this any less. "Okay."

Sam pressed the buzzer. "Not a lot about this is okay."

Her tone stuck with Hayden—haunted, sure. Sam's eyes were focused on the door, and the slope of her mouth made Hayden sad. All she could do was link their fingers and squeeze for a second before dropping them as the door opened. Not having her ring on felt strange, which in itself grated.

They were going to appear as friends throughout the meal and tell them afterward. Hayden had asked why they didn't tell them right away. And Sam had said she wanted them to see that Hayden was an average, nice person.

Sometimes, Hayden wondered if Sam was hoping they wouldn't reject her for this, even as she also planned for it.

That thought left an ache behind.

The door opened.

"Good evening, Miss Thomson."

"Merry Christmas, Ron."

The man who opened the door was dressed in a suit. He had a moustache. A hand was held behind his back with perfect posture. He looked every bit the stereotype of a butler. Incredulous, Hayden couldn't help but grin.

"This is my friend, Hayden."

Hayden held her hand out, and he stared at it for a moment, before slowly shaking it. "Nice to meet you."

"You too, Miss." He turned to Sam. "Your family is in the evening lounge. Drinks?"

"Whiskey. With ice. Hayden?"

"Wine—*please.*"

A note of desperation was in her voice, and she could swear she saw a small smile on Ron's mouth as he nodded and they walked through the door. When Hayden took off her jacket, he whisked it away from her, along with Sam's and that adorable hat of hers, and disappeared. The entrance was all shining, polished wood and high ceilings. A chandelier even hung above them, glittering.

"You have a butler," she whispered out of the corner of her mouth.

Sam rolled her eyes again and turned. Hayden followed her down the hallway and toward the lion's den.

"But seriously, Sam. You. Have. A. Butler."

They paused outside a huge, carved double door. It was so ornate. This was bizarre. Hayden could barely fathom how people lived like this. And her childhood had not been poor by a long shot—her family home was spacious and nice and well looked after.

But this was just ostentatious.

And now they had to go devastate Sam's parents and, Hayden was thinking, devastate Sam. Maybe they should back out and not do it. But this wasn't Hayden's call. Besides, as far as Hayden could tell, a lot of this was also about Sam not wanting to hide a part of herself anymore. And Hayden could understand that. To not...be herself, every day? To have to hide a huge part of her life? Unimaginable for her.

Again, she felt so lucky for that.

Yet they didn't walk through the door.

"Sam?"

Sam's hand hovered over the handle. "Hm?"

"We don't have to do this. If you're not ready, there's time later."

"I know."

"I don't mind. I—I signed on for a year. It's not even been half that." Hayden was whispering, not wanting their secrets to be sucked up by this ridiculous house.

"Yes. But that's in case it gets...difficult."

"I don't mind if it drags on longer. If you're not ready—"

Sam turned her head sharply. "You'd what? Put your life on hold for more time?"

Her eyes were bright, sharp. Hayden swallowed. "Well, yeah."

Sam cocked her head. "You would, wouldn't you?"

Her voice was such a soft murmur Hayden could barely hear her. The words settled deep in her and Hayden wanted to forever remember how Sam looked after she'd said them.

Before Hayden could gather a response, Sam pushed the door open and walked through. Squaring her shoulders, Hayden followed, keeping close to her.

The room was half-lounge, with squishy leather couches and armchairs, and half-library, with the walls covered in bookshelves. Her fingers twitched, wanting to sort through the titles and see what they held. But that faded quickly as a woman walked forward and wrapped her arms around Sam, pulling her into a hug. It was short, very short, but warm, and was finished with the flourish of two cheek kisses. When she pulled back, lines fanned around her eyes as she smiled with her hands on Sam's shoulders. A string of elegant pearls sat around her neck. Her clothes were neatly pressed and expensive-looking. But her face was kind, her eyes the green of Sam's.

"Hello, darling." Sam's mother's voice was so genuine. "Did work run late?"

"It got busy." She pulled back, and a man with hair as red as Sam's hugged her. However, his hair was streaked with gray, and the stubble on his cheeks was salt and pepper. Sam pulled back and turned to Hayden. "This is Hayden, the friend I said was coming. Hayden, these are my parents, George and Irene."

It was as if Hayden had tripped on a step that wasn't there. She'd pictured cold. Awkward. Uncomfortable. This was warm, welcoming, and bordering on familiar. She was wrapped up in a handshake from George and air kisses from Irene. Hayden kept herself looking polite until Ron appeared with her wine, which was thankfully very full, and Hayden took a gulp that was probably too large. Sam pursed her lips, almost imperceptibly, at her and George hid a smirk that reminded her of Sam's and made her wince.

"I was supposed to wait to toast, wasn't I?"

"You're fine, dear." Irene patted her on the shoulder, and Hayden's head swam.

How were these people the type to kick out their son for being gay? They could be described as a bit stiff and, okay, a hug didn't have to mean much, but the picture wasn't fitting with the image Hayden had put in her head.

Maybe that was the point. Villains didn't always look the part. Hopefully there was more wine.

"Merry Christmas." George raised his glass, and they all followed suit. "It's nice to have you here, Hayden, and to have all the family together."

Sam was like a statue next to her, and Hayden's eye actually twitched. Except his son? But he glossed over it as if it didn't even matter.

Jon was at home that night. He'd told them he planned to binge TV in his underwear and would wait until the twenty-fifth to have dinner with them both, like they'd planned. Was he sitting there wondering if his family was having a wonderful evening without him? Even though he knew Sam's coming out plan, he must feel that. How much must that hurt? To know Sam could walk in and he was sent away at the door?

Hayden's heart ached, and she had another long sip.

"We read your article, Sam. In the latest journal you were in." Irene was hovering at Sam's side as if anxious to share her warmth. Hayden knew that smile.

"Yes, good work there." George had dropped into one of the armchairs and had his whiskey balanced on his knee. It looked like he took it the same way as Sam. "Still hardly understood a word, but good to see you're keeping your professional portfolio buff."

He was almost jolly. A wink added to the effect.

Irene sat on a couch and patted the edge, so Sam sat near her and Hayden plopped into one of the other armchairs. Her drink almost sloshed over, so she took another sip, purely to prevent that from happening again, of course. It had nothing to do with trying to manage the twilight zone she was in.

"Hayden." Irene's smile was on her now. It was like Sam's, but there was something fake about it. As if it was there for appearances. Or was Hayden inventing ideas about them? "Tell us something about you."

"Uh—" Hayden had no idea where to start with a question like that. She had a cranky cat? She liked pears? Bananas freaked her out? Why was she thinking about fruit? Sam took a sip of her drink, her eyes on Hayden.

"Are you from New York originally?" Irene asked, her eyes warm. She'd clearly realized Hayden was floundering.

"No, actually. I was born in Miami."

"Oh, how nice." Her voice made Hayden believe she didn't really think that. "What brought you here?"

"College, and work." Hayden's finger traced over the rim of her glass. Everyone's attention was on her. "And then I guess I just fell in love with the city."

"New York will do that to you." George grinned at her, dimples on his cheeks. Jon was so similar to him. It was uncanny. "Great city."

"It is. Are you a native New Yorker?"

"Born and raised." His chest puffed out. "All of us are."

"And where do you live at the moment?" Irene crossed her legs like Sam, looking as if she belonged exactly where she sat.

"Do you mean what area?" Hayden asked.

Before Irene could answer, Sam cleared her throat. "Hayden's been staying with me."

Oh no. Hayden raised the glass to her lips with two hands and drank some more.

"Oh?" Irene looked at George then quickly back at Sam. "Aren't you too old for a housemate?"

Sam actually didn't look like she belonged here now. Months ago, Hayden would have thought she did—slightly stiff, surrounded by stiff people and stiff things. But now, Hayden had seen her in sweatpants and thick socks, legs pulled up on the sofa as she watched television and absently stroked Frank.

She didn't look comfortable here with her parents, in her childhood home.

The heaviness of Sam's gaze landed on her for a second, and Hayden wasn't sure if she was going to blurt it out, to get it out. But instead, she offered a small shrug.

"No."

"Don't shrug, Sam."

If someone had said that to Hayden, she would have shrugged again. But Sam straightened.

"So," George said, "are you dating anyone?"

Hayden resisted the urge to glare at George, who was clearly trying to brush over whatever was going on between Irene and Sam.

"No, Dad."

"Well, the son of the Jamesons is single. He's divorcing his wife."

"Because he was caught with his secretary."

"Sam." Irene's voice was indulging now. "Gossip isn't always the most reliable."

Sam sipped her drink, and Hayden realized the glass was as empty as her own. As if on cue, Ron appeared and topped up all the glasses, moving as if he weren't even there. Hayden flashed him a smile in thanks.

"It's hardly gossip. He was caught with his pants down in his office."

"Samantha!"

"Well, I'd like to think you'd want to set me up with someone who can at least keep it in his pants."

"Fair enough," George said abruptly. "What about you, Hayden? Are you seeing anyone?"

Hayden's gaze flicked to Sam, but Hayden had no idea what to say.

"Dinner is served."

Hayden jumped, wine almost sloshing over the sides of her glass again, and turned to see Ron standing behind her, his arm held behind his back. She narrowed her eyes at him, and she could swear his eyes were laughing at her. No one else seemed to notice.

Good timing. Avoiding that question helped everyone.

Sam's parents stood up and led them through a door on the right. Sam gave Hayden a tight nod. She wanted to reach out and tangle their fingers together and squeeze. To watch that hardness in Sam's eyes melt away as she huffed a laugh at something silly Hayden said. Instead, Hayden walked a step behind, and they entered a dining room.

With another chandelier.

The dining table looked decorated for dinner with royalty. Gleaming plates with glints of gold rims, crystal glasses, and what Hayden was pretty sure was real silverware. Holly and Christmas decorations sat in the middle. Hayden followed Sam when she slipped into her seat across from her mother. In front of her was more cutlery than she'd ever think she would need, including three types of forks.

Three.

Hayden barely used one fork.

Bowls of soup had been filled and were waiting, the steam rising—thick pumpkin, from the look and smell of them. Just the thought of soup for Christmas dinner was strange to her.

"So, Hayden." George settled his napkin on his lap, so Hayden quickly did the same. "Sam tells us you're a friend from the hospital?"

"We met there. I'm a nurse in the ER."

"Ah." He nodded, and Hayden wasn't really sure what for.

"You never considered doing something more ambitious?" It was hard to hear a question like that from Sam's mother, framed so differently from how Sam had asked the same thing so many months before.

No one had started to eat, so Hayden waited.

Sam reached for a glass of white wine that had already been at her place setting when they'd walked into the room. "Mother—"

"Not really." Hayden cut in, because there wasn't any point. She had nothing to prove to them. "I like being a nurse."

"Charming." And the smile she gave then was anything but.

Hayden was used to chatter and the clanging of plates and cutlery at Christmas dinner, the sound of several types of food being dished up and passed back and forth all at once. She guessed they were having courses here.

Hayden took a deep breath. She had to be there for Sam. And to be someone Sam's parents could relate to. Or something like that. "I started in medicine. But for personal reasons, I switched to nursing."

"And why not go back?" Irene asked.

"I like being a nurse. It's rewarding."

"Hm," George said. "Well, let's say grace."

And they did. They all bowed their heads and said thanks for the food and to the Lord for bringing their family together. Hayden's cheeks burned as she thought of Jon again, alone at his place. She didn't say *amen*. Abuela was religious, but they never really said grace. And here, in this house, it didn't sit well. Hypocrisy was something she had a hard time stomaching.

When they looked up, they started eating and Hayden wished the soup didn't taste as good as it did.

"So what do your parents do?" George asked.

The questions weren't going to stop, it seemed. And was that question really important? "My parents were both in law. It's how they met."

"What area?" A spark of interest lit him up. Was this a respectable job?

"Well, my father was in fiscal law. And my mother worked for the DA for a while. She did a lot of pro bono work."

A muscle twitched in his jaw, and Sam's foot slid next to Hayden's under the table. Nothing more than that, but it was enough for Hayden to remember why they were here and to take a deep breath. And a sip of her wine.

"Well, that's nice." His tone said it was anything but.

"Have you heard from Jon?"

Hayden whipped her head around to stare at Sam. Her soup hadn't been touched. But her glass was half-empty. Well. That escalated quickly. Sam took another sip of her drink, her eyes on her parents. Hayden sucked in a breath and looked back across at them.

Their faces were like stone.

"No," was all Irene said. She delicately raised her spoon to her mouth.

"Are you even going to ask how he is?" A tremor in Sam's voice gave her away. Hayden pushed her foot harder against Sam's. Anything to show support.

Apparently this was happening now.

Why had the plan changed?

George swallowed slowly, as if thinking. He rested his wrist against the edge of the table, his spoon held like royalty, delicate in his hands. "No."

The silence stretched over the table. A server, not Ron, walked in and went around, topping up their drinks again. Another gulp. Hayden wished none of this had been necessary. Not because it was awkward for her: she would get over it. This wasn't going to have a long-term effect on her or her life. Or her feelings.

But Sam's fingers trembled as she reached for her glass, and something fierce rose up in Hayden's chest. She clenched her teeth and looked back to Sam's parents. Irene caught Sam's eye and gave a short shake of her head. George was eating again.

Red crept up Sam's neck.

"He's doing well," Hayden chimed in. "He's such a nice guy."

Three sets of eyes bore into her, and Hayden had another sip of her wine. Probably not what she should have said. Maybe she shouldn't drink anymore.

They were really staring at her. So that's where Sam had gotten that shielded, impassive, impossible-to-figure-out look from. They could be wishing for her death right now and she'd have no idea.

"You've met him?" George asked. His voice was too measured.

"Yes."

He looked to Sam. Maybe Hayden shouldn't have said anything. But it was clear Sam had been ready to start the conversation, and Hayden had never been very good at not saying what she was thinking. "Why would your work friend have met that boy?" he asked Sam.

That boy?

"Because she's not my work friend."

Oh no. Here it went. It was happening. Hayden reached for her wine again.

"She's my wife."

All the air sucked out of the room and there was a thump as someone's leg jumped under the table and hit the wood. Hayden almost laughed. Mostly to relieve the hysterical feeling in her chest, but also because it was so ridiculous that this statement could cause such a reaction.

Irene's hand slammed down on the table, her spoon hitting her plate with a clang. George's face was absurdly red.

Hayden sipped her wine.

Sam sipped her wine.

"Your what?" Irene's voice was low, and in contrast to her husband's, her face was drained of color.

"My wife." Sam's voice was steadier than Hayden would have thought. She was looking from one parent to the other, her eyes like stone. "We're married."

"No, you're not," Irene said.

"We are." Hayden smiled. "Very."

Sam's foot twitched next to hers.

Both ignored Hayden, attention unwavering from Sam.

"You're a—" George looked as if he'd swallowed something extremely bitter.

"Lesbian. Yes."

"No, you're not." Irene shook her head. "You're intelligent, beautiful—you're too old to think this about yourself."

"I assure you, I've always known this about myself. I also assure you that there is no correlation between being a lesbian and your intelligence or looks."

"You're making a joke." There was a hard edge to George's voice that made Hayden think that even if it had been a joke, this would not have blown over quickly. "To punish us for your—your brother."

"No joke." Sam's voice was still steady. "We're married. I have all the paperwork."

"Stop this, Samantha. Immediately." George's face was as pale as Irene's now.

A slash of angry red was on Sam's cheeks that made the green in her eyes almost luminescent. "Or what? You'll tell me to go to conversion therapy or I'm out of the family? Like you did with Jon?"

Stomach roiling, Hayden stared at Sam's parents, her mouth hanging half-open. Conversion therapy? She knew they'd backed the idea, but not that they'd said that to Jon. "You tried to make your twenty-year-old son go to conversion therapy?" Disgust crept into her tone, and she couldn't care less. "You know all it does is teach vulnerable groups to hate themselves, right? That it has a disturbingly high rate of attempted suicide—like, fifty percent?"

George's jaw was set, his look hard. It was nothing like Sam's now. Hayden felt ill. She could almost hear what he was going to say to that.

Don't say it. Not that.

But he did. "Better off that way than carrying this sickness around."

Hayden reeled back as if slapped, and Sam's chair scraped as she stood, her palms flat on the table. She leaned forward over half the width of the large table. "You would rather us dead than accept that we're gay?"

The silence was deafening, Hayden's heart thumping so hard she could feel it against her ribs.

"You're not—you're not *like* that, Samantha." Irene's voice was shaking. "You're not like *them*."

"I promise you, I am."

"I don't believe it."

"You should. My college roommate? Who I lived with through med school? Not my roommate." Sam didn't spill secrets like Hayden did, in gushes of words and a mess of thought. She fired them as facts, as if she'd been holding them back for years, readying to shoot them in the perfect way. "She was my girlfriend. For eight years."

Irene's knuckles were white where she gripped her glass.

George stood slowly, looking his daughter in the eye over the table. "You come into our house and tell us you're—you're one of *those*. After everything we've given you, have done for you—you bring a lesbian in here—"

"Actually," Hayden interjected, her wine almost empty. "I'm pansexual."

They blinked at her, and Hayden could swear Sam's lips twitched.

"What?" Irene asked. Clearly not in the way that she cared about the answer, but the way people did when they were shocked you spoke at all.

But Hayden went for it anyway. "Pansexual. I'm not a lesbian, because I'm not only attracted to women. I'm attracted to people without their gender really playing a role. But I'm not attracted to kitchen pans, like some people joke."

She laughed dryly, and it echoed strangely in the room. It sounded hideously awkward. She winced, swirling the dregs of wine in her glass. "Not that that fact probably makes any of this better for you."

George's face twisted, and he looked at Sam as if he had never seen her before. Not necessarily angry, but twisted with disappointment. It was a look that would make most people flinch. Hayden certainly did, and it wasn't even directed at her. But Sam met him head-on, with mere feet between them on the table. "You're not a—a lesbian, Sam."

"I am. I've always known."

Irene placed a hand on George's forearm, fingers curling around it. "You don't have to be. There are things out there to help. Can't you, try, to date a man? Get married, have kids—even if you've got this idea that you're...one of those, you don't have to choose that life."

It was like watching every cliché she'd heard about homophobic statements spill out in front of her. She hadn't known people could really say them all. She'd read comments online, knew this vitriol existed. But to see it?

"I'm already married. And it's not a choice. It's who I am."

For a moment, parents and daughter didn't break eye contact.

"This," George said, his voice almost a whisper, "is your final chance to tell us this is a joke before you leave this house like your brother."

"Yes, let's speak about Jon." Sam's voice didn't waver and Hayden had no idea how she managed it. "The son you threw out and cut off."

"He's no son of mine."

"So I'm no daughter of yours?"

His lip actually quivered. "No child of mine is a queer."

Sam didn't even recoil, but Hayden had to stop herself from throwing her drink in his face. She'd never even heard someone use that word like that. Hearing a word she adored come out of his mouth in a way that was laced with disgust made her want to write it on a shirt and walk down the street. How dare he?

Sam looked down at her mother, still in her seat. "Mom. That's it? Because I married someone?"

Irene's face twisted in the same way George's had. "You didn't marry *someone* Samantha. You married a woman. It's—It's not right."

Hayden wanted to slap them both. She'd never been attacked for her sexuality. Not like this. She'd had comments and creepy guys in bars, and her family had taken a while to really understand Hayden dating women, and then to understand what pansexual was—hell, so had Hayden in the early days, unsure what label really worked for her. But nothing like this. With people who truly believed to their very core that who Hayden *was* was wrong. That who their own *children* were was wrong.

"Nothing has ever felt so right," Sam stated.

Irene's face fell. Maybe she'd expected it to be a joke, or for Sam to beg her to help her change. She clenched her jaw at Sam, looked to Hayden, who refused to look away, and back to Sam. "I don't believe you."

Sam pulled a piece of paper, folded small, from her back pocket and thrust it over the table. George stared at it as it skittered toward him as if he thought it would bite him. When he took it, he opened it slowly, a sneer forming on his face. He thrust it at Irene, whose lips went bloodless at the sight of it. The flash she saw told Hayden it was a photocopy of their marriage certificate.

Tears were in George's eyes.

"Get out." Irene's voice was so low it was almost a whisper.

"Mom—"

"You heard her. Out." The words were scraping out of George, the harshness like a punch, the wetness in his eyes a contrast. "You're no child of mine."

Hayden stood slowly, her chair barely making a sound. She curled her fingers around Sam's arm, whose palms were flat against the table again. She was almost vibrating. "Come on, Sam." Hayden kept her voice low, her eyes on Sam's face, even as Sam's gaze didn't leave her parents. "Let's go."

Her arm was taut under Hayden's palm. Finally, Sam exhaled heavily through her nose and straightened, showing no emotion beyond flaming cheeks. "Okay."

Hayden followed Sam past the table and toward the door. They didn't look back, and in the entrance, Ron was waiting with their jackets. They pulled them on without speaking, and Hayden wanted to grasp Sam's shaking fingers in her own.

"I ordered you a cab," Ron said. "Merry Christmas, Miss." His expression was sincere and his tone soft.

Sam gave him a tight-lipped smile. "You too, Ron. Thank you."

And Hayden remembered she could do it now: she slipped her fingers into Sam's, who linked them together and squeezed.

Her shoulders straight, they walked out the door.

~ ~ ~

The taxi ride home was silent. As was the trip up in the elevator.

Opening the front door seemed to echo in the apartment. Sam walked straight to the kitchen, eyes forward, dropping things on the floor as she went. Her coat pooled, and her bag slapped onto the ground.

Hayden watched her, shutting the door quietly.

Sam poured a generous glass of whiskey, plopping ice in after it. She stared down at the drink, shook her head, and grabbed a second glass, pouring in the same amount and adding ice. With a gentle push, she slid it down the countertop toward Hayden, picked up her own and walked out to the balcony, the door sliding closed.

Silence. Still.

Frank wandered out of her room and butted his head against her leg. She picked him up and clutched him to her chest. In true cat form, he pressed his paw into it and pushed back, staring at her wide-eyed. She hugged him tighter until he had to give in with a purring complaint.

Hayden had been warned this was what would happen.

But witnessing it was different. It was as if a switch had gone off in Sam's parents.

If she'd met them without seeing that, Hayden would have thought they were nice enough—maybe bordering on pretentious and clearly concerned with appearances, but warm with their daughter. Interested in her.

In the kitchen, Hayden considered the balcony door. Was that whiskey an invitation to join Sam? Or had she gone to the balcony to be alone? Sam wasn't one to enjoy a long chat about her feelings.

But not acknowledging how she was seemed wrong.

Hayden put Frank down, who meowed immediately, so she put some food out for him and washed her hands, taking her time, in case space was what Sam wanted. To give her a bit more time, Hayden swapped out her contacts for her glasses.

Whiskey in hand, she slid the balcony door open and was hit with a blast of air so cold she was glad she hadn't taken off her coat. Sam's stance was like the last time she'd found her like this: against the rail, glass in her hand. This time, though, she had a blanket around her shoulders.

"Do you want to be alone?"

Sam shook her head, and Hayden walked over to stand next to her. The whiskey burned in her throat. It wasn't her favorite drink, and the world was already a little blurry after her panic-wine at the house. But it gave her something to do with her hands to stop her from running one of them down Sam's cheek until she turned and faced Hayden and saw the ache in her eyes.

When Sam finally broke the silence, Hayden started.

"I never really thought they'd do it." Sam adamantly looked down at the street. Her voice sounded raw. "I know that's incredibly naïve. I watched them do the same with Jon. But I think some part of me still thought it was impossible."

"I'm sorry." Hayden, whose head was buzzing with wine and the need to comfort, would close the small gap between them and run her lips over her cheek, if she dared. She longed to shape Sam's jaw with her mouth.

"Thank you for being there." The sincerity was almost too much. "I don't think you'll ever know how much it helped."

Sam put her glass on the table and leaned against the rail again, so Hayden put hers own down too. She really hadn't wanted it anyway.

This was where Hayden pointed out that it was all part of the deal for her to be there. Except that she didn't. Because, for Hayden, it wasn't about that anymore. "I was happy to be there," she said. The one eyebrow Hayden could see rose. "Well," she amended, "you know what I mean."

Sam turned, and Hayden's breath caught at the shock of her steady gaze. Her brow was drawn, as if trying to puzzle out everything Hayden had said, though it didn't seem complicated to Hayden. "No. I don't. What do you mean?"

"I—" Hayden's voice was a whisper, and their faces were too close. Distracting. Sam's expression was the most vulnerable Hayden ever thought she'd see. "I was glad I was there and that you didn't have to do it alone."

Sam swallowed. The night was so still. Flakes of snow had fallen on the street earlier, which seemed to have stifled everything. Right then, they could have been the only two in the world.

And that gap was almost gone.

Sam's lips were there, barely brushing over Hayden's, whiskey on her breath. Hayden wished she could swallow this moment and keep it somewhere forever—the feel of Sam's body almost touching hers, the warm breath skimming over her lips.

"Hayden," Sam murmured, and Hayden was unsure if she was imploring or simply saying her name because she needed to. Either way, Hayden wanted to hear her name like that again and again, to coax it out of her and listen to her draw a shuddering breath straight after.

Sam's fingers threaded into Hayden's hair, fingertips scraping over her scalp. Hayden would melt into nothing if she didn't move forward soon.

Normally, Hayden wouldn't hesitate. She'd push forward, her lips desperate on the other person's. But Sam was hovering, and as much as Hayden craved more, this moment was everything, and she was terrified it would disintegrate, right there; falling between her fingers when it was so close. Her hand grasped Sam's shirt, sinking past the blanket to wrap her fingers in the material. Sam's stomach muscles jumped under her hand and Hayden let out a soft groan at the sensation.

Sam closed the gap.

Her lips started delicately on Hayden's. Nothing like before, when both of them had kissed for show and there had been nothing behind it. This one was full of something Hayden didn't have a word for, because she had no idea what it meant for Sam.

But it meant something to Hayden.

That knowledge should have been enough to make Hayden pull back, to untangle her fingers and press Sam away, her hand over her chest, an insincere no on her lips— to protect herself, even if just a little.

But instead, she tugged Sam closer. The blanket fell to the ground, and Sam's hands were cupping her cheeks, thumbs grazing them. Their lips parted, and Sam gasped into her mouth at the flick of Hayden's tongue.

That was all it took for Hayden to tug her back, to stumble toward the door. Hands slid along Hayden's back, under her coat, and under her sweater, fingers sliding over bare skin. It was enough to make her shudder, and Sam arched into the motion.

Somehow, they got the door open, even with Hayden's teeth grazing Sam's neck, her fingers at her buttons.

"Upstairs." Sam's voice was hoarse, and something throbbed low in Hayden's stomach.

Her coat was a puddle on the floor next to the stairs. Her sweater tugged after it. There were lips on her collarbone, a tongue between her breasts.

Sam's name fell from Hayden's lips too easily, proof of how readily it had been there, but Hayden didn't think to stop it.

CHAPTER 23

There were a lot of reasons Hayden didn't usually drink too much.

She hated being hungover. That was a big part of it. An entire day was lost—even if all she wanted to do was sit and watch television or read, she didn't want to do it feeling like Death, in the form of dehydration and regret, was flying toward her.

Another reason was she made terrible decisions. Way back in her first year of college, when she did her first and only body shots—big mistake—she'd thought it was a great idea to steal a sign that said *Slippery When Wet* and hang it on her dorm room door.

It had not been a good idea.

Another reason was she hated that first second she woke up and didn't quite know where she was.

Like right now.

The wall was really white. Light was filtering in. This wasn't her room. A weight pressed down on her feet.

An ache between her legs.

Her eyes opened wide, despite the jabbing pain her skull lodged in protest.

Oh shit.

She'd had drunken sex with Sam last night.

Hayden sat up, clutching the sheet to her chest like a modest gal in a B-grade rom-com. And came eye-to-eye with Frank, sitting on her feet and *glaring* straight at her. Hayden blinked. He didn't. Just stared.

And judged.

Sam *did* say he liked to sleep up here.

Sam.

Hayden looked to her right, the sheet still clutched to her very naked chest. Sam was sprawled on her stomach, her face buried in her pillow. Her hair was a nest at the back. The image of Sam throwing her head back onto her pillow slammed into Hayden's brain, and she closed her eyes for a second.

Well. None of that had been a dream.

Not that she wanted it to be.

Her eyes opened again, and she grimaced at what she saw. Faint red lines ran over Sam's shoulder blades. Running her hand over her face, Hayden sucked in a deep breath. Or *did* she want it to be a dream?

She looked around her. Sam was an utter neat freak. Her room was immaculate, even in Hayden's blurry vision. The heavy wooden dresser had very little on top of it, and what was there was lined up perfectly. A painting hung on the wall to her left, all splashes of blues and greens.

Hayden should stay, be an adult. Talk this over. Communicate. She should establish between them what she knew—that this had been Sam looking for some comfort, some distraction—and smile and be fine with it. Which, she was. Kissing Sam, really kissing her, sleeping with her—none of that had amplified this weird crush thing. At all. Nope.

So Hayden would wait until Sam woke up, and they'd be very mature and talk about this.

Three seconds.

That was all it took until Hayden was slipping out from the bed, ignoring Frank's growl of protest as her feet went out from under him. Her feet tangled and she hopped, almost falling, and turned. Sam was still asleep. One by one, she scooped up her bra and underwear and pieces of clothing that trailed down the stairs. Naked, and clutching her clothes to her front, she dashed through the living room and kitchen.

The only thing that would make this more perfect was if Jon walked through the door.

Hayden froze and stared at it.

He didn't. Of course he didn't. It was barely—she glanced at the clock—before six. Ugh. Way too early. Enough time to get sorted before work. Sam started an hour or so after her, so with luck, she'd be able to avoid her completely.

Oh, and it was Christmas.

She groaned and clutched her clothes harder, running through to her room and closing the door. With a sigh, she slumped back against it. The wood on her bare skin was freezing, but she just put up with it. Closing her eyes, she let her head fall back against the door. Too heavily. It thumped. "Ow."

Something scratched at the door and Hayden opened it, letting Frank run in, his belly wobbling. He jumped on her bed. She slammed the door shut again, flinching and glancing upward as if she could see if it woke Sam up.

Silence.

Frank was glowering at her.

"You can stop judging me now." He didn't. "Seriously. I know I'm an idiot. Stop it."

He winked at her.

"Merry Christmas to you too."

Despite her laundry basket being full, she dumped her clothes in it. When it all rolled off the top, she turned around and pretended not to notice.

Hayden had a shower. She turned the spray on as hot as she could tolerate and let the steam fill the room in a billowing cloud. She washed her hair and stayed in as long as she could.

She'd literally left Sam to wake up alone. After the night she'd had.

Biting her lip, Hayden shoved her head back under the water and rinsed the conditioner out.

She had really failed at the mature thing. Or maybe it was what Sam would prefer? No messy strings. It was clear Sam hated strings. And mess. And emotions.

And Hayden was definitely having some of those.

Which was inconvenient.

A lump was in her throat, swelling with each passing second. She kept her head under the spray. Emotions. That was not something she should have in this situation. They had a deal, one Hayden had agreed to. Willingly. For money.

Friends was one thing.

But this? Sleeping together and then Hayden wanting to cry in the shower? That was not part of the deal. It was not what Sam wanted from her.

And that was okay.

Sex could just be sex. Hayden could deal with her feelings. Privately.

A few more months and this deal would be over. She was only—she was pushing emotions into this situation because she had nothing else going on. That was all. They wouldn't sleep together again and they'd handle this and it would all be fine.

And Hayden would ignore this weird tightness in her stomach.

When she was drying off, she simply didn't look at the small red mark over her breast. Or the purple one on the sensitive skin under her belly button.

She also in no way thought about the way Sam's lips had whispered over her hip bone, chasing her fingers over the skin of Hayden's thigh. Or about the nip of her teeth in places Hayden hadn't even known she'd liked.

But she'd definitely liked it all last night.

She also didn't think about the vibrant ring of green in Sam's eyes, barely visible around her blown-wide pupils.

With her hair towel-dried and put on top of her head, Hayden realized she'd left her glasses upstairs next to Sam's bed. Sighing, she dug up her old pair, which were scratched on the left lens, and jammed them on her face. She needed a walk. Outside air. Something to clear her mind of last night before she had to work. Throwing on some thick, black leggings, an oversized long-sleeved top, and some boots, she went to the kitchen, switched the coffee machine on, and made herself a cup. The smell wafted into the room, already calming the headache still sitting in the back of her skull. Before letting herself have a sip, she chugged a huge glass of water. Feeling bloated, she took a sip of her coffee.

It was bliss.

Bliss was interrupted by a tapping on the front door.

She ignored it, knowing exactly what would happen. And she was right—the door crept open, and Jon popped his constantly stylishly-disheveled head around it. He grinned when he saw her—though smudges were under his eyes, the same kind Sam got when she was exhausted. With a stab in her gut, Hayden remembered he'd been alone last night.

"Morning," he said.

Hayden stayed in the kitchen, cup still in her hands and warming her fingers. "Morning. Happy holidays."

"Happy holidays." He pushed the door open and walked through with two groaning bags of groceries, which he dumped on the counter. He wrapped his arms around her in a hug that clung more than she had expected. She only just managed to put her mug down. But she returned it in kind. The burst of affection felt good after her whirlpool of thoughts from the shower.

When he pulled back, his jester face was gone. Seriousness had replaced it, and Hayden saw it, more than ever: the similarity between him and Sam. "How was last night?"

Hayden felt her heart still in her chest and she went to say something, anything, but came up empty. Right as her heart started again, racing far too quickly, it dawned on her and she could have kicked herself: he was asking about the dinner. "Last—last night? It was…"

"As expected?"

He let go of her shoulders and started unpacking the bags, vegetables and packages littering the counter.

"I guess you could say that. Did you go to the shop so early?"

"Couldn't sleep." He wasn't looking at her now. There was something purposeful in it. "And how's Sam?"

"I, uh, haven't talked to her this morning."

"Yeah but—" He turned, and Hayden could see the concern in his eyes, in the press of his lips. "How was she when you got home?"

Hayden cleared her throat and reached for her coffee, her excuse to not look at Jon. Heat crawled up her neck, into her cheeks. "She was—quiet."

Except at certain moments in her bed.

Hayden really wanted to kick herself. Not the thought to have when Jon was staring so intently at her. "You should really talk to her about it," she tacked on somewhat lamely.

His eyes widened. A grin grew on his face, and Hayden literally wanted to push it down with her hands. An impossible thought, but it didn't stop her from raising them in panic.

"Holy shit," he said. "You two slept together."

"What?" Hayden's voice was too high. "No—no we didn't."

"Wow. You absolutely suck at lying. How have you sold this to people?" His eyes lit up. "Is it because you have a secret crush on her and didn't have to lie at all?"

"*Jon.*" Her gaze flicked to the stairs to make sure there was no sign of Sam descending from upstairs in her post-ill-advised-sex state. "Don't be stupid. We didn't have sex."

"You so did." He was whispering now, delight coloring every word.

"How do you know?"

"So you don't deny it?"

"I did deny it, but clearly it didn't help much. How did you know?"

"You read like an open book. Was this the first time?"

Their heads were ducked together, and they hissed words at each other like teenagers sharing gossip in the school corridors. And all Hayden felt was relief. It felt good to be sharing a small part of this. She clutched her coffee closer. "Yes."

"Were you both drunk?"

She nodded.

"Do you... Holy shit, Hayden, do you *like* her?"

Too much. Too many feelings being revealed. She shook her head quickly. "No, I—I, no. It was, I don't know. We drank a lot at the dinner, and Sam was sad, and—"

"Jon, why do you have a turkey big enough to feed a family of ten?"

They leaped apart at the sound of Sam's voice.

"Sam!" The name tumbled from her lips: not at all as it had the night before.

But Sam barely glanced at her; rather, her focus was on the giant turkey Jon had left on the counter. How had Hayden missed that?

Jon glanced at Hayden, then back to Sam. "You gave me cash to buy the food for today."

"I was thinking a chicken."

His shoulders slumped. "Oh. Well, I thought whatever we didn't eat we could take out to people on the streets like we did other years with Mo—ah, other years?"

Sam wasn't even glancing at Hayden. "That's a good idea."

"How was last night?"

Sam straightened. Her face was washed out, her freckles a prominent smatter over her nose. "As we expected. Exactly so, actually."

He stared straight at Sam, and Hayden felt like she was witnessing something private. "I'm sorry," he told her.

The smile she offered him was small. Hayden's gaze was fixated over her collarbone, where a mark like the one on her own breast lay. "It's me and you now, kiddo," she replied.

"Wouldn't have it any other way." He clapped his hands together once. "Right. Cooking." His attention returned to the layout of ingredients scattered over the counter. "Food and stuff."

"You still want to be the one to cook?" Sam's voice clearly showed she didn't really want him to be.

"Damn right. I googled. I'm all over how to roast this turkey."

"You're not going to cause an explosion in my kitchen, are you?"

"Hey, I've cooked before."

"In the microwave. You know we won't be eating until tonight? Hayden and I work today."

"I wanted to get a head start. A, you know, really early head start."

More like he didn't want to be alone in his apartment anymore, Hayden thought. She backed out of the room slowly. "Uh, speaking of work, I should get there."

Jon looked at her, but Sam's concentration stayed right on the food she was organizing in front of her. "Okay," he said. "Is everything all right?"

Hayden's eyes fixed on Sam. Indifference poured from her, and Hayden's stomach ached. "Oh, yeah." She nodded vigorously. "Fine."

No way was Hayden going to go collect her coat from the balcony, or wherever it had ended up. She grabbed another one from her closet and dropped a kiss on the fast-asleep Frank's head. He didn't even move.

Ready to leave, Hayden slipped out the door while the two siblings in the kitchen continued to bicker over how to cook a holiday meal.

~ ~ ~

"You look like shit."

Hayden turned around as she pulled her gloves off, snapping them into the bin and washing her hands. "Why, thank you, Luce. I appreciate it."

Luce put their weight against the cart they were pushing over to restock the emergency carts with. "I noticed it this morning. But seriously, what's up?"

It was a day like yesterday before everything went to hell: barely any patients, the ER mostly quiet, the day spent restocking and performing checks. So far there'd been two kids with things stuffed up their noses, another with a huge bump on her head from riding her new bike down some stairs, a few broken bones from climbing ladders, and a scalp laceration on one man who insisted it was an accident despite smelling strongly of sherry.

Hayden dried her hands. "Nothing's up." She glanced around, but no one was in earshot. "I had a few wines and feel a little hungover."

Luce smirked. "Meeting the family was stressful?"

"You could say that." Hayden tried for casual and to stop thinking about last night. She kept replaying the scene on the balcony over and over, as well as the few hours that followed. Each time she did, her stomach throbbed, and not unpleasantly. She wished it wasn't such a blur, that she hadn't drunk anything. But would it have happened if she hadn't? Would that be a good thing? "How was meeting Clemmie's parents?"

"It went really well, actually." Luce was almost glowing. "They were lovely and we ate until we couldn't move, and her three brothers told me embarrassing stories about her."

"That sounds pretty textbook. And tonight she meets yours?"

Luce blanched. "Yeah."

Hayden chuckled. "Good luck."

"Thanks. You sound super sincere."

"I am." Everything slowed down as Hayden looked across the ER and saw Sam walk in, a different intern behind her, holding files.

Luce followed her gaze. "Oh yeah. Someone has a patient they think has an aneurysm. Wow—Sam looks as tired as you. Did you two really drink that much?"

Hayden gave a small, nervous laugh. "Something like that."

Watching Sam was the worst thing she could be doing. Hayden knew that under that shirt were marks she'd left with her fingers and mouth the night before, when Sam had panted in her ear and asked for more.

"I'm taking my break," Hayden said. "Can you keep an eye on my one patient? Bay twelve. He's waiting for a bed upstairs."

"Sure."

Hayden knew Luce's gaze followed her out, and Hayden didn't even care that she was all but fleeing the room.

~ ~ ~

The house smelled delicious.

"Jon, don't tell me you pulled off the turkey?" Hayden walked into the kitchen and peered into the oven. Of what she could see, it was golden brown and delicious-looking.

"I think I totally did."

Hayden turned, and he was at the dining table, placing plates around three spots. Wait, no, four.

"Jon? Why are you setting four places?" His cheeks were a deep red, and Hayden's mouth dropped open. "Have you got a hot date coming?"

"What? No. No. Just a friend."

Hayden snorted.

He narrowed his eyes. "Keep that up, and I'll make you continue that conversation from this morning." Hayden's mouth snapped shut. "That's what I thought."

Holding a glass under a tap, Hayden called over her shoulder, "Is Sam here?"

"Nice try at nonchalance."

Hayden was not stealthy, so she took a sip, turning back around.

Jon winked. "She's upstairs."

That would explain why he was at least keeping his voice low while he tortured her.

"Do you need a hand?" she asked.

"No. I'm sorting it out. I got this."

The table was set simply. A candle in the center with some strange Christmas holly decoration. Other than that, there were knives and forks and a glass each.

"It looks great."

"Thanks." He paused at the table. "You miss your family at this time of year?"

"Yeah. Especially Javi. He gets so excited. I called them on the way to work and again on my lunch break. I'll go home next Christmas."

"Your family sounds pretty cool."

Hayden slumped against the counter and watched him fuss over the table some more. "They are. I mean, they can drive me crazy. But I'm pretty lucky."

"How were they when you came out?"

"They were…fine, mostly. I mean, I came out in different stages. I had a boyfriend first. And I hadn't really thought much about it all. But then I met this girl—"

Jon gave a wolf whistle, and Hayden laughed. It died off when she saw Sam had padded down the stairs and was standing with a hand on the banister, watching them. But she plowed on, ignoring the way her heart stuttered. It had nothing to do with the tailored pants Sam was wearing, nor the low-cut top. "And I told them I thought I was a lesbian. They had a lot of questions, and Abuela especially—I think she thought I was going to have a really sad life? But they told me to bring her around for dinner and got to know her…"

Jon was watching her, as if thirsty for this story that didn't end sadly. "But you're not a lesbian?"

Hayden shook her head. "No. It was the year after high school I kind of figured it out. I used bisexual at first, and then discovered pansexual. Which took some explaining, but by that point, they just wanted me to be happy." She cocked her head and tried to ignore the way Sam's eyes were boring into her. "I'm really sorry that isn't how your family feels."

He gave an awkward shrug, but no anger reddened his cheeks. "I've spent the last year accepting it all. I have Sam, which means more to me than it should, considering she's a boring old lady." He grinned at the last sentence, and his eyes lit up.

It was apparently what got Sam to push off the banister and walk into the kitchen, her arms crossed. "I can hear you."

Jon turned around and covered his mouth. "Sam! I mean, of course it means a lot since you're just so utterly fantastic."

Hayden snickered and tried to ignore the warmth in her chest as Sam walked over. For the first time that day, she met Hayden's eye, and Hayden couldn't see anything there about last night. She held her hand out over the counter, Hayden's glasses in it. Hayden glanced down and swallowed hard.

Sam didn't say a word as Hayden took them. "Thanks."

Their fingers brushed past each other, and the feeling crawled up Hayden's arm. Her body utterly sucked. It was getting goose bumps at a mere brush of their skin. Sam barely reacted.

"How was your day?" Sam asked.

Sam was fine. So completely fine. And Hayden thought she was going to vibrate apart on the floor. "Slow. No one used the curse word today."

"It wouldn't have mattered if they did."

"You say that, but let's consider this: it was used yesterday, and the shift went to hell. It wasn't used today, and I had the laziest shift I think I've ever had."

Sam shook her head, but that smile she used when she thought Hayden was being funny but didn't want to admit it was there. It was small and cute, and damn it, Hayden had it bad. "The two are not related."

Hayden's chest felt all breathless, the surprise of it leaving her with the wind knocked out of her. "You don't know that."

And Sam shrugged and turned away, the curve of her neck meeting her shoulder at a place where Hayden wanted to trail a kiss, her breath hot over the skin just like last night, and leave a mark, faint like the one Hayden could see now. Sam picked up a thin scarf from the counter and wrapped it around her neck.

Hayden drank the rest of her water.

CHAPTER 24

Sam was avoiding Hayden.

Or Hayden was avoiding Sam.

Maybe they were avoiding each other?

Either way, there was avoidance.

Hayden was on night shift over New Year—something she'd volunteered for—so it had been easy to hide. Or so she'd thought. It turned out that Sam was on call and she was consulting on a patient who'd coded, and Hayden spent over an hour brushing elbows with her as they saved the patient's life.

It was the stuff made of romance novels, and Hayden was left with her stomach in knots, her skin on fire, and her brain imprinted with the memory of Sam issuing orders in a cool and calm voice, her eyes flashing over the scene.

They kept up the charade in public the few times it was an issue. Stood close and gave each other wifely looks, and all the time, Hayden's heart was racing in her chest. They left together some days from the hospital. Their rings stayed on their fingers. From the outside, nothing changed.

But at home, they managed to rarely be in each other's space. It were as if they'd both taken a huge step back and had a radar for how to avoid each other.

And that went great for a few weeks. With lots of snide comments from Jon.

Who Hayden mostly managed to avoid too.

Then Luce managed to get her alone, their eyes all lit up. "So, you're still coming, right?"

Hayden's hand stopped, coffee halfway to her lips in the cafeteria where she knew Sam rarely went. "Uh…"

Luce slid into a chair opposite Hayden, raising that one judgmental eyebrow perfectly as they did so. "You forgot."

"No…"

"You really did."

Hayden finally sipped her coffee. "A little?"

Luce grabbed a grape from Hayden's tray, and considering the circumstances, Hayden didn't think she should even be grumpy about it. "Hayden," they said, "we spoke about it before Christmas."

So much had happened since then. The words that would give that away to Luce built in Hayden's throat, pressed against her tongue. Hayden wanted to spill them out all over the table and not even care what she left behind for the entire hospital to see. But she and Sam had gotten this fake marriage this far, had gotten through Christmas, and Sam had her lawyer dealing with the process for the inheritance thing.

They couldn't mess it up now.

"Uh..."

Luce huffed. "Clemmie's photography exhibition opening?"

"Oh!" Hayden straightened. "I do remember it. I do. It's—" she turned sheepish "—it's tomorrow."

"So glad to see you're with me." Luce's voice was deadpan, and Hayden flashed them a sheepish smile. "Are you still coming? You said you and Sam were in."

"Yes, yes of course."

Hayden tried to look natural while inside trying not to die. Maybe Sam would be working—no. Hayden had seen her roster on the fridge the other day. They were both free from seven. Maybe Hayden could avoid mentioning it... No. Because then Luce could mention it to Sam. Or Clemmie. Clemmie and Sam often chatted when Sam bought coffee. Apparently, they were almost friends.

"Great." Luce brightened. "It'll be a fun night. There's bad wine, but it's free. And cheese."

"Two of my favorite things."

"I knew that would sell it for you." Luce paused. "Hey. I haven't seen you much, and didn't want to ask over the phone. Are you okay?"

"What? Me? I'm fine." Hayden's voice was far too high. She cleared her throat. "I'm fine."

That eyebrow was back. "Are you sure? You've been, I don't know, quiet?"

"I can be quiet."

Luce just shook their head.

"Luce." Hayden smiled as naturally as she could. "I'm fine."

"Really? Because..."

"What?"

"I don't know. You seem down. And you're not with Sam very much."

Damn it, Hayden thought she'd managed to keep it normal-looking.

"And, well, she's in the ER sometimes when I don't think she needs to be, and you make yourself scarce," Luce added.

So, Hayden failed at subtle avoidance, it seemed. Had Sam really been there when she didn't need to be? "I think you're imagining things, Luce." Hayden swallowed down her internal panic. "Sam and I are fine, really. It must have all been a coincidence."

"Okay." That was not the voice of a friend who believed her. Luce stood up. "I have to run. But I'll text you the address, okay?"

"Great. I'm looking forward to it."

Luce left and Hayden sagged into her chair. Well. An evening out with Sam. It would be good for their married image. Not that Sam was going to enjoy it. She'd been avoiding Hayden like the plague, no matter what Luce thought. Not that Hayden had been doing much better. Or, well, at all better. Would Sam even want to go? She didn't have much choice, though. Both of them needed to put a bit more effort into their public-appearance side of things, especially now that the ball was rolling toward Sam getting the inheritance.

Hayden plucked her phone out of her pocket.

Did you remember Clemmie's exhibition opening is tomorrow?

The reply back was fast. Sam must have been at lunch too.

Yes.

That was super conversational, Sam, thank you. Really painted the picture of her interest in the event. Hayden huffed and typed a reply.

Do you still want to go?

The salad on her plate was wilting. It had started that way, but still, Hayden stabbed at it half-heartedly as she waited for Sam's reply.

We told them we were going.

Hayden narrowed her eyes at the phone. This really was so helpful. The rest of their text conversation was going to be painful if it continued like this, so Hayden decided to get it over with.

Wonderful. So, shall we leave from the hospital when we both finish? Say 7:15 p.m. at the entrance?

See? Hayden could do upper-class indifference with the best of them. She chewed on her soggy lettuce with too much vigor and watched her phone. It lit up seconds later.

Yes.

Hayden growled at her phone, then looked up to see if anyone had heard. No one had. She jammed it back in her pocket and dropped her fork on her plate. Her appetite was gone. She might as well get back to work.

Sam was infuriating.

~ ~ ~

"Are you ready?"

Hayden turned and almost swallowed her tongue. Sam was standing in suspenders and a white shirt. With tailored pants. And suspenders—there were actual suspenders, cutting straight black lines down her shirt. With her short hair, she looked like a nineteen twenties lesbian. Not that it had been a fun time for anyone, really. But wow, did Sam carry the fashion well.

"Yeah."

Her throat was actually dry. It was strange, to be facing each other after a couple of weeks of avoiding exactly that. As much as Hayden had enjoyed that night, she wished she could take it back. She had been enjoying the ease with which they'd started to move in each other's space: the conversations they'd started to have, the smiles over coffee, Sam curled on the sofa in sweats and with sleepy eyes and Frank.

Ever since that night, it had been weeks of awkward.

Hayden pulled her coat on and wound her scarf around her neck. Sucking in a breath, she held her hand out. They were in public, after all.

Sam's eyes were intent on her own, and she took her hand, fingers entwining together. Hayden's ring pressed into her finger, and she hated that the sensation wasn't uncomfortable.

They headed outside and slid into a taxi. Their hands slipped apart, and Hayden wanted to reach over and pull Sam's into her lap but didn't know if she should. Actually, she knew she shouldn't. And, frankly, that sucked.

Once Sam gave directions, the taxi pulled out, and Hayden couldn't sit in this kind of awkwardness for the rest of the night.

She managed to wait ten minutes. "So, how was your day?" The taxi was dark, but Hayden turned to look at her anyway, watching the streetlights play over Sam's face. Her expression was hard to read in this light.

"Good."

When nothing more was forthcoming, Hayden replied, "Right. That's...good. Mine was busy. We had three strokes come in today."

"I know. I saw two of them."

Conversational. Once more. "How did the older lady's surgery go?"

"Well."

"She live?"

"She did."

"Sam." Hayden let the annoyance creep into her tone.

"Yes?"

"Do you have any other responses?" Sam didn't even react to the repetition of her own words from months ago. Hayden huffed. "You could try and, I don't know, talk more."

Hayden might not have been able to see Sam's face clearly, but it was impossible to miss the flash in her eye as they narrowed. "So now that you want to talk, I'm expected to?"

Hayden's mouth dropped open. "Now that I want to talk?"

"I think I spoke quite clearly." She looked back out the window.

"What do you even mean by that?"

Sam's head whipped around, and Hayden almost pulled back at the hard look on her face. "What do I mean? You've been quite clear in not wanting to speak with me."

"That's—that's not true."

"I thought you didn't like lies, Hayden."

"Oh my God, Sam, you—"

"We're here." The cab driver didn't even turn around to speak to them. He was probably too scared to after listening to the hissing frustration in Hayden's voice.

Hayden fished out the money, and when Sam went to interject to pay, Hayden sent her a dirty look that actually worked. Sam got out of the car with a face like steel.

They stood outside a funky building, people already spilling out the door. Anger flashed in Hayden's veins, and she took in a deep breath. Tonight was not the night to let that get the better of her.

But Sam was really so infuriating.

And then Sam was beside her. Jazz filtered out, fairy lights outlining the windows. Their sides brushed, both of them standing too straight.

"Clemmie has done well," Sam said.

Hayden sucked in a breath. She could tell from Sam's voice that she was frustrated and trying to push through it. Hayden could play that game too. "She has. She was invited to show months ago, Luce said."

"This is her, what, eighth exhibition?"

"Mhm."

"She's starting to get noticed."

"And I'm starting to get cold."

Fingers brushed Hayden's again and, after a moment's hesitation, she linked their hands together. "Shall we go inside, then?" Sam asked.

"Okay."

And Hayden didn't look at her. Because, even with her annoyance, looking at Sam wasn't a safe thing to do. Though here, in public, she was supposed to look at her wife with adoration on her face.

She was starting to get a headache.

They walked in and checked their coats, Hayden trying not to stare at Sam's forearms, annoyingly sculpted and on display with her sleeves rolled up.

It should be illegal for her to wear suspenders.

"Hayden." Hayden spun around at Luce's voice. Their eyeliner was flawless, and they looked so happy Hayden felt some of her frustration ebb away. "You made it."

Sam stood along her back, her left side against her, and Hayden felt her breathing hitch. "Of course I did."

"Hey, Sam. Whoa. Nice suspenders."

The chuckle was warm in Hayden's ear, and she thought she might turn into a puddle right there. Which made her more annoyed. "Thanks. I like the tie and the black tutu skirt."

Luce winked. "Me too."

And now they were getting along. In what millisecond did that happen? Hayden needed a drink. Except not, because that meant drunkenness and confessing stupid things.

"Where's the person of the hour?" Hayden asked instead.

"She's over there." As Luce jutted their chin in the direction over Hayden's shoulder, the look on their face went completely, grossly smitten. "She's super busy schmoozing, but she'll grab you later. Want the tour?"

Luce took them around the space, and Hayden took a bottle of water with her. Sam declined a wine, and Hayden couldn't help but wonder if it was for the same reason Hayden was avoiding alcohol right then: she didn't want to say anything she'd regret. But in what way? Did she really regret that night?

Or was Hayden being completely egocentric, thinking it was about her at all?

It took all her strength to focus on the photos. Clemmie was talented. Hayden had no idea about any of it but was amazed at how Clemmie had blended the reality of photography with fantasy aspects. Following Luce around, it was obvious how proud they were of their girlfriend. They gesticulated wildly and dragged them both to their favorite pieces. At the back of the room, once they'd walked through everything, Sam slipped away to the bathroom and Luce rounded on her.

"Okay, what's going on?"

Hayden took a second to follow the sudden change. "What?"

"You've been weird for weeks. And like, the two of you seem normal enough, but, well, is everything okay with the two of you?"

"If everything seems fine, why would you presume there was something wrong with our relationship?"

Luce was hiding something. Or was at least not saying what they were thinking. Hayden could tell.

"Look." And there it was. Straight to the point as ever. But then they crossed their arms and stood closer. "It's only—" They even lowered their voice. Something was going on. "I was at work yesterday, and some guy showed up while I was in the cafeteria. He was really friendly, said he knew you and Sam. But then he was asking all sorts of questions about the two of you. Your relationship, how long you'd been dating. I told him to get lost, and he gave me this card."

Luce pulled a plain white card out of their back pocket, hand dipping under the skirt and to the black jeans they had on underneath, and handed it to Hayden. Simple black lettering spelled *Ryan's Investigations* along the front, with a phone number on the back. "He said to call if I thought of anything I wanted to talk about. It was really, really weird, Hayden."

All Hayden could do was gape at the card. So Sam's parents had really hired someone to investigate their relationship. Could they do anything with that? Sam didn't think so; all of this was a precaution. But their relationship was being seriously questioned.

At least it wasn't hard for Hayden to act besotted. Not that this fact was all that consoling to her. "I'm sorry that happened." Hayden tried to smile but knew it would be failing.

"Why? I'm fine. What I don't get is *why* it happened. Are you two okay?"

Luce's face was full of concern. All Hayden wanted to do was spill everything in this shadowy corner. To finally come clean and tell Luce everything and cap it off with the fact that Hayden was embarrassingly head over heels for Sam, and it was all a huge mess.

Instead, she said, "Yeah, we're fine. This is to do with Sam's family. But I can't really tell you about it, since it's not my stuff."

Luce visibly relaxed. "But you two are really okay?"

"You sound almost disappointed."

"No, no." Luce grabbed her elbow and squeezed. "Not at all. Sorry. I just thought I'd figured out why you'd been weird the last few weeks. But I'm glad you and Sam are fine."

"Why wouldn't we be?"

And of course Sam walked up right at that moment.

Luce grinned at her. "Good question."

The card felt heavy in Hayden's hand. Sam needed to know some guy was investigating them. Or maybe she knew? No, she would have told Hayden. But here wasn't the place, in case she reacted badly or they drew any attention to the situation. Though Luce already knew *something* was going on.

Before Hayden could decide, she felt her phone vibrate in her bag. She crammed the card into her back pocket and pulled her phone out.

"Will you two excuse me? It's my sister."

Both nodded at her, Luce making a "go away, already" gesture. Hayden would have pulled a face, but she was too busy being distracted by Sam in those suspenders again.

She hit the *answer* button and raised it to her ear. "Sofia? Hey."

"Hayden." She sounded breathless. A catch was in her voice at Hayden's name, and out of nowhere, the hair on Hayden's arms stood on end. "Can you talk?"

"Of course." Hayden stepped away. "What's up?"

"Mom—Mamá is in the hospital." Now Hayden's blood ran cold. "She's in the ER. She'd been asleep in the living room, and we thought she'd be fine. But she disappeared."

"What? How long for? What happened?" Hayden tried to control the panic crawling up her throat.

"She was gone maybe thirty minutes. Less." Sofia was crying, or at least tearful. That alone was jarring—Sofia never cried. Hayden had sobbed when their dad left, and Sofia had set her face into armor it took years to chip away at. "We found her, but she'd fallen. We have no idea where or how. She was just walking down the street with blood on her forehead and holding her arm."

"Shit." It was as if nothing else around her existed, until Sam stood behind her and Hayden relaxed back against her, one of Sam's hands on her hip. "Is she okay?"

"She's gone for a CT. They suspect a bleed. She may need surgery."

"Sofia..."

Hayden had no words. No way of comforting her. There was no point saying that Sofia should have paid more attention. That first year, Hayden's mother had ended up in the corner of the backyard within minutes and had no idea what she'd been doing there.

"Can you come?" Sofia's voice was small. "I mean, I know you won't be able to get a flight until tomorrow. And you work. But, I don't know, could you?"

Hayden swallowed. "I should be able to. I have to call the coordinator, but for emergencies I may be able to get two days. And I'm off work after tomorrow, so I can probably come two nights. Can I call you back?"

"Yeah, I'll be here."

"Are you okay?"

"No."

"I'll be there as soon as I can."

Hayden hung up because listening to her sister's voice crack like that for too much longer was going to make her crack herself; it already felt as if something had, something deep within her.

Hadn't she been waiting for something like this to happen?

Sam's warmth was still pressed into her back, and she turned, the front of their bodies now nearly together. It was hard to swallow, and she clutched her phone to her chest. Luce was to her right. Both were watching her, hovering, as if uncertain of what to do, and Hayden just wanted to drop her face into Sam's neck. To breathe her in. To lose herself in something that wasn't this sick feeling in her gut.

Had her mother been scared? Wandering around alone? Hurt? Had she hurt herself, or had someone else hurt her? Her coordination was going. Most likely it was the former.

"My mom's in the hospital. She, uh, she wandered and was hurt. They think she'll need surgery."

Sam's hands were on her biceps, her thumbs stroking the skin there. Hayden had to organize things, to call her coordinator and make sure she didn't have to be at tomorrow's shift. To book the flight and make sure Sam would look after Frank.

She would have to call her sister back. Brain surgery was a big deal. Not in her world, in the hospital, where it happened every day. But to her own mother?

Hayden didn't like being on the other side of this. She never had.

"What can I do?" Luce asked.

Hayden shook her head. "I just have to call to get tomorrow's shift off." Were her hands shaking? Her voice definitely was. "I'm off for two days after that."

"I'm not working. Tell them I'll cover."

Hayden almost burst into tears. "Luce—"

"No, really, it's fine. That's done. So you can book your tickets."

Sucking in a breath, Hayden slipped out of Sam's grip, her body missing the warmth immediately, and slammed into Luce. She wrapped her arms around them. "Thank you."

Luce's hands ran over her back. "It's really no problem. I'll call in ten minutes, after you've called, to confirm that I'll cover." They gave Hayden one more squeeze and pulled away. "Call me if I can do anything, okay? I'll explain to Clemmie; don't worry."

"Tell her it's amazing."

"I will."

And when Hayden stepped back again, Sam's hand slipped into hers, their fingers linked. Hayden settled into her side right away and let Sam lead them through the throng of people. Leaving her for a moment, Sam reappeared with their coats and scarves, and Hayden tugged hers on robotically. As they walked out the door, she already had her phone to her ear, Sam's hand back in hers.

While Hayden talked to the coordinator and explained the situation and that Luce would cover, they sat in the back of a taxi, Sam's hand still in hers. Even when she hung up, Hayden had no urge to let go, so she started tapping at her screen with her thumb, pulling up flight details.

One had free seats at ten a.m. the next morning. Earlier would be better, but she couldn't complain. She booked it, tugging out her card one handed and tapping in her details. She checked in as soon as she had the confirmation, and called Sofia.

"I'm all set. I sent you my itinerary. I'll come straight to the hospital. Any news?"

"She has some kind of bleed. She's on the emergency list."

Hayden's heart skipped over. "What kind of bleed?"

"I—wait. I have no idea. I don't really understand. I can get the nurse?"

Somehow, Sofia managed to get the nurse to speak to Hayden. None of it reassured her very much, and when she got back on the phone, she reiterated everything to Sofia again as plainly as she could.

"Please," Hayden asked when she was finished. "Message me when she's out of surgery? Call me if there's an emergency?"

"I will. I love you."

"Me too."

And Hayden hung up, feeling completely useless. Being there was all she wanted. To be able to kiss her mother before she went into the operating room. She wanted to hold Sofia's hand, to murmur with Abuela, and to sit with Javi on her lap, heavy and warm and just so solid.

Sam didn't say anything and melted back into the seat. She'd obviously heard everything on the phone and knew the bleed was a grade high enough to be worrying and that they wouldn't know anything for hours. She had to know that this opened up the question of moving Hayden's mother into more permanent care much sooner than any of them had wanted.

All too much and not worth talking about. Those words all hung between them anyway. Why discuss them? Why pull them apart and hold them up, exposed and needing to be acknowledged?

Her hand was still in Hayden's, and it was like an anchor on the seat between them, stopping Hayden from floating up and too far away. The lights from outside flashed inside the taxi, illuminating them before dropping them back into darkness only to light them up again. Shadows danced over Sam's face, and Hayden wanted to push forward and lose herself in them. The air was all gone again, and she had no idea how to bring it back.

Sam paid for the cab, her hand finally falling away as she dug out the cash. Inside, they stood side by side in the elevator, arms touching and Hayden's fingers twitching with the need to find Sam's again, to feel tethered to something. She checked her phone repeatedly, but she only had a message from Luce, confirming that they were scheduled to work for Hayden tomorrow and urging her to message at any time if she needed anything, and one other from her sister that was another message of love.

The house was quiet, with Frank nowhere to be seen.

ially, Hayden didn't mind opening the door to find Jon on their sofa. But relief ~~flooded~~ her that tonight nobody else was in the house. They stood, measuring each other in the entrance. Sam opened her mouth like she was about to say something, but closed it again. Crossing her arms around her middle, Hayden resisted the urge to shiver.

She'd never felt so useless.

Where she wanted to be was miles upon miles away and impossible to get to until the next morning. Her mother was in the hands of surgeons Hayden didn't know. Right now, she would have paid all the money she had in her bank account for it to be Sam in there, operating on her mother. Ethic laws would prevent it due to the rings on their fingers, but she wanted it anyway.

It was strange, really, that the first time Hayden had really touched that forty thousand dollars was for an emergency plane ticket home.

Was she trembling? She might have been trembling. Sam was watching her, her brow furrowed, as if she was trying to puzzle out how to help, how to do something.

"Sam." Hayden's voice cracked, and she absolutely hated it. But the fissure that had opened up in her chest was aching, widening, and Hayden was afraid she was about to fall into it. She swallowed heavily, her throat raw with the feeling. The motion did nothing to push down the lump there.

Sam strode forward, and Hayden almost fell into her; Sam's arms wrapped around her in a hug so tight Hayden thought Sam might be trying to hold her together. Hayden buried her face in Sam's neck, her skin warm, pulse thumping against her lips. Without thinking, she pressed her lips harder to the soft skin there, letting the warmth soak into her. With the slightest movement, Sam tilted her chin up, and Hayden pulled her lips away, brushing Sam's skin, only to press again slightly higher, trailing kisses up Sam's neck. For the slightest of seconds, Sam tensed until her head listed to the side, as if to give Hayden more room. The quietest sigh brushed over Hayden's ear.

"Hayden." A warning was in her tone: subtle, but there. A longing too. The sound of it left pooling heat in Hayden's stomach, spreading out toward her limbs.

Need. That was the sound, the sound of something that echoed within Hayden, that was bounding through her veins. It was so strong that she closed her eyes as she nipped at Sam's earlobe.

"Sam?" Hayden's voice was a hoarse whisper, and she didn't even care. Her breath washed over Sam's ear, and Hayden felt her shudder in response. "I—I need…" Her voice was pleading, and for a second, she wondered if Sam didn't want this, if she'd step away.

But fingers fluttered onto Hayden's waist, and Sam tilted her head, her lips hot on Hayden's. No alcohol was on her tongue this time, no regret lathering her movements; just the soft silk of her mouth and the way she returned Hayden's kiss with as much force as Hayden gave. Hayden wrapped her arm around Sam's neck and pushed up on her toes, her body arching in.

The groan Sam gave... Hayden swallowed, and she started pushing Sam back toward the stairs, toward her room.

They stumbled up the steps, their coats pushed off somewhere in the living room. Hayden's back hit the wall halfway up the stairs, and Sam pressed along the front of her body, her arms a cage around Hayden's face. All Hayden could do was grip fistfuls of shirt and pull her in tighter. In the bedroom, her fingers slipped under Sam's suspenders, pushing one then the other over her shoulders to dangle down the back of her legs. Her fingers grappled with Sam's buttons and they tripped as they kicked off shoes, Hayden's jeans a puddle on the floor.

Hayden bounced as she sat on the bed, hands never leaving Sam's body as she tugged Sam with her. Sam's thighs slid along her hips, and Hayden's hands pushed up her now-bare back, palms and fingers splayed over the slight arch of her spine, her shoulder blades, her shoulders. Their kiss slowed, Sam's lips languid, her fingers threading through Hayden's hair. Hayden let her hands glide back down, resting over the slight sharpness of Sam's hip bones. With a slow movement, Hayden's hand left Sam's hip, the other hand moving further around Sam's waist, her fingers digging into the small of Sam's back. Everything was all smooth skin, and Hayden wanted to lose herself in it, to trace her fingers over more than that small patch. She wanted to run her tongue along Sam's spine and see how fast she shivered. But she had later to do that, because right now, she wouldn't have moved Sam for anything, not when there was the press of her thighs around Hayden's hips, the sheer contact of skin against skin. It all kept Hayden in the moment.

The backs of Hayden's fingers ran up Sam's side, over her ribs, over her breast, and brushed over Sam's cheek. With a flutter, Sam's eyes closed, her face turning, ever so slightly into Hayden's palm. Hayden's fingers danced over her ear, the skin behind it, and she trailed them down Sam's cheek, the tip of her index finger stopping over her lips. Warm breath washed over it, and Hayden's lips parted.

Sam was a picture as she straddled her, with the light filtering up the stairs in the background. When Sam's lips parted, she opened her eyes at the same time, and Hayden ached, a throb low in her belly, as Sam took her finger into her mouth, her tongue flicking over it. Hayden surged forward as Sam began to suck on it, her hand falling to rest on Sam's chest. Sam's heartbeat was a drum against Hayden's palm, and she kissed her so hard that Hayden wondered if they would both shatter.

None of this was gentle anymore.

There were teeth and scraping nails, a hand digging into the back of Hayden's neck as her fingers glided over Sam's ribs, fingers trembling when Sam shivered. She wanted to see the expression on Sam's face, to take in the image of her entire body as something only for her. But that would have meant breaking the kiss, and Hayden was lost in it—in the tug of Sam's lips, the pant of her breath. The way Sam held her close, as if she thought at any moment Hayden might disappear.

"Hayden." She panted into her mouth, the word almost breaking Hayden.

Hayden had to shift her hips, anything to relieve the ache between her legs.

"Touch me," Sam said. Her hips were rolling, seeking friction from Hayden's stomach, and Hayden pushed her hand between Sam's legs, the other still clinging to the small of her back.

With their foreheads together, Hayden asked, "Is this okay?"

"Yes," Sam breathed. "Yes."

It was an impossible angle, an uncomfortable twist of her wrist, but it was worth it when she pushed past Sam's underwear and her fingers glided through wetness and warmth. Sam gasped at her touch, and Hayden groaned, their lips pulling apart as Sam's head lolled back. There was no way Hayden would stop her fingers from stroking Sam, nor stop her teeth from grazing the beating pulse under her mouth. Sam's hips, flush against her, guided her movements, and she thrust more as Sam's movements sped up.

"Hayden." And her name turned into a grunt that sent fire through Hayden's veins as she slipped a finger inside. "*More.*"

So she did.

The skin under Hayden's lips tasted like salt, and she swiped her tongue from Sam's collarbone to behind her ear, Sam's entire body arching into her. She curled her fingers, and if given the opportunity right then, Hayden would have stayed there forever.

Sam's hand fell to her shoulder and pushed, and Hayden let herself fall back against the bed, Sam following her down. Sam's hips didn't stop rocking, her mouth on Hayden's throat. She turned her head to bite down on Hayden's shoulder when Hayden swiped her thumb. Sam pushed up on one hand, hips still moving, her lips falling into a kiss that was all desperation, her breath nothing more than panting. Nails dug into Hayden's side, grazing down along her stomach until her fingers were in Hayden's underwear, and Hayden thought she might shatter apart on Sam's hand.

Hours later, Hayden lay awake, Sam warm and naked behind her, curled along her back. From the floor, her phone beeped with a text message from Sofia. Their mother was out of surgery and stable. Relieved, she set an alarm and fell asleep with Sam's arm around her middle, her fingers splayed over her belly.

~ ~ ~

It was not like Hayden to wake up with total consciousness. It normally took some time and copious coffee.

She blinked at the wall on her left, the night before crashing over her: Sofia's phone call.

Her mother in the hospital. Surgery.

Sam.

Sam, who Hayden was very aware was behind her. She was no longer curled around Hayden but merely had a foot thrown over Hayden's.

Hayden's phone had been on the loudest possible setting, and her sister would have called if anything had happened, but she grabbed it anyway, moving as little as possible to avoid disturbing Sam. She only had another message from Sofia, saying she'd gone home to get some sleep and would call if there was any change.

It was six a.m. Almost. Hayden quickly turned off her alarm. She needed to charge her phone. She needed to shower and pack some clothes.

Sitting up on her elbows, she looked over at Sam. Much like the last time, she was fast asleep, her hair a mess, her face buried into her pillow. Red lines were down her back again, over her shoulder blades. Unlike last time, Hayden hovered, unsure about doing what she wanted—running her lips down Sam's spine, kissing the back of her neck, falling into the safety of her before she had to get up and face everything that was headed her way.

But she couldn't do that.

She had no idea what last night was.

The first time, Sam had so obviously needed something. Had Sam just been returning the favor? The idea left Hayden feeling hollow. It was possible. Hayden had all but begged. Warmth flooded her cheeks at the memory.

That was all it was: Sam had felt bad for her.

Hayden pushed the sheet aside and swung her legs over the edge. She sat there for a moment, looking around for her clothes.

"Please don't leave this time."

Hayden stopped. The voice was hoarse. When she turned, Sam was looking straight at her, half-asleep, still on her stomach.

Hayden had been caught in the act. She swallowed. "You don't want me to?"

Sam pushed up on her side, resting her head on her hand. She was delightfully naked and didn't seem at all inclined to pull the sheet up from her hips. Her skin was flushed from sleep.

"No."

So here they were, the early morning light starting to filter in, and Sam didn't want her to leave.

Sam always said things as if the answer was so simple. Like it had been obvious. Hayden lay back down, mirroring Sam, their faces a foot away, her head in her hand with her elbow pushing into her pillow.

"Okay," Hayden said.

"I think we should talk." Those words were never good, and something in Hayden's face must have shown that thought, because Sam added, "Don't panic, Hayden. Just. We should talk."

Hayden chewed at the inside of her lip. "Okay."

"What was last night for you?"

Hayden sucked in a breath. Talk about starting easy. What was last night for her? She'd been lost in a storm of emotions she'd had no idea how to sort through. "I just—I needed…"

Sam nodded, once. "It was only sex for you?"

Her face could be called impassive. Her voice neutral. But Hayden liked to think she knew Sam, now. At least a little. And her voice was almost too neutral, her face too impassive.

"No."

Sam's look was too intense, and Hayden dropped her gaze to the sheet underneath her.

"It wasn't only sex. I—I needed something. But it wasn't," she raised her gaze, not wanting to finish the sentence just yet. "What was the first night for you?"

Sam's eyes widened. "Touché." The was a flush in her cheeks now that had crept up from her neck. Hayden liked her like this—in the morning, with none of the day wearing down on her. She was more real. More present. In her bed, with her clothes all over the floor and not even a sheet between them, Sam was almost vulnerable. A word Hayden would never have used for her before this. "I guess I needed something too. We were also a bit drunk."

"We weren't drunk last night."

"No. We weren't." Sam studied her. "You were going to leave again."

Hayden huffed and dropped face-first into the pillow. Of course she'd been going to leave. Staying had seemed way too scary last time, and now, nakedness be damned. Even now Hayden wanted to run down the stairs, out the door, down the street, and away from the discussion of feelings.

"Hayden." Sam sounded exasperated, and it made her smile into the pillow.

"I didn't know what you wanted."

"What?" Sam asked.

To be fair, Hayden had said that completely into the pillow. She turned her head, enough that she could still hide yet be understood. "I didn't know what you wanted."

"So your solution was to run away?" Even in hiding, Hayden could hear the frustrated tone in Sam's voice.

"Yes." Hayden dropped her face fully back into the pillow.

Sam sighed.

A hand stroked over the back of Hayden's head, fingers tugging gently at the tangles in her hair. It was so unexpected from Sam, but it was exactly what Hayden needed.

"Maybe," Sam said, her voice exceedingly soft, "we should talk when you get back?"

Hayden turned her head, one eye peeking out from the pillow and up at Sam. "Yeah?"

"Yes. You have a flight soon, and a lot to think about at home. And this is… complicated."

"Do you regret it?" Hayden certainly regretted how words spilled out of her as soon as she thought them.

Sam's hand was still resting on her head, and her fingers curled into Hayden's hair, her palm warm and weighted against her neck. "No."

Hayden had never liked two letters more.

CHAPTER 25

Her mother was small in the hospital bed.

It wasn't like seeing her in her bed at home.

There were tubes. A drain was in her head, and Hayden couldn't stop herself from checking everything, eyes restlessly moving over the machines and the pulse oximeter readings, watching the rise and fall of her chest. They'd sedated her for now to stop her tugging on the various plastic things coming out from her body.

Once upon a time, her mother had been funny. And stubborn. Strong. She'd liked old black and white films. She'd cry in romantic movies and used to throw a couch cushion at Sofia and Hayden if they laughed at her. She'd liked cooking even if she wasn't the best at it. Things were always undercooked. She used to sing, always off-key, when she cleaned.

Some of those habits, those little pieces of her, continued the year Hayden had looked after her. But slowly, one by one, they'd fallen away, peeled back and lost somewhere. And her mother had become someone Hayden didn't recognize. She'd flash in anger, get confused over small things. Yell. And it was all the disease; Hayden knew that. But watching her mother fade away into someone else had been the most painful thing Hayden had ever experienced.

But her mother was fine.

She'd be fine.

Abuela, Sofia, and Hayden, however, were not.

And that was something they all needed to talk about.

In the cafeteria of the hospital, they sat with coffee that was as thick and stale as the one in the hospital in New York. Abuela put in three sugars and still made a twisted face when she took a sip.

"This tastes like ass," she stated.

Hayden snorted, thankfully right before she took her own sip, whereas Sofia was not so lucky. She choked and started coughing.

Abuela clicked her tongue at her. "You should be more careful."

"And you shouldn't say 'ass.'" Sofia took the napkin Hayden handed over and swiped at her chin.

"I am seventy-two. I say what I like."

Who were they to argue with that?

"Say 'ass' all you want, Abuela." Hayden smiled and hoped her exhaustion didn't reach her eyes. "I for one think it's hilarious."

Abuela sniffed and looked from Sofia to Hayden and back with a stern eye. "It is time we talk."

Hayden was hearing a version of those words a lot today, it would seem.

"Agreed," Sofia said.

"Me too," Hayden agreed.

"I think the time is coming that we need more help with your mother." Those words cost Abuela a lot to say. Hayden could see it in the way her jaw was set, in the way the words rasped out her throat, as if she wanted anything more than to say them.

Hayden reached a hand over the table and laid it over hers. Only a second later, Sofia put hers over both of theirs. Abuela's eyes were misty.

"Oh, my girls. *Mis buenas nietas.*" She drew in a shaky breath. The fluorescent lights made her squint, emphasizing the deeply etched lines around her lips and eyes. Hayden had no idea how she considered putting her own daughter into care. "I wanted... I wanted to look after her. For always. This is what we do with family. We do not—not, give family to someone else."

Hayden's throat tightened at the disgust that was thick in Abuela's words at the thought of doing so. Both Hayden and Sofia opened their mouths, starting to speak, but Abuela held up one hand.

"But—we know. We know this disease. The prog—the prog?" She looked at Hayden.

"Prognosis."

"*Sí.* The prognosis. The time is not long. Like with your *abuelo.*" Her voice was tight, her eyes wet, as she looked from one to the other. Sofia's hand squeezed tightly, Hayden's wedding ring digging into her fingers. She pressed her leg to Sofia's under the table. "But I think I must accept that I cannot do it. That I am being *egoísta*—I am being selfish. We are. And it is better for your mother now, and for us, for Javi, if she go somewhere they can look after her more."

Hayden looked at Sofia, whose eyes were as wet as Abuela's, and the lump in her throat grew. She tried to swallow it down, but it did nothing.

"My girls. How does this sound?" She looked at them so earnestly.

Hayden nodded, as did Sofia.

"I called two places from the airport today." Hayden sounded raw. She felt it too. This decision would sit heavy on all of them. "Two years ago, I researched the best care facilities in Miami. We can go and see them tomorrow. Together."

Sofia's hand was too tight, but Hayden wouldn't complain.

"Of course you do that." Abuela's smile was watery. "You like to organize these things."

It wasn't often Abuela would say Hayden liked to organize. Hayden had never been known to be organized as a teenager. But it was an easier way to cope with this, to do something, to have something else to think of.

Sofia swiped her free hand over her cheeks. "Okay. Good. We can take Javi. I think it would be good for him to see where she'll go. So he knows it's somewhere nice and won't be scared when we visit. Now. How are we going to pay?"

"We sell the house." Abuela pulled her hand away and straightened. "We can buy something much more smaller. That money will help."

"And I have some." They both looked at Hayden. "I have some money I've been saving for this, plus the money I've been sending."

A tiny lie. She had been saving. But only recently. The money and its too many zeros, sitting in her back account and staring at her when she checked it, like lots of judgmental eyes. She had always known where that money was going to go. It would help them afford somewhere nicer than what they could have otherwise, with only the house money.

Months ago, she'd been sure she couldn't make her family sell the house, that she'd married Sam and found a solution to that. Because years of care was going to be painfully expensive, and the plan saved them from that.

But now?

No way Hayden could take that money.

They spent the next day going between the hospital and the two facilities that Hayden had found.

It was exhausting and daunting, and it left them all on edge.

Javi, though, saw it like his grandma was going to live in a hotel.

"A pool." He bounced on the sofa, the piece of pizza in his hand flopping everywhere. None of them had the energy to tell him to calm down. "But it smelled funny in there."

Hayden checked her phone again. She had three messages, all from Luce: one a funny photo and the others seeing if Hayden was okay. Hayden sent a photo of Javi with pizza sauce all over his chin, then sent a message asking for a coffee date the day after next. Her flight was getting in late tomorrow night.

Nothing from Sam, and Hayden tried not to think about her; she had been trying not to the entire time. It was surprisingly easy when she was so distracted. But still, something in her gut twinged at the thought of her. She ignored that too.

"I like the second one," Abuela said. She sat back in her armchair, frowning at the congealing cheese on her piece of pizza. "It has a pool, like Javi says. Paola likes the pool."

It was true. She really did.

"But the first had bigger bedrooms." Sofia wiped at her fingers and tried to hold Javi down to wipe his face. He slipped under her arm and grinned at her from the other side of the couch.

"But a pool, Mami." He wiped at his mouth with the back of his hand, and Sofia closed her eyes and took in a breath.

"You really think she'll like the pool, buddy?" Hayden asked him.

His big, sincere brown eyes turned to her. He nodded, sauce smeared up his cheek where he'd missed. "I do. Big rooms are nice. But she can see friends in the pool."

"Tiny child has a point."

"I'm not tiny!" He stood on the sofa. "I'm a giant."

"Sit down," every adult in the room said in unison.

He dropped onto his bottom, bouncing and taking a huge bite of pizza, one that he shouldn't have been able to talk through. *Shouldn't* being the operative word. "I'm not tiny," he insisted; at least, it sounded like that.

"Well. If Abuela and Javi like the second," Sofia put her plate on the table, "I'm happy with it too."

"Great. I'm in." Hayden knew her mother probably wouldn't use the pool for long, with how things were going. But even if it was just a month of something nice for her, it would be worth it. She poked at her pizza slice, gave up, and put her plate down too.

When Hayden looked up, Abuela was blinking rapidly. "Yes. Good. It is decided." She stood up abruptly. "We need tea."

Tea was not something Hayden wanted right now, and she doubted Sofia did. But they weren't going to tell her that.

"Should we go after her?" Hayden asked when she'd left.

"I think she needs a moment."

They spent the evening on the sofa, and Hayden sat with Javi in her lap, watching kids' movies and trying not to think. When he went to bed, later than usual, Hayden wandered out to the porch swing. Sofia joined her not long after.

"Want me to call?" she asked, as she slid under the blanket next to Hayden.

"No." The backyard was dark, quiet. It was soothing. "I can call in the morning. This one is good, too. It has some free spaces."

They didn't talk about why there were free spaces. But the thought of it left an aching hole in Hayden's chest. This disease was not a nice one. On average, people lived seven years after diagnosis, some for much longer. But they were in the seventh year of the disease, and their mother was declining.

"This sucks," Sofia breathed.

Hayden threw her arm over her shoulder, her cheek resting on Sofia's head. "Yeah. It does."

Hours later, crawling into bed, Haden plugged in her phone and lay watching the dark ceiling covered in shadows thrown by the window. She wasn't tired. What she wanted was to be at home and curling around Frank in her bed, letting his purrs settle her heart rate. She wanted to be on the sofa with Sam.

As the feeling of missing Sam, missing Frank—and missing her mother something fierce—started to creep over her, overwhelm her, that was when Sofia knocked on her door and padded in. They talked for hours under the covers like they would when they were silly, giggly kids and had sleepovers. They voiced whispers out into darkness, saying things without light shining on the bare-boned truth of it all.

Until one of them started crying and got the other going. When finally one of them hiccupped so hard that they farted, they had to smother their peals of laughter with their hands. Abuela came in, tiny in her cotton nightgown, huffed at them, and crawled in between them both.

"Shush, and go to sleep, *nietas*." After a pause, she said, "Why it smell in here?"

And that set Sofia and Hayden off laughing again.

They slept squashed together, all with puffy eyes, but Hayden's chest felt lighter. Hayden woke up with Abuela throwing too much heat over her back. The room was dark, morning clearly a while away. But her phone was flashing.

Hayden tapped her screen to open a message from Sam, warmth flooding her chest as she read.

Frank misses you.

Swallowing heavily, yet warm to her toes, she replied.

I miss him too.

She put her phone down, dropping back onto the bed.

~ ~ ~

Rubbing her eyes, Hayden fell out of the taxi. Literally. She hit her knee on the curb and cursed her inability to be coordinated. She'd entertained the idea of taking a bus. But that would have meant waiting thirty minutes and changing twice, and her eyes felt like they were going to fall out of her head. She just wanted to be home. So she'd splurged.

She hefted her backpack onto her shoulder and closed the taxi door. It was too late for Nicolas to be working. The elevator ride up was quiet, the hum of the machine soothing. She avoided the mirror behind her. She knew she looked exhausted.

The apartment was quiet when Hayden put her bag down near the doorway. A single lamp in the corner lit up the living room and Sam on the sofa. She looked up from her book.

"Hi." Her voice was low, quiet.

"Hey." Hayden kept her own the same way.

Fur rubbed against her legs, and Hayden picked Frank up, already purring heavily. She pressed her face into his neck and walked over to the sofa, sitting down close to Sam.

It was strange, but a shyness was creeping up on her. Frank got up instantly and walked away back to Hayden's room. "Nice to see you too, Frank," she said.

Sam huffed a laugh, her head falling against her hand, her elbow on the back of the sofa. She wore dark-gray sweats and a soft-looking hoodie. She was so casual with her bangs falling over her eyes. The suspenders had been hot as hell, but Hayden liked her like this. Quiet and dressed down. Fewer edges.

"He's been moping, but now that you're back, I expect he wishes to punish you."

"That's what he always does." Hayden tucked her legs under herself and it left their knees brushing. She'd been in constant contact with Sofia, Javi and Abuela the last few days, but Hayden found herself craving more—skin and heat and something to lose herself in.

Sam. Who was watching her. "How are you?" Sam asked.

"I'm okay."

Sam just kept watching her. Slowly, as if unsure, she pushed some of Hayden's hair behind her ears, her fingers resting on one of the arms of her glasses for a second before trailing down her neck. Hayden's breath hitched. Sam didn't move away as Hayden thought she might. Instead, her gentle fingers stayed there in the crook of her neck.

"You look tired."

"Gee, thanks."

Sam huffed, and Hayden was delighted when she still didn't take her hand away. "You know what I mean."

"I do." Those fingers started to slip away, and Hayden wrapped her fingers around Sam's hand, keeping it against her collarbone. "Don't stop."

Sam's pupils blew wide as she drew a breath in sharply through her nose. Her fingers hooked into Hayden's sweater. She tugged, and Hayden let herself be pulled forward and into the distraction of Sam. Hayden's hand curled around the back of Sam's neck, and her lips started slow. Unassuming.

A kiss to get lost in.

But when Hayden pushed Sam back to lie down on the sofa, Sam's tongue glided over her own, and Hayden gasped into her mouth. Fingers were in her hair, and Sam's legs wrapped around her waist. And it was everything Hayden had been wanting. Sam's head fell back, and Hayden's lips grazed over her neck, her teeth nipping and her tongue soothing the skin.

"Hayden." Sam should always say her name like that—rough and raw and filled with need. "We were supposed to be talking."

Hayden paused, Sam's legs still locked around her waist and her mouth on the curve of Sam's breast. She raised her head, pushing herself up, her hands digging into the sofa on either side of Sam. The pink flush of Sam's cheeks and the way she bit her lip didn't really make Hayden want to talk.

"Okay." Hayden swallowed. "Hit me."

But Hayden's hand slipped from under her, off the edge of the couch, and she fell on a yelping Sam before she could stop herself. Hayden pushed herself back up, and before she could apologize, Sam laughed, the sound loud and real and grounding. It was delightful.

"Okay, if we're going to talk, one thing you should know is I'm a klutz."

"Good to know. Also, you warned me of this right from the start." Sam's eyes were bright. Her lips were still curved up, and her fingers threaded through Hayden's hair as she pulled her back down again.

Sam's lips were addictive.

The curving line of her jaw was too. Hayden kissed her, her breath washing over Sam's neck as she said, "I thought we were talking?"

"Tomorrow."

And she pulled Hayden back to her mouth.

CHAPTER 26

"Why don't you look…terrible?"

Hayden pushed the sugar over toward Luce. The café they were in had a pleasantly warm buzz. After a hectic day in the ER on very little sleep since coming back the night before, it was the perfect way to end the day. Well, almost perfect.

"You're worried because I don't look utterly destroyed?" Hayden asked.

"Well…when you put it that way…" Luce took a sip of their drink, then blew over the edge, eyes on her even over the rim. "You just look all, like, glowy? Warm. Don't get me wrong; you look tired—" they grinned as Hayden narrowed her eyes "—but I thought you'd be a little broken."

Hayden fiddled with a sugar packet, turning it over and over between her fingers. "Miami was hard. It sucked, essentially." She chewed on the inside of her cheek, wondering how to explain it. Especially after being so tight-lipped about it all for so long. "We're, well, we decided to put Mom in a home. Which was a difficult decision. She'll move in straight from the hospital in a couple of days. They think that will be a smoother transition than going home first."

Saying it out loud made it all too real.

Luce put their cup down and reached over to rest their fingers on Hayden's forearm. "That would have been really hard."

"It was. And all I wanted was to be at home." And now Hayden got to speak the truth. Her lips pulled up into a smile—she didn't know if it was for what she was saying or for the fact that, for once, she got to gush at Luce, and it was going to be about something real.

"Oh." Luce winked. "*That's* why you're glowy?"

Heat was creeping up Hayden's neck. "Well, maybe."

"Did you go home and have make-me-feel-better-about-life sex?"

"Maybe."

"You so did."

"Just three times."

Luce barked a laugh. "Good to know sex doesn't die after marriage like they say, though if it did with you two, I'd be pretty concerned, considering you've only been together for like, six months."

"We seem fine."

"You do seem happy." Luce cocked their head at her.

"So do you."

Luce grinned, Hayden grinned, and Luce tittered. "The two of us are pathetic."

And they really were.

By the time the café kicked them out at nine, Luce had gushed about Clemmie and her photography for twenty minutes, Hayden had teased Luce for being smitten, and so Luce had again pointed out the way Hayden mooned at Sam at work when she thought no one was looking.

And Hayden tried to ignore the twist in her gut at the reminder that she and Sam still hadn't talked.

Luce eventually left her on the bus for the rest of the trip home, and Hayden let the rumble of the engine soothe her as she sat near the front, shoulder against the cold window. There were only a few stops until home. Sam would be working late that night. Slipping out of bed that morning, leaving behind a sleeping, naked Sam for work, had not been easy.

The house was deathly quiet when Hayden got in, went to her room, dropped her bag on the floor, and flopped on her bed. She had too much to think about, but Hayden could feel sleep pulling her under. She was so tired. But a good tired, in a lot of ways. She hadn't gotten as much as sleep as she'd needed the night before. Snapping her eyes open and sitting up, she shook her head. She shouldn't sleep.

Shower first.

Frank glared at her for no reason. Back to normal, then.

She showered quickly and crawled into bed without clothes, tugging the covers over herself. For a second, she thought Frank would ignore her, but he walked over her back and lay down in the middle of it. The pressure was weirdly therapeutic.

It must have been hours later when something woke her up.

"Hayden?" The word was whispered, no urgency in it.

Sam.

Hayden didn't move her face from the pillow. "Mhm?"

There was a weight on the bed, legs on either side of her own, the blanket tugged away.

Soft lips trailed down her spine, and Hayden's breath hitched in her chest as Sam's fingers followed the same path. Her tongue was added, light and wet on her back. Sam didn't stop, slowly tracing her fingers over the sensitive skin of the planes of her back, her shoulder blades, up her spine, and finally the back of her neck. Hayden's nipples were taut against the fabric of the sheet under her, and she arched up as Sam's teeth bit into her neck and grazed over the side of her ribs. When Hayden groaned, she could feel the smile Sam gave against her skin, her chuckle rich and content.

Warm breath blew over the tips of her ear, and Hayden shuddered, her hips rocking, which matched the torturous rock of Sam's hips where she ground down on Hayden's ass.

"Are you awake?"

Hayden grinned, even as she gasped at Sam's tongue running over the shell of her ear. "Definitely."

Sam made a humming noise, and Hayden could feel her breasts against her back. The room was still dark, her body overloaded with sensation. Sam's hand spread over the back of her neck, her fingers digging into her hair, almost roughly.

Hayden's "*fuck*" turned into another low moan when Sam's other hand slid between her hip and the mattress, her fingers sliding down. Hayden's hips were moving in a rhythm that was completely devoid of Sam's. "Please."

Sam didn't move her hand, just left it still. "You do it."

She breathed the words into Hayden's ear and finally slid her hand low enough, and at the pressure of her fingers, Hayden pressed her forehead into the pillow, Sam's other hand still in her hair, tugging. When Hayden rolled her hips again, her clit rocked against Sam's fingers, and Sam moaned louder than Hayden at the sensation.

Heat. That was all Hayden could feel—heat spreading throughout her body and heat in the very core of herself. Every time she rocked her hips, Sam's fingers pressed against her, the hand in her hair clenching. Soon, Hayden was nearly a sobbing mess into her pillow.

"Sam." She choked the word out. "Please."

She didn't know what she wanted, had no idea. Her hips moved of their own accord, the fingers of one of Hayden's hands gripping the mattress, the other reaching up and behind her to dig her nails into Sam's thigh.

"Please what?"

"*Please.*"

The hand in her hair disappeared, and Hayden actually whined, Sam's chuckle into the back of her neck fading as Sam sat up. The warmth over her back was mostly gone, and Hayden would have missed it, but the fingers were still there, and Hayden ground down even harder. And then she knew why Sam had sat up, because her hand slid down Hayden's back once more, over her ass, down the back of her thighs. She ran them back up, and now fingers were inside her: curving, curling, thrusting.

It built leisurely, a wave that built higher and higher.

Hayden saw stars.

She came back to earth slowly, her breathing too loud and ragged. Sam's fingers were smoothing through her hair, her leg thrown over the backs of Hayden's. There was no way Hayden could move. She barely managed to turn her head. The room was still so dark.

"I can't see you," Hayden murmured.

A rustling sound, the feeling of the bed dipping, and the bedside lamp clicked on. When Hayden finally stopped squinting, Sam's face came into focus, at her side. Her head was pillowed on her forearm.

"Hey."

Sam brushed hair out of Hayden's eyes. "Hello."

Hayden licked her lips, her brain still fuzzy, limbs heavy. "What time is it?"

"After midnight. My surgery ran long."

"You must be tired?" Hayden asked.

"Not really."

"If you give me like, ten minutes, I'll regain control of my body and return the favor."

Sam's laugh was something Hayden wished she could bottle and carry around with her. "I don't think it needs to work like that."

"How does it need to work?"

Again, Hayden hated how her words spilled out. Like her brain and mouth weren't connected.

Sam raised her eyebrows, and Hayden wanted to pull her closer, even though her face was less than a foot away. "Sex? From my experience, you seem to have a fairly good understanding of how that works, Hayden."

Hayden pushed up a little, moving onto her side and propping her head up with her hand. "*Fairly?*"

Sam smirked. "You're extremely easy to wind up."

"And you're cruel."

"I didn't hear you complaining a few minutes ago."

Hayden's cheeks burned. "Maybe you have a fairly good understanding too."

"Good to know." Sam had pulled her shirt off at some point, and Hayden ran her hand over her shoulder and down her back, her fingers running over the waistline of her jeans. Sam closed her eyes, her face smooth and relaxed.

"And is that all this is?"

Sam's eyes snapped open, her eyes intent on her. "Is all what is?"

Hayden shrugged, feeling fifteen. "This. Us. Are we just...having The Sex?"

"*The* Sex?"

"Yes. The Sex."

"Are you sticking with that?"

"I am."

Sam sighed and pushed herself up so they were at eye level, her head propped on her hand too. Hayden's hand splayed over her waist, the curve of it under her palm. "Hayden, what do you want this to be?"

"I—" Why was Sam so calm and able to ask these questions without wanting to hide? Hayden already wanted to pull the blanket up over her head. "That's not fair. You go first."

And now she *sounded* fifteen.

"Right. Should we write it down on slips of paper and pass it to each other at the same time?"

"You're an asshole."

Sam was looking insanely sassy. "I was under the impression that this was... something. Not just sex. Is that true for you?"

"I—well. Yeah."

Why was Sam making this sound so simple?

"The first time, I thought maybe it had just been an accident," Sam said. "A slip. I was a little bit of a...well, a mess that night, and we'd been drinking. So I assumed that maybe that was all it was for you. And you?"

"Uh, yeah."

"And then it happened again, but no alcohol was involved, and you spooned me all night."

Well, pointing that out was just rude.

"I've never done that with someone when it was just about sex," Sam said.

"Me neither. And you spooned me back."

Sam deigned to ignore that. "And then there was last night. Hayden, only the most insecure person has to be unsure at this point."

"Um…"

Sam's hand fell over Hayden's own against her waist, her thumb swiping over the digits. "I understand being unsure after that first time. But are you still?"

And that was when Hayden realized it. "No. I'm not."

Sam's pushed at her hand and entwined their fingers. "Were you unsure the first time?"

Hayden dropped into the pillow, hiding her face before turning it to look at Sam who was staring down at her, amused. "Shit, yes. I had no idea what was going on. Weren't you?"

"You hide in your pillow a lot."

"Do not."

"Once at your family's house, the other day, and just now."

"Okay, fine. I do. I feel safe."

Sam looked at her as if she thought Hayden was kind of adorable and it left a flutter in Hayden's stomach.

"You're ridiculous," Sam said.

Which Hayden knew meant she was adorable. "I really am. And you didn't answer my question."

Sam swallowed, and if she had been anyone else, Hayden thought Sam might have looked away. She didn't, though. Her eyes stayed on Hayden's, a steady well of green. "You weren't there when I woke up the first time. Which I think is a pretty clear sign of regret. And then you avoided me completely."

Hayden sucked in a breath, not expecting the fragile edge to Sam's tone. She tugged the hand linked to her own, rolling onto her back so Sam was pulled on top of her, her legs falling between Hayden's and her weight comfortable. Hayden brushed the bangs out of Sam's eyes. "I'm sorry. I completely panicked. I thought that, well, you were sad, and…"

"You thought I was using you."

Hayden swallowed. "Maybe? Not in a really bad way. So I thought I'd save you the trouble of having to get rid of me and just…"

"Completely avoid the topic, like an adult?"

Hayden bit her lip. "Well, yeah."

Sam sighed, then wriggled down and dropped her chin onto the back of her hand on top of Hayden's stomach. Hayden put her forearm under her head to see her better. "I followed your example. I told you at the very beginning that I was not the best at all of this; at, well, people." Sam blinked up at her. "I generally take my cues from others."

"So you avoided me because I was avoiding you?"

"I thought it was what you wanted. I did try. You can be extremely frustrating."

"You only realized this then?"

"No. But more so after. Every time I went to the ER to try and start a conversation, you disappeared. And you were never home."

"Sorry." And Hayden meant it. Hayden bent her legs, and Sam pillowed herself between them. Hayden liked her there, her eyes calm and looking up at Hayden, all honesty and open questions.

"Have you thought about what this means?" Sam asked. "Us actually being together?"

Hayden's breath caught. Sam looked at her like silence was exactly what she expected. So Hayden said, "I never really thought it would happen. So, uh, no."

"We aren't exactly in the most uncomplicated situation."

"Not the most complicated, either."

The fingers of Sam's other hand were tracing patterns over her sternum. "True. But, Hayden, you're young, and—"

"I'm not young."

Sam's eyebrows shot up, and Hayden's cheeks went hot. Sam looked smug.

"Okay, I'm aware the high-pitched denial made me sound young. But that's not fair. Age isn't important."

"I'm fifteen years older than you."

Hayden gasped, throwing her hand over her mouth and widening her eyes. "No? Are you? I had *no* idea."

"I may be an asshole, but *you* are maddening."

"It's probably because I'm fifteen years younger than you."

Sam huffed again and sat up. Which she should always do shirtless, Hayden decided then and there. Hayden pushed herself up to sit against the headboard, pulling a pillow into her lap. She was a lot more naked than Sam.

"Hayden—"

"Sam, look. Yes, you're fifteen years older than me. I don't care. Can I say I'll always not care? No. But right now, and as far as I know myself in the future, I really don't care. Do you care that I'm younger?"

"No," Sam said instantly. "I feel I'm getting the better side of the deal, though."

Hayden laughed and let her gaze rove down Sam's neck, her chest, over her stomach. "You aren't sitting where I'm sitting."

Hayden pushed the pillow away and sat up on her knees, putting her hand on Sam's shoulder and pushing backward until she gave in and lay down. Hayden straddled her thighs, her hands on either side of her shoulders and her hair falling down around them. Slowly, she bent down, running her nose over Sam's, grazing it over her cheek until she finally kissed her once, slowly.

Hayden bit her lip. "I kind of like you."

Hayden was breathless, and she traced her fingertip over Sam's cheek. Sam huffed through her nose as if she wanted to say Hayden was ridiculous, but her smile betrayed her. By now, Hayden knew Sam's eyes, and the way they'd softened as Hayden said it spoke volumes. She felt giddy with everything exploding within her at that moment.

Against her lips, Sam murmured. "Me too."

And Hayden let herself swallow those words, in the hopes they'd nestle deep within her.

CHAPTER 27

It was still dark outside, yet the kitchen was filled with the smells and sounds of eggs and bacon frying on the stove. Hayden took a sip of her coffee and wove her foot around the rung of her stool, watching Sam move things around the pan with a spatula. She yawned as quietly as she could.

"You really didn't need to get up to make me breakfast," Hayden said. "You could have had an entire extra hour of sleep."

Sam didn't even turn around. "Well, it was me who prevented you from sleeping."

Hayden put her elbows on the counter and kept her coffee cup near her face. Even the smell helped. "I really wasn't complaining."

"I know."

The arrogance that had once driven Hayden up the wall was less annoying now. More kind of sexy. Okay, less eye-roll inducing. Still, when Sam winked at her and went back to the stove with a slight flick of her hips, Hayden almost melted into a puddle.

"I don't want to work today," Hayden said. "Let's just stay home all day. In bed. Naked."

When Sam turned around with empty plates in her hands, she caught Hayden staring at her ass. Hayden grinned shamelessly. Sam put the plates down on the counter across from her. "And what about our patients?"

"To be fair, I don't have specific patients. Another nurse can cover."

"I do."

"They can wait?"

Sam leaned over the plates, across the counter and Hayden met her partway, the kiss lingering. Then Sam shook her head and pulled away, and Hayden groaned. "No. I have things that can definitely not wait."

"Someone else can do them?"

Back at the stove, Sam picked up the pan, carried it over, and dropped the eggs and bacon onto the plates. "And deny them my genius?"

"You're full of yourself."

"Partly, yes." The pan now in the sink to soak, Sam grabbed the pieces of toast she'd kept warming in the oven and placed them on the plates as well. "But also, every time I walk in that OR and know I have to open someone up, I have to believe I'm the best."

"Okay." Hayden took a bite of her toast. "And besides, you *are* the best."

"Now you've noticed."

"I always had. You're the best neurosurgeon in the state. It's not really debatable."

"Yet—" Sam stood opposite her, picking up a piece of crispy bacon, and Hayden strangely loved that she wasn't using her fork to eat it "—you didn't like me at all." She took a bite and chewed it like she had all the time in the world. It was kind of hot, actually.

"Maybe I was secretly harboring pent-up sexual feelings for you?"

"Were you?" Sam looked particularly interested in that answer.

"I *did* stare at your collarbones the first time we went out. And I kind of have a thing for those, so…"

"I hadn't noticed." Sam's voice was extremely dry. "Each time we've slept together, I've had to wear shirts that go up to my neck."

"Stop having biteable body parts, then."

Sam hummed in response, and they ate in silence. When Frank appeared and meowed loudly at Sam's feet, Sam dropped some bacon in his bowl. Hayden could hear his purr from where she sat.

"There's something else we have to talk about," Sam said. She put down her knife and fork, her plate clean.

"We're married," Hayden supplied.

"That, yes. We're married—and now involved. That is something we also need to talk about at some point. But I was thinking about the money."

"I don't want it," Hayden blurted out.

"I knew you were going to say that."

"Well, I don't. I have the original forty, which I also don't want, by the way—"

"You're keeping it."

"I knew you wouldn't take it back. So I have that. I don't want the rest."

"Yes, well—"

Then something occurred to Hayden and her mouth dropped open. She swore she could feel the blood draining from her cheeks as a memory hit her. How had she not told Sam about this yet?

Sam's brow furrowed. "What?"

"Um, I forgot to tell you something."

"Hayden?"

Hayden winced. "Luce told me at the gallery, and then—well, I forgot. Some investigator was asking them questions about us."

Sam had looked as if she'd been waiting for a bomb to drop. But at Hayden's words, she relaxed and waved a hand in the air. "Oh, I already know."

Hayden relaxed back against the counter. "You do?"

"He's poked around work, and he even cornered Jon. But he'll find nothing. We're married. Everyone thinks we're married, whether people think it was fast or not. I spoke with my lawyer yesterday, and he's received absolutely no indication that the paperwork to start processing the fund is being blocked."

That made something occur to Hayden.

She straightened, the hair on her arms almost standing on end. "Sam, what if he can see the money transfers in our accounts?"

Waving a hand airily, Sam looked far too relaxed at the thought that had Hayden panicking. "Their ability to do that is a fallacy. It's completely illegal for him to do so."

"Oh."

"So don't worry. And don't change the subject."

Hayden fiddled with the ring on her finger. It didn't feel foreign to her anymore. She kind of liked it. Last night, their hands had been linked over Sam's hip, and their bands had matched. "In my defense, changing the subject wasn't what I set out to do."

Sam pushed her plate aside and watched her, intent. "That money is yours. It was part of the deal."

"Well, the deal's changed now." Hayden pushed forward, resting her hand on Sam's forearm. "Sam, I don't want to take your money. It feels weird and gross and uncomfortable."

"But what else do I need it for? You have no idea the amount in that trust; it's obscene. Jon will get half. I don't need the other half. I'm donating most of it."

"You are?"

Sam got a small, self-satisfied smirk on her lips, and Hayden liked it far more than she should. She was about to say something great; Hayden could feel it in the wicked glint in her eye. "Yes. To various LGBT organizations. My parents will love it."

"That's awesome."

"I'm going to donate in their names so they get certificates thanking them."

"Seriously?"

"Yes. Jon almost wet his pants laughing when I told him."

Hayden laughed so loudly that Frank jumped where he was sitting on the kitchen floor, looking up at them, clearly waiting for more bacon.

"It's genius." It really was. Hayden could just imagine them opening up the letter and seeing the certificates. "Donate the two hundred thousand there too."

"No. I want you to have it. You can use it to help your mother or study or whatever you wish."

Sam was incredibly annoying. "I don't need it. With the money I already have, and when we sell her house, we can—"

"But why sell it? Why make your family move when they don't need to? Plus, if you sell the house, you'll have to make sure they have a new place, smaller or not, so you lose some of the money there. This way, everyone is looked after. No new mortgages, and your mother can have the best care. You know for a fact that you may need to pay a nursing home for years."

Hayden swallowed and shook her head. "I can't take your money."

"You would have before."

"Yeah, and now it's different."

Sam huffed, throwing her hands up and straightening. "It's in the prenup. I'm required to pay it. I'll divorce you anyway, and pay it straight out."

That just sounded harsh.

"I can refuse it. Dispute it in court."

"You'll go to court to say, 'No, thank you. I don't want the money my prenup promises me'?"

"Uh—yeah. Yes."

"Hayden, stop being difficult."

"I'm not being a stubborn child."

"Yes, you are, a little."

"Is this because I'm fifteen years younger than you?"

Sam laughed, even though her cheeks were pink with irritation. "Don't be a smart-ass."

"I thought you knew by now that's impossible for me?"

Sam looked as if she didn't know whether to laugh or throttle her. "Take the money. Use it for your mother. If you end up with some left, donate it. Give it away. Pay off any debt you have. I don't care. But take the money, Hayden." Sam paused. "Please."

The look on her face was so sincere. "But my family thinks they have to sell the house."

"What were you going to tell them before? Before you and I happened, and you knew you'd have the money?"

"I don't know." Hayden really needed to learn to plan better. "I thought it would be another year or two until Mom would need permanent care, and I could have just said I'd saved."

"Okay." Sam nodded slowly. "Tell them I'm helping. We're married. It's normal that I would. Exaggerate how much you've put aside waiting for this."

"More lies?"

"Well, me helping is not really one. And the other is an exaggeration."

"A lie."

"A very small one."

"I hate lies."

"I know. You told me that in the bar, and I thought for sure this was all going to fall apart."

"Did you think, then, that we'd be having mind-blowing sex months later and arguing that I didn't want your money?"

"Not even a little."

Hayden reached over and wrapped her fingers in Sam's shirt, beckoning her forward to kiss her. She rested her forehead on Sam's. "Yet here we are."

Sam's laugh was disbelieving. "Yet here we are."

~ ~ ~

Hands were up Hayden's shirt, and she kicked the remote to the floor. Not that she cared. She and Sam had both had late nights and too much work the last few days.

Teeth grazed Hayden's neck, and Sam's hips were between her legs, rocking against her insistently. She felt like a teenager having a make out session, and it was positively awesome.

"Oh, my fucking hell."

Sam froze. Hayden froze. They both turned their heads as one. Jon stood at the front door, gawking.

"My eyes!" He clapped a hand over them and turned around dramatically. Sam dropped her head on Hayden's chest for a second, then pulled her hand out of Hayden's shirt and sat up. Adjusting her shirt, Hayden did the same.

"You can uncover your fragile gaze now, Jon," Hayden said.

Without dropping his hand, he turned around. "Are you sure?"

"Are you really that grossed out by two women?"

He dropped his hand and rolled his eyes, looking the spitting image of Sam. "I'm not that juvenile. That's my *sister* you're half-naked with."

Hayden had once walked in on her sister and her boyfriend. She shuddered in commiseration. "Fair enough. Though my shirt riding up is hardly half-naked."

Sam crossed her legs, perfectly poised except for the red of her neck. "Is there a reason you're just letting yourself in, dear brother?"

"Dear sister, you told me to come round at eight."

"I did?"

"You did. You were distracted by kissing, I think."

Hayden grinned. "I *am* a good kisser."

"Gross. I'd like to know," Jon said, "since when did this thing become a *thing*."

"Don't act like you didn't know."

Jon scowled at Hayden's comment and flopped into a chair.

Sam looked at him. "You knew?"

"It was so obvious that you two slept together after that dinner with our parents. You may as well have done it in the hall."

Hayden wrinkled her nose. "Ew."

"Yet you said nothing." There was something strange in Sam's voice, and she was looking at Jon like she looked at Hayden sometimes, as if trying to figure him out.

Across from them, he shifted uncomfortably. "Well. Yeah. We don't, you know, do that—talk." Sam kept watching him. "Our family doesn't do that."

"Our parents don't. But perhaps we should."

"Okay," he shifted, as if uncomfortable, "so, you start." He winked. "Are you two just banging, since your deal involves not dating other people, and it's been a while? Or are you together? Are you in *lurve?*"

"I retract my statement." Sam stood up and walked past him to the kitchen, not looking at either of them. "We shouldn't talk."

Hayden chuckled and Jon smirked.

"Oh, come on, sis." Jon watched her movements in the kitchen. Hayden buried her knuckles in her mouth to stop herself from laughing out loud. "Tell your dying-of-curiosity brother: are you two just going to stay married and have tiny children? And, years from now, will you tell them the charming story of how you fake-married, then met your soulmate?"

Hayden gave up and snickered. Sam's sigh could be heard from the kitchen.

"Do either of you terrible people want a drink?" she called.

"What's on offer?" Jon asked.

Sam had opened the fridge, and Hayden couldn't really see her from her position. "You will have what you're given," she called from inside the fridge, her voice muffled.

Jon turned to Hayden. "Is that what she says to you?"

Hayden laughed. "Would you really like to know?"

He shook his head. "No, no. I take it back. I'll be good."

"Are you sure? I can tell you details. Lots of them. Right before you came in, I—"

He covered his ears. "Lalalalala."

Sam walked back over, carrying a bottle of champagne in one hand and three glasses by the stems in the other.

"Champagne?" Because Hayden always liked to state the obvious.

Jon turned quickly, dropping his hands from his ears. "What have we done to deserve champagne?"

"You? Nothing," Sam said.

"Are we toasting to your newfound love?" he asked.

Sam stopped and narrowed her eyes at him. It was actually slightly terrifying, and Hayden remembered the course she went to that Sam had spoken at years ago. Someone had asked what was, admittedly, a stupid question, and she'd leveled that exact same look on the poor guy, who had almost liquefied in his seat. Everyone there almost had.

Jon met the look without even a cringe. "No? What, then?"

Sam put the glasses down and unwrapped the foil over the cork, her fingers nimble. She untwisted the metal ring. "Well," she started, the cork popping while Jon held up a glass to catch the overflowing bubbles. "I spoke with my lawyer today. The final paperwork was completed. The trust is in my name. It can't be contested now."

Jon handed Hayden a glass, who half sat up to take it. "Seriously?" he asked.

"Yes." Sam poured another glass. "Seriously." She passed the other to Jon and poured her own. "Half is already on its way to you."

"Really?"

"Really. It's yours."

He stood up and held his glass out. Hayden quickly got to her feet and did the same. With bewildered smiles, they all clinked their glasses and took a sip. It fizzed all over Hayden's tongue and down her throat.

"So... It's done?" she asked.

"It's done. And you," she turned to Jon, "need to figure out what you're doing."

He shrugged. "I'm going back to school."

Sam went very still. "You are?"

"Yes. I've been thinking a lot about everything. You're right. I should use the opportunity and get my degree, then use what I have to help later somehow."

"You're going back to school?" Sam was grinning.

Jon held his hand up for a high five. "I really am."

Sam blinked at his hand.

"Come on." He waggled his fingers.

She raised her hand and he clapped his to hers, the slap ringing out in the room. She shook her hand. "You're a brute."

"Sometimes. So it's done." He looked at Hayden, who had sat back down, and to Sam. "That means you don't really have to be married, except to carry it on for a couple of months. What the hell does that mean for you two now that you're together?" He dropped back into his chair again, taking a jovial sip of his champagne. "I mean, you've lied to everyone about being married. I imagine if this hadn't happened, you would have just gotten divorced, and that'd be that. But what do you do now? Tell everyone the truth? Get divorced? Though, that would be hard to explain if you're together. Stay married?"

He looked from one to the other, a smile plastered on his face and far too comfortable in his chair.

Neither Hayden nor Sam said anything.

"Have you two just not talked about it?"

Hayden cleared her throat. "Well, we've been busy."

"Sex is not an excuse."

Sam sat gracefully next to Hayden. "Stop talking about my sex life, Jon, or I'll talk to you about brain surgery."

He paled. "No. Don't do that. Also, don't change the topic."

Sam looked at Hayden. Hayden looked at Sam.

They looked at Jon, who sighed. "You're both useless."

~ ~ ~

It was hours later, on the balcony, and Hayden was shivering. The air had a bite to it, painfully cold, but it was so peaceful outside. Only the sound of traffic, muffled, and the lights flickering around the city. The door behind her slid open and closed again. There was no reason to turn around. She knew who was there.

Arms wrapped around her waist, encased in a blanket, and Hayden gave a contented hum, pushing back into the warmth of Sam's body.

"Jon's left," Sam murmured in her ear, her chin on Hayden's shoulder. The front of her body was entirely draped over Hayden's back, and Hayden's shivering finally eased. "What are you doing out here?"

Every word she said whispered over Hayden's ear and cheek and sent an entirely different kind of shudder down her spine. "Enjoying the calm."

"It's nicer in summer."

"I like it now. Everything is so still when it's so cold."

Sam kissed behind Hayden's ear. "That's true."

Hayden's fingers traced over Sam's against her stomach, warm under the blanket. Her nose was cold against her cheek. They stood, the night closing around them.

"Are you okay?" Hayden asked.

She'd wanted to ask since Sam had announced the successful transfer of the money. Sam had been smiling, yes, but also distant, something about it not sitting right with Hayden.

Silence, and the feeling of Sam's breath over her cheek, her fingers running over Hayden's.

"I thought there'd be...something more from them. My parents, I mean. I thought there'd be a final challenge, some form of contact. But there's been nothing."

Hayden's chest ached. To get nothing from your parents, to be turned away like that. Hayden couldn't fathom it. Even after her father, her mother had done nothing but love her and Sofia fiercely. To be hated so viscerally by your own flesh and blood, for something you couldn't change about yourself?

Hayden turned her head, her nose brushing over Sam's cheek and her mouth pressing to her jaw.

"I'm sorry," she said. Because what else could she offer?

Sam turned her head, her lips finding Hayden's and Hayden turned completely, her back against the railing, Sam keeping the blanket around them both. Everything was warm. Comfortable. Sam moved closer against her, their thighs falling between each other's, and Hayden gripped Sam's sweater to bring her in tighter. There was something about kissing Sam, something she could happily lose herself in with no need to find her way out. She loved the way her hands cupped Hayden's cheeks or her fingers ran through her hair, the way she'd give a small moan for Hayden to breathe in, to swallow.

Sam pulled away gradually, her forehead against Hayden's. "We do kind of need to talk about the issues Jon brought up."

Hayden kept her eyes closed and tilted her mouth toward Sam's, their lips brushing by each other. Sam laughed, nothing more than a puff of air, and pulled back further. Hayden pouted at the sense of loss. "No distracting each other with sex?" she asked.

Sam shook her head. "No."

"Okay. Well. We're married."

"We are."

Hayden still clutched fistfuls of Sam's sweater, and she tugged her closer again. "And we're together, but newly, not marriage-ready, type of together."

"Yes."

"Plus, I don't really, you know, believe in marriage as a necessary thing to do."

"You've mentioned that."

"And yet we live together. And everyone thinks we're married."

"That they do."

"What a weird predicament."

"Unique, I'd say." Sam brushed her lips over Hayden's, simple, nothing much, but enough to leave Hayden wanting more.

"So... What do we do?" Hayden asked, honestly not caring, right then.

"I guess we make a plan."

Plans. Right. That thing that Hayden had been telling herself she needed to get better at. "Any ideas?"

"One."

"And that is?"

"Well, you don't believe in marriage. So we simply get divorced, but not tell anyone else we're divorced. If we ever break up, we'll then pretend it's a divorce."

Hayden chuckled as Sam's lips now grazed her neck. "So just..."

"Act like we have been all the time anyway."

"Okay."

And apparently, they were done talking, because when Hayden kissed her, Sam responded eagerly.

CHAPTER 28

"Want to get a coffee?"

Hayden grinned and turned around. Sam was against the break room door, hands in her pockets.

The sludge she'd resigned herself to drinking almost sloshed out of the coffee pot as Hayden put it down with too much enthusiasm. "Oh, yes."

"That's what you said last night."

Hayden laughed, the sound spilling out of her. Discovering this side of Sam had been the best thing since starting their relationship. A giggle almost joined her laugh at that thought. Their relationship.

She was a giddy mess.

"I'm pretty sure you said something similar."

She walked forward until they were standing in front of each other, Sam's eyes alight. "I did. Though I was thinking." She cocked her head, and Hayden was glad no one was around, because Sam was not looking at Hayden in any kind of platonic way. "You were right, months ago."

That made Hayden pause. "I was?"

Sam had a wicked grin. "Yes, when you put your foot in your mouth and said you'd been told you're loud? It's true." That grin was going to be the end of Hayden, even as she clued into what Sam was saying and felt heat crawling up her neck. "You really *are*."

Hayden could almost disappear into the floor. Except that Sam looked like she kind of loved it. "Well, I did warn you."

Sam turned to walk toward the stairs, and Hayden fell into step with her. She wrapped her fingers around the handle of the door to the stairs and held it open for Hayden. This was all something she could get used to. Especially when Sam paused one flight of stairs up, looked around and pushed Hayden against the wall. Hands clenched at Hayden's scrub top and Sam ran her nose over Hayden's before dipping her head and kissing her. Her lips were soft, gentle; the kiss chaste. When she pulled back, Hayden gave a breathy sigh that should have left her embarrassed.

"Hey," Hayden whispered.

"Hello." Sam smiled at her, her finger against Hayden's chin. "You didn't wake me up when you left this morning."

"You looked so happy asleep."

Sam hummed and kissed her again before she pulled away slowly, leaving Hayden against the wall and wishing they were at home.

"Coffee?" Sam asked, her voice full of innocence.

Hayden followed her up the next flight of stairs, and it would have been far nicer to tug her back onto the landing than to emerge out where there were people and light and Sam slipping her hands in her pockets.

Did she do that to stop herself from wanting to touch Hayden? Because Hayden's fingers were itching to run down Sam's arm and trace over the back of her hand. Maybe it was better when Sam wasn't in her space, because it would seem Hayden turned useless when she was.

Not that she really cared.

In the line, their shoulders brushed and Hayden stepped closer, Sam's lips turning up even as she didn't look at her.

"Clemmie isn't working today," Sam said.

"Luce mentioned she had the day off. Luce has an early finish and they get to spend the afternoon together."

Sam turned her head, their faces barely a foot apart. Hayden wanted to close the gap, right there. Sam's gaze lingered on Hayden's lips. "Lucky them."

"Next!"

Good timing, because Hayden didn't think she would have cared about much right then and would have kissed Sam exactly where they stood. Sam ordered for them both and got Hayden's coffee order spot on. Maybe there was something to fake-dating your girlfriend before you actually started.

Girlfriend?

Right as they sat down at a table, Sam's pager went off at her hip. Of course it did.

"Got to go?" Hayden asked.

Sam plucked it off her waistband and looked at it. "Yes."

With a droll smile, Sam stood up, her coffee in hand. Hayden stared up at her. "Okay. I'll see you tonight?" Hayden's face fell. "Wait, tonight isn't your turn on call, is it?"

"That's tomorrow."

"Good."

They shared a smile and Sam hovered. "I really have to go."

"Go, then." Hayden shooed her with her hands. "Go save some lives."

With a last look at her, Sam walked away and Hayden picked up her coffee, hoping her face didn't look as dreamy as she felt.

That would just be humiliating.

The coffee was too hot, but she sipped it anyway. She only had about fifteen minutes before she had to go back down, her lunch a sandwich she'd eaten far too quickly while waiting for the coffee pot to drag through the grossness she'd been about to drink before Sam had appeared.

And then someone was slipping into the seat opposite her, the one Sam had barely vacated.

Hayden didn't care as much about space as Sam, but she still didn't exactly love it when hers was invaded. A quick glance around confirmed it: most other tables were empty. She looked back at the man who was smiling nonthreateningly at her. He was in his forties, a thick head of hair and eyebrows to match, brown eyes. The kind of guy she wouldn't look twice at.

Yet he was staring straight at her like he knew her.

"Can I help you?" Hayden asked.

"Hayden Pérez?" The syllables rolled off his tongue perfectly.

"Uh, yeah?"

Her hackles were up, and she had no idea why.

"My name's Nathan Ryan. I'm a private investigator."

Hayden went cold.

"Your face tells me you know who I am."

Hayden flicked at the lid of her coffee cup. "I do. You haven't exactly been discreet."

"Well, there wasn't really any point."

"I suppose not." Hayden swallowed. She had no reason to be nervous. The trust paperwork was finalized. She straightened her shoulders. "Find anything interesting?"

He held his hands out and shrugged. "Nothing except a married couple. Though that's not why I'm here to talk to you."

What?

"Why else would you want to talk to me?"

"We both know why Samantha's parents hired me. To find holes, proof that their daughter wasn't really a lesbian." He looked so comfortable, relaxed, and sure. "They wanted to prove it was a sham to get them back for what happened with her brother."

"Why are you telling me all this? Surely this is some kind of violation of privacy."

"It would be, usually, but they asked me to speak with you."

That made no sense. "Me? Why me?"

"They have a proposition for you."

"A proposition?"

"Yes." He spoke blankly. "Leave Sam."

Hayden reeled back as if she'd been slapped. "Excuse me?"

"Divorce Sam, and leave her. For good. Out of her life."

Hayden stood up, her jaw clenched. "I think *you* should leave."

He looked up at her, not even remotely surprised at the venom in her voice. "Leave her, and they will compensate you."

Compensate. That word. Sam's ad online.

"You think I would leave Sam for some money?"

"Not simply *some* money. They would like to offer you enough to look after your mother for as long as she'd need. To make sure your nephew can go to any school in the country. Your debts would be gone."

Hayden fell back into the chair, her heart in her throat. "How do you know about my life?"

"It's my job. All of that information was easy to find, if you know where to look." He slipped a folded up piece of paper over the table and left it in front of her. Hayden just looked at it. "Here is a number you can contact them on, and the figure they're speaking of."

He stood up, and Hayden didn't take her eye off the paper. "They expect an answer as soon as possible. They wish to give their daughter the help they know will set her right. Oh, and Hayden." He looked down at her, his expression so benign. "Getting married after a month? It's obvious this was a setup, even if I couldn't prove it."

And he left.

Hayden felt ill.

She picked up the paper and unfolded it with trembling fingers. A phone number was printed on it, as he'd said.

Then the figure.

One million US dollars.

Her mouth fell open.

She almost laughed. A million dollars? That wasn't even a real figure.

Someone sat opposite her again, and Hayden jumped, looking up, half expecting the cool smoothness of the man who had just walked away. Instead, she was met with Luce giving her a concerned look.

"Are you okay?"

"Yeah." Hayden cleared her throat and gave a shaky smile. "I'm fine."

She shoved the paper into her pocket, down as far as it could go.

~ ~ ~

Frank was purring next to Hayden on the sofa, a contented ball. That piece of paper, lead in her pocket all day, now lay next to a glass of wine that had mostly been untouched.

What to do?

The door opened and Sam stepped through it, tugging her jacket off as soon as the door closed behind her and walking into the kitchen. Her movements were so fluid, so confident all the time. Sam put her jacket down and looked up from the counter.

"Hey." Her face had warmed considerably at the sight of Hayden. "You beat me home."

The paper on the table in front of her may as well have been covered in neon lights. "I did."

Sam put her bag down on top of her jacket. "I was about to get a drink. Do you want anything?"

Hayden pointed at the glass. "I have something. Thanks."

Rather than turn to the fridge, Sam paused and really looked at Hayden. "Are you okay?"

Hayden nodded. Then shook her head. "I need to talk to you about something."

"Oh." Sam didn't move. "Do I want my glass of wine before you do?"

"Probably."

Sam moved around the kitchen, getting herself a glass of wine while Hayden tried to calm her heart rate down. She could actually feel her heart slamming away. When Sam sat next to her, she tucked a leg under the other and turned to face Hayden, her glass next to Hayden's.

Was this the right thing to do? Hayden really had no idea.

"What's going on?" Sam tilted her head. "What's happened?"

"I—" Hayden had no idea where to start. Or even if she should. "Someone visited me at work today, right after you left to answer your page."

"Okay?"

"It was Nathan Ryan."

Sam's face instantly darkened. She knew his name. "He offered you something?"

Hayden snapped her mouth shut. "How did you know that?"

Reaching for her wine, Sam said, "Well, the trust is done. There'd be no undoing it, and they really wouldn't have been able to before, anyway." She took a sip, her eyes bright over the rim, her gaze glued on Hayden's. She lowered the glass slowly. "So that's the only option."

"Well, you're correct."

"How much did they offer you?" This time, Hayden's mouth dropped open. "I imagine they wanted you to leave me. They either still think it's not real, or they think if you leave, they can 'fix' me."

Sam's voice was monotone.

"One million dollars," Hayden blurted out. Sam's head twitched back. Hayden grabbed the paper and handed it to Sam. "That's how much to leave you and never come back."

"That's a lot." But Sam didn't take her eyes off the paper she'd opened, so Hayden couldn't see her expression.

"I didn't know what to do." Sam didn't look up, so Hayden waited a second. Still nothing, so she kept going. "I didn't know if I should even tell you they did it. I thought maybe it was better not to, but then I couldn't keep that from you, so—"

Sam looked up sharply. "That's what you didn't know?"

"What?"

"You didn't know if you should tell me they'd done this?"

"Not telling you wasn't a serious thought, but I just—I didn't want you to be hurt even more. It wasn't that I wanted to lie to you—why are you smiling?"

"Hayden." Sam sounded disbelieving. "You weren't conflicted about whether or not to take the money? You were conflicted about telling me what they'd done? Because you didn't wish to see me hurt?"

"Well, yeah?"

Sam dropped the paper next to her, put her glass down and pitched forward, colliding with Hayden almost painfully. Her arms wrapped around her, and she kissed her once, twice. In shock, Hayden let herself fall against the back of the sofa. Sam's lips parted, and her tongue brushed over Hayden's in the best kind of kiss, full of emotion. But it all sunk in, and Hayden pulled back.

"Wait? You thought I'd accept that gross offer?"

It seemed to take a moment for Sam to catch up with the sudden movement and the question. "I didn't really think much at all." She was looking at Hayden's lips and it was very distracting, even as Hayden wanted to feel indignant. "But it sounded that way." Her eyes flicked back up to Hayden's, genuine. "And I, well—my entire family thinks about money first. And that was a lot of money."

Hayden shook her head, her fingers grazing Sam's cheek before she cupped it in her palm. "You're an idiot. I'm afraid you're stuck with me."

Sam's grin unfurled, slow and delicious. "That's agreeable."

She ducked her head to kiss Hayden again, but Hayden pulled back, and Sam made a sound that was almost a growl. "Wait." She chuckled at the frustrated look on Sam's face. "Sam. He knew stuff about my family. My mom. My debt. Everything. It was creepy."

How quickly Sam's expression changed was amazing, her look clouding. "I'm sorry. He was clearly told to find whatever he could to manipulate this."

"So, should I just message them a very friendly 'fuck off'?"

Sam smiled, in spite of herself. "How is that friendly?"

"I can put a smiley face before and after."

"As tempting as that is, I think I have a better idea." Sam's expression went distant. "Hand me your phone."

Hayden stared at her.

Clearing her throat, Sam said, "I meant, can I have your phone?"

"Still not what I was looking for. What are you planning?"

"Something more satisfying than a simple text message."

Eyeing her, Hayden grabbed her phone blindly and held it out.

Sam took it, a glint in her eye.

"You look a little scary right now." And by scary, Hayden meant hot.

"Good."

~ ~ ~

An hour later, they sat at a table that faced the entrance of the small café they'd chosen, and Hayden tried not to bounce her knee.

"Relax, Hayden."

And failed, apparently. "Sorry."

Sam's hand slid over her knee under the table, her fingers squeezing enough that Hayden calmed down. Being touched by Sam was one of her favorite things. Now they were actually together, their PDA had calmed down, especially as they weren't trying to prove anything to anyone. The few and far between moments Sam reached out when not at home left Hayden lightheaded.

She turned. "I thought you hated affection in public."

Sam squeezed so that Hayden's ticklish leg jumped. "I would hardly call these simple touches excessively affectionate."

Hayden bumped their shoulders together. "Still, it's more than you made out that you liked to do in the beginning."

Pink spread over Sam's cheeks, and she was very interested in looking anywhere but Hayden's face. "Maybe I started to enjoy it a bit—with you."

Hayden tried to smother her smile but was probably failing miserably. "Oh. Is that so?"

Sam looked at her, her eyes clear, and she gave a nod.

Hayden dropped a kiss on Sam's shoulder. "Right back at you."

The door opened, a bell tinkling, and they both jerked their heads to look at it.

Just a young couple.

"Are you sure you want to do this?" Hayden asked.

"Yes."

Well, that was definitive. Not that Sam did things any other way.

"Okay. And you're not nervous?"

Sam sighed. "No. Mostly, I'm angry. I've spent a year working up toward all of this. I thought, maybe, they would change their mind when they realized they were losing both their children and would want to speak to us. But this?" Sam pressed her lips together. "I'm done."

Before Hayden could say anything else, the door opened again, and this time, Hayden could feel Sam straighten in her chair, though her hand stayed where it was.

George had spotted them from the doorway, based on the hard look on his face. When he started to walk over, Sam didn't stand up. He stopped at their table, his glance flicking over to Sam, and back to Hayden to address her. "I had assumed from your text message that we were to meet alone."

Hayden shrugged. "You assumed wrong."

"Am I right to assume, then, that you're saying no to my offer?"

He definitely nailed the *ass* part of assume.

Hayden waved a hand airily. "I'm actually a multibillionaire. Your offer was a pittance, really. Sorry. Not even worth thinking over."

In the future, Hayden thought, she should maybe think more about what she said. But it had been satisfying to watch his eyes widen ever so slightly before he took another look at Sam. He didn't even flinch under the stony look that made most interns almost wet their pants on sight.

"Samantha."

"Dad."

He sat down.

"Where's Mom?" Sam asked.

He sat ramrod straight, his suit and posture not fitting well into the eclectic, relaxed café's ambience. "She only wishes to be a part of this mess when it is straightened out."

It was so tempting to make a joke about only one third of the people at the table apparently being straight, but for once Hayden told herself that now really wasn't the time.

"Lovely," was all Sam said, voice steel.

"Sam." He wasn't even remotely looking at Hayden now. "Stop this whole homosexual nonsense. Your brother has refused, multiple times, the help we've offered him. We know you're not really like this. And if this, this *marriage* was for real, we know people who can help you. There are many people that have had success with therapy."

Hayden scoffed with disgust, but he wasn't interested in her anymore.

"Dad." Sam's voice was completely measured. "I did not come here to have a long conversation. I know, now especially, that this is who you and Mom are. That you will never think any differently. I came here—" if her voice had been steel before, now it was ice "—to tell you to stay the hell away from Hayden. You do not contact her or pry into her life. You leave her alone. By extension, you leave us alone."

She stood up, and Hayden followed suit. Something was ballooning in her chest. She felt breathless, light at Sam's words. Sam's hand slipped into hers.

"Samantha." George's voice turned pleading, and Sam, about to walk out, paused. She looked down at him, her face blank. "Darling, your mother and I, we can help you."

Sam shook her head. "This is something you can't seem to grasp. I don't need any help. Unless you and Mom can accept Jon and I for who we are, you'll leave us all alone."

Sam walked away, their hands still linked. As they reached the entrance, Hayden looked back one more time at George. His jaw was so clenched, she could see it from the doorway. His gaze caught hers.

"Great seeing you again, George." Hayden beamed at him.

Sam didn't falter, and when they stepped outside, the air was cold and frigid, but Sam's hand was warm in her own. Snow was falling, the flakes tiny and barely there, and their hands fell away from each other as they tugged on their coats and scarves, then slipped back together again immediately. Hayden's cheeks felt overheated, and all she wanted to do was have Sam closer.

A block away, she stopped and made that happen, pulling on Sam's hand so that she turned, and they stood, hands between them, watching the snowfall. Sam's eyes weren't glistening. No angry red slashed her cheeks. Rather, she gave Hayden a tentative smile.

"You okay?" Hayden asked anyway. Her hands were trembling, and George hadn't even been her family.

Sam stepped closer. "I am. I've been making my peace with this for a very long time." Sam brushed her lips over Hayden's, just once. "I have Jon. And you. I'm much more than okay."

With fragile bits of snow falling between them, Hayden gripped Sam's coat and kissed her, soft and slow. And Samantha Thomson, whom Hayden had written off as rude and cold, cupped Hayden's cheeks with gentle fingers and kissed her back: leisurely, sweetly, with no need to rush. Hayden could really get used to this.

Ironic, really, that a sham marriage done for money had led to *this*, something that left Hayden breathless and—who'd have thought—seemed to have left Sam the same way.

Turns out this year *was* the weirdest of her life.

In all the best of ways.

EPILOGUE

A no-fault divorce was the best thing ever invented—it was fast and easy, almost too much so.

Once they decided to get divorced, the process began with barely any effort. They weren't even required to appear in court for the hearing. The only thing they had to do was to file the paperwork together.

Although she had apparently gotten to like small amounts of PDA more, Sam was still much better at not appearing smitten than Hayden. At the notary, Hayden had to avoid looking at Sam too much in front of the stern-looking woman who witnessed them signing. With a pen in one hand, Sam's knuckles grazed hers, and Hayden had to resist the urge to trace her fingers over the back of Sam's hand.

They submitted everything to Sam's attorney to put together the official paperwork on a day when Sam had to rush back to work, and Hayden to the continuing education day she was supposed to be attending. Even as petitioning for the divorce got closer, that hyperinflated feeling in Hayden's chest that had been there for months whenever she thought about Sam remained.

Sam left her buoyant.

One evening, Sam walked in with a rattle of keys, and Hayden startled up and half-off the sofa. Frank slipped off her chest and fell onto her lap with a mostly good-natured growl.

Sam stood in the kitchen, flicking through letters. "Were you asleep with your cat at seven in the evening?"

Hayden cleared her throat, peering around the room. It had been bright as day when she'd lain down with the idea of watching a movie. But the light had clearly shifted; it was dark outside. "Uh, no."

Sam didn't even look up from the mail in her hand. "You're a terrible liar."

"This is not new information."

But Sam had stopped listening to her, focused on something in her hand.

"Sam?"

She dropped all but one of the letters in her hand on the counter and walked over, dropping onto the sofa and throwing a leg over Hayden's lap. Hayden tugged her leg closer and lazed back against the sofa.

Sam held the letter out, and Hayden almost went cross-eyed to stare at it. "What's that?"

"Open it."

Hayden's brain felt filled with cotton wool. Night shift had only ended the day before, and she was still coming back to the real world. That morning, she'd poured juice into her coffee instead of milk. "Okay."

The letter was heavy. It was more of a packet. Sam propped her head on her hand and watched Hayden, something soft in her eyes.

"What?" Hayden asked.

"You look so sleepy." Sam brushed hair off Hayden's face, tucking it behind her ear. Her fingers trailed down Hayden's neck.

"I really am."

"Want me to cook tonight?"

"That would be amazing."

"Would you like carbonara?"

"That would be even more amazing."

"Done." Sam nodded. "Now, open it."

Hayden flipped it over and obeyed, pulling out the stack of paper—a summons and an index number for their court date.

"Is this—?"

"It is."

"This is the paperwork, ready to file?" Hayden was grinning.

"It is."

Hayden gave an incredulous laugh and dropped the letter, hooking her finger into Sam's shirt and tugging her in to kiss her. "Do you think everyone reacts like this to impending divorce?"

"Probably not." Sam was pushing her back on the sofa, and Hayden let herself go willingly, their legs falling together. Sam's lips grazed her neck, making Hayden arch into her. "We could file it all tomorrow, if you like?" Sam offered.

"We can. And when we get the certificate, we could have it framed," Hayden suggested as Sam's teeth bit teasingly at her neck and Hayden's fingers grazed over Sam's back in response. "We could hang it over the bed." Sam's lips rested against the swell of Hayden's breast. "We should have lunch to celebrate once we get it," Hayden declared.

"Hayden?" Sam murmured.

"Mm?"

"Stop talking."

"Or what—you'll divorce me?"

But her witty riposte came out with a wavering delivery. Sam had slipped her hand up her shirt.

Hayden found herself happily wordless.

~ ~ ~

"This courthouse is a maze."

"It really is," Sam answered.

When they finally found the right place to file the paperwork, they stood in a line that absolutely crawled.

"You excited?" Sam murmured.

Hayden turned to look at her. "Is that a weird question about a divorce?"

"Most likely. But are you?"

Nodding, Hayden let their hands brush. "I am. Not that anything really has to change."

Sam was watching someone sitting in a chair in the corner who was flicking through a pile of paper with angry mutters. She hummed. "I suppose that's true."

And it kind of was. True.

Hayden clutched the documents closer and stared at the back of the man in front of her as he stepped up to the booth.

This was the final step. File the divorce papers, wait for the hearing date, and *bam*. They would be divorced once it was processed.

"Hayden?"

Snapping back to reality, Hayden focused. The man in front of them had gone, and Sam had stepped up to the booth. The woman behind it eyed her tiredly.

"It's our turn," Sam said.

"Right." Clutching the documents to her chest, Hayden stepped forward.

Sam twitched an eyebrow at her and turned back to the woman. "We wish to file our divorce package."

The woman cracked her gum. "Slide the papers under the window, please."

Hayden looked down at the yellow packet. She put it on the desk but didn't push it forward.

"What if we didn't?" she blurted out.

Sam blinked at her. As did the woman behind the glass.

"Excuse me?" Sam asked.

"What if, uh," Hayden swallowed. "What if we didn't get divorced?"

Sam had paled, and Hayden knew the pattern of every freckle that stood out on her skin. She knew a lot, now. She'd learned that Sam liked to go slowly in the morning, no matter how put together she looked when she was finally awake. She knew that Sam stuck up for her brother, and now for Hayden, before she defended herself. She knew that Sam liked chocolate but thought white chocolate was an abomination. She knew Sam didn't like being interrupted when she was working. She knew Sam preferred a real book to an e-reader.

She knew they were married; the entire world knew they were. And they acted like it too.

"You don't want to get a divorce?" Sam asked, and Hayden didn't remove her hand from the papers, as if scared the woman would yank them away and process them. "But—this is what you wanted, Hayden."

"Maybe—maybe it's not."

Sam turned to the woman, whose tired look had faded and was now chewing her gum rapidly, gaze fixed. "One moment."

She actually looked disappointed as Sam tugged Hayden out of the room and back through the maze of corridors until they were standing on the steps of the courthouse. Weak sunshine spilled around them as Sam faced her. Hayden tucked the papers into her bag.

"You don't want to get divorced?"

Hayden opened her mouth, then closed it. She shrugged. "Apparently?"

"Apparently? What does that even mean?"

Hayden swallowed. "It's just, why bother? I mean, we're happy, and together, and everyone thinks we're married anyway. Why not—why not just stay married?"

"But you don't believe in marriage."

Hayden shrugged again, hand rubbing at the back of her neck, wondering why this discussion made her so nervous. "I know. And, well, if we'd started dating and gotten together the usual way, maybe I never would have wanted to. But we *are* married now, and well, it's been working out pretty well so far?"

Sam was staring at her as if she'd never met her. "So we…wouldn't divorce?"

"Not if you don't want to."

"Well…" Sam looked lost in thought.

"You're thinking about it?" Hayden's tone rose with incredulity. "I'm asking you to stay married to me, and standing here like an idiot because I love you, and you're just gonna—"

"You *love* me?"

Shit.

Hayden winced. "Yeah?"

Sam looked stunned. "You've never said that to me before."

Hayden felt herself mirroring Sam's expression. "I guess I haven't. But I, uh, I do."

Was that a smile? "You love me and want to stay married?"

"Yeah?"

Sam stepped right into her space, on the steps of the courthouse, with her hands cupping Hayden's cheeks, her lips curved up still, even as she kissed her.

It was like their first kiss, a laughing one. Except this one was incredulous because she was just so damn happy and not because she had no idea what she was doing. This was one Hayden wouldn't forget as long as she lived. The day Hayden had accidentally blurted out that she wanted to stay married and she loved Sam.

Who hadn't said it back, come to think of it. Hayden pulled away, and before she could even say anything about it, Sam rolled her eyes at her.

"I love you too, of course."

It was the most utterly unromantic declaration of love Hayden had ever heard of.

Or maybe it was entirely romantic.

Whatever it was, Hayden wouldn't change it for anything.

"You do?" Hayden asked.

"Yes."

"I thought we weren't meeting you here for another twenty minutes?"

Both of them jumped and turned to see Luce and Clemmie. Sam and Hayden stepped back from each other but stayed touching.

"Hi," Hayden said weakly.

Clemmie and Luce looked at each other, then back at the two of them, clearly confused.

"You do remember messaging me and telling us to meet you, don't you?"

Right. Sam had suggested last night that, since Hayden hated lies so much, why not come clean to Luce, now that it wasn't so important? After kissing Sam and doing some things that had distracted both of them for a few hours, Hayden had messaged Luce to meet them for lunch.

And, with everything, she had promptly forgotten.

Hayden still felt a little high from Sam's sweeping kiss.

"Uh, yeah. I suppose we did." Hayden chewed the inside of her cheek, looking to Sam. This had not been the plan. "Why are you two early?"

"Why is that even important?" Luce was eyeing her down, suspicion in their eyes. "You've been so mysterious. What the hell is going on?"

"You two look seriously high right now," Clemmie said.

Hayden caught Sam's eye. Should they tell them? They'd meant to come clean at lunch about everything and their new divorce, and the start of their "newly dating" status. Now they weren't getting divorced?

Sam seemed to pick up what Hayden was saying with the widening of her eyes and gave the smallest, one-shouldered shrug, as if to say "why not?"

Hayden looked back to the two of them. "So, lunch? We have some celebrating to do."

She stepped forward and dropped her arm over Luce's shoulder, and they fell into step.

"We do?" Luce asked.

"Sam and I have a *really* funny story for you. One that has to stay between us four."

Luce's head whipped around.

"Hayden, what did you do?"

###

About G Benson

Benson spent her childhood wrapped up in any book she could get her hands on and—as her mother likes to tell people at parties—even found a way to read in the shower. Moving on from writing bad poetry (thankfully) she started to write stories. About anything and everything. Tearing her from her laptop is a fairly difficult feat, though if you come bearing coffee you have a good chance.

When not writing or reading, she's got her butt firmly on a train or plane to see the big wide world. Originally from Australia, she currently lives in Spain, speaking terrible Spanish and going on as many trips to new places as she can, budget permitting. This means she mostly walks around the city she lives in.

CONNECT WITH G BENSON

Website: www.g-benson.com
E-Mail: gbensonauthor@gmail.com

OTHER BOOKS FROM YLVA PUBLISHING

www.ylva-publishing.com

FLINGING IT

G Benson

ISBN: 978-3-95533-682-0
Length: 376 pages (113,000 words)

Midwife Frazer and social worker Cora have always grated on each other's nerves, but they have to work together to start up a programme for at-risk parents. Soon, the unexpected happens: they tumble into an affair. However, Cora is married to their boss, and both know it needs to end. But what they have might turn out to be much more than just a little distraction.

YOU'RE FIRED

Shaya Crabtree

ISBN: 978-3-95533-754-4
Length: 193 pages (61,000 words)

When poor college student Rose Walsh gives out an inappropriate gag gift at her office Christmas party, it backfires horribly. The gift's recipient is her boss, the esteemed president of Gio Corp., Vivian Tracey, and the only thing that can save Rose now is her smarts.

Instead of firing her, Vivian blackmails math major Rose into joining her on a business trip to New York to investigate an embezzlement. A week out of state with a woman she can barely stand seems like the last thing Rose wants to do with her winter vacation. Only, maybe Vivian is not as bad as she seems. Maybe they can even become friends...or more.

COMING FROM YLVA PUBLISHING

www.ylva-publishing.com

Falling into Place

Sheryn Munir

Romance is not for Tara. Embittered after a college fling, she vows to never fall in love again—especially since she believes there's no future for same-sex love in her home in urban India. Then, one rain-drenched evening, an insane decision brings the bubbly Sameen into her life and everything changes. Sameen is beautiful, a breath of fresh air...and almost certainly straight. All Tara's carefully built-up defences start to crumble, one after the other. But is this relationship doomed before it can even start?

The Brutal Truth

Lee Winter

Australian crime reporter Maddie Grey is out of her depth in New York, miserable, and secretly drawn to her powerful, twice-married, media mogul boss, Elena Bartell, who eats failing newspapers for breakfast. As work takes them to Australia, Maddie is goaded into a brief, seemingly harmless bet with her enigmatic boss—where they have to tell the complete truth to each other. It backfires catastrophically. A lesbian romance about the lies we tell ourselves.

Credits
Edited by Michelle Aguilar and Zee Ahmad
Proofread by Louisa Villeneuve
Cover Design by Adam Llyod